THE
BRITISH
LION

ALSO BY TONY SCHUMACHER

The Darkest Hour

THE
BRITISH
LION

TONY SCHUMACHER

wm

WILLIAM MORROW
An Imprint of HarperCollinsPublishers

THE BRITISH LION. Copyright © 2015 by Tony Schumacher. All rights reserved. Printed in the United States of America. No part of this book may be used or reproduced in any manner whatsoever without written permission except in the case of brief quotations embodied in critical articles and reviews. For information address HarperCollins Publishers, 195 Broadway, New York, NY 10007.

HarperCollins books may be purchased for educational, business, or sales promotional use. For information please e-mail the Special Markets Department at SPsales@harpercollins.com.

FIRST EDITION

Library of Congress Cataloging-in-Publication Data has been applied for.

ISBN 978-0-06-243919-2

15 16 17 18 19   OV/RRD   10 9 8 7 6 5 4 3 2 1

Printed and bound in Great Britain by Clays Ltd, St Ives plc

For the greatest generation, who gave me the freedom to write this and you the freedom to read it

I have never accepted what many people have kindly said—namely, that I inspired the nation. Their will was resolute and remorseless, and as it proved unconquerable. It was the nation and the race dwelling all round the globe that had the lion's heart. I had the luck to be called upon to give the roar.

—WINSTON CHURCHILL, PARLIAMENT, NOVEMBER 30, 1954

THE
BRITISH
LION

CHAPTER 1

November 1946
Queen Alexandra's Military Hospital, London

ERNST KOEHLER'S INDEX finger and thumb on his left hand ached like they'd been hit with a hammer.

Which surprised him, because he no longer had an index finger and thumb on that hand to ache.

He squeezed what remained of his fist tight and looked at his watch. He reached into the pocket of his trench coat for his cigarettes, then opened the top of the pack with his teeth before shaking one free.

"There is no smoking here, Major," the English hospital orderly said quietly.

The little man was already looking down at the floor, away from the death's-head badge on Koehler's SS cap, before he finished the sentence.

"Shut up," said Koehler, cigarette already in his mouth.

Koehler produced a box of matches and passed them to the Gestapo officer to his right.

Schmitt looked at them for a moment, and then back up at his boss.

"Light me," Koehler said, cigarette bobbing, left hand held up as proof of its ineffectiveness.

Schmitt fumbled with the box, nerves on edge, before finally managing to light a match and put it to the cigarette. Koehler grunted, drew deeply, and closed his eyes, agitation eased for a few minutes.

He held out his hand for the matches, and Schmitt passed them back.

"Thank you," Koehler said in German.

Schmitt didn't reply.

"Are you okay?" Koehler tried again.

Schmitt looked at the orderly, then back to Koehler.

"He doesn't speak German—none of them do, it's the rules."

"I still don't want to talk in front of him," Schmitt whispered.

"Do you have a problem?"

Schmitt shook his head unconvincingly.

"If you have a problem, you need to tell me," Koehler tried again, then took another drag on the cigarette.

Schmitt looked at the back of the orderly's head once more, then at Koehler.

"This is wrong, what we are doing. It's wrong."

"Visiting Rossett is wrong?"

"Yes. Well, no, but yes. After the damage he caused—" Schmitt broke off and looked at the orderly again, then shook his head. "We shouldn't be here. Now isn't the time."

Koehler stared at the Gestapo man for a moment, then leaned in close.

"How long have you worked for me?"

"Technically I don't work *for* you."

It was Koehler's turn to frown.

"Am I your boss?"

"Technically, yes."

"So, technically, how long have you worked for me?"

Schmitt looked at Koehler.

"A month or so, although I'm Gestapo liaison, so technically—"

Koehler cut him off.

"It's been eventful, hasn't it?"

"What has?"

"This month, it's been eventful?"

Schmitt shook his head.

"If you call chasing Rossett and some Jewish kid all over London for the last week eventful? Well, then, yes, it has; but personally, I'd say it's been more madness than anything else. Madness that has nearly cost me my job, and my life."

"But you are alive, Schmitt, and if you want to stay alive, you'll stick with me while I sort this out."

"We're German officers." Schmitt looked at the orderly again, subconsciously lowering his voice as he continued, even though he was still speaking in German. "We shouldn't have to sort things out. Things should be done correctly in the first place."

"You just follow my lead. If you want to stay alive, follow my lead."

Schmitt shook his head.

"When this is over I want out of your department."

"I want out of your department . . . *sir*," Koehler replied, then regretted it.

"I want out of your department, *sir*. I can't operate like this, this way that you work, breaking rules, running wild. I can't do it. I want out. If you give me your word I can go, I'll do as you say."

Koehler put the cigarette back in his mouth as he looked into Schmitt's eyes. He pondered the offer, taking the time to take a deep drag and weigh up his options; finally, he exhaled and spoke.

"You follow my lead this morning with Rossett, and then I'll recommend your transfer."

"Thank you."

Koehler nodded, then nudged the orderly.

"How much longer?" Smoke drifted from his nose and mouth as he spoke, this time in English.

"I don't know, sir, maybe ten minutes."

"Ten minutes?"

"Maybe less, it all depends . . ."

The orderly didn't finish his sentence. Koehler had already pushed through the double doors and was limping up the middle of the half-empty ward. Schmitt sighed heavily and followed.

There were eighteen beds, occupied by men in various states of distress, but Koehler didn't pay attention to them. He headed straight for the one at the top of the ward on the left-hand side. The bed that had curtains drawn around it and two bored SS guards sitting at its foot.

The two guards stood up when they realized there was a uniformed SS major limping his way toward them. One of the guards dropped a newspaper on the floor, made to pick it up, then thought better. He eventually made an awkward attempt at standing to attention, half up, half down, MP40 swinging in its sling in front of him.

Koehler ignored the guards, pulled back the curtain around the bed a few inches, and stepped inside. A doctor was bent over the patient and another orderly stood behind him, holding a tray of bloodied bandages and cotton wool. Both men turned to Koehler, who looked first at the tray and then at the doctor.

"Get out," Koehler said.

"I'm treating this man." The doctor turned to face Koehler.

The orderly was less belligerent. He stepped backward through the gap in the curtains without a word, like a bad comedian glad to get off the stage.

The English doctor held a thick cotton wool wad in front of him, bloody proof of his need to be there.

"You need to wait until I'm finished." This time the doctor's voice was stronger, given weight by years of telling people what to do and them doing it.

"Get out," repeated Koehler flatly.

"I'll do no such thing. I'm—"

"Schmitt."

Schmitt appeared through the curtains and stared at the doctor.

"Herr Major?"

"Take the doctor outside," Koehler said in English for the doctor's benefit.

"I'm treating this man; you can't just walk in here. I refuse to leave. This man is my patient. He—"

"And shoot him?" Schmitt said in English, staring at the doctor, who fell silent, lowering the bandage slowly to his side.

"Not yet," replied Koehler flatly, eyes still on the doctor.

The doctor looked at Schmitt, then at Koehler, and quietly stepped out through the curtains. Schmitt nodded to Koehler and followed the doctor out of the gap before closing it quietly behind him. Koehler listened to their footsteps fade away farther down the ward, Schmitt following his earlier orders to move everyone out of earshot. Koehler waited, then turned and looked down at John Henry Rossett, who stared back at him through heavy-lidded eyes.

"Hello, John," Koehler said in English, well aware that Rossett's German was terrible.

"Ernst," Rossett replied through cracked lips.

Koehler took another drag of his cigarette. He noticed Rossett's eyes following the smoke as he took it out of his mouth.

He held up the cigarette to Rossett.

"Can you?"

Rossett nodded, so Koehler held the cigarette to his lips and watched as he took a drag.

Rossett closed his eyes before letting the smoke rise back out of his lungs and float to the ceiling. He finally looked up at Koehler, managed a half smile of thanks, then closed his eyes again.

Koehler put the cigarette into his own mouth before lifting the loose cotton wadding from Rossett's stomach to reveal an inch-wide open wound. The wound had a faint whiff of infection, and Koehler softly tutted before gently placing the dressing back down.

"How's the hand?" Rossett whispered, eyes still closed.

"Fucked. Index finger and thumb gone." Koehler held up his gloved left hand, but Rossett still had his eyes closed.

Koehler shrugged, looked at it himself and then dropped it to his side.

"Sorry about that," Rossett whispered.

"You didn't do it."

"No."

"How's the stomach?" Koehler put the cigarette back to Rossett's lips.

Rossett took the barest of breaths, struggling to breathe life into the ember at the tip.

"It went straight through, came out clean the other side," he finally said after giving up on the cigarette.

"I'm sorry."

"You didn't do it."

"No." Koehler smiled, then sat down on the edge of the bed. His weight caused the mattress to sag, and Rossett groaned as gravity made him shift slightly. Koehler half rose, then settled again, this time more gently.

"I need to sit. I'm sorry, this leg is killing me," Koehler said. "I took a round through the calf in the firefight at the pub, when you were trying to get away with the boy and Kate."

Rossett opened his eyes.

"Me and you got pretty banged up."

"Lucky to be alive."

"Are you sure about that?"

Koehler chuckled.

"I think so."

They sat in silence for a while until Koehler spoke again.

"I can't believe you threw it all away. You had a good job, good living, quiet life, and you go and throw it all away for one Jewish kid."

"Throw it all away?"

"We had it good, and you risked screwing it up like that." Koehler looked around for somewhere to get rid of the cigarette. "You threw it all down the drain."

"I was already down the drain."

"You had everything."

"Everything?" Rossett opened his eyes again. "I worked for you rounding up Jews, just so you could cart them off to . . . well, God knows where." Rossett paused as he drew another shallow breath and looked at the ceiling above his bed. "I have no family, no home, no future, and no friends." Another pause, another shallow breath. "I didn't throw anything away, Ernst, because I didn't have anything to throw away. That child, Jacob, he . . . I don't know." Rossett looked for the words. "He made me feel human."

Koehler gave up looking for somewhere to put the cigarette and settled for dropping it on the floor. He leaned forward slightly so that he could rest his elbows on his knees, staring at the butt that was still smoking next to his boot.

His head hung low on his weary shoulders.

"I was your friend," Koehler finally said.

"You were trying to kill me."

"I was doing my job."

Rossett chuckled, then grimaced as his stomach tightened.

Koehler looked up from the cigarette butt, waiting for Rossett's pain to pass before speaking again.

"We're part of a machine, John. I don't like it any more than you do, but the fact is, we are part of a machine. We're told to round up the Jews in London, so that's what we do. What happens to them, where they go, it isn't our concern. You taking that child, helping him, stopped you doing what you were supposed to do, and that nearly caused the machine to break down." Koehler rubbed his hand again. "If I didn't try to fix what was broken, it would have been fixed by someone else. I had no choice but to do what I did. You have to remember: whatever I think about the machine, how I feel about what it does, it doesn't matter. If I don't do what I'm supposed to do . . . I die." Koehler rummaged in his coat pocket for his cigarettes again, then thought better of it. He looked back at the cigarette butt on the floor before continuing, his voice lower this time, softer. "I still have my family, John. They mean everything to me. I couldn't risk their future, not for you, not for the Jewish kid you were trying to help, and not for the Jews we round up. I'm sorry."

"I know."

"I'm here to fix things—between us, and between you and my bosses. We need to get you back in the machine before it is too late," Koehler said, half turning his head to look at Rossett again, checking his reaction.

"What if I don't want to go back into the machine?"

"You don't want to start thinking like that, trust me. You need to get back on board and quickly, while we can still keep some sort of lid on this."

"How?" Rossett opened his eyes again.

"It's complicated."

"Am I going to prison?"

Koehler shrugged, removed his cap, and ran his right hand through his thick blond hair.

"I still don't understand. Why did you do it?" Koehler looked at his cap. He gently straightened the death's-head badge as he waited for Rossett's answer.

Rossett swallowed, staring up at the ceiling, looking for the words before he finally replied.

"Saving the boy, getting him away from it . . . from this . . . this place."

"London?"

"England, Britain, what it's become."

"One kid? You've helped send thousands to . . . wherever they go to."

Rossett looked at Koehler. "I wanted it, helping him . . . I wanted it to save me. I woke up, looked around at what I'd done, what I was doing. I wanted him to save me from what I . . . what we were doing."

"If you don't mind me saying so, John"—Koehler nodded his head to the injury on Rossett's stomach—"you don't look much saved." Koehler spun his cap in his fingers slowly.

The edges of Rossett's mouth twitched and he went back to staring at the ceiling.

"I feel saved. I feel better inside than I've felt in years. Doing something good, instead of doing what we usually do. Whatever happens to me from now, I know I did the right thing for Jacob."

"But not for yourself?"

"You don't get it, do you?"

"Apparently not."

"I had someone other than myself to think about, for the first time since my wife and son died. When they were blown up by the resistance, something in me . . . stopped working. Some part of me changed. I thought I was broken forever." Rossett paused, and then went back to looking at the cracked hospital ceiling. "I don't know, Ernst. That kid brought me back to life; he made me see what I'd become. I had someone to care about, to look after, and to do the right thing for. All this . . ." Rossett pointed at his stomach. "It was worth it. It was all worth it to find myself again."

They sat quietly as someone at the other end of the ward called for a nurse. Nobody answered. Schmitt was doing his job.

"So, what happens to me now? Do I go to prison?" Rossett said.

"No."

"Executed?"

"What's the point? You're already half dead."

"So what, then?"

"You're the British Lion, John, the Führer's favorite Englishman, remember? You're a hero, and the Reich needs heroes." Koehler spun his cap again, then looked at Rossett. "So the Reich needs you."

Rossett raised an eyebrow. "The Reich needs me or you need me?"

Koehler waved his hand and continued.

"The statement the British High Command will release is going to say that you were shot by the resistance as you tried to stop gun smugglers at Wapping docks. You were working for the Reich, assisting in the glorious battle against the cowardly communist and royalist resistance, who are determined on undermining the glorious future of Great Britain and the British Fascist Party. You bravely tackled a group of men who were about to launch a terror campaign against the civilian population. You nearly died protecting a platoon of German soldiers." Koehler turned to Rossett. "The diary we found on you, the one you had in your pocket? It was pretty water damaged, but there were a lot of useful names and addresses we can use. That alone has given the Gestapo enough reason to celebrate."

"No mention of Jacob?"

"Nobody will miss one Jewish kid."

"Kate?"

"If anyone asks, she's been transferred up north."

"But nobody will ask?"

"Probably not. It's best not to when people disappear, you know that."

"But *I* don't disappear. Why?"

"You're a hero, and you will be rewarded for your heroism."

"Rewarded."

"You're getting a medal."

"What if I don't want it? What if I don't agree to this?"

Koehler shook his head and puffed out his cheeks.

"That is where things get tricky. If you don't comply with this arrangement, all of this arrangement, I've been authorized to explain to you that you'll tragically die of your wounds, probably here, probably today."

"And you?"

"No doubt I'll succumb to infection as well, or, if I'm really unlucky, I'll end up out east fighting the Chinese and the Russians."

Both men sat in silence, surrounded by curtains, amid the smell of hospital food and disinfectant.

The patient down the ward called out again, this time louder, but with no more success than before.

Rossett looked at Koehler.

"Die of my wounds?"

"Yes."

"Maybe that would be easier?"

"Don't be stupid, John. Just nod your head and we come through in one piece. Shake it and things will be exactly the same, except you'll be dead and my wife will be a widow."

"Why are they doing this for me?"

Koehler clenched his fist again and leaned forward, looking down at his boots once more.

"This hand hurts like hell."

Rossett looked at the hand, then at his stomach.

"Swap?"

They stared at each other for a moment before Koehler's eyes seemed to dim, the bright blue turning a sad shade of gray.

"If you die, the English High Command have to explain why they let the British Lion, the Führer's favorite Englishman, charge around getting shot, just before the Führer sends someone to London to give him a medal. The Führer needs you, and he wants you standing up, not lying in a box. Keeping the Führer happy, that's the number-one rule of being a high-ranking German officer. And the high-ranking German officers I answer to know this; that is why you will come through the other side of this." Koehler straightened up again and looked squarely at Rossett. "The last few days have been—well, let's just say they haven't gone well for me. The shootings all over London, the dead soldiers—none of it looks good for my bosses and me, unless we can put a positive spin on the events. If we can paint you as a hero, things will improve, and my bosses can stand behind you. You get to take the glory, and we get to fight another day. If you die, I die, either in a cell in London or a trench in Russia. I'll be honest, I don't fancy either much."

"If I die, what do I care?"

"Not a lot, but . . ."

"But?"

"They'll follow up on Kate. She was my secretary, and she was seen with you before she fell off the face of the earth. We know she was helping you; we aren't idiots. You might have got her out of the country with the kid, but they'll track her down easily enough if they want to." Koehler shook his head. "They can make things go badly for her over there." Koehler leaned in close. "They know what strings to pull, John. They'll let it be known to the Americans that she worked for the SS, for me, rounding up the Jews. They can also let it be known that she still is working for us. That'll soon make its way to Canada. They can make her look very bad, very, very bad."

"Even though it isn't true?"

"Some of it is, some of it isn't. All you need to know is that the British government abroad hangs traitors. You don't want that for Kate, do you?"

"She wasn't a traitor."

"Maybe not at the end, but whether you like it or not, she was a traitor, same as you are. You were both working for the Germans, and you were both involved in rounding up Jews. That'll get you on the end of a rope. Your agreement to the official explanation I'm offering you now will make certain she is left alone."

"So I lie?"

"Doesn't everyone?" Koehler tilted his head.

"Traitors to the truth," Rossett replied, closing his eyes again.

"You got very close to her, John, in the madness of what was happening with the kid. I know you did. She was a special person. I was ... well ... I was very fond of her myself. If you have feelings for her, you'll agree to what I'm offering."

Neither man spoke for over a minute until Koehler tried again.

"Do we have a deal?"

"What about Schmitt, and the men who died?"

"If I go down, Schmitt goes down. He knows that; he isn't an idiot. Shit rolls downhill, and if it doesn't I'll give it a push. He knows why I'm here, he knows what I'm saying, and he knows if we can make this stick we all stay alive, and maybe, just maybe, we'll look good in the morning. If he keeps his mouth shut I'll let him move on out of my office, which will buy his silence."

"And the men?"

"This is war. Men die."

"A dirty secret," Rossett whispered.

"Our secret," Koehler replied, looking longingly at the now long-dead cigarette butt. "You get your medal; I get to give my bosses the resistance men you

killed and the timber yard full of guns we uncovered. You just need to agree
with the account of what took place."

"The man who shot me?"

"He's an old soldier, don't worry. Just nod your head, come on . . . please,
John, for me, for my family?"

Rossett opened his eyes again and looked sadly at Koehler.

"I can't decide what would be better, to live or die. Isn't that terrible?"

"Live to fight another day."

"I'm tired of fighting, Ernst; I can't go back to that job, what we do . . . I
can't, not anymore. I've changed. I'm not that person, the man who loads the
trains. I can barely live with the thought of what we did, what we do. I won't
do it again."

"I can get you a nice quiet job, little office with some paper to shuffle, out of
the way? I could maybe get you back in the police, just like old times? You just
have to nod your head, take your medal, sign a statement. That's all. Then you
get a quiet life."

"I want to be a policeman again. I want to go back to my old job."

"Fine."

"I'll not put another soul in a boxcar. I want to do some good again, be a
better man."

"Okay, you can be a policeman."

Rossett shut his eyes and rested his head back on the pillow. For a moment
Koehler thought he'd fallen asleep, and he leaned forward slightly to check.

Finally Rossett spoke. "All right, I'll sign."

"It makes sense. We'll be heroes, John, smelling of roses."

"We'll never be heroes again, Ernst, not after the things we've done."

Koehler didn't reply. He stood up off the bed and smoothed his tunic before
looking down again at the man he hoped was still his friend. After a second or
two he nodded silently and turned to leave through the gap in the curtains.

"Ernst?"

Koehler stopped and looked back at Rossett, who had opened his eyes
again.

"Yes?"

"The boy, have you heard?"

Koehler rubbed his hand again before struggling to button his coat against the cold November afternoon that waited outside.

"They are on a plane to America. My contact in Dublin says the boy is well and has an American passport."

Rossett closed his eyes and rested his head back on the pillow.

CHAPTER 2

ERNST KOEHLER TRIED punching some life into the pillow for what seemed the thousandth time that night, then rested his head on it once more.

In the distance Big Ben started to chime.

Six. He was an hour early.

He grunted, rolled out of bed, and picked up his dressing gown before crossing to the window.

He flexed his toes as he pulled back the heavy curtain an inch and looked out.

No snow: the forecast was wrong again.

He put on his dressing gown.

"Ernst?"

Koehler smiled, crossed back to the bed, and bent to kiss Lotte, his wife, softly on the forehead.

"Go back to sleep, it's early," he whispered.

"Come back to bed." Lotte didn't open her eyes. Just half her face was visible above the blankets, the rest hidden under her thick blond hair.

"I might as well do some work, now that I'm awake," Koehler whispered as he brushed her forehead with his lips.

Before he could rise, Lotte reached with her arm and pulled him close. They kissed before she set him free, her arm snaking back under the blankets.

"I love you, Ernst Koehler." Lotte's voice was thick with sleep.

"I love you, Lotte Koehler," Koehler replied as he pulled the blankets up further around her.

"I'm so happy, together again," Lotte said, drifting off to sleep.

Koehler smiled, traced a fingertip across Lotte's cheek, and left the bedroom, carefully closing the door behind him. He padded through the plush living room of his apartment and into the small kitchen, where he lit the stove and filled a kettle.

A small, sleepy-eyed black kitten appeared at the door. It yawned, flicked its head, then padded across until it was weaving around his legs, like long grass in a breeze.

Koehler felt the brush of the kitten's tail and looked down. He smiled at the get-well-soon gift from Anja, his daughter. She had christened the kitten "Schwarz," and Koehler had a feeling that when it was time for his wife and daughter to go back to Berlin, little Schwarz would be going with them.

Koehler hoped he would be going, too.

"We've got a big day ahead of us, little Schwarzy. Today we find out if I'm ever going to leave this shithole, England."

Schwarz purred even louder.

"Maybe we'll get a house with a garden for you?"

Schwarz sat down, staring at Koehler.

"Or would you sooner leave me here, and go back to Germany with just Lotte and Anja?"

Schwarz meowed and Koehler smiled, as the kettle started to boil.

"Yeah, sure. You just want your breakfast."

CHAPTER 3

YOU WANT TO come back?"

"I'd like to."

"You want to come back here?"

"Yes."

"Be a policeman?"

"Yes."

"Here?"

"Yes."

Chief Superintendent Bernard Reade leaned back in his chair. He looked at Rossett's written request, then back up at Rossett, who was standing directly in front of his desk.

"Here?"

"Yes." Rossett tried not to frown.

"Wapping?"

"Yes . . . sir." Rossett heard his nerves stretching in his reply.

"There is nowhere else you'd rather go? A desk at Scotland Yard, maybe? Nice office, secretary, spot by a teapot?"

"No, sir."

"You want to come back here?"

"I do."

Reade tapped his index finger on his top lip, adjusted his position in his seat, and leaned forward so that his elbows were back on the desktop.

"It's just that, well—and please remember, this isn't me saying this, Rossett, this is just me letting you know that . . . well . . ."

"People might not want to work with me, sir?" Rossett filled in the blank.

Reade nodded, opening his hands as he did so.

"It's not that you aren't a good policeman. I've read your record." Reade looked around his desk for the folder, gave up, and smiled at Rossett. "Plus there is all that medal-winning stuff in France, which was exceptional work."

Reade waited for Rossett to reply, but Rossett was staring out of the window at the Thames, watching a barge battle the wind, as he waited for whatever was going to come next.

"Inspector?"

Rossett looked at Reade, who tried again.

"Your exploits in France, they were exceptional."

Rossett nodded.

Reade chewed his lip and scratched behind his ear, then gestured that he wanted Rossett to say something.

Rossett blinked, turned his head a quarter of an inch, sighed, and then spoke.

"I was told I could apply to any station that I wished. I was told that my application would be a formality. I was told that I would be allocated a detective role commensurate with my rank."

"But here?"

"Yes, here."

"Why?"

"This is where I started my career, this is where the challenge is, and this"—Rossett paused, fixing Reade with a stare—"is where I want to be."

Reade removed his spectacles and rubbed his eyes with his finger and thumb, then squinted up at Rossett, who had returned to staring out of the window.

"I've had no official confirmation of this, Rossett." Reade sounded tired.

"One phone call can get you that, sir."

"I don't even know for certain if you're still a policeman." Reade offered up his hands to Rossett, then flopped them back down.

"I've still got my warrant card."

"But you work for the Germans. I've checked. We don't pay your wages; you don't have an office, or a department, or men working under you." Reade gestured to the window.

"Find me a job, sir." Rossett looked at Reade.

"It isn't that easy, Inspector."

"I can do anything. My record speaks for itself."

"That's part of the problem, John." Reade used Rossett's first name for the first time. "Your record does speak, and what it says is, quite frankly, terrifying at times."

Rossett raised an eyebrow as Reade wiped a hand across his mouth, regretting what he had said, aware that Rossett was still very much connected to his Germans.

He tried again, conciliatory this time, leaning forward, letting his chair rock with him.

"Look." He glanced at the request. "John, this is difficult for me to explain to you, but you're well known here. From your time before the war and since you've been working for the Germans."

"And?"

"And that has made some people reluctant to be associated with you."

"I don't care."

"But I do, John. I have to look after you. I have to worry about your safety."

"I look after myself."

"I can see that from your personnel file." Reade cast an eye around the desk for the file again, then looked back at Rossett. "Look, I don't know how else to say this."

"Just say it."

Reade frowned, scratching his cheek as he took a deep breath. "If you return to policing, you will be in danger." The words finally tumbled out.

"Every policeman is in danger; it's the nature of the job."

"Yes, but you'll be in danger from everyone, John. Criminals, resistance, and, even though I hate to say it, you'll be in danger from fellow police officers."

Rossett went back to staring at the dirty black barge banging its prow against the incoming tide of the muddy brown Thames.

He knew how it felt.

Reade tried again.

"I don't know how else to tell you, but you're hated here. And not just here: you're hated all over London."

"I've just been following orders."

"It isn't just about what you do with the Germans. Let's be honest, John, you weren't exactly popular before the war, either."

Rossett looked at Reade, who gave a slight shake of his head.

"Don't shoot the messenger; just try to understand the problem from my point of view."

"I just want to be a policeman."

"As that may be, I have to be careful."

"So I just carry on floating around?"

Reade leaned back in his chair again, his hands now holding the edge of his desk, as if he were expecting Rossett to snatch it away.

"Go back to the Germans. They'll have you."

"No."

"You'd do well with them; you've done well with them. Promotions, nice easy job, maybe they'll give you an apartment?"

"I want to be a policeman."

"Why?"

Rossett shifted his weight onto one leg and then, for the first time, wandered to the window. It was colder by the window, and across the south side of the Thames Rossett could see black snow falling from a gray cloud miles away. It looked like charcoal shading in a picture of the sky, and he squinted, trying to see it more clearly than the distance and dirty glass would allow.

Half a minute passed until finally he spoke without turning around.

"To be good again."

"What?"

"I want to try to make up for what I've done."

"You've been doing your job; you've done nothing wrong."

"You don't know what I've been doing," Rossett replied, becoming aware that he could see himself inches away, reflected in the glass.

He needed a shave.

"You said it yourself: you've been following orders. No one will criticize you for that."

Rossett turned and faced Reade, who stared back at him.

"You don't know what I've been doing."

ROSSETT DIDN'T HAVE many friends left.

In truth, although he tried not to think about it too much, he'd never had many friends to start with.

As time had passed, and he had slipped further into the machinery that made up the Third Reich, his Christmas card list had gotten shorter and shorter, until finally there were only one or two names left on it.

Not that he bothered sending cards anyway.

One of those names was walking toward him as he stood next to his Austin, finishing his cigarette, staring at the Thames, as the first snow of winter fell steadily outside the station.

He'd known Bill Fraser for over ten years. First they'd been young coppers together, walking the beat and dodging the sergeant on night shift. Then, after years of those shifts had passed by, they'd become the sergeants searching for lazy bobbies.

They were that rare thing, friends who could pick up where they left off. Years could pass and a conversation would continue as if one of them had paused for breath.

"Gi's a fag, John?" Fraser flicked his fingers toward the cigarette Rossett was holding.

Rossett smiled, took out the packet, and passed it across the roof of his car.

He waited for Fraser to light up, then caught the cigarettes when Fraser tossed them back.

"How you doin'? I heard you were in hospital?"

"You didn't come and see me."

"German hospitals give me the creeps."

Rossett nodded and gave a slightly thinner smile. "Stiff and sore, but getting there." He took a drag on his cigarette, watching his friend.

"You back on the job?" Fraser jerked a thumb toward the police station.

"Not yet." Rossett noticed for the first time in their long relationship that the conversation seemed stilted, hanging awkwardly between them.

"You ain't missing much."

"You'd be surprised."

Fraser leaned against the roof of the car and rolled the cigarette in his fingers, studying it.

"Everything all right, Fraze?"

Fraser tilted his head and then gave a tiny shake; he frowned.

"No, mate, I'm sorry."

"What's up?"

"I wanted to say . . . well, I heard you was looking to come back 'ere."

"And?"

Fraser shrugged and shoved his hands in his pockets against the cold. Here and there patches of gray cobbles poked through the snow, like mountaintops through thick cloud.

"It's not like in the old days, mate." Fraser's cigarette bobbed as he spoke.

"So I keep hearing."

Fraser shifted his feet in the snow, scratching away until he could see a cobble under his boot.

"The whole place has changed, John, it isn't like it was. The crooks are crookeder, most of the bobbies are worse, even the magistrates ain't averse to a little touch or two, if you know what I mean." Fraser winked.

"What about the sergeants, Fraze?"

Fraser looked behind him and then joined Rossett on his side of the car, leaning in close enough that their shoulders touched. He took the cigarette out of his mouth.

"Things are tough round here, John. We've got resistance and smugglers, on top of the usual thieves and vagabonds we knew back in our day. Christ almighty, most of them are the same people who've stepped up a gear." Fraser looked over his shoulder at the station and then continued. "When you worked here it was a picnic. Nowadays you don't know who you're talking to. You've got to be careful; there is a lot of money to be made, inside the law or outside the law. It isn't just money, either: one wrong word, a dirty look, or a rumor spread can have you up in front of the Gestapo, and I don't need to tell you about them."

"If you do your job the right way, you've nothing to worry about. It's very simple," Rossett said softly.

Fraser chuckled.

"Simple for you, maybe. Not so simple for the blokes who want to go home to their families at the end of their shift."

Rossett looked at Fraser, who immediately regretted his words.

"I'm sorry. I didn't mean . . . your family. I'm sorry."

Rossett stared at the river, putting his cigarette into the corner of his mouth. The cigarette glowed orange, the only color for what seemed like miles around.

Rossett breathed out the smoke through his nose as Fraser tried again to explain his position.

"All I'm telling you is it can be dangerous."

Rossett nodded, then looked at Fraser again.

"Are you a bent copper?"

Fraser opened his mouth as he took half a step away from Rossett, their shoulders no longer touching.

"What?"

"Are you a bent copper?"

"You're asking me that?"

"I am."

"I can't believe you'd ask me."

"You can't believe I'd ask you because we're mates? Or because nobody asks that question?"

"Because we're mates."

"I'm sorry." Rossett finally blinked.

Fraser nodded, then followed Rossett's gaze across the river.

"This place is all changed. Time was, if we knew who was up to no good we would just go and lift 'em. Now, well . . . we know who runs the manor and we can't touch 'em."

"Who is that?"

"What?"

"You know who runs the manor—who is it?"

Fraser took the cigarette out of his mouth.

"No, mate. Seriously, no . . . I want to go home of a night, and you want to be careful."

Rossett thought about the answer as he lowered his head and flicked away his cigarette into the snow to smolder and die.

"You've got to learn, John, things have changed around here. Do you understand?"

"I thought I understood." Rossett pushed himself off the car and turned to face Wapping Police Station with its bare brown brick, topped off with a limp Union Jack, hanging next to an even limper bloodred swastika flag. "I'm not so sure now."

"You take care, John, you hear me? Take care about what questions you ask and where you ask them. It's dangerous, even for someone like you." Fraser tapped a finger on the roof of Rossett's car and turned to head back into the station. Rossett looked up at the heavy gray sky and the dots of snow that were falling faster from it.

He looked back at the station where he had learned to be a policeman all those years ago.

It seemed the same on the outside, all except for the swastika.

Rossett fingered his own swastika lapel badge and then looked down at it. He and the station had a lot more in common than he cared to admit. He watched as Fraser jogged up the steps and pushed against the heavy entrance door.

"Fraze!" Rossett shouted. Fraser stopped and turned, half in, half out of the building, one hand holding the door open.

"What?"

"I just want to be a policeman again."

Fraser stared at Rossett, then let the door swing shut behind him, leaving Rossett alone in the snow.

CHAPTER 4

January 1947

YOU'VE FULLY RECOVERED, Ernst?"

"Yes, sir. Thank you, sir."

"The hand?"

Koehler lifted his left hand and studied the black glove before wiggling his remaining fingers.

"It'll never be the same, sir, but it is better."

"Good, that's very good." Oberführer Adolf Hahn studied Koehler, who sat stiffly in front of him on an uncomfortable wooden chair, before looking down at the file on the desk and half turning a page. A minute passed before he spoke again, this time not bothering to look up.

"So you're totally healed?"

"I think so, sir."

"How long have you been on restricted duties now?"

"Just over two months, sir."

"Hmm." Hahn returned to reading the file.

Koehler silently puffed out his cheeks once he was sure his boss wouldn't look up at him. He looked around the office, noting how bare it was compared to his own: no books, no pictures, no plants, no soft settee, no rugs, nothing.

"I don't understand." Hahn interrupted Koehler's sightseeing.

"Sir?" Koehler whipped his eyes back to his boss.

"If you are fully fit, why are you asking to go back to Germany?" Hahn removed his wire-framed spectacles from his nose, signaling he'd finished with the written request Koehler had spent days composing.

"As I say in the report, sir, I feel, with respect, that I could do more for the Reich back in Germany."

"You do say that, but you don't say why."

"Sir?"

"You don't say why you think you'd be more useful in Germany than in London. If it was because you were no longer fit enough to do the job, well, I could understand that, but this . . ." Hahn lifted his index finger and then rested it on the file, as if it were a dagger jabbed into the tabletop. "This doesn't tell me anything."

"I feel . . ."

"You feel? Feelings don't come into it, Major. Tell me what you *know*."

Koehler shifted on the chair and looked at the brown carpet for inspiration; there wasn't any there.

"I just thought, sir . . ."

"What you *know*, Major, what you *know*."

Koehler tried again.

"I know, sir, that I've been here a long time."

Hahn nodded.

"I also know," Koehler continued, "that my work has been to the highest standard."

"Without doubt." Hahn nodded.

"And I think—"

Hahn held up his hand for Koehler to stop speaking, and Koehler obliged.

"That, Major, is the problem. You think. You don't know, you merely think. Thinking, feeling, wanting: none of that matters when you are a soldier. *Knowing* matters. Knowing is the key."

"I know I am tired, sir."

"We are all tired."

"I know I miss my family, sir."

"Many men miss their families, Ernst. You still haven't told me why you are different." Hahn rested his finger on his temple, waiting for Koehler to continue.

Koehler rocked slightly to the side and then shook his head, looking again at the carpet.

"I want to go home, sir; it is that simple. I need to go back to Germany. I can't do this job anymore. The last few months have shown me that I am not the right person for the role that I've been given. I can't do it; I'm finished."

Hahn shook his head.

"You have been ordered to do your job. The person who orders, it is he who decides when a job is finished, not the person doing it."

Koehler kept looking at the brown carpet. Tiny lines in the weave made it look like the plowed fields Koehler had seen far below when he had flown out of Moscow back to Berlin all those years ago.

Another lifetime.

Hahn opened Koehler's file once more. He picked up a pencil and tapped it on the desk.

"Your family are visiting you, are they not?"

"Yes, sir."

"When do they go back?" Hahn said without looking up.

"Four days, sir." Koehler's mood lifted along with his head.

Hahn leaned back in his chair studying Koehler, who stared back, unsure of what was coming next.

"You are a good soldier, Ernst. Your men would do anything for you, your superiors speak highly of you, and you run a tight ship. Your work with the Jews has been extremely efficient and is to be commended." Hahn toyed with the pencil again. "Your adventure last year with this Rossett character, exposing those resistance cells, was unconventional but effective. For that work, the Reich and the Führer are extremely grateful. You are being awarded Oak Leaves, aren't you?"

"Yes, sir."

"Good. Well deserved." Hahn clasped his hands in front of him again, still holding the pencil, which stuck out the top like the plunger on a firing box.

"Thank you, sir."

Hahn stared at Koehler without speaking, for so long Koehler found himself shifting in the chair.

"Am I dismissed, sir?"

Hahn leaned back from the desk, then tapped the pencil against his teeth before speaking again.

"You're not losing faith, are you, Ernst?"

"Faith, sir?"

"In what we do, and the people we do it for?"

Koehler stiffened and suddenly regretted writing the transfer request.

"No, sir."

Hahn frowned.

"Germany calls on us. The Fatherland makes great demands. Demands that many find difficult to live up to. You've been tasked with an unpleasant job—a vital job, but unpleasant nonetheless." Hahn leaned forward again and lowered his voice. "It would be understandable if your work with the Jews in London became a difficult cross to bear. If you'll pardon the pun." Hahn smiled thinly at his own joke.

"My record speaks for itself, sir."

"Records are history. It's the present I'm talking about, so I'll ask you again. Are you losing faith?"

"I'm not losing faith, sir."

Hahn smiled before standing up and wandering over to the window.

Koehler twisted to look at his boss as he spoke.

"Does the business with the Jews offend you, Ernst?"

"Not at all, sir. It is important work that needs to be done," Koehler replied, surprised to find his eyes straying toward a portrait of the Führer.

He looked away quickly and scratched at his ear.

"You can speak freely, Ernst. You have my word as an officer that nothing will leave this room," Hahn said, still staring out the window.

Koehler didn't reply, for fear of falling into a trap. He noticed his left hand was aching again, and he had to fight the urge to rub it.

"It's been a long war, Ernst," Hahn said at the window. "For some, longer than others. You are one of those others. I understand that you are tired, and when people are tired, they make mistakes."

Like asking for a fucking transfer, Koehler thought to himself.

"But you can relax with me here. Here and now, Ernst, in this room, you can speak freely. I'll ask you again: does this business with the Jews offend you?"

Koehler turned to look at Hahn, swiveling slightly in his chair. He paused, looked down, and then back up again at Hahn, who still stared out over London from the window.

Say nothing, Koehler thought. Just say nothing and get the fuck out of this office as soon as possible.

Silence sat on his shoulders like a shroud. Hahn didn't move an inch. Somewhere down a corridor a phone started to ring.

Eventually Hahn turned to look at Koehler and smiled like a grandfather—warm, soothing. His face was half in shadow as he waited for an answer.

"It seems vindictive, sir," Koehler heard himself say. His heart pounded, one, two, three. He swallowed and spoke again. "We've won the war, these people are pathetic, and yet . . . and yet we keep punching them like . . . playground bullies. It seems so pointless. I've seen them, I see them every day." Koehler looked at the carpet and lowered his voice to a whisper. "They aren't a threat."

Hahn nodded.

"You think the job is done?"

Koehler looked up. "I don't know, sir . . . I'm just struggling to do it. I can't sleep, I feel guilty, so guilty about it all. I've turned into a monster." Koehler paused, feeling his cheeks flush and pressure build behind his eyes. "Having my family here, it's made me see myself. What I do to others . . . and what it does to me."

Hahn crossed the room and sat down on the corner of his desk near to Koehler.

"Why did you join the SS, Ernst?"

"To be the best, sir. I wanted to fight with the best, and to be the best."

"Not just the uniform?" Hahn smiled.

"Well, a little of that, sir, yes," Koehler smiled back.

"I joined in the early days, back in '33; we had real enemies then, real threats. The Jews and the Bolsheviks were destroying Germany. The enemy was real. You could see them, punch them in the nose, and they punched you back. Now . . ." Hahn chuckled. "The enemy is some frostbitten Russian peasant sitting in a ditch waiting to starve to death. Soon he'll be gone and we'll have nobody left to fight." Hahn took a deep breath and let it out slowly. "Do you know what happens to a warrior who has nobody left to fight?" Hahn didn't wait for an answer. "He gets fat, fat and lazy, and he starts to question the point of his existence."

"I . . . I don't . . ." Koehler trailed off, aware he was lost in a minefield of his own making.

Hahn continued as if he hadn't spoken.

"My son died in Moscow, did you know that?"

"No, sir."

"My son." The smile slipped from Hahn's lips and Koehler felt his cheeks flush at the intimacy of the moment. Hahn was the third most important German in the country, and one not renowned for his emotions. "Just after the communists fled the city, a sniper they'd left behind got him."

"I'm sorry, sir."

Hahn turned to look at Koehler.

"Yes."

Koehler didn't know what to say. His hand hurt like hell and he squeezed it tightly into a fist.

"So much waste."

"Yes, sir."

"I'm tired, too, Ernst. I'll let you into a secret: I also sometimes question our role, what we are doing. The question vexes me as much as it vexes you." Hahn looked at Koehler, waiting for a reply that didn't come. He stood up again, wandered around his desk, and sat back down in his chair.

"Do you love your family, Ernst?"

"Of course."

"More than the Führer?"

Koehler blinked.

"I love the Führer and my family."

"You didn't answer the question."

"I—"

Hahn held up a hand, stopping him.

"Let's hope you never have to answer that question, Ernst. Thank you for speaking freely. I'm glad we've had this conversation."

Hahn picked up the pencil again and wrote something in the margin of one of the documents, then shut the file with a flourish.

"Your request for transfer to Germany is denied. I'm going to bounce you upstairs for a few months; you can join the national planning team."

"Planning team, sir?"

"Railway timetables, census work, just paperwork regarding the Jews throughout the country. Basically the sort of stuff you've been doing in London, on a slightly larger scale."

Hahn smiled as Koehler slumped a fraction in his chair.

"It isn't as bad as it sounds, Ernst. You'll be deskbound, so you'll not have to work directly with the Jews. You can just slide them across the tabletop on sheets of paper and keep your hands clean."

"Thank you, sir," Koehler said unconvincingly.

Hahn paused, then steepled his fingers and leaned forward, elbows on the desk.

"I know this is difficult for you, Ernst, but whether you like it or not, you are good at your job. Stick with this for a while and I'll get you some leave back in Germany with your wife and child. How does that sound?"

"Thank you, sir."

"It'll keep you away from the Jews, and give me a man I can trust working there to keep an eye on things."

"Yes, sir."

"You will report for duty in five days. That'll give you time to get your Oak Leaves and say good-bye to your family when they return to Germany." Hahn slid the file to the far side of his desk and pointed at the door. "You are dismissed."

Koehler sat and stared at Hahn for a second, then nodded slowly. He rose, put on his cap, and saluted before making his way to the door.

"Ernst," Hahn called, and Koehler turned to face him.

"Sir?"

"You are a stunning soldier. You really are one of the best. Germany needs you and I need you. This is important work. We're sowing the seeds for the future here, remember that. You've plenty of fight left in you, you just haven't realized it yet."

"Thank you, sir," Koehler said.

For fuck all, Koehler thought, closing the door behind him.

CHAPTER 5

IT WAS SAID that the diplomatic quarter of London was one of the safest places on earth.

Maps now featured a thick black line that signified the German ring of steel, an impenetrable phalanx of checkpoints within which roaming squads of German soldiers patrolled, ready to sweep up those foolish enough to be inside without good reason and the correct papers.

A circle of safety for those on the German payroll, and a place where swastikas and portraits of the new leadership remained safe from resistance paintbrushes.

Inside the ring security was tight; at its edge it was tighter still. Ever since the Waterloo Station bomb a few years earlier, the Germans had taken care to protect their own. Now, just a few years later, it was said that the pigeons in Trafalgar Square had to show their papers every morning before landing on Nelson's Column.

All this meant that Lotte Koehler felt safe as she walked with Anja along Regent Street toward Piccadilly. The snow was falling beautifully, silently sliding past the swastikas that hung from every other lamppost, virginal bright white against the bloodred flags that hung limp, barely drifting in the gathering breeze.

A few nervous-looking cars crept down the road, back ends slipping this way and that on the compacting snow, their occupants rushing home before the storm closed the roads. Lotte noticed that the buses were almost all empty; the city was battening down. It made her wonder how Ernst's meeting with Hahn was going and whether he'd be home before them.

Maybe they'd be heading back to their real home soon?

Back to Germany, back to being a family.

"Can we build a snowman tonight when Daddy gets home?" Anja tugged on her hand.

"Aren't you a little old for snowmen?"

"You are never too old for snowmen, Mother, even you," Anja teased, and Lotte realized how much her little girl was growing—thirteen, nearly fourteen, not nearly a young woman but already her best friend.

Anja beamed at her mother, red cheeked, strands of blond hair escaping from under her woolen hat.

"Frau Koehler?" A young man in a smart suit and overcoat approached from where he was standing next to an Opel parked at the curb. "Your husband sent me to collect you." The man pointed to the open rear door of the car.

"My husband sent you?"

"Yes, ma'am. He said I was to pick you up and take you home." A smile, and almost impeccable German.

"He said that?"

"Yes, ma'am." The man took a shopping bag from Anja. "The weather, he was worried." The man pointed a finger up at the snow falling around them, just in case Lotte hadn't noticed it.

Lotte looked into the Opel. Another man was sitting in the driver's seat, also smiling.

"My husband Ernst sent you here to collect me?" Lotte turned to the first man.

"Yes, ma'am." The smile now didn't quite reach his eyes.

Lotte stepped back from the car, taking hold of Anja's hand once more.

"Who are you?"

"We're attached to your husband's office; we provide low-key security, ma'am."

"I've never seen or heard of you."

"That shows we're doing our job." The smile again.

Lotte looked at Anja and then back at him.

"Do you have identification?"

"Of course." An ID card swept into sight from where it had been waiting in his right hand. "We do need to get moving . . ."

"I have one more thing to buy."

"Allow us to take you to the shop. This is awful weather to be walking in."

Lotte lowered her head to take another look at the driver, who was now staring straight ahead, hands on the wheel, waiting.

"The shop is just across the road; we can walk."

"I must insist, Frau Koehler."

Lotte took another half step and Anja, sensing tension, looked first at her mother and then cautiously over her shoulder at the half-empty street behind them.

"There really is no need, the shop is just across the road." Lotte pointed to a nearby tailor's shop, barely visible through the plummeting snow that was getting heavier by the minute.

From out of the shop two uniformed army officers appeared. They paused to light cigarettes in the doorway.

Lotte stepped off the curb and started walking toward them; behind her the man took a step forward and then stopped. He rested a hand on the roof of the car, glancing toward the shop and then smiling.

"We'll wait for you here."

Lotte was already halfway across the road, Anja a few steps behind. Anja glanced back over her shoulder at the young man and smiled. He was handsome, tall, well built, and well dressed.

His smile was gone; he was now watching the German officers on the other side of the street, tugging at their collars and heading off toward the bright lights of Piccadilly Circus.

LOTTE KOEHLER WASN'T a normal officer's wife.

Lotte Koehler had shot her first wolf when she was nine years old.

When she was eleven she and her father had tracked a wounded boar for two days. She had finally killed that same boar after it thundered out of the blackness of the forest and into their camp at midnight before goring her sleeping father as he lay next to their dwindling campfire.

Lotte Koehler knew how to fight, she knew how to look after herself, and she knew how to look after those whom she loved.

But most of all she knew when something felt wrong.

As she walked toward the tailor's shop with Anja, watching the men in the Opel in the reflection of the shop window as she approached it, Lotte Koehler knew something was seriously wrong.

She knew that Ernst would have told her about a plainclothes security service. She also knew that while the young man spoke excellent German, really excellent German, it wasn't his first language. It sounded like someone from the movies: perfect, too perfect, clipped and polished so that it was cut like glass.

Cut glass with a tiny trace of an American twang.

The other thing that wasn't right was that they had said Ernst had sent them; it wasn't right because Ernst didn't know where they were.

She hadn't told him she *was* shopping. It was her and Anja's little secret, time to buy a present for their dearest Ernst before they left him to go back to Berlin.

Something was wrong, and she knew she had to do something about it, because if she and Anja were in danger, Ernst was in danger, and this lioness protected her pride.

THERE WAS A deep mahogany gloom inside the tailor's shop. What light struggled through the windows seemed to be sucked up by the dark red carpet and the solemn tick-tock of the old grandfather clock that was standing sentry by the door.

Only one member of staff was visible as Lotte pushed Anja ahead of her. Anja turned to look at her mother.

"What is it?" she asked, but Lotte looked back out through the door and didn't reply.

Across the street she could see that both men were now standing on the pavement, talking and ignoring the snow that was bucketing down around them. They were staring at the shop, and neither seemed pleased with the way events were unfolding.

"May I help you, madam?" the shop assistant said slowly in English, speaking clearly, as if addressing a child.

"*Sie verfügen über ein Telefon?*" Lotte replied, still looking through the glass at the men outside.

The shopkeeper smiled, holding out his hands apologetically.

"I'm terribly sorry, madam. One doesn't speak German; I normally have an assistant who does, but with the weather . . ." The tailor's statement trailed off redundantly with a shrug.

"Do you have a telephone, please?" Anja translated for her mother into perfect English. Lotte breathed a sigh of relief that she and Ernst had chosen to employ a British nanny back in Germany.

"If you would like to step this way."

Lotte and Anja followed the tailor to the back of the shop. They'd barely made it halfway when the door behind them opened and the two men from the car entered.

The first smiled at Lotte as he brushed some snow off his shoulders and then looked past her to the tailor. Behind him, the driver stared out through the door toward Regent Street, in the manner that Lotte had done a few moments earlier.

"Frau Koehler, really, we must insist you come with us now; your husband is waiting." The same immaculate but not-quite-right German. He tapped his wrist and shrugged an apology.

"I need to make a telephone call," Lotte replied, opening her handbag while still walking through the shop.

"Now, Frau Koehler. We need to go now." The driver spoke for the first time, his German rougher around the edges, his hand resting on the handle of the door, the other held out, inviting Lotte to leave the shop.

She stopped, turned, then tilted her head. "I must also insist," she said, an edge creeping in.

Lotte stared at the man before following a nervous Anja to the back of the shop. Light and sound from the street were virtually nonexistent as the shopkeeper finally reached the telephone. It sat on a glass display case that contained ties, handkerchiefs, and a selection of brightly colored socks.

Lotte was fumbling in her bag, looking for the number of Ernst's private office, when the first man reached around her and rested his hand on top of the receiver.

"Now, if you please," he said quietly, intimately, his lips a few inches from her ear.

Lotte paused, looking at the hand on the receiver in front of her. A second passed before she half turned and jabbed her silver Walther PPK pistol hard into his side.

"Get away from me and my child," Lotte said quietly, pushing hard with the muzzle of the PPK, so hard he felt it dig right through his overcoat and separate two of his ribs a fraction.

He looked down and then back up into Lotte's eyes.

"Frau Koehler, please . . ."

Behind him, the driver, confused by the quiet conversation between Lotte and his colleague, moved closer.

"She has a gun," the first man said quietly in English, looking down at the pistol.

Nobody moved.

The tick of the clock was the only reminder that the earth still turned, until Lotte shouted.

"Go!" She looked at Anja. "Out the back, run!"

As Lotte shouted to Anja she remembered another time. Long ago, another life almost. She remembered opening her heavy eyes, seeing the smoldering campfire, and hearing her father screaming.

Lotte remembered the sound of the boar, the smell of it, the sparks kicking up from the fire, and the flecks of spittle as her father shouted one word.

One final word to save the life of his precious daughter before he was overcome.

"Run."

Back then, all those years ago, Lotte hadn't done as she was told, either.

Anja launched herself at the man next to her mother with all the fury a thirteen-year-old girl could muster. She gripped his coat collar with one hand and pushed as hard as she could. Clawing at his face with her other hand, she gritted her teeth and felt her nails dragging across his skin.

She was screaming, slapping, kicking, and pulling now, her words just animal sounds and fury.

ERIC COOK'S DAY was going from bad to worse.

He tried to ignore Anja and her fingernails ripping at his cheeks. He tried to focus on the gun as the blows rained down on him; he flicked his head, this way and that, shoving with his shoulder, but still Anja fought, and still Lotte twisted the pistol, trying to pull it free from his hands. He'd managed to grab the top slide of the pistol, jamming the webbing of his thumb under the hammer to stop it from falling.

Anja was like a dervish as she slapped and scraped at his face. He felt a finger in his eye and then his eyelid stretching under the drag of its nail.

He shook his head, squeezing his eyes tight as he called for help.

"For God's sake, King, help me here!"

The second he shouted he knew he'd done wrong. He knew there was no going back, no escape, no denial, and no doubt that he had made the biggest mistake of his life.

Eric Cook had called for help in a broad American accent, and Eric Cook had used a name.

Frank King winced.

They'd blown it.

King stepped forward and attempted to drag Anja away from his partner. He grabbed one of her arms, pulling it up, but the maelstrom twisted and turned, and then the girl started to scream as she felt herself being dragged from her mother.

Cook felt the girl finally slide off him. His eye was watering and his nose was sore from where she had smacked him hard in the face. He gasped a breath and felt Lotte jerk the pistol again, trying to pull it free from his grip.

The battle wasn't over yet.

Lotte tried to twist the pistol as Cook worked the muzzle out of his ribs, both hands still clamped around the slide and hammer, clinging on for dear life, desperately squinting down to see where the gun was going as they wrestled it between them.

Lotte dropped a shoulder and Cook thought he would overbalance; she ducked in low at his hip and then twisted. He felt the pistol slipping in his hands as he looked toward King for help again.

Help wasn't forthcoming.

FRANK KING WAS suffering his own private nightmare with Anja. Punches, shin kicks, scratches, and shrieks rattled around him as he dropped his chin into his chest and tried to grab at her free arm.

Anja was still screaming, higher now, painful to the ears, setting King's teeth on edge. He couldn't take any more; he gave up trying to grab her arm and pulled back his hand to slap her face.

He stopped when he heard the shot.

Time stood still.

Everyone froze for the briefest of moments as their ears rang and they waited for sense to return.

King looked at Cook and then at the tailor, who hadn't moved throughout the entire pantomime. Cook suddenly started to struggle again, the respite from the shock of the shot over. He grunted, jerked, then grunted again before he finally managed to rip the Walther from Lotte and point it up at the ceiling.

"You okay?" King asked.

Cook nodded, his face pale. He looked at Lotte, who took a half step back, the fight gone along with the pistol.

Anja started to cry. She tried to move toward her mother, who stared watery eyed at King and then at her daughter.

"Don't do anything stupid and your daughter can come to you, understand?" King said in his leaden German.

Lotte nodded, and King allowed Anja to go to her. She held her mother close, her head buried in the fur coat Lotte had worn against the cold weather that morning.

It took everyone except Lotte by surprise when she slowly sank to the floor, Anja desperately trying to hold her up.

"Mama?" said Anja, confused.

Lotte's head lolled and Cook dropped to his knees next to her, quickly pulling open her coat. Just below Lotte's groin, blood was leaching out, staining her white dress.

Anja moaned at the sight of the blood and Lotte looked down, an almost curious expression on her face.

"Oh, no," Cook said in English as he looked up at King and then quickly lifted the dress to find the wound. "She's bleeding to death. Fuck, oh fuck, give me a tie." Cook looked up at the tailor, who meekly stared back.

"Give him a tie!" King shouted at the little man, who suddenly burst to life. He almost ran around the glass display counter and dropped the flap at the back. King watched him grab a handful of brightly colored ties and hankies and toss them over the counter to Cook. The tailor rubbed a dainty pink palm across his forehead and then looked at King.

King stared back, then gave a tiny nod of his head.

The tailor nodded back and swallowed.

King checked on Cook and saw his hand was thick with treacly blood.

"Can you see it?" he leaned forward to get a closer look.

"What?"

"The wound, can you see it?"

Cook didn't reply.

"I'll call an ambulance." The tailor lifted the phone, but King spun around and slammed his hand across the cradle.

"Wait." King raised a finger and stared deeply into the tailor's eyes. "Wait," he repeated quietly.

The tailor took a step back and shot a look at Lotte and Cook. King read the look and sighed inwardly. Things were going from bad to worse.

"How is she?" he asked quietly.

"It's bad, Frank." Cook looked up and King thought he saw tears in the younger man's eyes.

King leaned forward again and looked into Lotte's face. She looked confused, bewildered by the blood that was sneaking out of her. This really wasn't what King had planned. He ran his hand through his hair and looked back toward the door before bending down and picking up the gun. He studied the Walther and then lowered it to his side.

"Well?" he asked Cook while looking at the tailor, who stared back silently.

"I've found where it went in, but it's bleeding like a bitch." Cook looked up and shook his head at King, who sighed and looked away, pondering his options.

"Can you stop it?"

Cook shrugged.

King tapped the Walther against his leg, then looked over his shoulder at the door again.

He squeezed his lips together as he looked down at Cook, the pistol still knocking against his leg as if it were eager to get away from the scene of the crime.

King knew how it felt.

"I'm sorry," Cook said.

"So am I," King replied as he looked at the tailor, who slowly started to raise his hands and then gave a slight shake of his head.

"I'll not say anything. I'm all for the resistance, I swear I'll not say a word."

"We're not the resistance," King said, just before he shot the tailor dead.

The little man dropped like sand.

King looked down at Cook, Anja, and Lotte, who all stared back, open-mouthed.

"Go get the car. Park it on the curb by the door," King said quietly to Cook.

Cook looked at Anja and then at his bloodstained hand, still gripping the silk necktie tourniquet on Lotte's leg.

"Go get the car," King repeated, very quietly.

Cook nodded, looked at Anja again, and then stood up, wiping his hands on his coat.

He stepped over Lotte and hurried past King to get to the car. The bell above the shop door rang brightly after a second or two, causing Anja to lift her head and look at King.

He saw her cheeks were wet, and he licked his lips and felt a thud in his chest.

"Why?" Anja said softly in English, her hand now holding the tie tightly around her mother's leg.

King could feel his own pulse pounding in his neck, and he looked at the dead tailor on the floor. He opened his mouth, but the first word caught in his throat and he had to cough it free.

"This will be okay. You just need to do as you are told. Believe me, you'll both be okay."

"Just go. We don't know who you are." Lotte surprised King by speaking, and he had to move slightly so that he could look into her face.

She blinked back at him, paler than before but strangely beautiful with her blond hair spread across her shoulders where it had fallen during the struggle.

"You will be fine. I'll see to it. We have doctors. Trust me."

"Let my daughter go."

King looked toward the front of the shop, suddenly afraid that Eric was going to run away.

"She is only a child. Please, let her go."

King raised a hand, motioning that she should be quiet.

"I promise I'll give you no trouble if you let her go," Lotte tried again.

"That isn't going to happen. I'm sorry."

The bell sounded above the door.

Cook jogged back toward them, stopping just short of King.

"Get the woman and put her in the car," King said in English, now that there was no point in pretending to be German.

Cook nodded, then nervously approached Anja and Lotte.

Anja tensed, half turning to Cook as she hunched across her mother, causing Cook to look at King, unsure of what to do next.

King lowered the pistol. "Help him to put your mother in the car, and then we'll get her some help."

Anja looked unsure as Cook nodded, holding out his hands, palms out. He gestured that they should lift Lotte together. Anja nodded and Cook approached cautiously before crouching down. He tugged on the tourniquet once more and then grabbed an arm; with Anja's help, he lifted Lotte from the floor.

King stepped back as Anja and Cook supported Lotte between them. They headed for the front door. He looked briefly at the tailor on the floor and then bent down to pick up Lotte's handbag. He saw a cash register at the back of the shop and quickly moved around the counter to open it.

There was less than three pounds inside, but he took the money and then knocked the register onto the floor. He looked once more at the dead man and gave a slight shake of his head. It was time to go.

CHAPTER 6

YOU SAID YOU were going to take us to the hospital." Anja's face was wet with tears.

Her mother's head lolled in her hands as the car thudded through a rut in the snow.

Lotte moaned softly.

"I didn't," King replied as he eased the car to a halt at a red light.

"You did! You said you would!"

King looked over his shoulder at Anja and then at Cook, who was crouching in the footwell of the backseat, pressing against the wound at the top of Lotte's leg.

Cook's hands were wet with blood.

"I said I'd see to it that she was okay." King turned back to looking at the traffic lights, which were still resolutely stuck on red.

"She needs the hospital, please!" Anja shouted, tears tumbling, looking first at the back of King's head and then at the top of Cook's.

"Maybe we should call the embassy, Frank?"

Cook sounded panicky. King glanced at Anja in the mirror and then at her mother. He could see that Lotte's cheek was daubed with some blood off Anja's hands.

The snow, which was still falling, had cleared the streets of pedestrians and traffic. King lifted his foot from the brake and thought about driving through the red light, before changing his mind again and deciding to wait.

He pressed down again on the brake. He didn't want some bored cop pulling him over when he had a woman bleeding to death on his backseat. The windscreen wipers juddered on the glass as the snow lessened; he switched them off and looked again at Anja, who was whispering to her mother as she stroked her face.

"Keep an eye on her, Eric; they're whispering."

Cook looked up at Lotte and Anja. "She's out cold." Cook shifted his position so that his head was inches from the back of King's. "We really need to get her to the hospital, she's bleeding out."

Anja started to cry again.

The lights finally changed and the car started to move.

"Just keep her alive; maintain pressure on the wound. We'll sort things out when we get to the flat and I get to speak with control."

COOK LOOKED AT Anja and Lotte, chewed down on his lip, then returned to pressing on the wound. King had collected a handful of woolen scarves as they had left the shop, and Cook picked up another to wrap around the three blood-soaked ones that were already on Lotte's leg.

A rainbow of colors that was slowly staining deep bloodred.

Blood pooled around his fingers when he pressed the wound. He looked up to check if Anja had seen how bad things were. She had. She sniffed and wiped her nose, then met Cook's gaze.

"Please," she whispered. "My mother is dying, you have to help her."

The car jolted and Lotte groaned again. Cook looked down at her and then wiped his face, smearing it with blood.

"She needs a hospital, please," Anja tried again, reaching forward to help Cook tie off the scarf he was wrapping. Her hand brushed against the back of his, he looked up at her, and she took hold of his fingers. "Don't let her die. She's my mummy."

"Stop talking to her, Eric."

Cook flinched as King spoke to him from the front seat. He shook his hand free before placing it back onto Lotte's wound, eyes downcast, unwilling to meet Anja's.

ANJA STARTED TO cry again, quietly this time, shifting in her seat so that she could better cradle her mother's head. She felt the car turn and looked up to see that they were now in a very different part of London than Regent Street.

Dark, brooding, run-down blocks of buildings seemed to crowd in on the narrow road. The shop windows were empty. Anja saw an old man in an apron, watching them through distorted glass that made him seem to ripple as they drove past. Streetlamps were flickering to life in the gathering gloom, struggling to light the inside of their lenses.

Anja caught sight of a name above a shop: COHEN BROS BUTCHERS, WHITE-CHAPEL. The shop was boarded up but the sign remained, gold on blue paint, snow covering its edges. A yellow star of David was painted vividly on the boards across the windows.

The paint had run at the tip of the star; Anja thought it looked like it was crying.

Whitechapel? She'd heard of it, but couldn't remember where. She tried to guess how long they'd been in the car. Twenty minutes? Maybe more?

Anja twisted her head. Each house looked the same: cold, closed, unwilling to help.

She stroked her mother's hair; they were alone.

Over King's shoulder, through the windscreen, she saw a public telephone box at the end of the road. It sat on the corner, outside another boarded-up shop, bright red in the white and gray. The car started to slow even more and she dared to imagine that King was stopping to call for help.

He eased into the curb at the call box, then switched off the engine.

Silence.

Nobody spoke. There was no wind, no voices out on the street, nothing but silence.

Anja looked at Cook, who seemed to be staring at the back of King's head. She followed his lead and saw that King was moving slightly, an inch this way and that, checking the street around them in the car's mirrors.

Their reflected eyes met. He held her gaze a moment and then carried on searching the street. Anja did the same; she looked over her shoulder out of the back window of the car, and then back at King, who finally spoke.

"Stay here." King got out.

He left the door open as he took a few steps onto the snow-covered curb. He paused by the call box and then fished in his pocket.

"He's going to call an ambulance," Anja whispered down at her mother, then gently traced some hair off her forehead with her finger.

King turned from the call box and went to the narrow, peeling black door next to the boarded-up shop. He pulled out a key, which Anja could see glinting in his hand, and opened the door. He had to push against the swollen wood a couple of times to get it to open. When it finally did, he pushed it ajar and returned to the car.

King surveyed the street, then opened the car's rear door and looked in at Anja.

"How good is your English?" King asked in German.

"Excellent," replied Anja primly.

King nodded and then spoke, this time in English.

"You will help him carry your mother; she needs to get inside quickly so we can look after her. Do you understand?"

Anja nodded.

"The tailor at the shop, he didn't do as he was told. Remember what happened to him?"

Anja nodded. King stared at her a moment and then flicked his head, gesturing for Cook to get out of the car.

"Push her toward me," King instructed Anja as he took hold of Lotte's legs and dragged her forward. When she was half out of the car King gripped the semiconscious Lotte under the arms, and turning, swiveled her so that Cook was able to grab her upper body, taking her from him.

King turned back toward Anja as her mother slid the last part of the way out of the backseat.

"Take her legs." King gripped Anja's arm, pulling her toward her mother.

Anja did as she was told, and she and Cook carried Lotte into the building. Behind her she heard the car doors slam.

King entered the building and kicked the front door shut behind him, then flicked a switch that turned on a bulb at the top of the staircase. The stairs were narrow; Cook had to twist his head to look over his shoulder as they climbed, feet echoing on the wooden boards with each hesitant backward step. Anja, still holding Lotte's legs, stared up at her mother's gray face.

She could feel King's hand occasionally on her back as they silently made their way up to the first floor. The naked bulb above lit a tiny landing. Two doors greeted them, once white but now faded and dirty, one left, one right.

"Back room," King said.

Cook kicked open the door on the right and shuffled in. The room was dark; it smelled of damp and seemed colder than outside. Anja shivered, lowering her head as if the weight of the gloom was pushing it down. King must have flicked a switch behind her, because another bulb flickered hesitantly into life, even dimmer than the one on the landing. There was a stained mattress on the floor, under a boarded-up window. Anja and Cook shuffled automatically over and laid Lotte down upon it.

Anja looked toward King, who was still standing at the door, hand on the light switch.

"The man at the shop?" Anja said quietly.

"Yes," King replied.

"He was doing as he was told; you killed him anyway. You are a liar and a murderer."

King looked at the floor and then looked back at Anja.

"I am. And you would do well to remember it," he said before leaving the room.

Cook watched King go, then leaned down to check the scarves tied around Lotte's leg.

He looked up at Anja.

"Did you bring the other scarves?"

"No."

He got up from the crouch and stared at Lotte a moment, wiping his hands on his coat again.

"I'll go get them." He walked to the door and paused at the threshold. "Remember, Frank is out here. Don't try to leave."

"I wouldn't leave my mother." Anja didn't look around at Cook as she spoke. He nodded, as much to himself as anything, then closed the door.

Anja heard his boots banging down the stairs and looked up at the boards on the window.

"If you get the chance, run. Run as fast as you can."

Anja gave a start and looked down at her mother, whose lips were blue, her skin white like paper.

"I won't leave you," Anja whispered.

"You must go. These men, they'll kill you."

"I won't leave you." Anja smoothed her mother's cheek.

Lotte smiled, but it soon faded, like a ripple on a pond. Her face relaxed to nothing but a slow blink. When her eyes reopened Anja could see only the whites flutter for a moment before the iris reluctantly rolled back into sight.

"I'm dying, my love."

Anja started to cry and wiped her mother's forehead, then looked down at the leg wound.

"No."

"Don't give up, whatever they do. Don't stop thinking about how you can get away. You must run." Lotte closed her eyes again and Anja heard a creaking breath inflate her mother's lungs.

"Shush, rest."

"Don't give up. Go to your father." This time Lotte's eyes didn't open.

"Rest, Mummy."

The breath rattled in.

"I love you, Anja."

"I love you, too, Mummy."

The breath rattled out.

Lotte Koehler was dead.

CHAPTER 7

BY THE TIME Ernst Koehler got home the cat had shit on the rug.

"Jesus Christ" was all Koehler could manage as he skirted the mess and opened the floor-to-ceiling French windows on the far side of the room. Clean, cold evening air wafted across his face as he looked out across the deserted South Kensington street, three floors below him, and then back to his feet, where Schwarz innocently stared back up.

"What are they feeding you?"

"Miaow," the cat replied, ignoring the question.

Koehler turned away from the window and dropped his SS greatcoat onto a chair. He cleaned the floor, washed his hands in the bathroom, then wandered back into the living room. He stopped, looked toward the kitchen, then to the half-empty coat stand by the door.

Anja and Lotte weren't home.

Koehler looked at his watch: 9:15 P.M. He turned to look into the small kitchen of the apartment again and saw that there was no food prepared.

"Miaow," Schwarz tried again.

Koehler looked down at the cat.

"Where are they?"

"Miaow."

Koehler frowned and headed to the kitchen, followed by Schwartz, who high-stepped behind with a patter of tiny padded paws, his tail almost overtaking his head.

Koehler saw both the cat's bowls were empty, water and food.

"They've been out all day?"

"Miaow."

Koehler fed the cat and picked up the water bowl. He was holding it under the tap when the phone rang in the apartment behind him. He put the bowl on the floor and went to the phone, picking it up with his wet hand.

"Hello?"

"Outside."

"What?"

"Outside."

The person on the other end of the line hung up.

Koehler's hand holding the phone felt cold in the breeze coming from the open window. He put the phone down slowly, walked to the edge of the window, and gently eased back the net with his index finger. The snow was still falling; the street was Christmas card white, picture perfect. High, gray stone Georgian terraces stared back, sharp edges softened and frosted like cake.

Koehler looked down, through the narrow, waist-high wrought-iron balcony, to the street directly below. A few cars were parked for the night, his included. He could see two German soldiers, trudging through the snow on a routine patrol, walking away from his apartment block.

Across the street, like a figure out of a painting, stood a man. Hat pulled down low, collar up high, a cigarette in one hand, the other in his coat pocket.

The man stared back at him.

Koehler squinted and then stepped fully into the window, defiant, embarrassed at hiding to the side a moment before.

The man took a drag on his cigarette, flicked away the butt, and stared back.

Equally defiant.

KOEHLER HIT THE stairs at a run, hard and fast, three at a time, hammering down as quickly as his still-stiff calf would allow. On the ground floor the stairs opened out to a forty-foot marble entrance hall.

Koehler skidded, slipped, and then ran along the hall, one boot clapping on the marble while the other hit the long red carpet down its center. At the end of the hall was a dark-wood-and-glass revolving door, to its left an equally dark concierge desk.

The door was turning, slowing to a stop.

Someone had just passed through it.

"Major Koehler, sir?"

Koehler heard the call as he hit the first compartment of the revolving door, pushing hard, fighting its inbuilt resistance with gritted teeth and a barging shoulder.

The sentry on the steps flinched as Koehler erupted through, leaping down the four stone steps to the street, then sliding slightly to an ungraceful stop in the snow.

He was just in time to see the back end of a long, low black saloon car drift away around the far corner. Koehler grabbed his pockets, searching for his car keys, then remembered he'd left them in his coat in the apartment.

He felt impotent on the pavement in the falling snow. He looked at the sentry, who was now standing at attention, doing his best to ignore the panting SS major in front of him.

"That car?"

"Yes, sir?"

"Who was in it?"

The sentry turned his head to look toward where the car had gone.

"A man, sir, he looked like a civilian, in a suit."

"How long where they here?"

The soldier shrugged. "He arrived not long after you, sir, had a smoke, and went into the—"

The door behind the sentry started to turn again, slower this time. Koehler looked and saw through the glass that the concierge, an old Englishman whose name he could never remember, was leaning against the bar coming toward him.

Koehler stepped up to the door and gave it a shove with his good hand, speeding up the old man, who barely managed to get out of the compartment without getting his heels clipped.

The concierge held out an envelope. "I was calling you, Major. A gentleman left this, sir," he said in English to Koehler, who stepped forward and snatched the envelope out of his hand.

It felt empty and had no name on it. Koehler ripped it open and noticed that its gum felt damp.

He looked back to the corner where the car had disappeared, then opened the flimsy piece of airmail paper inside, which read "MAYFAIR 6266."

He looked at the other side, then back at the front.

"Did the man say anything to you when he gave you this?"

"No, sir."

"Was he English?"

"I don't know, sir."

"How do you not know? He must have spoken to you; there is no name on the envelope."

The old man wrinkled his nose and looked worried at the question, trying to think of the right answer to give.

"He just walked in, sir. He said 'Major Koehler,' gave me the envelope, then walked out. I couldn't say where he was from, sir."

Koehler looked back to the corner of the road, then ran a hand across his mouth before looking at the note again.

"Should I call for the officer of the watch, sir?" the sentry asked nervously.

"No," Koehler replied, crossing the street and looking up at his apartment.

The snow was falling hard again and he blinked as flakes dodged and danced in front of his eyes. Some landed on his face. He wiped his cheek, then looked down at the pavement, where he saw the half-hidden cigarette butt the man had dropped.

He bent to pick it up; it was smoked low to the end. Across the street the sentry and concierge watched him. Koehler stared back. The concierge looked away and ran a nervous hand across his waistcoat.

Koehler looked down at the snow again; he squinted, then flicked a finger across where he had found the cigarette butt.

There was a bullet.

He picked it up; it looked like a 9mm round.

Shiny, new, unfired.

Koehler stood up, squeezing the round tight in his hand. He looked up to his window, imagining how he would have looked staring down moments ago.

He shook his head, angry all over again that he had stood to the side. He walked back across the street, then stopped on the steps.

"Have you seen my wife today?"

"Yes, sir. She wanted a cab for one o'clock this afternoon, sir," replied the concierge, still rubbing his stomach.

"Where was she going?"

"She didn't say, I—"

"She hasn't been back?"

"Not that I'm aware, sir."

Koehler checked his watch again.

He looked back across the road, as if expecting the ghost of the man he'd seen earlier to still be watching him.

"Thank you." Koehler pushed against the revolving door.

"I can call the officer of the watch, sir; he won't mind."

Koehler didn't reply; he was already back in the building.

THE APARTMENT SMELLED of cat shit. Koehler closed the door and crossed to the window, followed by a still-complaining Schwarz.

Koehler pushed the window open wider, checking the street outside again.

The breeze blew the net back into his face and he swiped it away like a cobweb.

Everything was back to normal. No silent watchers, no smoking men.

Just bored sentries and snow.

Koehler took the note out of his pocket and went to the telephone next to the settee. He sat down, but before he could reach for the phone Schwarz plopped into his lap, head butting his hand while pawing his stomach. Koehler reached for the phone with one hand while stroking the cat with the other.

The phone rang four times before it was picked up.

"Hello?" a voice answered in English.

"Who is this?" asked Koehler, also in English.

"Major Koehler?"

"Who is this?"

Schwarz nuzzled his chin, so he pushed the cat down, twisting his head as he did so, struggling to hold the receiver against his ear.

"We have your wife and daughter." The voice switched to German.

"What?"

"We have your wife and daughter. They are safe as long as you do exactly what we say. Do you understand?"

Koehler sat forward, squeezing Schwarz down tightly into his lap.

"Who is this?"

"You are to leave your apartment and drive to the corner of Bayswater Road and Queensway. There is a public telephone there. Enter the call box. There will be an envelope for you. Bring nobody; tell nobody. If you break these rules your family dies."

The phone went dead.

Koehler looked at the receiver. He leaned back an inch and then realized Schwarz was digging his claws into his leg. Koehler put a finger over the cradle of the phone, killing the call before dialing the number again.

The phone rang, unanswered, eight times before he put the phone down.

He stood, pushing Schwarz onto the floor. Koehler paused, looking around the apartment for ideas as Schwarz rubbed his head against his boots.

Koehler looked at the phone.

"Should I phone the police?" he said out loud.

"Miaow."

Koehler pushed a hand against his forehead and crossed to the window again. There was nobody there, just as he knew there wouldn't be. He looked back to the phone and then down at Schwarz, who had followed him to the window.

Koehler knew he had no choice. He closed the window, grabbed his cap and coat, then left the apartment to go and get his wife and child.

KOEHLER GUIDED HIS car into the curb and killed the engine. The sudden silence seemed to drop the temperature inside of the car.

Queensway was thirty seconds' walk from the north side of Hyde Park, in an area not dissimilar to the one he lived in himself. The drive had taken him less than seven minutes, and he was now sitting outside Queensway tube station, staring at the phone box on the corner of the street.

He wanted to get out and run to the box.

He wanted to search the area, look for clues, bang on doors, ask about strangers and strange cars. But he was too much of a soldier; he'd set and seen too many ambushes to run anywhere, regardless of how desperate he was.

He scanned the park.

Iron railings, dark hedges topped with a layer of snow.

Full of shadows, which were potentially full of snipers.

He took his Mauser out of his pocket and worked the slide.

The street was quiet, the snow keeping people at home. The tube station was still open, but aside from a light in the ticket office, there was no sign of life. A red London bus hove into view in the distance, coming toward him slowly. Koehler could make out the top deck's milky white lights over the headlamps as it drew closer.

As the bus crept past at ten miles an hour on the empty street, Koehler rolled out of the car door, using it to protect him from any potential threat in the park. By the time the bus had gone by, Koehler was standing in the shadows of the entrance of the tube station, being watched warily by the ticket seller in the window.

The ticket seller's eyes took in Koehler's uniform and then dropped to the Mauser. He slowly slid off his stool, disappearing behind the CLOSED blind he lowered as he went.

Koehler stood behind the pillar at the left side of the entrance, eyes back on the park. He frowned, wondering if it was too late to call in the police to help him.

Some snow blew in from the street, tumbling over his feet.

He'd spent the drive over silently debating the pros and cons of what to do next. In the end he'd taken the easiest option and done as he was told.

He'd play along, learn what he could, wait and see, and then make a decision.

He dodged out of the station entrance and ducked around the corner toward the call box.

There were no snipers.

Why would they shoot me? he asked himself, embarrassed at his extra precautions but keeping hold of the pistol all the same.

The telephone box, like the bus, was bright red, and like the bus it was lit inside by the same milky white light.

Koehler pulled back the heavy door and stepped inside. He looked down at the concrete floor and saw that someone had been there recently. Wet footprints: he wondered how long they would last on a damp cold night like tonight. He looked through the windows at the intersection outside.

Both roads were major thoroughfares, but tonight they were deserted, the shops all closed. In the distance Koehler could see a green neon sign blinking on and off, as if the city had a pulse. He checked the upper windows of the nearby buildings, but even the ones that were lit revealed no movement in the flats behind them.

He turned to look at the phone, which sat on a shelf in front of him.

There was no message, no envelope, nothing.

He ran his hand under the shelf, bending to look as he did so.

Nothing.

He picked up the telephone directory that sat next to the phone and flipped through the pages.

Nothing but numbers.

He lifted the receiver, holding it to his ear. It purred, and he thought of Schwarz.

He put the phone down and took a tiny step back, as far as he could go in the tiny call box.

He looked up.

A brown envelope was jammed into the frame of the door just above his head. He pulled it down and ripped it open.

Another sheet of airmail paper: "WHITECHAPEL 6168."

Koehler put the note in his mouth as he searched through his pockets for change; he came up empty.

He pushed the call box door open and charged out into the snow, running toward the tube station through the steady fall that had started again. He skidded around the corner, then skidded again on the wet floor tiles, before tapping the muzzle of the Mauser on the glass of the ticket office.

He waited five seconds and then tapped again, harder and faster this time. Beneath his feet he felt the vibration of a passing tube train and he turned to look toward the steps that led down to the platforms.

Adolf Hitler stared back, holding a laughing child in a sunlit pasture;

behind him a tractor tilled the land and some farm laborers waved toward whoever was looking at the poster they were in.

"WORKING FOR THE FUTURE TOGETHER, WORKING FOR A UNITED EUROPE!"

Koehler looked at the laughing child, then hammered on the window with the Mauser again.

The blind shot up and the ticket collector stared back, first at Koehler and then at the Mauser.

"Give me money for the telephone."

The man nodded dumbly and then grabbed some change and notes out of his cash drawer. He tossed the money through the slot at the bottom of the window, then raised his hands.

Koehler slid the change off the counter into his palm, then looked at the ticket collector's raised hands.

"This isn't a robbery, you idiot."

The man lowered his hands as Koehler ran out of the tube station, back toward the phone box.

He dialed the number, waited for it to answer, then dropped the money into the slot and pushed the call lever.

"Hello?"

"You took your time."

"I had to be careful."

"No, Major, not had: *have*. You have to be careful. You have to be careful that you don't mess me around. You have to do as I say, exactly as I say, and when I say it. Do you understand?"

"I do."

"Good."

"Lotte and Anja?"

"They are well."

"I want to speak to them."

"In good time."

"What do you want?"

"You to do something."

"What?"

"We want a Jew."

"You can have them, any of them. If I can get them you can have them."

"Don't make promises you can't keep, Major."

"I want you to know, I don't have a problem with the Jews. I just do my job. I don't hate them, I just do my job; do you understand?" Koehler realized he was babbling. He took a breath and looked around the street outside through the windows of the box.

"We don't care about the Jews, Major. We care about a Jew. I want you to get me that Jew and bring her to London, and then you can have your wife and daughter back."

"Who is it? I'll get her. Just tell me who it is."

"Ruth Hartz."

Koehler searched frantically for a pencil in his coat, jammed the receiver under his chin, opened the phone book, and wrote the name in a space on the first damp page.

"The address?"

"Cambridge."

"Do you have a street or anything? Something to help me?"

"St. Catherine's Hall, Coton. It's a village just outside the town. She stays there when she isn't working at the Cavendish Labs, the physics department at the university."

"She's working? I thought you said she was a Jew."

"She is a special Jew, which is why we want her, and why you will get her. Do you see the post office on the other side of the street?"

Koehler put the pencil in his mouth as he scanned the street and found the post office.

"Yes."

"When the girl is in London, go to that post office and collect a parcel that will be waiting for you there. Further instructions will be inside. Do not deviate from these instructions or the ones in the parcel. Do you understand?"

"Yes."

There was a pause on the other end of the line.

"You've been chosen carefully, Ernst. None of this is accidental. Do you understand?"

"Yes." Koehler leaned an elbow on the shelf and rested his forehead in his hand.

"Ernst, the bullet, the one you picked up outside your apartment."

"Yes?"

"I took three out of a box this morning. I selected them myself, the first three, right next to each other, out of a fresh box."

"Yes."

"Don't make me use the other two."

The phone clicked dead and Koehler lowered his own receiver into the cradle. He ran a hand across his mouth and looked up and down Queensway through the windows of the box.

The neon sign pulsed; life went on as the snow slowly fell.

The ground under his feet rumbled. Koehler looked down at his boots; it felt like the devil was coming up to take his soul.

He shivered. It was going to be a long night.

CHAPTER 8

ANJA COULDN'T STOP shaking. She hugged her arms around herself and squeezed her eyes tight, but still she shook.

It was as if her clothes were made of ice and the blankets she lay under were soaked in water.

Her breath came in gulps, and though the tears had stopped, her eyes still ached as if they'd been wrung out and then dipped in vinegar.

"Be quiet," said King, who was standing at the door.

Anja wondered if she'd made a sound.

She shook again.

"Crying isn't going to bring her back. You must be quiet," King said again.

"I'm not crying."

"Well, be quiet then."

Anja opened her eyes and turned on the mattress, away from the wall with its dirty gray damp stains, toward him.

"I'm a child. I'm allowed to cry," she said, and King surprised her by smiling.

"I'm sorry."

"I want my father."

"Soon."

"Where is my mother?"

"She is being looked after."

"She's dead. I'm a child, not an idiot."

King tilted his head a fraction and nodded.

"Of course, I'm sorry."

Anja bit her lip and felt another shudder building in her chest.

"Why are you doing this?"

"We need you, just for a while."

"Why?"

"You don't need to know. Your father will collect you soon."

"My father will kill you."

"So be it," King replied.

"You'll be sorry," Anja said.

"I've been sorry a long time. A little longer won't make much difference. Now please, try to be quiet."

Anja stared at him and he stared back until she rolled over again to face the wall.

The mattress squeaked, but Anja was silent.

She wasn't going to cry anymore. She was going to do what her mother had told her.

She was going to fight.

She was going to get to her father.

"SHE'S DEAD?"

"Yes."

"Are you sure?"

"Yes, I'm sure; I'm not an idiot."

"Don't get smart with me. Remember who you are talking to."

"I'm sorry." King rubbed the bridge of his nose with his fingertips before resting his forehead on the cold window of the call box.

"How did she die?"

"She had a gun, hidden. When we tried to lift her, she became suspicious and pulled it. She was struggling with Eric and it went off; the round caught her in the leg and she bled out. There was nothing we could do."

"Jesus," Allen Dulles said softly.

King lifted himself off the glass and stood up, waiting for his boss, across the city in the American embassy, to collect himself.

"Did you tell Koehler when he rang?"

"No, sir."

"Good. How is the girl?"

"She's fine. Upset, but fine."

"Will she give you problems?"

"She's a kid. There'll be no issues."

"Are you keeping a low profile?"

"Absolutely. We're at the flat, and we haven't made a noise since we got here. The streets are deserted and the weather is helping keep them that way."

"Good."

Small mercies.

"I need to tell you, sir . . . there was a shop assistant." King rested his head against the glass of the call box again.

"And?"

"He's dead."

"How?" Dulles mumbled on the other end of the line.

"I had no choice."

"Is there anything else you need to tell me?"

"No."

"You sure?"

"Yes."

"Where is her mother?"

"We put her in the trunk of the car. We couldn't keep her in the flat; it's too small."

King waited, all the while staring at the darkened half-derelict shop next to the call box. "What about the shop assistant?" Dulles finally asked.

"We left him there. With all the snow nobody saw us come out, so I figured it wouldn't matter if he was found."

"You're sure?"

"Yes. I took some money from the register and messed up a few things to make it look like a robbery." King looked at the car, which was now coated in a half an inch of fresh snow. "What should I do with the woman's body?"

"Lose her tonight, do you understand? We don't need some bored cop stopping you and finding a body in the trunk."

"And the child?"

"Stick to the plan. There is no reason she shouldn't be able to go back to her father at the end of this."

"She knows our names, sir; she could talk."

"We'll have what we want, and you'll be out of the country with the scientist by then."

"Or dead."

"What?"

"Or dead by then."

"Frank, I don't have to tell you how important it is that there are no more mistakes, do I?"

"No, sir."

"We are out on a limb here; we've got no safety net if things go wrong."

"We?" King raised an eyebrow.

"I might not be on the ground with you, but I'm just as much on the line with you. I've pushed for this operation, there aren't many people in Washington on our side, and there is nobody going to stick up for us if things go to shit. Add to that there is nobody at the embassy here who knows what we are doing, and Ambassador Kennedy is further up Hitler's ass than Goering. You have to remember that we have no room left here, none whatsoever."

"There's even less on the streets of London, sir."

"I understand that, Frank, and I'm sorry."

King accepted the apology without speaking; he listened to Dulles give out a long sigh on the other end of the phone.

"Okay, so you've told him to get the Jew. What next?"

"We wait, sir; either Koehler will go get her, or he won't. I'm guessing with the snow things will take a while, but I think he'll get it done."

"We don't have long."

"Neither does he. He won't hang around."

"You sure he can do it?"

"Koehler's the best they have in London, sir; I didn't just pick him out of a hat. He works in the right office. His whole job is about shifting Jews around the country. His family were in London, which gave us leverage, and he has a history of operating outside of the rules. We are also aware that he has been having a crisis of confidence in what he is doing at the moment; he isn't the usual rabid SS officer, sir. I chose him carefully. He's the man, he knows the game, he knows he has one chance to get it right, and he'll get it right."

"All right. Just remember how important that girl in Cambridge is, Frank. Just remember what will happen if we don't get to her soon."

"I'll remember, sir."

"We need her. If we can get her back to America and show the president what she knows, what she and her team have been doing, maybe we can wake some people up."

"I know."

"You call me if you need me, understand?"

"Yes, sir."

"Take care."

King put down the receiver, pushed the door of the call box open, and stepped out. The city was silent, muffled by the snow.

He looked up and down the street. Nobody moved. It felt like he was the only person in the world, and for a moment he wondered what it would be like to just walk away, be on his own.

Start again? He had his passport in his apartment, money for a ticket; he could be out of this shithole of a country in ten hours and en route to the U.S., far away from dirty tricks and political games.

How important could this Jew be?

He let the door swing shut behind him and looked up at the falling snow.

No time for dreaming; Dulles would have him killed.

He knew it; he knew it because he'd done the killing for Dulles before.

He trudged across the pavement to the narrow door at the side of the shop, shouldered it open, then kicked it closed behind him. He clumped up the wooden stairs and noticed some fat dried drops of blood on the timber.

He pushed open the bedroom door and nodded his head at Cook, who was sitting on a low chair opposite the mattress where Anja lay under a thin brown blanket. King looked at Anja, face to the wall, trying to ignore them, and then at the floor. He noticed that his breath was misting in the chill of the room.

"What do we do?" Cook leaned forward like a nervous schoolboy desperate for information.

"We get rid of the body." King looked at Anja again.

"Now?" Cook said.

"Later. We'll take her to the river. The snow is due to keep coming and going all night. We can use the storm to cover us."

"Was he upset?"

"About what?"

"The woman and the tailor?"

"What do you think?" King turned to look at Cook, who stared back, face pasty white, worry draining it of color.

Cook shook his head.

"How was I to know she had a gun? Did you blame me?"

King tilted his head. "It doesn't matter who is to blame, Eric, okay? None of that matters. What matters is that there are no more mistakes. We're already out on a limb here; if anything else goes wrong we will get dropped and left to get out of this ourselves. You need to remember that: there will be nobody coming to help us. Do you understand me?"

"Yeah."

"Okay, try to get some sleep. This is going to be a long night."

CHAPTER 9

DEATH HAD A habit of being dramatic.

Police Generalmajor Erhard Neumann had seen enough murders in his career to know this.

He was on speaking terms with death; he knew its tricks, its sleights of hand, its clever way of pulling you one way and then spinning you the other.

He knew that death favored a flourish of wide strokes. A strong palette of reds, blacks, and ghostly whites splashed and dashed onto the canvas. Death favored shadows. It skulked in corners surrounded by gloom, bodies scattered around like leaves on the ground after a strong wind had dislodged them from the tree of life.

Like an art critic he looked at the background and the foreground, he looked at scenery, he looked at the frame, he looked where fingers pointed and heads were turned.

He looked at the past, the present, and the future.

And then, when he knew it inside out, he decided who'd painted it.

He lived murder, he lived death.

He looked up and down a darkened Regent Street and then back at the tailor's shop to which he'd been called.

The telephone call had said "robbery gone wrong," but Erhard Neumann wasn't ready to agree until he'd seen the body himself.

He felt Lieutenant March shift in the snow next to him. The younger man was rocking backward and forward, impatient to get into the shop to show his boss what he had found. Neumann looked left and right again. He could see German soldiers and English policemen fanned out, blocking the road in either direction.

"Maintaining the scene," March had said when Neumann had arrived, causing to him frown and feel old.

"The getaway car was parked here." March pointed to the curb and Neumann inwardly shuddered at the use of the word *getaway*.

He thinks he's in a movie, Neumann said to himself.

"How do you know?" he said to March.

"When the first patrol attended, he said there were still marks in the snow, as if a car had bumped onto the curb as it turned around."

"We're on one of the busiest streets in London and it's been snowing all day. Why wouldn't there be marks in the snow?"

"There were drops of blood by the marks. The snow was still coming down, but it had stained red from below." March pointed at the pavement. "Here there was a larger pool, as if someone had waited with an injury." He looked at Neumann. "Dripping in one spot."

Neumann nodded. It was a good answer.

The snow started to fall again as they went into the tailor's shop. Neumann made a mental note of the CLOSED sign. He pointed to the little gray fingerprint guy, who was hovering by the door, and then at the sign.

The man nodded and started to work on the sign as the detectives moved through the shop.

"It looks like the shooter surprised the tailor at the back, a long way from the entrance. There doesn't seem to be anything touched at the front. There is a cash register at the back which has been emptied." March kept up a commentary as they walked.

"How much?"

"We don't know yet. I've an English bobby going through the sales ledger. Not much, though, not with this weather, plus a place like this does a lot of work on account."

"Is there a safe?"

"In the back storeroom. Untouched."

"Key or combination?"

"Key."

"You find the key?"

"In the cash register."

"Did you check it?"

"Yes, after the fingerprint guy took a look. Eight pounds, a checkbook, and some papers."

Neumann nodded again; March was doing well, learning his trade.

They arrived at the back of the shop. It was darker, the lamps suspended from the ceiling barely lighting the floor. The five or six policemen standing around seemed to dull it further still, sucking the light into their grimy raincoats, dark suits, police tunics, and cigarette smoke.

Nearly everyone turned to see who was arriving; Neumann gestured that they should all get behind him so he could see the scene inhabited by only the important person in the building.

The dead tailor.

Everyone silently filed past and took up station behind Neumann and March.

March made to speak, but Neumann shook his head.

Neumann looked at the tailor on the floor. He then turned and looked at the assembled officers, but he didn't seem to see them.

His mind moved back in time, where he heard the report of the gun, smelled the cordite, and felt the thud of a falling man.

He looked at the register.

He lifted the curtain at the back of the shop, peered into the gloom of the sewing room, and then back at the man on the floor.

Neumann walked around the counter and took his position next to March, who finally spoke.

"Okay. I reckon the robber or robbers came in, found the tailor at the back of the shop or maybe closing up because of the weather. He's pulled a gun. I'm guessing an accomplice was waiting in the car outside. There was a struggle and the shooter copped a round himself, hence the blood on the ground outside and the two shell casings we found." March pointed to the blood on the floor, a small distance from the tailor's body. "He shot the tailor, did a bit of first aid on himself, rifled the register, and fled the shop."

"Who found the body?"

"The tailor obviously never went home. His wife waited a while and eventually called a friend who lived nearby to come take a look. She tried the door, found it was open, came in, and . . ." March held out his hands toward the body.

"Do we know how long he's been here?"

"He's pretty cold, and the blood is almost dry, even the pools."

"A few hours," Neumann said and March nodded.

"There was a case up in Coventry last year, do you remember?" March slipped his notebook back into his pocket. "A couple of Ukrainian SS privates robbing local businesses and selling whatever they got on the black market. That might explain how a robbery has happened in the German quarter of London."

"I don't think this was a robbery."

"Why?"

"There is a jeweler's shop next door. Why would you rob a tailor when a jeweler is next door?"

March nodded, disappointed he hadn't thought of it first.

"Maybe the snow, sir? Maybe the jeweler closed early?" someone said behind Neumann, who half turned and responded, "Go find out."

The policeman who had spoken dropped his shoulders and left the shop. Neumann crossed to the body of the tailor and looked at him.

The man had fallen straight down, crumpling on his legs. His eyes seemed to stare back at Neumann. Neumann looked at the wound. It was a good shot, center of the chest.

"Sudden death, probably gone before he hit the ground." Neumann looked at March. "He dropped straight down. He wasn't turning away—no momentum except the one that gravity gave him. If he'd been pleading, fighting, or running I'd expect a defensive wound at least, possibly a raised hand."

March looked at the corpse and then back at his boss.

"But the blood, on the carpet there." March pointed to a spot to their left, next to the display cases. "I don't think it's his. There must have been a struggle."

Neumann knelt down by the blood.

"Torch." He raised his hand and clicked a finger.

Someone obliged and Neumann pointed it at the carpet, found the edge of the bloodstain, then traced it with the beam of the torch all the way around until he came to a stop, back at where he'd started.

He leaned forward, shone the beam into the middle of the stain, and then with his other hand placed his fingertip onto the carpet into the middle of the spotlight.

He pushed down and for a moment his finger cast a shadow like an actor on an empty stage. Around the tip, fresh wet blood was forced through and up to the surface; Neumann lifted his finger and looked at it, then held it up for March to see before wiping it next to his foot.

He stood up.

"Somebody else was hit. They might have even died here—there is enough blood."

"Someone else?"

"They bled out, or they were bleeding out. I'll wager an artery. There's no way they walked to a car."

"But if there was no struggle?"

"I didn't say there wasn't a struggle; I said the tailor didn't struggle."

"But if you leave the tailor, why would you take the other person?"

Neumann looked at March and then back at the blood.

"I don't know." He stared at the stain and then called over his shoulder. "We need to check the hospitals, see if anyone has been brought in with a gunshot wound or bleeding heavily."

Two of the detectives behind him, one English and one German, nodded and left the shop to make the inquiries.

Neumann knelt down again and then looked at the display case in front of the assistant.

"Why is that case open?"

All eyes turned to the case. Sure enough, the glass door hung open with keys still in its lock.

March looked into it.

"Handkerchiefs and ties." He looked back at his boss.

Neumann stood up.

"They used a tie to stop the blood, a tourniquet."

March looked back down, and then back at the blood before nodding. "They used it to keep him alive."

Neumann knelt, looking at the blood from the back of the shop, a new angle. Fresh perspective.

It was then that he saw it.

Slipped under the cabinet next to the blood: a sliver of white beneath the dark wood.

He stepped around the blood and tried to pull whatever it was out of the tiny gap. He cursed himself for biting his nails, then dug in his pocket for his penknife.

He used the blade to flick at the card, easing it forward until he could finally pull it free from under the cabinet.

"No," he finally said, turning to look at March and holding up a German citizen's identity card. "They used it to keep *her* alive."

CHAPTER 10

ROSSETT HAD TRIED to stop drinking many times before.
And failed.

He'd battled the bottle and ended up bruised, but that last time—that time he thought he'd done it. He'd seen the light at the end of the tunnel, so close; he almost made it.

It was the boy.

Losing a child had made him start drinking, and finding a child had nearly made him stop. They hadn't found his son's body after the resistance bomb at Waterloo, and although he would never say it, Rossett was glad.

He knew what explosives did to people; he'd wiped enough blood off his face and picked up enough pieces to know that some things should never be seen.

And the body of your son was one of those things.

The boy's mother had died that day as well, and Rossett missed her dearly, an aching loss that called across the years.

He could remember her voice.

Someone had once told him the first thing you forget when a loved one dies is the sound of their voice. Rossett knew that wasn't true.

He could close his eyes and listen to his wife singing in the kitchen, he could hear her laugh, and he could feel the whispering breath of her words in his ear anytime he was alone.

But the boy, his dear sweet boy: the boy he'd never touched, never heard, never met, and never known.

That was why the pain was greater; the boy would never know how much Rossett loved him.

The boy would never hear him say it.

And then came Jacob, a little Jewish child hiding in the dark, praying to be saved.

A bit like Rossett himself.

Rossett had nearly died for Jacob. He'd done the right thing for the first time in years, and as a result he thought, for a moment in time, that he could love again.

He'd saved the child, and a woman he thought he might love, and in doing so he'd lifted the cloud and seen the sun again.

He'd felt human again.

He'd done a good thing; away from the misery of his job and his loneliness, he'd done a good thing.

There had been one glorious, aching afternoon. He'd come out of hospital and rounded up the collection of half-empty bottles that littered his room and his life.

He'd thrown them into the bin at the back of his lodgings. He knew it was over, he knew the cork was back in the bottle.

He'd woken up.

He realized what he'd been doing—to himself, to the Jews, to his soul. He was going to change, do better, and earn forgiveness for his sins by doing good work. He would become a policeman again; he would protect the weak, not persecute them. He couldn't turn the country around, but he could turn himself around.

He had purpose, he had his soul again, and he knew, more than anything else, he was never going to drink again.

It wasn't long before he also knew he was wrong.

First it was beer to take the edge off the pain of the damage he'd caused to his body.

Then it was a Scotch to take the edge off the pain he'd caused to his mind.

He'd been a fool to think the wounds had gone just because he couldn't see them. They were still there, waiting in the darkness when he fell asleep. The dreams returned, the faces, the blood, the shouting; the tossing, the turning, and then the worst part.

The staring at the ceiling in the small hours.

He couldn't remember the exact date the bottle reappeared. But he could remember sitting on the edge of his tossed bed, the bottle cool, smooth in his hands as he rested it against his forehead. His body covered in sweat, but still shivering in the light from the streetlamp outside.

The soft ticking of the clock in the corner of the room.

Then the rattle of the bottle on the edge of the glass.

The burn of the Scotch.

The back of the hand across the mouth to cover the cough.

He drank that night to push himself off into the river of sleep, and then again when he'd gotten tangled in his nightmares once more.

He was numb when he passed out.

He'd been numb many nights since.

He wasn't numb now.

The knocking sounded far away on the other side of a dream. His head banged with it as he slid, squinting, into consciousness. Rossett felt like he was rising up from deep water, and then he was awake, and the knocking was still there, along with the banging of his hangover.

At his door.

He coughed, rolled onto his side, and coughed again, clearing his throat.

"Okay, I'm coming."

The knocking stopped.

Rossett grabbed the alarm clock off the chair next to his bed: 11:35 P.M. He was surprised. His head felt like he'd been asleep all night. He must have started drinking earlier than he thought. He put the clock back down, knocking some loose change onto the bare floorboards.

There were three more knocks on the door.

"All right!" Rossett shouted as he kicked his legs out from under the blankets. "Fuck's sake," he muttered to himself as he padded across the room.

Subconsciously he touched the barely healed scar on his stomach as he opened the door.

The hallway light was on and the glare made him squint.

Koehler stood on the landing in a black woolen civilian coat, open over black suit, white shirt, and black tie, black leather gloves, pale skin, and blond hair.

Immaculate.

Worried.

Rossett didn't speak. He was surprised to see his boss and his friend; he'd never visited before. He stepped back and let Koehler in. As he closed the door the light on the landing went off. He flicked the switch for the light in his own room and considered shouting down to his landlady for tea, but then decided against it.

He still had some whiskey left.

Koehler was standing by the window looking out. Rossett rattled another smoker's cough and then ran his hand through his sleep-stuck hair, suddenly aware that his room smelled musty.

"What's up?" His voice was gravelly and he coughed again as he scratched his scar.

"I'm sorry to wake you. I need your help." Koehler's English carried the barest whiff of a German accent; he turned from the window toward Rossett. "Jesus, John, you look terrible."

"Thanks." Rossett looked around for his undershirt. He found it over the back of the solitary armchair and pulled it over his head. The muscles in his stomach pulled tight as he raised his arms, a legacy of the hundreds of sit-ups he was doing to help repair the damage.

The pain felt good.

"Do you want a drink?" Rossett gestured toward where his whiskey had been the last time he had seen it.

"Are you drunk?"

"Mostly," Rossett replied as he made another attempt with his hair.

"No, I don't want a drink. Can I sit?"

Rossett nodded and redundantly pointed to the armchair. Koehler passed close and Rossett thought he heard his boss inhale as he went by, checking for the smell of booze. Rossett saved him wondering: he sat down on the bed and picked up the bottle that had fallen on the floor from his hand when he had collapsed a few hours earlier.

He unscrewed the top, then looked across at Koehler.

"You sure?"

"Yes."

"I've a hangover brewing."

Koehler didn't reply and Rossett took a drink, then scratched at his scar again, this time through the shirt.

"What's up?" Rossett said after half the Scotch had gone down.

Koehler stared at Rossett and then reached into his coat and pulled out his cigarettes.

"Are we friends, John? I need to know before I tell you. I need to know, because if we're not, I've no right to burden you with this."

Rossett shifted slightly.

"You're about the only friend I have." Rossett took another sip and reached for his own cigarettes off the chair. "I don't know what that says about you or about me, though."

Koehler shook his head. "I don't know what to do."

Rossett paused midway through opening the cigarettes.

"What?"

Koehler ran his hand through his hair again and then shook his head. "This was a mistake. I'm sorry, go back to bed."

He pushed himself out of the threadbare armchair, and as he crossed the room Rossett stood up.

"Ernst, what's going on?"

"Nothing. It's okay, go back to bed."

Koehler had the door open; his shadow reached the top of the stairs.

"What's the matter?"

Koehler looked out into the darkness of the landing. Someone was snoring behind one of the boardinghouse doors. The smell of boiled cabbage, body odor, and sweat filled his nostrils.

He looked back at Rossett.

"They have Lotte and Anja, and I don't know what to do."

"Who?"

"Lotte and Anja have been taken."

"The resistance?"

"No."

"Who is it?"

Koehler looked at his friend, his only friend.

"I've been driving around, trying to think. I don't know what to do, I'm . . . I've no right to be here. I've no right to ask you for your help."

Rossett shook his head.

"Close the door."

Koehler paused, then stepped back, shutting the door quietly. Rossett sat down on the bed once more, giving Koehler some space.

Koehler sat, removed the unlit cigarette from his mouth, ran a weary hand over his eyes, and shook his head.

"Lotte and Anja are being held hostage. If I want to see them again I have to do something."

"What?"

"I have to get a Jew from Cambridge and bring her to London. I've got a name and a place of work, and that is it."

"And then?"

"When I have her, I get further instructions."

"From who?"

"I collect a parcel or an envelope from a post office."

"So you don't see who the instructions are from?"

"Yes."

"Why you?"

Koehler shrugged. "I don't know. Maybe because I've got . . . I had my family here? There aren't many officers with family in London; it gives them leverage over me, plus it's my job to move Jews. I'm the obvious choice."

Rossett nodded.

"Can you think of anyone you know who might be connected to this?"

"No."

"How did they get in touch with you?"

"At my flat, a message with a number. I called it, and they told me to go to a call box by Hyde Park. I went there, got another number, and spoke to them."

"They wanted you out of the flat in case your line is monitored."

Koehler nodded. "It's an open secret the Gestapo monitor calls, and after last year, the trouble with you and the boy . . ."

"Jacob."

"Jacob . . . well, let's just say I'm sure to be of interest to them."

Rossett took a drag of his cigarette and looked at the whiskey.

"Did you see them drop off the note? Did you get a description?"

"I saw one of them, across the street; I didn't get a good look."

"Was he in uniform? Did he have a car? Did anyone else see him?" Rossett was coming awake, turning back into a policeman.

"No uniform, black car, no make, nobody else has a description."

"That's a lot of nos."

"I know."

Rossett looked for the saucer he used sometimes as an ashtray; he tapped his cigarette and then leaned across to pass the saucer to Koehler.

"I can't believe the resistance would just walk up to your front door and leave a note. Tell me everything you can think of, everything: voice, sounds in the background on the call, everything."

Koehler passed back the saucer and paused, staring off into space. Rossett gave him as long as he needed, silently watching with his head still pounding behind his eyes.

Eventually Koehler broke the silence. "He spoke German and English."

"A lot of people do nowadays."

"No, no. It was excellent German, perfect . . . almost. There was an accent."

"What accent?"

"I don't know. It sounds crazy, but . . . he sounded like an actor."

"An actor? Which actor?" Rossett looked at the Scotch again.

"Not a specific actor. He sounded like . . . like one of those ones in a movie, you know? The ones who try to sound American, or who are playing Americans?"

"Yes?"

"Yeah, but he wasn't trying." Koehler looked up. "I think he was an American."

Rossett shook his head. "A Yank, are you sure?"

"The more I think about it . . . yes, I think he was an American."

"The Americans are allies of Germany, especially since Lindbergh got into power. Why would they be doing something like this?"

"Maybe it's nothing to do with the government. They have anti-Nazi factions."

"It explains how they got to you," Rossett added. "The diplomatic quarter is right next door."

"They could drive right in and right out and all they would get is a salute."

Rossett drew on his cigarette again; it crackled in the silence of the room. He let the smoke fill his lungs as he slowly scratched at his scar.

"Why do they want a Jew?" he finally said, staring at the wall, his fingers moving back and forth, tugging at his undershirt.

"I don't care. They want her, they can have her."

"Who is it?" Rossett looked up.

"Ruth Hartz. She works at Cambridge University."

"Doing what?"

"Physics."

"Physics?" Rossett stopped scratching his belly. "Why do all of this? Kidnap your family, force you to go there and get her? It would easier to go and get her themselves."

"Maybe they can't go?"

"They've got transport; they must have diplomatic plates to get into . . ." Rossett trailed off.

"What?"

"They're spies."

"Who are?"

"The people who called you. If she is a Jew who is still working, she must be important. There are hardly any of them still in employment, other than the ones who police the ghettos. So if this Hartz is working, she is important to Germany."

"It doesn't matter. I don't care about Germany. I want Lotte and Anja."

"I know you do, but we need as much information as we can get. We have to understand the situation. If the Americans want her but can't risk getting her themselves, she is important to them as well. And if she is important she'll be guarded. It'll be tough, maybe impossible."

"I know," Koehler said quietly. "That's why I'm here."

Rossett looked at his friend. He understood Koehler was there because he knew if anyone could get the scientist, Rossett could.

"THE BRITISH LION." That was what the newspapers had called him around the time of the collapse at Dunkirk.

A country clinging on by its fingertips, its navy beaten back by bad weather as it tried to rescue a battered army off the bloody beaches of Dunkirk.

Not many had kept fighting in France once the evacuation had failed.

Rossett had.

He hadn't given up, crossing the channel in a stolen torpedo boat twice with injured men and fleeing soldiers. He'd have gone back a third time if the boat hadn't been sunk in the bombardment of Dover.

Churchill, desperate for heroes to rally an almost broken nation, had stood next to Rossett for the pictures at Buckingham Palace as the king pinned on Britain's highest military honor.

John Henry Rossett, Victoria Cross.

King George saluted the British Lion as the papers took his picture and the sound of artillery crashed in the distance.

Over the king's shoulder Rossett could see the packing cases being loaded on the trucks parked behind the camera.

The king knew the game was up, and he was running to Canada.

Rossett wasn't.

Just as Churchill had asked, Rossett fought on the beaches, he fought on the landing grounds, and he fought in the fields and the streets.

He never surrendered.

But the government did.

Germany won, Rossett lost.

When he finally was captured, the Lion was caged, then broken, as his family were annihilated at Waterloo Station.

By the time he was released, the Germans were at home in London. Swastikas hung next to Union Jacks around the city. King Edward and Prime Minister Mosley waved shyly from the balcony at Buckingham Palace next to a triumphant Hitler.

There were crowds in the Mall.

That was the thing that had surprised Rossett when he saw the pictures.

Crowds.

Waving, cheering, saluting the new king and the devil who had put him there.

THEY PULLED UP outside Koehler's apartment building in Kensington about forty-five minutes later. Rossett could smell the booze on his own breath, mixed with the stink of cheap tobacco; he wiped his hand across his mouth as they stopped. A miserable, cold, solitary SS guard, the one Koehler had spoken to earlier, was standing under a damp, drooping swastika flag. He recognized Koehler and sprang to as soon as he climbed out of the car.

Koehler ignored him and leaned back into the vehicle.

"Wait here. I'll get changed and get some cash and a couple of pistols."

Rossett nodded, not wanting to say that he already had a knife and his Webley .44 in his pocket.

Koehler jogged up the steps and entered the building via the revolving door. He felt his cheeks burn with the warmth of the central heating. Through force of habit he looked across at the concierge's booth and was surprised to see it empty.

It had been a tough call whether to go to his office or to the apartment first. As he saw it, there were arguments in favor of both. He needed to go to the office to write the order that he would use to bring Ruth from Cambridge to London.

But deep inside he had wanted to check the flat again just to be sure that this wasn't a bad dream or sick joke, inflicted by someone with no heart, before he set off on a crazy adventure that he knew, in the deepest, darkest part of his soul, was never going to end well.

Rather than wake the building by using the rickety, clanging elevator, Koehler jogged up the stairs to his flat. His feet whispered through the thick red carpet as he thought about Anja and the races he always let her win on the same set of stairs.

A good memory.

He blotted it out.

The mission, always remember the mission. Look forward, never back. Eyes on the target.

The mantra he'd taught a thousand different men under his command.

"Focus," he said out loud as topped the stairs on the third floor before walking along the corridor to his apartment.

He unlocked the door, entered the flat, and turned on the light.

Generalmajor Neumann was sitting opposite him in an armchair, stroking a sleeping Schwarz.

"Major Koehler, I was beginning to worry." Neumann smiled.

Schwarz lifted his head, blinking.

"Who the fuck are you?"

"I am Police Generalmajor Erhard Neumann of the Kriminalpolizei. Excuse me for not getting up; I don't want to disturb your delightful kitten," Neumann rubbed a knuckle behind Schwarz's ear and the cat leaned back into it and started to yawn. "The gentleman behind you is Lieutenant March," Neumann continued, holding up his ID with the hand that wasn't stroking Schwarz.

Koehler turned. He'd not seen the younger man. March nodded but didn't speak.

"What is the meaning of this?" Koehler turned back to Neumann, who lifted Schwarz from his lap and lowered him to the floor.

Schwarz gave a low moan of disappointment, stretched, yawned, sat down, and then stared at Koehler while licking his lips.

All eyes in the room were on Koehler.

"I'm sorry for the intrusion, Major. We had to search your flat and you weren't home." Neumann rose stiffly from the chair and Koehler realized they had been there for some time.

"My flat? What for?" Koehler looked back at March, nervous with him standing behind him.

"Your wife."

Koehler rocked and then turned back to Neumann.

"My wife?"

"This is your wife's identity card?" Neumann fumbled in his inside jacket pocket, theatrically looking into it, playing the game, then smiling and approaching as he held up Lotte's card.

Koehler squinted at it and nodded.

"How did you get that?" His heart raced.

"I found it at the scene of a robbery this evening."

"My wife has been robbed?"

Neumann frowned. "When did you last see your wife?"

"This morning. I've been out all day and ended up working late. I . . ."

Koehler was gulping for air. The police being involved changed everything. They were one step down from the Gestapo, and almost as dangerous. He heard a snatch of panic in his voice, but then Neumann rescued him by holding up his hand, gesturing for Koehler to slow down.

"Please, Major, take a breath. When did you last see your wife?"

Koehler paused, breathed, and then spoke.

"This morning at about eight o'clock, when I went to work. She was still in bed."

"So you've been out all day?" Neumann slipped the ID card into one pocket and pulled out a notebook and pencil from another.

"Yes, as I say, I've been working." Koehler glanced at March, then back to Neumann.

Neumann nodded, put the pencil into his mouth, and then flicked through the notebook looking for the final page of writing. Finally he removed the pencil from his teeth and looked up.

"The concierge said you came home around nine this evening, and that you remained here a short time before rushing out again?"

Schwarz licked his paw, wiped it across his face, and then looked back at Koehler before flicking his head to rid himself of an itch.

Neumann pointed to the door with his pencil.

"Is the concierge lying? I can have him brought up; he is downstairs with my men."

"He isn't lying."

"So you came home?"

Koehler nodded.

Neumann scratched his cheek with the pencil, then sighed before looking back at the notebook.

"Maybe the major would like to take a seat?"

Koehler nodded. He crossed the room slowly, mind racing. He sneaked a glance at the French window that opened out onto the wrought-iron balcony, briefly considering jumping.

Lunacy.

Three floors down.

He was no good to Lotte and Anja dead.

He sat down in an armchair, rubbing a hand across his face as Neumann dragged a dining chair across the room toward him.

March stayed at the door, watching.

Neumann sat down directly in front of Koehler before flipping through the notepad again. Koehler stared at the top of the policeman's head, wondering if playing with the notebook was just a ruse to make him uneasy.

If it was, it was working.

Neumann looked up. "So, when did you last see your wife?"

"I told you, eight o'clock this morning. Can I have a drink?"

"Soon. Are you sure?"

"Yes."

"It's just that you've already lied to me, Major."

Koehler shook his head.

"I didn't lie. I forgot. I was confused. I'm not used to coming home and finding detectives in my apartment."

"Of course," Neumann replied and looked at March. "Who is?"

"Criminals," replied March, speaking for the first time since Koehler had arrived.

Schwarz stood up and sauntered across the room, jumped up onto the settee, and pulled with his claws a few times. The sound of the fabric being dragged caused Koehler to look across; Neumann followed his gaze and then looked back at him.

"He'll ruin the furniture," Neumann said.

"He's a kitten."

"It's being locked up all day, it drives them crazy," said March quietly.

Koehler looked at March, then Neumann, and shifted in his chair.

"You said there was a robbery?"

"Did your wife say what her plans were today?" Neumann gave nothing away. Koehler shrugged. "No."

"You didn't ask?"

"No."

Neumann frowned, wrote something down, then looked up again.

"I checked. Your wife normally lives in Germany?"

"Yes."

"She is on holiday here?"

"Yes, while I've been recuperating. I could really do with that drink."

"Of course. Your wounds, how are they?" Neumann gestured with the pencil toward Koehler's damaged hand.

"As well as can be expected."

"You're a hero."

"I'm a soldier."

"Yes." Neumann smiled. "Of course you are."

"Is my wife all right?"

"Interesting," March said from behind Koehler, who had to shift in the chair to see the other man.

"What is?"

"You're asking how your wife is."

"I'm concerned."

"You weren't concerned when she didn't come home this evening." March spoke flatly, matter-of-factly, no accusation in his tone, just a simple statement of fact as he saw it.

Koehler had to swallow down a lump of anger that caught in his throat; he turned away from March and looked back to Neumann.

"I remember now, she said she was staying with a friend." As the words came out Koehler was aware how pathetic they sounded, and regretted them immediately. He stood up, crossed to the drinks cabinet, and poured a brandy. He turned, holding the bottle to the two policemen, who both ignored it, but watched him.

"Who?" Neumann said after Koehler took a sip of the brandy and then topped up his glass again.

"I'm sorry?"

"Who is your wife staying with?"

"I . . ." Koehler floundered and Neumann leaned forward.

"Yes?"

"A friend. I didn't catch her name, someone she met in my office. I wasn't really listening. I'm very busy." Koehler flushed.

Can I tell them what has happened? he thought. Maybe they can help?

Neumann leaned back and looked at Koehler.

"A friend?"

"Yes."

Neumann rubbed a finger across his top lip while staring at Koehler. Eventually he spoke again.

"I'm surprised you weren't worried enough by her absence to call us. After all, London is a dangerous city."

"I was going to call you. I went out looking for them, and then when I couldn't find them, I was going to call you."

Neumann nodded, doubtfully and slowly.

"Forgive me, Major, but I don't believe you." The words hung in the air and Koehler left them there, unanswered.

"Where did you look?" March said behind him, but this time Koehler didn't turn around. His eyes stayed on Neumann, aware that the older man was pulling the strings, not March.

"It doesn't matter if you don't believe me, it is the truth," Koehler said, his voice steadied by the warmth of the brandy, his mind made up. He'd figure out a way to get Lotte and Anja, and say nothing to these two flatfoot idiots.

Neumann sighed, looked at the notebook, and nodded.

"Fine, thank you, Major. I'll be leaving March here tonight, in case your wife returns. She may have information about the robbery, which will help us greatly if we can speak to her as soon as possible."

"I'll call you when she comes home."

"March will stay with you." Neumann pointed to his colleague at the door.

"There is no need."

"Oh, but there is, there really is."

"He isn't staying here."

"The only alternative is we arrest you now, I'm afraid."

"This is an outrage. I'm an officer of the SS. You have no right."

"What is an outrage, Major, is that you are an officer of the SS whose English secretary disappeared without a trace last year. The same English secretary you were having an affair with for eighteen months, I hasten to add. Now, your wife and daughter disappear in the same manner? That, I'm afraid, is the outrage, and, more important for you, sufficient grounds for us to arrest you."

The breath seemed to evaporate in Koehler's lungs as he looked at Neumann, who gave a weary smile in return.

"I've been asking a few questions this evening, Major, so I'm sure you will understand my concerns. Your secretary disappears in mysterious circumstances, closely followed by your wife . . . well, I'd be a fool if I didn't leave March here with you, wouldn't I? Just in case you're the next one to disappear."

Neumann nodded to March, who opened the door. Koehler took a step forward and then stopped. Their eyes met.

"You haven't asked where the robbery was, or if anyone was injured," Neumann said.

"I'm sorry." Koehler touched his forehead and nodded. "I'm . . . I'm a little confused by this. Please, tell me what happened."

Koehler saw the lump of the policeman's tongue run across his teeth behind his closed lips as he thought.

"A man died in a tailor's shop on Regent Street," Neumann finally said. "A tailor's shop you have an account with."

"Brown's?" Koehler remembered the name of the shop.

"Mr. Brown died."

"Oh . . . oh, that's such a shame." Koehler felt his heart beating so hard he thought it was going to erupt out of his chest.

"I'm not sure it was just the tailor who died. Someone else took a round in the shop; I'll wager they are hurt pretty bad, if not—"

"Who?" The word came out, soft as a breath, as Koehler's heart suddenly stilled.

"We only found blood. It wasn't far from where your wife's ID was lying." Neumann shrugged. "There was no body, but a body's worth of blood. I don't know whose, but as soon as I do, Major, so will you."

Neumann nodded to March and then walked away toward the lift.

He didn't care who he woke up.

ROSSETT WAS FREEZING. He looked at the half-frozen sentry standing on the step that he'd been watching for the last ten minutes and shook his head.

He took out his cigarettes and looked for his matches.

He didn't have any.

The boy didn't look old enough to smoke, let alone have any matches, but the heavy hangover Rossett was carrying around was craving nicotine.

The sentry eyed him as he approached, so Rossett forced a smile to relax the boy. He guessed he didn't look his best, because the sentry took a half step backward.

"Do you speak English?"

"A little," the sentry replied.

"Do you have a light?" Rossett held up his cigarette. The sentry's eyes darted toward the door, then back to Rossett, who read the signal.

"There is nobody coming. I'll keep a lookout."

The sentry changed hands with the rifle, then took out some matches and passed them across. Rossett nodded thanks, struck up, and then gave them back.

Rossett offered a cigarette to the German, who took it and lit up.

"Cold," the sentry said, his English clunky and simple, smoke slithering out of his nostrils as he stamped his feet in the snow.

"The major?" The sentry pointed over his shoulder. "You wait?"

Rossett nodded.

"The police." The sentry rolled his eyes and jabbed his thumb back at the door again. "They talk and talk."

"The police?" Rossett looked up at the building.

"Yes, police, inside, nice and warm." The sentry smiled, but this time Rossett ignored him.

He took a few steps back toward the car and looked up to where he guessed Koehler's flat was on the third floor. "Did they say what they wanted?" he asked while still looking up, blinking at the snow.

"No."

Rossett flicked his cigarette into the snow, where it hissed, still smoking, sitting on the surface four inches above the blanketed pavement.

"How many?"

The sentry held up four fingers.

"You're sure they didn't come back out?"

"Yes." The sentry was frowning now, uncertain about his new English friend.

Rossett didn't try to reassure him; he walked into the foyer of the building through the revolving door.

IT WAS HOT.

So hot he had to pull at the scarf around his neck to get some air. He looked at the empty concierge desk and then carried on toward the lift. The indicator over the cage doors told him it was on the third floor; he reached for the call button, but before he had a chance to push it, with a noisy clatter the lift started to descend.

Rossett wavered, debating whether to walk back out to the car or stand his ground.

He stood his ground, just like he always did, for better or worse, for his friend.

The lift was coming slowly, banging in the shaft.

Rossett saw the bottom of the car rattling down. He stepped back from the cage doors and watched the sole occupant's feet descending into view.

The man inside opened the cage and paused when he saw Rossett.

Plainclothes, fifty-odd years old, gray mustache with a yellow tinge that could do with a trim, and a raincoat that could do with a wash.

Policeman, thought Rossett.

"May I help you?" said the man with fairly good English.

"You the lift operator?" replied Rossett.

"No."

"No, then."

Rossett moved to step past Neumann, who had taken a pace forward himself.

"I'm Generalmajor Erhard Neumann of the Kriminalpolizei."

"Good for you."

"It is gone midnight, and you don't live in this building, and you are English. This is a German officers' accommodation block. So, I'll ask again, may I help you?" Neumann produced his ID from his pocket and flashed it at Rossett.

Rossett held up his own ID, finger carefully covering his name, years of practice coming into play.

Neumann squinted at Rossett's warrant card and then smiled.

"I think you will find my card trumps yours, so once again, for the last time. May I help you?"

"I'm visiting a friend."

"Who?"

"Major Koehler."

"Why?"

"We have work to do."

"At this time of night?"

Rossett looked at the floor, sighed, and then punched Neumann hard in the mouth.

The force of the punch drove the older man hard into the back of the lift, which rang like a bell in its shaft. For a split second Rossett thought he had knocked Neumann clean out and he looked over his shoulder toward the concierge's office, half expecting a squad of policemen to come running out.

They didn't, so he turned back to Neumann, who was folded at the waist, his left hand drunkenly reaching for the thin brass handrail that ran around the lift. Rossett was impressed Neumann was still functioning. He punched the German again, this time on the left temple with a chopping right hand at half power.

Just enough for the job.

"You ask too many questions," Rossett said as Neumann finally went down, face sliding down the side of the cage with his feet sticking out into the hallway beyond. The old elevator clanged again once or twice against its workings as Rossett crouched down, looking toward the concierge's office as he dragged the unconscious Neumann's legs into the lift.

He pulled the door closed, then pressed the button for the third floor several times impatiently. Neumann groaned as the cage started to rise, and Rossett knelt down, roughly searching through Neumann's pockets.

He found a Mauser and some cuffs. He slipped the Mauser into his own pocket, snapped one cuff onto Neumann's left hand, and then, pushing hard on the German's shoulder, managed to free the other arm and cuff both wrists to the rear.

Neumann blinked and gave a tiny shake of his head as the lift shuddered to a halt on the third floor. Rossett, still crouching, gently tapped him on the side of the head with the Webley.

"Do you see this?"

Neumann struggled to focus his eyes on the gun; he blinked a couple of times and then nodded.

"Who is in the room with Koehler?"

"Are you mad?" Neumann finally spoke, his voice weak but incredulous.

"Who is in the apartment?"

"You'll hang for this."

Rossett thumbed the hammer on the pistol and jammed it into the temple he'd punched moments ago.

"Who is in the apartment?"

"My assistant, just one man, that's all," Neumann replied, his eyes now closed.

"Is he armed?"

"Yes."

"What are you doing here?"

Neumann didn't reply, so Rossett pulled back the pistol an inch and then jabbed the barrel forward again, hard.

"Answer the fucking question. What are you doing here?"

"We are looking for Koehler's wife and daughter. They are missing, and he's up to something. I'm trying to figure out what."

Rossett tapped the pistol against Neumann's temple, lighter this time.

"Shush now."

Neumann fell silent.

The lift arrived at the third floor. Rossett pulled open the cage and looked along the silent, red-carpeted corridor. Four gold-numbered doors led off to either side. The contrast with Rossett's own accommodation couldn't have been greater, but that didn't matter right now.

His friend needed help.

"Is Koehler locked up, handcuffed?"

"No. This is crazy. We were only questioning him. This is crazy." Neumann shook his head, his voice stronger now. "Uncuff me and we can sort this out."

"Where are the uniforms?"

"What?"

"Where are the uniformed policemen?"

"In the office with the doorman. I didn't bring them up. The major is an officer; I didn't think it was correct."

Rossett looked back along the corridor and then down at Neumann.

"Get up."

Rossett half dragged, half pushed Neumann to his feet. The German flopped against the wall of the lift until Rossett took a handful of his collar and pushed him out into the corridor.

"What door?"

"I thought you were his friend," Neumann replied. "You don't know where he lives?"

"Which door?" Rossett shoved Neumann forward a few steps more.

"You're taking a big risk for someone who wouldn't invite you to his flat."

Rossett pressed the gun into Neumann's neck.

"You're the one taking the risk. Which door?"

"Pull the trigger and March will know you are coming. I thought you English policemen were supposed to be the best in the world?"

Rossett looked at the back of Neumann's head, sighed, then hit him with the butt of the Webley just behind the ear, knocking him down again.

"Smart arse," muttered Rossett as he lowered Neumann to the floor.

He didn't do it quietly enough. The door to his right opened. March stood framed in the light, looking down at Rossett and the unconscious Neumann.

In a second he was also looking at the Webley.

Rossett rose up from the crouch and pointed at Neumann with his other hand. "Get your boss into the flat."

March did as he was told. Quickly and quietly he gripped Neumann's arms and dragged the older man unceremoniously into the apartment.

Koehler emerged from the kitchen holding a china teapot, which he almost dropped as he watched March, under the eye of Rossett's Webley, drag Neumann out of the corridor.

"What . . . ?"

"This wasn't the plan," Rossett replied.

Neumann groaned, so everyone looked at him.

"You had a plan?" said Koehler.

Rossett looked down at March and then back at Koehler.

"Not exactly, no."

CHAPTER 11

EVEN UNDER A fresh fall of snow, Whitechapel still had the grit and grime of two hundred years of soot powdered to its face. The narrow streets and the tall tight houses squeezed the people who lived there like mortar between bricks.

The occupation of the Nazis had done nothing to improve Whitechapel; the place had just gotten worse. When the Germans arrived there had been a fair-sized Jewish population. At one point there had been talk of a ghetto being established, but the clearance had been too efficient: the residents were thrown away rather than thrown behind barbed wire.

Frank King had been sure he'd chosen their hiding place well; there were no Germans or police prowling these streets when he had originally scoped the area. But looking out the window at their snow-covered Opel outside, he was suddenly feeling less certain.

No other car had been up or down in hours. There had been one solitary strolling policeman, who had stopped and stared at the car, then around at the houses in the street. King had watched from behind the curtain, in the darkened room, as the bobby had scraped off some snow to inspect the tax disc in the Opel's windscreen.

King had squeezed to the edge of the window, breathing a little faster when the bobby turned and stared at the car again before continuing on his way.

Suspicions aroused, a silent conversation going on his head, decisions being made that King wasn't party to. The copper hadn't wanted to get involved, but King knew policemen gossiped, and King didn't want that gossip drawing attention to their location.

The car, and the body of Lotte Koehler in its trunk, had to go.

He walked to the back room and looked at Anja. She looked like she was sleeping, although he doubted that she actually was. The girl hadn't spoken since he'd helped Eric Cook carry her mother downstairs and put her in the car. She had silently watched them, face blank, too blank, worryingly blank.

King didn't trust her. He considered giving her her mother's coat, but decided it would be in poor taste, so he went back to looking out of the window to check on Cook, whom he'd sent out to ready the car.

Cook looked up toward King and gave a thumbs-up before quickly wiping the snow-covered windscreen and side windows.

King checked his watch: 3:30 a.m. He should have gotten rid of the body earlier, but the policeman had worried him. He'd stared out the window for two hours before finally calling Cook and sending him downstairs.

King was angry with himself.

He squeezed his hand in his pocket tightly and dug his nails into his palm.

"Come on," he said out loud, and behind him, through the open door, he heard the mattress springs groan at the sound of his voice.

Cook started the Opel, leaned out of the open door, and waved again.

King drew a deep breath and took out his pistol. He went to Anja and shook her roughly. Her eyes opened wide and stared into his so quickly, he was certain she'd been awake all along.

He lifted his pistol and showed it to her.

"Do as I say, do you understand?"

Anja nodded, head still on the mattress, blanket still pulled around her shoulders.

"We are going to leave the flat and go somewhere else. You must be very quiet, very, very quiet. If you make a sound I will kill you." King whispered the threat, which hung in the air with the white wisp of breath that carried it.

Anja nodded again.

"Get up."

King stepped back from the bed. Anja slid off the mattress and stood, staring at him, hair ruffled.

"Get your blanket, it'll be cold."

Anja did as she was told and pulled the blanket around her shoulders. King gripped her arm, then pushed her out of the room and down the steep, narrow stairs that led to the front door.

He could hear the engine running on the Opel. At the bottom of the stairs he pulled Anja to a halt and stepped past her to open the door. He looked out into the street, then roughly dragged Anja across the pavement to the rear door of the car and pushed her onto the backseat. He stepped back to the front door of the building, slammed it shut, then clambered in next to Anja.

"Go."

The Opel's engine gunned and the back wheels slipped slightly on the snow, then found purchase. The car slithered forward.

"Slowly." King reached forward and rested his hand on Cook's shoulder. In return Cook nodded and flicked on the windscreen wipers to combat the snow that was whipping off the hood.

"To the river?"

"Like I told you," King replied, looking now at Anja, who was pressed into the corner of the backseat against the opposite door. The car slipped and slid for a few minutes before it finally made it onto Commercial Road and headed in the direction of Limehouse Docks, next to the River Thames. Cook drove slowly and carefully through the snow until finally, they arrived at their destination.

"Go take a look," said King, and Cook got out of the car.

Anja and King sat in silence, ignoring the cold and each other for nearly two minutes. Cook came back, opening the door next to Anja; she flinched as he leaned across her to speak to King, keeping his voice low.

"Here is good, there's a hole in the fence where we can get straight down onto the river."

"Get out." King pushed Anja toward Cook and then followed her out of the car.

In the distance a dog barked as the falling snow pattered onto their shoulders and hair. Cook and King were wearing long black woolen coats; Anja watched as King slotted his pistol into his pocket and then pulled up his collar.

Cook took Anja's arm, less aggressively than King had done earlier, then guided her to the rear of the car.

"Pull the blanket over your head," he whispered, and Anja did as she was told.

"Right over," King said behind her, and Anja found herself closing her eyes as he roughly pulled the blanket fully over her head and her face.

She heard the trunk of the car open and wondered if she was about to die. A curious calm overcame her, a sense that things would soon be over, and she surrendered to it, feeling the knot in her stomach unravel.

She heard Cook grunt and realized they were getting her mother.

The knot returned, and so did the anger.

King took hold of her arm again.

"Keep the blanket down," he said, surprising her with the gentle tone of his voice. Anja didn't want to watch; she pulled the blanket tighter around her head and squeezed her eyes tight.

Anja hadn't watched when they had struggled to lift the body off the mattress earlier. After they had taken her mother from the flat, Anja had lain on the spot where she had died, feeling the warmth fade away underneath her cheek.

She knew her mother was gone.

But she wouldn't mourn yet.

Her mother wouldn't want her to.

Her mother had wanted Anja to wait until she was in her father's arms.

Right after he had killed the two men who had caused this misery.

Anja would watch that.

The dog stopped barking and a horn on the river took its place, then silence fell around them once again. Anja could see her feet if she looked down, so when King told her to walk forward she was able to watch her step by lifting the front of the blanket slightly.

Behind her she heard a curse from Cook, who must have slipped.

King grabbed her head and shoved it forward.

"Duck," he said, as they made their way through the fence, then onward to the river.

The snow grew heavier, falling in curtainlike flurries as the smell of the muddy, brick-strewn, oil-washed riverbank of the Thames sneaked under the blanket and filled her nostrils. Anja listened to her feet crunch, and for a fleeting moment she thought about the snowman she and her mother would never build.

King jerked her again, keeping her moving.

She heard a bird somewhere, calling on the river. She lifted the blanket so she could look up. Across the water, the lights of South London twinkled in the falling snow. A breeze stroked her face as she caught a whiff of the sea from far beyond where they stood.

She shivered.

The splash to her left sounded cold.

Crisp.

All too short.

Her mother's good-bye, the final sound Anja would ever hear her make.

Cook gently took her arm this time, and they turned back to the car.

"I'm sorry," he said.

"You will be," she replied, matter-of-fact, no doubt in her voice.

KING ALLOWED ANJA to remove the blanket from her head as they walked back to the car, so she wore it like a shawl across her shoulders, wrapping it tightly, keeping the shivers in.

King shoved her through the fence, and as Cook took her arm he finally looked at her.

"Are you all right?"

Anja ignored him and he looked hurt.

She wanted to spit in his face, kick his shins, scratch his eyes, but instead, she ignored him.

"I want you to know, we're sorry for what happened," he tried again.

Anja looked at him, holding his eyes with hers until he could bear it no more and looked away.

CHAPTER 12

KOEHLER PULLED ON his coat, then took forty pounds out of the small wall safe that was hidden behind a picture in his bedroom. He counted the money, then reached back into the safe and took out three passports—his, Lotte's, and Anja's.

Just in case.

He closed the safe, switched off the light, and went back into the living room.

Rossett was standing behind the settee, upon which sat the handcuffed Neumann and March. Rossett looked at Koehler and tapped his wrist.

Time was ticking.

Koehler went through to the small kitchen and opened a can of food for the cat; he knelt down as Schwarz bounced into the room, summoned by the sound of the opener.

He looked into the living room from the kitchen and saw Rossett watching him.

"I can't let him starve," Koehler said, shrugging.

Rossett returned to watching the two policemen.

"Be safe, little boy, they'll be home soon," Koehler said softly before leaving the kitchen to join Rossett and the two policemen.

He grabbed his overcoat off the arm of the chair, then started toward the door of the flat, but he stopped when Rossett spoke.

"What are we doing with these two?"

Neither policeman looked up.

"Leave them. They are handcuffed."

"They'll raise the alarm."

"What else can we do?"

Rossett didn't reply, and it took a moment for Koehler to realize what that silence implied.

Koehler shook his head. "We're better than that."

"You might be."

"I can't hurt them."

"They'll get in the way."

March risked a half turn of his head to look at Koehler but didn't speak.

"I can't do that."

"Anja and Lotte?" Rossett said quietly, leaving the question for Koehler to ponder.

"No," Koehler eventually said. "Get up." He dragged the still-groggy Neumann to his feet. Rossett followed his lead, pulling up March.

Koehler led the group into the small bathroom of the flat and sat Neumann down on the toilet seat; he rested a hand against the side of Neumann's face and inspected the lump on his head. The wound was superficial. He looked at March.

"No noise, nothing at all. Sit quietly and wait till we have left the building; otherwise your men downstairs will pay a heavy price. Do you understand me?" Koehler still held on to Neumann but spoke to March, who nodded before sitting down on the edge of the bath.

Koehler leaned Neumann back against the wall, where his head lolled before coming to rest on the cold tiles. Koehler crouched in front of him for a second to make sure he didn't fall off the toilet, then stood up and turned to March.

"Do you have a wife?"

March nodded his head.

"Children?"

March didn't reply.

Koehler nodded. "My wife and child? I haven't harmed them. You have to believe me; I'm trying to save them. I can't let you get in the way. They are precious to me and I will kill you if you put them in danger or try to stop me.

This is your only warning: I'll kill you stone dead and walk away without a backward glance. If you've got a child, you'll understand that."

March stared back and Koehler nodded before walking past Rossett out of the bathroom.

Rossett remained in the room for a few seconds. He stared at the lowered head of March and then Neumann.

"Hey," Rossett called to March, who looked up. "Make sure you feed that cat."

ROSSETT OPENED THE apartment door and looked down the corridor.

"Is there a fire escape?"

"No."

"Front door, then?" He looked at Koehler.

"The car is at the front. It'll be the quickest and easiest."

"Let's hope so."

"Thanks for coming for me," Koehler said as the door clicked shut behind him.

Rossett didn't reply. He was already halfway down the corridor, coat billowing, feet soft on the carpet.

They hit the stairs at a run, quickly and quietly, two, sometimes three at a time, traveling fast without words.

At the bottom they burst into the entrance hall of the building and took the hard right that led to the revolving door.

Neither slowed when they saw the two uniformed German policemen leaning against the concierge's desk drinking tea. The policemen turned at the sound of Rossett and Koehler approaching. One of them put his mug on the counter and pushed himself upright, unsure whether to stop the two men jogging toward him or not.

His colleague half lowered his cup but relaxed slightly when Koehler smiled and said, "Warmer in here than out on the streets?"

"Yes, sir. May I ask, is the generalmajor finished upstairs?"

Koehler and Rossett kept moving briskly toward the doors, full of purpose.

"Very nearly. He is questioning a few other people. He'll not be long."

The policemen saluted as Koehler and Rossett exited through the revolving door.

The cold hit them hard on the steps as the sentry snapped to attention, eyes ahead, a dusting of snow still on his shoulders. Koehler and Rossett ignored him and made their way to the car.

It was then they heard the smashing of glass.

Shards landed around them, falling stars catching the light and landing in the snow.

They both looked up toward Koehler's flat.

March was half leaning out over the balcony, straining to look down past the window ledge toward where the sentry was standing.

"Stop those men!"

The sentry took a half step forward, still looking up, trying to see where the shout was coming from.

Rossett backhanded him hard on the jaw. The sentry went sideways and down in a heap at the bottom of the steps, a pile of military gray, his helmet dislodged. Rossett grabbed the sentry's rifle before it hit the ground and, turning in one fluid motion, worked the bolt, driving home a round, then bringing the gun to bear on the revolving door.

The two policemen stared openmouthed on the other side of the glass.

Nobody moved.

Rossett heard Koehler's shoes crunch in the snow as he took a backward step to the car. He stared at the two policemen on the other side of the door, aiming his rifle through the glass, shifting the sights from one to the other.

"Somebody stop them!" the shout from above came again.

Rossett heard the car door slamming shut. He watched the eyes of one of the policemen, the younger one, flicking from the car to Rossett and then back again.

These men weren't going to wait.

Damn them.

Rossett tightened his grip on the rifle, pulling it into his shoulder, ready for the kick when it came.

The young policeman took a quick step to the left, ducking slightly as he went, half turning, right hand rising to the leather holster high on his belt.

Too high for a quick draw.

Rossett fired through the door, the bullet slamming through two sheets of thick glass. Spinning, off target, the bullet was still close enough to catch the policeman high on the shoulder, half turning him as he ducked.

Rossett didn't bother taking time to work the bolt for another round; he threw the rifle into the door to jam it and shook his Webley free from his pocket. The young policeman had hit the floor, showered in glass, scrabbling to get clear and out of sight of Rossett and his Webley.

The second, older policeman stared at the pistol, mouth open, hands half raised, as Rossett took aim at his chest. The policeman didn't move as the car started behind Rossett; he just stared at the gun.

Koehler shouted for Rossett to get into the car, so he took a pace backward, Webley still high. He risked a glance over his shoulder and saw that Koehler was holding his Mauser, pointing it at the revolving door. Rossett walked quickly around the car, checking up and down the street.

A few curtains were flicking on either side of the road. A curious concierge appeared, nervously watching them from a building farther up the street, squinting through the falling snow, one hand shielding his eyes.

Rossett opened the passenger door as a bullet slammed into the front of the car twelve inches from where he stood. He felt the door handle twitch in his fingers as the car shook from the impact. His reflexes caused him to dip his head as another round fizzed past. Rossett felt the shock wave as the bullet missed him and ricocheted off the building behind. He ducked, looking for whoever had fired the shot, hoping to mark a target before the shooter could fire again.

He spun, checking windows, unwilling to get in the car until he was certain he wouldn't be a sitting duck.

"Come on!" Koehler shouted, but still Rossett spun, searching for the shooter.

Another shot.

Rossett felt the car buck next to him and turned once more, looking for the shooter, wanting to shoot back.

He looked toward the door of the building they'd just left, but neither policeman was in view. The sentry outside was still on the ground, stomach in the snow.

Koehler gunned the engine.

"John!"

Rossett held his ground, looking left and right, up and down the street. He'd once been in the passenger seat of a car when the driver had been shot dead traveling at thirty miles an hour; it wasn't an experience he wanted to go through again.

There, top of the street. A soldier, crouching down near some railings about seventy yards ahead. Rifle poking round the corner, not wanting to expose himself. Rossett guessed he was probably a sentry from another German officer's apartment block who'd heard the shot and the smashing glass and come to investigate.

"We need to turn around. Shooter ahead," Rossett said as he got into the car.

"Fuck's sake."

Koehler revved the engine, slammed the car into reverse, and started a J-turn away from the threat.

The two policemen opened up with their pistols through the revolving door, closer than the sentry but firing fast and loose.

"You might want to get a move on," Rossett said quietly.

Koehler eased off on the accelerator as the rear wheels found some grip, then the car pulled away from the curb.

The younger policeman appeared at the top of the steps and Rossett aimed at him with the Webley, causing him to duck back out of sight.

Finally the car made its way across the road, turning away from the soldier on the corner, who fired again, this time hitting the back door on the driver's side. The bullet passed through the thin metal before lodging in the dashboard, missing Koehler's arm by half an inch. Neither he nor Rossett registered it; both men had been in combat enough times to know that the ones that missed didn't matter.

They'd worry about it later, if later ever came.

The two policemen in the apartment block opened fire again. Window glass shattered around them and Rossett involuntarily ducked, then returned fire at the doorway with the Webley. Its mighty boom deafened him as the car finally started to pull away down the street.

As their speed picked up, Rossett watched out of what remained of the back window as the policemen, and the now distant sentry, ran into the middle of the street still firing. One round pinged off the inside of the roof, into the back of Rossett's seat. He felt the heavy thud and for a moment thought he had been shot.

The car skidded in the snow around the corner and Koehler slowed slightly before looking across at Rossett and shaking his head.

"Jesus." Koehler whistled and took a deep breath. His face broke out in a broad smile.

Rossett just stared blankly back at him.

Rossett had seen it a thousand times, the laughter of soldiers who'd just survived by the skin of their teeth. Men rejoicing because they'd lived to fight and die another day.

He'd once worried that he never experienced that postbattle euphoria. He fought, he finished fighting, and then he fought again.

No emotion, no terror, no rush of adrenaline, no glory.

Just do the job, kill or be killed, and if you are still alive, do it again.

Koehler finally spoke, his voice almost level again.

"We need another car; we can't drive around in this thing full of holes."

Rossett didn't reply as he removed the spent cartridges from the Webley, replacing them with fresh rounds. He clicked the revolver shut and looked over his shoulder again before settling into his seat more comfortably.

"Pull over."

Koehler did as he was told. The car slid the last few feet into the curb. Rossett got out and jogged across to the line of cars parked on the opposite side of the street. In the distance the sound of police-car bells rang out as they made their way to Koehler's apartment block. Rossett guessed they had minutes to get moving again; he signaled for Koehler to stay in his car with the engine running as he made his way along the line of cars, pulling on door handles.

The fourth car, a tiny, battered, dark blue Austin Seven, was the only one he found to be unlocked. It sat like an ugly duckling at the end of the line, half buried in snow and barely the size of a shoebox.

Rossett waved Koehler across, then went to the bonnet and pulled up one of the side panels.

"This? We go in this?" Koehler said as he approached.

"Pull the choke and I'll try to start it."

Koehler shook his head and climbed in. Inside of three seconds the little engine turned over a few times and then caught. Rossett dropped the bonnet and quickly brushed the snow off the windscreen before jumping into the passenger seat.

The car was so narrow that their shoulders banged together as Koehler looked down at the gear lever and fumbled for first.

"As soon as we can, we ditch this thing," he said as the gear ground home and the car dug its way out of the four inches of snow that had half buried its narrow tires.

They had barely got moving when the first police car sped past, not slowing to take a look at the comical little car and its occupants. Rossett looked over his shoulder and then wiped at the windscreen with the back of his hand before lowering his window an inch or two.

"What do we do now?" said Koehler.

Rossett lit a cigarette and took his time blowing the smoke out of his nose and mouth, then turned to look at Koehler.

"We go get your family back."

CHAPTER 13

ALLEN DULLES TOOK another drink from the glass on his desk. His mind was wound like a spring. He'd already drunk a quarter bottle of brandy, but his shoulders and back still ached as if he'd been beaten with a bat.

He stood up and walked to the window.

All was quiet; the snow cast a pink glow on the street outside as he watched two guards share a cigarette at the checkpoint barrier. The barrier was a new addition, set up to protect the embassy from threats unknown.

Dulles didn't like it. He argued it sent out the wrong signal; it was as if they were under siege, hiding from the Germans, scared.

Dulles stared at the barrier and realized he *was* scared.

The telephone rang on his desk. He crossed the room and picked it up before it had the chance to ring twice.

"It's done, she's gone," King said, his voice faint, echoing in the call box.

"What about the girl?"

"She's fine. Cook is with her."

"That boy is an idiot. I want both of you to be with her. We can't lose her as well. Do you understand?"

"What happened to Koehler's wife wasn't Eric's fault."

"I don't care. I want both of you with her, do you hear me?"

"Yes."

Dulles sank down into his chair and leaned forward, resting his forehead in his hand.

"I'm sorry, Frank." He lifted his eyes and stared through his fingers at the brandy glass.

"I understand, sir."

"This has to work, you understand?"

"Yes."

"We can't afford any more mistakes. The future of our country depends on it."

"We're very exposed here, sir. Maybe if I could take her to one of our safe houses?"

"We're off the books, Frank; you know that."

"Maybe if I had some backup out here, sir?"

"You knew there was no backup when you signed up, Frank."

"I didn't sign up to kidnap children, sir."

Dulles lifted his head out of the palm of his hand.

"You listen to me, Frank, and listen well. You signed up to defend the United States by whatever means necessary. What you are doing now *is* those means, you understand me?"

"Yes, sir."

KING PUT DOWN the phone and checked the street outside the booth before exiting. The door creaked loudly behind him as he crossed the pavement back to the house.

He stopped.

Did he hear something?

He waited.

He watched the darkness, not sure what he was waiting for. He waited so long he felt the chill start to eat into his bones; he shook his head, and then headed back up the stairs to the bedroom at the back.

Anja was back under the sheet on the mattress, and Cook was sitting, arms folded, hands tucked into his armpits, dozing in the tattered red armchair next to the door with a Thompson machine gun in his lap.

The ceiling light was off. King had been worried it might leak through the loosely nailed boards across the window, so a fat stub of a candle was flickering at his feet. Cook opened his eyes and looked at King as the floor creaked under him.

"Did you speak to him?"

"Yes."

"What's happening? Can we go to the embassy?"

King scowled at Cook, held a finger to his lips, and pointed at Anja.

Cook shrugged in the half-light.

"What does it matter if she knows? We'll be gone by the time she says anything."

King ignored him and looked around the room for somewhere to sit. It was a hovel; the place reeked of squalor. King had chosen the building because he knew some Jews had been recently evicted. Normal practice was that it would have been left empty for a few weeks until the civil service had finally gotten round to letting it out. He wondered how long the poor people had been forced to live there?

Waiting for the next step that took them nearer to never having existed at all.

It stank of damp and dirt, and King was reluctant even to shift Cook out of the armchair for fear it would be infested with fleas.

He sighed.

"I'll be in the other room, on the settee. Do not sleep. I'll have a few hours and then you can."

"Fine." Cook yawned and shifted slightly in the armchair, adjusting the Thompson.

"Don't sleep, understand?"

Cook held up a hand of acknowledgment. King shook his head before going to the front room and its damp settee. He pulled his overcoat tightly around him and realized just how cold his nose was.

He breathed out, attempting to loosen the stress of the day and failing badly.

How could things have gone so badly wrong? He shifted again on the settee and closed his eyes. He needed to sleep; he needed to think clearly tomorrow. It was going to be another long day, and he needed it to go better than the one that was coming to a close.

He sighed, shivered, pulled the coat tighter, and closed his eyes.

And then he heard the smash of glass outside.

He was up off the couch and at the window in a flash. He pulled back the tattered net curtain and looked down to the car.

All looked well; he wiped at the window to clear the mist from his breath and looked up the street both ways as far as he could see.

Nothing.

He looked back down at the car.

Nothing.

Except . . . there . . . a flicker, a flash of orange and then it was gone. He wiped again and adjusted position, shielding the glass with his hands as he tried to improve his view.

There, again, the flicker of orange.

The inside of the car was on fire.

"Eric!" King shouted as he turned from the window and grabbed his own Thompson off the floor next to the couch. "Eric!" he shouted again as he ran down the stairs, two at a time, working the bolt on the machine gun as he went.

As he reached the front door he heard Cook on the landing above him.

"Stay with the girl!" King shouted up the stairs as he pulled open the door.

The car interior hadn't quite caught; whoever had set it alight hadn't used enough fuel for the fire. Thick black smoke was rising from the smashed window as King ran toward it. Cook came out of the front door behind him.

"The girl!"

"She's all right."

Cook looked up and down the street and then back at the car as a dancing flame licked around the broken window, reaching for oxygen outside the choking car.

"Get some water."

King struggled to keep his voice low. He dropped the Thompson and started to scoop up snow to throw through the smashed window and onto the burning seat.

Cook ran back into the house. King scooped another armful of snow and pitched it into the car, then tried the door. He fumbled in his pocket for the keys, cursing when he remembered Cook had them.

Another four scoops of snow had gone through the window by the time Cook returned, balancing a metal bowl of water, which he emptied through the window onto the smoldering seat. The flames died and then sprang up again, not quite extinguished.

"The keys, give me the keys." King held out his hand as Cook dropped the bowl and put his hand in his coat pocket.

Someone opened up with a machine gun from the alleyway across the street.

Cook and King both dropped to the pavement. The firing across the street stopped and silence fell, punctuated only by the occasional pop and crackle from the fire, which was threatening to take hold again.

King grabbed his own weapon out of the snow and looked under the car toward the alley opposite.

It looked dark and empty.

Then he saw movement in the darkness. King fired a quick volley under the car. The muzzle exhaust from his Thompson blocked his view momentarily; he paused to let it clear.

Silence.

King rolled to the side and took up position, belly flat to the ground, partly hidden behind the rear wheel of the car. Cook got up to a crouch and risked a look over the bonnet.

"Who was that? Did you see them?" King called.

The machine gun in the alleyway let loose again. Cook barely ducked his head before the car jumped under the weight of the incoming rounds.

King returned fire with a three-round burst and then called to Cook.

"Did you see them?"

"It's not soldiers. I saw one of them, a scruffy bastard."

"Resistance?"

Cook shrugged. "I don't know. He didn't look like a German, that's for sure."

"Where is your gun?" King checked the buildings behind them.

"In the kitchen. I couldn't carry the bowl and the gun at the same time."

Everywhere was dark; another alleyway lay behind them on their own side of the street, maybe twenty feet away. King doubted he'd make it, even at a run; he'd be exposed with no covering fire.

"Fuck! Can you get back into the house?"

"If you cover me. On three: one, two, three!" Cook ran for the house as King let go with two short bursts toward the alley.

The gunman in the alleyway ignored him and fired a long tracing arc of bullets after the sprinting Cook, who slipped at the last moment and dived headlong into the open doorway.

The wood around the door splintered, rounds ripping into it as Cook disappeared from view, kicking the door closed behind him.

The firing stopped again.

King could hear the flames, and he knew the car was done for. He looked across the pavement, back toward the flat, watching the door a moment, hoping to get a sign that Cook was okay.

He shifted again in the snow to look at the alley again. Nothing moved. It was impenetrably black. He imagined whoever was in there was changing magazines.

He considered advancing in the lull but decided against it.

He wiped some snow off the barrel and bolt of the machine gun.

Then he heard the shooting behind him.

From the flat where Cook and Anja were.

A short burst, then a shout, then another.

As if on cue the alleyway opposite lit up again, rounds hitting the Opel and causing it to rock. The car lurched as a tire deflated and glass rained down on King, who buried his face in the snow that kicked up and danced around him.

King heard the muffled rattle of a Thompson behind him, in the flat, in addition to what he was now guessing were two Thompsons in the alleyway.

Finally all the shooting stopped.

He was caught in a pincer: he'd messed up basic field craft. He swore softly to himself as he listened to the fire popping in the car again.

He made up his mind.

He was running before either gunman in the alleyway had the chance to change their magazines. Away, away, as fast as he could run, a tactical retreat to buy him time to regroup and think. He dived into the alleyway on his side of the road, crashing into an old metal bin, tumbling with it and its contents into the protective darkness, hitting his head on the ground.

The Thompsons opened up again behind him.

He rolled onto his back and aimed his own Thompson down his body.

His head pounded.

He waited.

Not for long.

He hit the first man to appear at the end of the alley in the hip and across the stomach, two short rattles of fire as the Thompson kicked in his hand. He heard the man cry out. He didn't bother to fire again as the man thrashed and dragged himself to cover. King knew he had only a few rounds left in his weapon; he didn't want to have to resort to his pistol unless he had to.

He got to his feet and made his way backward down the alleyway, taking small, silent steps, keeping the machine gun pointed at the street. The other Thompson peeked around the corner of the building, letting rip with a high and wide salvo.

King cried out, even though he wasn't hit. He dropped to his knee and waited for the head he knew would follow when the shooting stopped.

It did.

He fired, low and to the left, feeling the Thompson lift and pull to the right as he squeezed the trigger. He saw the dust of the bricks as the rounds hit home. Whomever the head belonged to cried out and withdrew back behind the wall.

King guessed a stone chip had got the man, painfully enough to make him think twice.

King was on the front foot now, in charge of the fight. He advanced slowly toward the street, toward his attackers. Holding the machine gun with one hand, he opened his coat and pulled open the holster on his belt so that he could use his sidearm quickly if required.

He stopped short, some ten feet from the corner, leaning to the right slightly, and saw the legs of someone lying on his back in the snow.

He took a step to the right and then another, trying to get a better view of the man who was lying still. King was almost at the end of the alleyway by the time he was certain the man on the ground was alone.

The fire in the Opel had turned into a full-on inferno, as thick black smoke billowed from the orange flames inside. He craned his neck to see over the roof of the Opel into the alleyway opposite, but the smoke was too thick.

He pointed the Thompson at the man on the ground.

"Where did he go?"

"Gone," the man replied, his breath short, a bubble of blood on his lips. He was bleeding heavily. Around him the snow was staining red, and his breath was coming in short watery gasps.

He was as good as dead. King stepped over the man toward the bullet-splintered front door a few feet away and half pushed it open, keeping his head close to the frame for cover.

"Eric!" he called up the stairs, looking back at the car and then down at the dying man, who now had his eyes closed, his breathing quieter.

"Eric?" he tried again, this time looking up into the darkness of the flat.

"She has my gun!" Cook shouted back, his voice high, panicked.

King dropped to a knee and leaned back from the door; he risked another glance up into the darkness.

"Are you okay?" he called. He was nervous. If the resistance knew they were here and that there were only two of them, they'd be back.

He needed to get moving quickly.

"I'm in the front. She has me pinned down, Frank. I can't move," Cook called again, and King considered leaving him. He figured he could probably make it to a main road and flag down a car with his machine gun.

It would be the end of the operation, he'd have questions to answer, but he'd be alive. Maybe Cook and the girl would be killed by the resistance and the whole thing would blow over.

Who was he kidding?

He wasn't the sort of guy to abandon Cook. He'd gotten the kid into this, and he'd do his best to get him out.

Besides, this wasn't going to blow over.

He'd never get out of the country to tell his tale. Dulles would see to that, just to cover his own back. If he had any chance it rested on either success or no loose ends.

And he had none of one, and a lot of the other.

The man on the ground groaned and gurgled, and King looked down at him as he breathed his last. King felt something trickle down his own face. He dabbed the top of his scalp with his fingers and saw it was blood. As if to confirm his injury, his head started to ache again.

"Where is she?" he called up to Cook.

"The back bedroom!" Cook shouted back.

King stepped into the building and, keeping low, advanced halfway up the stairs. He could see the flicker of the candle in the bedroom. It danced on the wall of the hallway, throwing barely there shadows that made it hard for him to focus.

"Run for the stairs. I'll cover you," he called quietly.

"I can't—she'll have a clear shot."

"We haven't got time for this, Eric. Either run now or stay here and wait for the Germans."

There was silence.

The candle danced and King touched his scalp again.

Suddenly Cook broke from the front room, head down; he hit the top of the stairs flat out, slamming into the wall. Anja let off a short burst from the machine gun, firing mostly high and wide of Cook, who was shooting back blindly with his Browning pistol.

Cook dropped, scrabbled, and cried out. He half rose and then fell down the stairs toward King, who in turn emptied the last of his bullets at the bedroom wall above him, showering dust and plaster down the stairs behind the floundering Cook.

Cook kept falling to the bottom, half rolled onto the pavement, then turned a hard right away from the front door. He tripped over the resistance soldier on the ground. King dragged him to his feet and along the street away from the flat, only stopping to drop his empty weapon and to pick up the dead man's Thompson from the snow where it had fallen.

"The girl?" Cook gasped.

King didn't answer; she was the least of their problems.

CHAPTER 14

ANJA CROUCHED DOWN at the end of the bed and listened.

Silence.

She realized that her hand was burning where it was holding the barrel of the Thompson.

She didn't let go.

She hadn't heard a sound since her ears had stopped ringing from firing the gun. She'd seen Cook diving for the stairs but didn't think she'd been quick enough to hit him.

She hoped she had.

She crept forward, listened again, then peeked her head around the doorframe. Nothing. She ducked back again. She waited for a few seconds, chewing her lip, and then looked again, this time down the stairs at the open front door.

She could see the snow on the pavement outside. She sniffed the air, which smelled of smoke.

She remembered her mother's words: if you get the chance, run.

Whatever might happen next.

She moved forward, gun pointing at the door at the bottom of the stairs. Slowly, crouching, every step placed carefully like a hunter in a forest.

Toes pushing forward first, just as her father had shown her.

She put her foot onto the top step and paused, then slowly, ever so slowly, she took another step, then another, this one slightly quicker.

Closer to the door, closer to her father.

She was halfway down when a head popped around the doorframe and then back out of sight, much too quick for her to react with the gun.

Anja froze, her foot hovering an inch off the step beneath it. The Thompson in her hands rose slowly, pointing at the door. She stepped backward in slow motion, back up the stairs, unsure whether whoever had looked in had seen her in the gloom and the smoke. She took another step, quicker, and then another. The stair creaked, so Anja gave up all pretense at stealth by breaking into a stumbling backward run toward the landing above.

She'd barely made it to the top when the head appeared again, lingering this time. It was still there as she made it into the sanctuary of the bedroom. It was her turn to hide, shoulder to the wall, breathing hard, weapon clutched to her chest.

She turned and looked at the boarded-up window. She was trapped.

Maybe the people who were shooting at King and Cook were still out there? Maybe they could help her?

She looked out again.

The head was there; she couldn't make out the face looking up, so she leveled the gun, showing her ability to defend herself if she had to.

The head disappeared at the sight of the gun.

"Hey!"

Anja ducked back into the bedroom.

"You up there! Throw out the gun!" An Englishman, shouting in English, not angry, nervous.

Anja rested her head against the wall.

"Come on, it's the police! Throw it out!"

The voice grew in confidence, assured, used to people doing as they were told, and Anja felt an urge to comply.

She didn't.

She just sneaked another look around the doorframe, then ducked back into the bedroom.

Could she trust the English police?

Her father had told her, time and time again, "The English aren't our friends, they are our subjects. As long as you are here, be polite, but never trust them. They will turn on you like dogs if you let them."

Anja didn't care who the man at the bottom of the stairs said he was. If he tried to come up, she was going to shoot him like a dog.

She hugged the heavy gun to her chest to take the weight off her arms, then took up position next to the landing again, Thompson pointing down the stairs.

"Throw down the gun; don't make me come up there to get it."

"I'll shoot!" Anja heard herself shouting back, her voice high and light with nerves and adrenaline. She coughed to clear her throat in case she had to shout again.

"This is Police Constable Alf Harris! Come on now, love, throw out the gun and come downstairs before you get hurt." The Englishman held his helmet in the doorway for Anja to see. "Look here, see? I'm a bobby. Come on, throw down that gun before someone gets hurt."

Anja watched the helmet waving and bit her lip as it disappeared back out of sight. She ducked back into the bedroom. She didn't know what to do. She couldn't shoot a policeman.

Even an English one.

She looked up at the ceiling searching for a loft hatch or any other means of escape. The ceiling was stubbornly bare: nothing but yellowing paint and a damp patch.

There was a creak on the stairs.

Anja spun and pointed the gun out the bedroom doorway. Harris froze; Anja looked down at him with the gun held at her hip, pointing at his head.

He blinked, half crouched, and then slowly held out the hand that wasn't carrying his helmet.

"There now, put that down." He motioned with his hand.

Anja didn't reply.

"Come on, I'm here to help you. Please put it down."

Anja swallowed and felt her finger tighten on the trigger.

The bobby took another step up the stairs.

"Go," Anja said, barely a whisper.

"Give me the gun, girl."

He took another step up.

Anja pulled the trigger.

Click.

Empty.

Neither Anja nor Harris moved or made a sound.

A second seemed like a lifetime, then Harris exhaled and sprinted up toward Anja like a cork out of a bottle.

He caught the barrel of the gun with one hand and Anja round the throat with the other.

His helmet tumbled down the stairs and into the street, and they in turn tumbled into the bedroom, landing hard, Harris on top of Anja on the hard wooden floor. Anja tried to scream, but Harris's grip on her throat was too tight.

Harris shifted so that he was completely smothering Anja with his body. She felt an overpowering rush of panic flood through her as she realized that she couldn't move or break free of the weight on her.

Anja felt his hot breath gasping next to her ear. She smelled cigarettes. She struggled to release her arms from where they were pressed against her chest and tried again to scream, but his hand was still choking her. Harris's cheek rubbed against hers and sharp bristles caught and dug at her skin. She screwed up her eyes in frustration, wriggling underneath the great weight pressing down on her. The sound of Harris's breathing bellowed next to her ear; he was blowing hard through his nose.

Anja's panic eased. She turned her head and watched the candle, which seemed to dance slower and slower. She forgot she couldn't breathe.

Harris released his grip.

She gasped back to life, her hearing and vision returned, and the candle lit the room. She looked up into the eyes of the policeman, who blinked and then laughed loudly.

Anja saw he had a black tooth, left incisor. His breath smelled, and she turned her head as far as she could manage.

"I thought you'd bleedin' killed me then." Harris seemed to grab at the words as they fell out of his mouth, almost too fast to catch. He panted, another quick breath, still smiling. "When you pulled that trigger I thought, Hey up. You're a goner here, Alf." Harris laughed again; Anja looked at him and saw more rotten teeth in his mouth near the back.

He blew out his cheeks and then dragged Anja up with him as he stood. He gripped her harshly by the collar, almost lifting her off the floor as he held her at arm's length.

"You scared the shit out of me," he carried on talking as he roughly rummaged in the pockets of her coat and then quickly searched her for any other weapons, twisting her and pushing her face first against the wall, still holding on to her collar and keeping her on tiptoes.

Anja allowed herself to be searched without making a sound; she neither resisted nor assisted. She simply stood silently, aware that she was held firm by Harris and that any chance of escape was gone.

For now.

He dragged her across to the mattress and pushed her down so that she was sitting on its edge. He let go and slowly withdrew his hand, holding it palm down close to her face.

"Don't try and run away. I'm here to help you, understand?"

Anja nodded.

"Good girl." Harris took a few steps back and picked up the Thompson. He looked at the gun, then tried and failed to remove the magazine before looking back at Anja.

"What was going on here? I heard the shooting from a couple of streets away. Who was it?"

Anja didn't reply.

"Come on now, I saw the bullet holes all over the front of this place and I heard enough shooting to start a war. Was it resistance? I didn't see no Germans around."

Anja stared at him.

"Where are your papers?" Harris tried to free the magazine again, but he clearly had no idea how to operate the Thompson.

Anja didn't reply.

"Don't make me look for them, girl. Where are they?" He lowered the gun to his side, finally admitting he didn't know how to operate it.

Anja pointed to the inside pocket of her coat.

"Open your coat and take them out slowly." Harris took a step closer and held out his hand cautiously, ready to strike her if she tried to trick him.

She reached into her inside coat pocket very slowly, removed her identity card, and held it close to her chest.

Harris flicked with his fingers, looking into Anja's eyes.

"I'm the police, love, you can trust me. Come on . . . give it here."

Anja gently put her identity card into Harris's outstretched hand; he smiled at her and then looked down at it.

Harris whistled through his teeth. "You're a bleedin' Kraut.

CHAPTER 15

KING WAS OUT of breath. He stopped at the end of the alleyway and looked out onto the street beyond.

It was deserted.

He checked back along the alley he'd just run along, then back to the street. He was lost.

"Fuck."

He breathed deeply a few times and tried to slow down his heart, then took a few steps back into the darkness.

"Where are we?" Cook caught up to him, gasping for breath.

"I don't know, we've run too far. This place is a maze. Everywhere looks the same."

"Can't we just call the embassy? Have someone come and get us?"

"Nobody needs to know we are out here, Eric. We're on our own for now, just a little longer, okay?"

Cook slid down the wall and sat in the snow. King crossed the alley and knelt next to him, laying the Thompson down.

"I'm shot, Frank. It hurts."

"I know; you've told me. Lean forward and let me look again."

Cook rolled forward slightly. King reached around and ran his hand across the younger man's back. Cook stiffened when King found the wound, then lifted his hand to check for blood.

"Is it bad?"

"It can't be that bad; you've run half a mile. Just keep going a little farther and then I can fix you up. It might be just a graze."

"It stings like crazy, really bad, and I'm cold." Cook's voice sounded weak, and for a moment King thought he was going to cry.

"Of course you're cold, it's below freezing out here."

Cook shook his head. "I'm scared."

"You really aren't cut out for this sort of thing, are you?" King rested his hand on Cook's shoulder and looked back out to the street. "Wait here. I'll get us transport and come back for you." King stood up and walked back to the head of the alleyway. He looked left and right and then back at Cook. "I won't be long. Stay here. Keep hold of the Thompson just in case."

"I'll come..." Cook stopped. King was already gone, head down, into the night.

Cook shifted in the snow. His coat was damp and he was regretting sitting down. He tried to push himself to one side, so that he could get up to his knees, but the pain in his back caused him to give up and sink back down the wall.

He closed his eyes.

It wasn't meant to be like this. Frank had told him it would be easy: "A simple job for Dulles. We do this and we'll be made for life, part of the new security service they've set up to keep an eye on the Nazis back in Washington."

Eric Cook didn't feel made for life right now. He just felt scared.

Scared of dying, scared of being alone, scared of the bullet wound in his back, and scared of being caught.

King was right; he wasn't cut out for this sort of thing. He was a clerk, an intellectual, working his way up the diplomatic service and happy with his life. Sort of.

Sure, he didn't like Ambassador Kennedy and President Lindbergh's policy of working with the Germans, but he could have lived with it. He had his career to think of. He'd read the interviews with Churchill in the papers, demanding weapons, money, and action against the Nazis. He read them all, and while he quite liked Churchill as a guy, he also quite liked Hitler.

At least Hitler had seen off Stalin—communism was as good as dead thanks to him. Cook doubted whether Churchill would have done that. He guessed Churchill would have run to Uncle Joe for help just the same as he had run to Uncle Sam.

Plus Churchill was happy for his own people to die. He was always being asked in the press to condemn the bombs that went off all over Britain, especially straight after the invasion, and not once had he done so.

No, Churchill was the kind of guy you'd go for a beer with; Hitler was the kind of guy who owned the bar.

Hitler was the winner, and the USA liked winners, so the USA liked Hitler.

Eric had been excited to get Great Britain as his first posting overseas. It had seemed glamorous until he got here and saw the fog, the queues, the checkpoints, and the squads of soldiers lining people up against walls with their hands on their heads.

One night in a restaurant, four of the English fascist Home Defense Troops had dragged a guy out, just like that. One minute the guy was drinking soup, the next minute he was on the floor being pulled by his hair to the door.

The strangest part of it was the way the band just started playing again when he was gone, as if it had never happened, as if he'd never been there, as if the whole thing were a dream.

That was when Eric decided that he wanted to go home.

He'd found himself staying in the embassy more and more of a night, instead of getting the tube back to his flat. The way people ignored each other on the underground spooked him; they were like ghosts, lost in their own heads, dodging around each other silently looking away.

Just as everyone had done in the restaurant.

And then along came Frank King, the new military attaché, a uniform packed full of charisma and a bright light in a city in darkness. They'd fast become friends. Eric didn't really know what a military attaché did for certain, but it seemed to involve a lot of drinking and a lot of laughing.

Oh, and English girls. It involved an awful lot of English girls.

Frank King had changed Eric Cook's life in many ways.

Especially seeing as a few months after meeting him Eric was sitting in an alleyway, shot and bleeding, after kidnapping a mother and daughter.

Shot and bleeding, and on his own.

He still wasn't certain what a military attaché did, but whatever it was, he didn't like it.

He opened his eyes and looked up at the sky. Fat, heavy, pink clouds, which looked ready to let go of the snow they were barely clinging to, pressed down on him, and he shivered with the cold.

His back hurt, but the damp of the ground finally made him struggle onto all fours, in a preamble to getting up.

He paused, lifted his head, and saw them.

Two men stood at the end of the alley watching him.

Nobody moved.

Somewhere a dog barked as Cook's hands began to hurt from being half buried in the snow.

"I'm an American," he finally said, although he didn't know why.

One of the men took out an automatic pistol and walked toward him, feet crunching in the snow.

"Please, no. I'm an American." Eric raised one hand out of the snow.

"I don't care," replied the man as he lifted the pistol level with Eric's temple.

Eric Cook shut his eyes and lowered his head.

He wasn't going to cry.

Everything went black.

FROM THE CORNER at the end of the street, King watched them carry Cook out of the alleyway and put him in the back of the van. He hadn't heard a shot, but he'd only just arrived, after trekking a quarter of a mile across Whitechapel toward Bethnal Green. By the time he had flagged down the car, struggled with the driver, and eventually dragged him out, he'd been gone for over twenty minutes.

It was turning into one hell of a night.

King squinted; Cook could be dead, but there was no way of telling from this distance.

He drummed his fingers on the steering wheel, then chewed his thumbnail.

One of the men at the far end of the street climbed into the back of the van, where they had just put Cook; the other two closed the doors and got into the cab.

Why would you climb into the back with a corpse? If he's dead, there's no point.

He saw a puff of white smoke at the rear of the van, so he in turn started the car. He watched the van move off, then slowly followed it out of the street with his headlamps off.

They didn't travel far. King guessed they were heading back in the direction he and Cook had run from. They crabbed across Whitechapel through smoggy streets that seemed to suck the air out of your lungs.

His suspicions were confirmed when he saw the saw the sign for Stuffield Street pass by on his left-hand side.

They were passing the street where King and Cook had held Anja.

He craned his neck to look for signs of police activity after the shooting, but the street was silent. The only indication that anything untoward had taken place was the Opel, lopsidedly sitting on two flat tires, smoke drifting through the smashed windows, waiting for the local kids to pick it clean in the morning like buzzards would a carcass.

The van hadn't slowed at Stuffield Street; it continued another fifty yards before turning left, and then sharp right onto Providence Street.

King breathed a sigh of relief that he was traveling slowly enough to glide to a halt at the head of the street before he was seen. He watched the van pull over to the curb, halfway down the short street of terraced houses.

Before the occupants of the van had a chance to get out and go to the back doors, King was out of his own vehicle and crouching by the street corner. He watched as one of the men, carrying a Thompson submachine gun, climbed up into the box on the rear of the van and disappeared into the shadows.

A moment passed before Cook emerged, supported on either side by the men. King watched as Cook managed to climb down, slowly and gingerly, half lowered, half dropping the two feet to the floor, into the arms of the van driver.

They hadn't killed him; he was still alive, waiting to be saved.

Cook seemed to swoon slightly and the driver struggled to hold him up. The two men from the back of the van dropped down, then all three dragged Cook into the open door of the house next to the van.

Cook seemed to stiffen as he crossed the threshold; he turned his head and for a moment King thought he was looking right at him.

King pulled back from the corner and stood flat against the wall. He waited and then snuck another look along the street.

Except for the tracks in the snow at the back of the van, there was no sign anyone had been there. Every house was in darkness.

The one Cook had been taken into was tiny, one window downstairs, one window up, and barely big enough for a cat to fit into, let alone be swung around.

King wiped his nose with the back of his hand and looked back the way they had come. He realized that after all his circuitous traveling on foot and then driving, he was less than five minutes' walk from where they had held Anja.

He leaned back against the wall and cursed.

If the resistance had a safe house here, they would have noticed his Opel parked nearby.

"Fuck," he breathed. A simple mistake had ruined everything. He kicked his heel against the wall behind him and looked again at the house where Cook was.

The front door opened and the driver appeared. He'd barely stepped through before it closed again behind him. The driver went to his vehicle and King listened as it coughed into life, belching oily blue smoke as it did.

The van revved once or twice, then slowly pulled away from the curb and headed off into the darkness. King watched as brake lights shone dirty red at the end of the street, then the van disappeared as it turned left.

The exhaust smoke drifted toward him, irritating his nose with the sweet smell of burned oil. King looked at his own vehicle, ten feet away, and thought about his options.

Run or stay?

Fight or flight?

He looked back around the corner at the darkened house.

Dulles would want him to drop Eric, put distance between them and him. If the poor kid turned up dead in an alley in a week's time there was nothing that could connect them. Frank King had been careful of that; he'd taken a few weeks to spread rumors about Eric being a party boy, always on the arm of some young English broad. If the kid turned up dead in an alley, people would most likely think he'd just crossed to the wrong side of the tracks chasing a bit of skirt.

London was a dirty town with a dirty police force; violent crime was rife in certain quarters. King could be back in Washington before people started to ask questions, assuming they bothered to.

"Fuck," he said again before sighing and crossing to the car.

Frank King wasn't that kind of guy.

He should never have used the kid. He should have known he wasn't up to it. He was a clerk, for God's sake; he barely knew how to carry a gun. King silently damned Dulles for pushing the operation through. He knew he should have stuck to his guns, demanded proper backup, a chain of command, and an exit plan.

"Fuck."

He locked the car up.

He took out his 9mm pistol and checked that he could see brass in the breech.

He put the pistol back into his pocket and, keeping tight hold of it, walked quickly across to the opposite corner of the street, the same side where the house that held Eric was.

The kid was a clerk, for God's sake.

CHAPTER 16

ERIC COOK HAD tried to look around as they dragged him up the two low steps, off the street, and into the house. He'd wanted to see a street name, a landmark, even a smiling face, but his ears rang and his head ached, and he'd barely had time to catch his breath and see his own feet.

He had fallen across the threshold onto the floor in the narrow hallway of the house. One of the men shoved him farther into the hall with a boot against his backside. Eric heard the door behind him slam as he scrabbled his way across the floor.

He stopped maybe ten feet from where he had come in and sat with his back pushed into the corner, drawing his knees up to his chest and lowering his head, doing his best to ignore the throb of the wound in his back.

The front door opened and he risked lifting his head to see what was going on. One of the men left, and he caught sight of the street before the man closed the door behind him.

The outside seemed a long way away.

The other two men stared at Eric.

"I'm an American." He spoke quietly, aware that the same words had resulted in a blow on the head earlier.

The men stared at him some more, neither of them spoke, and he felt suddenly indignant.

He started to get up off the floor.

"Stay there or you'll get another crack," one of the men said quietly.

Eric slid back down the wall and lowered his head.

He'd attended a lecture in Washington that addressed situations such as these. He remembered the speaker had given a long list of dos and don'ts if one were kidnapped or mugged. Eric could remember only two things: "Don't resist" was one, and the blond girl sitting opposite who had smiled at him on the way into the lecture was the other.

He'd spent an hour looking at her, trying to think of a good line to use when he asked her out.

She obviously hadn't been listening to the lecture either, because she resisted, and he never got the date he was after.

One of the men approached Eric and lightly kicked his feet.

Eric looked up.

"Here." The man was a lot older than Eric, with a fat mustache that was turning gray at the ends. He held out an equally gray handkerchief in his dirty hand. "For your head."

Eric took the handkerchief, unfolded it, saw it was even dirtier than it first looked, and looked at Mustache, who was still standing over him.

"You're bleeding." Mustache pointed to the top of his own head.

Eric folded the handkerchief slowly, trying to find the cleanest part of it.

He pressed the rag gingerly against his head, then inspected the blood on it, a black dot in the dirt. He put the rag on his head again.

"Thank you," he said quietly, aware that he was thanking the man who had caused the injury in the first place.

Mustache nodded and returned to standing by the door.

"This is a misunderstanding. I'm an American citizen," Eric said, still looking at the floor, trying to not to be confrontational.

Neither Mustache nor the other man replied, so Eric tried again.

"If this is a robbery or something, you can have my wallet. I don't have anything else."

"Shush now," Mustache said quietly.

"I demand to be released."

"In good time."

"I'm an American, I'm not German . . . I demand . . ." Eric trailed off as the other man reached into his pocket and took out a Browning pistol. The man stared at Eric, who lowered his head, hating himself for doing so.

"Get up."

Eric looked up at the man with the gun.

"Get up," the man said again.

Eric looked at Mustache, who stared back sadly.

"Please, I'm sorry, I don't want any trouble . . ."

The man with the pistol charged forward and grabbed Eric by the lapel of his coat. He dragged him halfway off the floor, and Eric felt the pistol being jammed into the side of his neck. The man dragged and pushed him forward, bent double, to the foot of the stairs. With a final shove he sent Eric sprawling onto the bottom steps.

He felt a boot in the backside and stumbled forward again, eventually managing to propel himself on all fours up to the next floor.

The man pushed Eric into the back room, then down onto the floor again. Eric half lay, half crouched, shielding his head with his left hand, the one closest to the Browning that menaced him, so close he could smell the oil that had been used to clean it.

"Corner, go!" The man pointed with the Browning and Eric scuttled and crawled into the corner, eventually sitting with his back against the wall.

The room was empty of furniture and almost completely dark, except for a rectangle of light tossed in by the light on the landing. One of the walls was covered by peeling striped wallpaper, which had once been colored but now looked various depressing shades of damp. The ceiling that was lit by the landing light had the pallor of a corpse and was covered in hairline cracks that looked like black veins.

Mustache entered the room with a wooden chair, which he placed near the door. He sat down and nodded to the man with the Browning, who turned back to Eric, staring at him again with the same angry eyes.

"You aren't going to give me any problems, are you?" Mustache spoke to Eric, and Eric replied by looking confused and then burying his head in his arms.

Mustache looked at his mate and smiled. "He's not going to give me problems."

The second man nodded and left the room.

Eric listened as the other man jogged down the stairs, and then as the front door slammed shut behind him.

He was alone in the half-light with Mustache.

He risked looking up.

"If you look at me again, I will shoot you in the face," Mustache said, lifting his own Browning slowly so that it was pointing straight at Eric, who, in turn, immediately lowered his head again.

Message received and understood.

TEN MINUTES PASSED by in silence.

Eric's back began to hurt again, a high-pitched pain that burned every time he breathed in. He was aware his clothes were wet from blood, but he took some comfort from the fact that they didn't seem to be getting wetter.

He looked at the floorboards and chewed at his lip.

Eric knew he wasn't a brave man.

He knew he was in big trouble, off the grid, a long way from home with people who didn't appear to care if he lived or died.

The front door of the house slammed shut, then came the thumping of several pairs of feet on the stairs. Mustache stood up. Eric glanced at him and then back to the door.

A real dread, a painful certainty came over him: he was about to die, this was it, from small-town America to a grim room in London.

Not much of a life.

He felt like crying. Such a waste, it just wasn't fair.

He thought about the blonde at the presentation, wished he'd thought of a better line, wished she had said yes.

The door opened and Eric looked up.

The man who had left earlier entered, followed by another, much older man. Very tall, very thin, maybe sixty or seventy, all elbows and angles. He pulled off a black homburg hat and straightened his glasses before peering at Eric with a frown.

Finally a woman entered, in her late fifties, fat. The kind of fat that was too fat for ration books. Red cheeked from the cold, with a round, friendly, fleshy face and dots for eyes. She smiled at Eric as she unfurled the purple scarf from around her neck, then wound it around her hand before passing it to Mustache.

The room fell silent as everyone looked at Eric in the corner.

Maybe he was wrong. Maybe this wasn't the end.

They didn't look like a firing squad, that was for sure.

Eric felt himself blushing and his heart pounded. He could bear it no more, so he looked down at the floor again until the woman spoke.

"What's your name, love?"

Eric looked up. "Eric Cook. I am an American citizen and I demand to be released. I refuse to be some sort of hostage."

The words had sounded better in his head.

"Oh, Eric, I'm sorry, lover, not just yet. We have to have a talk first. I'm Ma Price, but they call me 'Ma' because I'm like everybody's own dear mum herself. Do you have a mum, my love?"

"Yes."

"Yes, *Ma*. Go on, try it."

"Yes, Ma."

"I expect she'll be worrying about you, so far away from home."

Eric nodded.

"Like I worry about my boys." Ma Price rested a hand on Mustache's arm, which he didn't seem to notice.

Eric looked at Mustache and doubted Ma Price needed to worry too much about him.

"Are you injured, Eric?" she asked in her singsong way.

"Yes, Ma."

The old man took his cue, and holding his black hat across his chest like a breastplate, he walked across the room toward Eric.

"My head and my back," Eric said. "I've been shot."

"Lean forward, please," the old man said quietly.

Eric did as he was told and felt the old man inspecting his back. Eric watched Ma Price as the inspection took place. She smiled at him, and he found himself smiling back, politely, like an idiot. The old man eased him back against the wall again, and then gingerly touched the swelling bloody lump on his head.

"Superficial, nothing to worry about. It'll need a good clean, but there is no serious damage to you."

"Thank you," Eric heard himself say.

The old man struggled arthritically to stand up, then crossed back to Ma Price and the men.

"You are safe for now, as long as you answer my questions truthfully. So, tell me, what is your name?" Ma Price spoke again.

"I told you, Eric Cook."

"What were you and your colleague doing in the flat two streets away?"

Eric paused and looked at Price and then the old man.

"You should answer the question while you still can," said the old man.

Eric shifted and then touched the wound on his head lightly.

"That has nothing to do with you."

Ma Price kept on smiling, but Eric noticed Mustache frown.

"I'll not give you many chances, lover, so you really need to take them when they come along. One last time now: what were you doing in the flat with your chum?"

"I'm an American citizen, I work at the embassy, and you have no right to hold me like this. You're going to be in a lot of trouble . . ." Eric stopped speaking as Ma Price lifted a finger.

"I can see, my love, that you're not a hard case. I've only got to look at you to see that, so don't go puffing out your chest and spouting off."

"Listen to her," the old man said.

"But I . . . I'm . . ."

Mustache crossed the room and stopped in front of Eric, who slid farther back into the corner.

"Answer the question."

"I'm . . . we . . . I'm an American." Eric swallowed, looking up into Mustache's sad eyes.

"All right, have it your way. Kill him," Ma Price said behind Mustache.

Eric didn't see the pistol until it was pressing into the center of his forehead. He watched Mustache's finger curl around the trigger and the pink of his knuckle turn white as he squeezed.

"I was guarding a girl."

"A girl?"

"Yes, ma'am." Eric stared at the trigger finger's knuckle, which stayed white.

"What girl?"

"She is the child of a German SS major ..." Eric paused; his mouth was bone dry and his tongue was catching on the roof of his mouth. "We kidnapped her."

Eric began to cry, and he felt the pressure of the muzzle lift. He sobbed and let his head fall forward, ashamed to let the others in the room see his tears and his humiliation.

"Please don't kill me, please, I can help you ... please ... I don't want to die, I'm just a clerk."

CHAPTER 17

KOEHLER HAD DRIVEN in snow countless times before. He knew all the tricks, braking with the gears, no sudden movements, early anticipation, and easy on the gas.

He knew them all.

It was just that none of them were working.

The little Austin Seven barely had the weight to push down into the snow, even with the combined weight of Rossett and him in it. The car seemed to be sliding from rut to rut, back end flicking this way and that like an excited puppy.

He wondered if it was because he was tense. Koehler rolled his head and breathed deeply, trying to stretch the tension away as he waited at traffic lights on the main road out of London, heading for Cambridge.

His mood wasn't helped by their decision to not set off too early. The reasoning had been that they were more likely to get stopped on an empty street than on a busy one. They had sat in Rossett's favorite café, waiting out the night.

Rossett had sat quietly, barely moving, eyes closed, arms folded, as the hours had passed. Koehler had twitched and smoked, fidgeting like the second hand on his Rolex, perpetual motion, unable to relax, cigarette after cigarette counting down the night.

The morning hadn't hurried; even now that they were moving the sun was still snoozing behind the heavy clouds that looked about to let go of another fall of fresh snow.

All around them now the city was waking up, stretching, and trying to shake off the night before. Koehler tapped the tiny fuel gauge set into the speedometer of the car.

They had a long way to go and not a lot of fuel to do it with. Koehler guessed the journey was about 120 miles, there and back, assuming they made it back.

They had to make it back.

For Anja and Lotte.

They had to.

The lights changed; Koehler lifted the clutch and the car slithered forward a few feet before the back end caught hold of the road, finally picking up what little speed it could muster. Koehler had been in an Austin like this before in dry, clear weather, and it had barely managed forty miles an hour; he guessed he'd be lucky to see twenty-five on this journey.

The car drifted, and Koehler found his mind drifting with it as his reflexes corrected the slide.

He thought about Lotte, how they'd met at a dance when he'd been at university in Munich.

So long ago now.

She had made him laugh that first night, really laugh, as if they'd been friends for years, immediately comfortable, fitting exactly, made for each other, pieces of a solved puzzle.

As they'd danced Koehler had found himself looking into her eyes and smiling like a man who couldn't believe his luck. She taught him to waltz, leading him, laughing with him, starting to love him as he started to love her.

He called her "Farm Girl" after she told him how she had grown up in the countryside. When she finally took him to meet her mother and father, halfway across the farmyard, his shoe came off in ankle-deep mud and he stumbled and blushed.

Lotte had laughed and called him "City Boy."

And he was.

Koehler smiled at the memory.

So long ago now.

They had made love for the first time that weekend. Softly, silently, in a loft in the barn, as beneath them animals stirred and above them rain thundered on the roof, an angry autumn downpour. Together, on winter straw, they had lain silently staring at each other, eyes inches apart.

In love forever.

Marriage, then Anja. Koehler finished university and found what he thought was his future in the classrooms of Munich, teaching history to children who didn't understand how important it was.

Lotte never followed her dreams of pursuing a career in science. She held on to them, though, waiting for Anja to grow before she took up her studies again and became the doctor she'd always wanted to be. Koehler had been so happy with his family around him; their little apartment just off the Marienplatz had become a kingdom of heaven, filled with laughter and joy.

They had learned together, grown together, loved and lived together as if every day was the start of an adventure.

And then the clouds came.

Lotte hadn't liked the idea of Koehler joining the Nazi Party. She had never enjoyed politics; she would frown at the sound of the Führer on the radio when she came home with Anja from walking or shopping.

He remembered their first real argument.

A letter had arrived, stating that old Mr. Cohen was no longer their landlord; the building had been seized as a result of the new laws.

"He is a good man, Ernst! He doesn't deserve to have his home, his livelihood, and his dignity taken away!"

Koehler had held his finger to his lips and shushed Lotte. She had thrown the letter on the fire before storming out of the apartment, going downstairs to help Mr. Cohen and his family pack their belongings onto the handcart in the street outside.

Koehler had sat on the sofa with a sleeping Anja in his arms, watching the curtain drift in the breeze.

So long ago now.

Rossett coughed, the first noise he'd made since they had set off. Koehler looked across but Rossett ignored him, just the same stare, straight ahead, emotionless, silent, as if he were alone in an empty room.

The Austin plowed on through the snow, doggedly going where it had no place to be. Koehler wiped at the windscreen with the back of his hand as the morning finally brightened.

Another red light, another fumble for the crushed damp cigarette packet in his pocket.

Empty.

"Do you have smokes?" He looked at Rossett, who moved for the first time during the journey to check his own pockets. A quick search and a packet emerged, which he offered across.

"I've one left."

"Shit, I need to smoke. My nerves."

"Take it." Rossett looked at him and then back out the windscreen.

"You sure?"

Rossett didn't reply, so Koehler took the cigarette and then tossed the empty packet over his shoulder onto the backseat of the car. He managed to touch the end with a flaring match, just before the lights changed.

He hadn't wanted to join the military. His conscription and basic training in the army had been tough, but his education and overall performance had marked him out early as a candidate for promotion.

"You could go a long way, Koehler. You are smart, charming, a good soldier. People like you inspire. Your men would follow you. I'm recommending you for officer training school." His CO had smiled at him, signed a file, and Koehler had gone to the academy, unsure of whether he was doing the right thing.

He'd known as soon as he got there that he wasn't.

The time wasn't right. He wanted to be home and in the arms of Lotte and Anja, so he flunked out on purpose. A map-reading exercise gone wrong, followed by a failed initiative test, and he was back in front of the CO in no time at all.

The CO had a portrait of the Führer hanging on the wall behind him, and they'd both frowned at Ernst as he had stood to attention, trying not to look either of them in the eye.

"I'm disappointed. You've let us down. Go away and come back in twelve months." The words followed him out of the door and back to Munich. He smiled all the way.

But Munich was changing; Germany was changing. His old friend Helmut from university visited with presents and a smart black uniform and boots that creaked when he walked.

"Don't leave it too late, Ernst. Germany isn't a place for schoolmasters and students anymore. You need to get on board with us, the SS. The Führer needs men like you to spread National Socialism across Europe. We won't be conquerors, we will be saviors!" Helmut had spilled schnapps on the kitchen table when he slammed down his glass to make his point.

Lotte had stood up from where she was sitting silently on their old sofa, then fetched a cloth to wipe up the mess before it stained the table.

As he drove the car that morning, far out of London through the snow, Ernst Koehler wished he had heard what Lotte had been saying with that silence.

Instead he had followed Helmut into the SS. This time there was no failed map-reading exercise. This time there was no failed initiative test.

He'd tried his best for Lotte, Anja, the Führer, and Germany. He became a Waffen SS officer. His boots had creaked across the floor of their Munich apartment, and then they'd creaked across Europe and beyond.

From Dunkirk to Dover.

From west to east, through Munich on leave, then on to Moscow and beyond.

He earned his Knight's Cross the hard way. He had led men, lost men, killed men, and been a warrior for the Reich and for the Führer he'd sworn to die for.

But now, right at that minute, driving through England, blood was on his hands, staining his soul and causing his conscience to physically ache when he thought about what he had done.

He knew Lotte had been right all those years ago. Slamming the door, loading Cohen's cart, she'd been right.

And he'd been so terribly wrong.

He was trapped and wrapped in a nightmare he'd helped to create.

He was a reaper, and he hated himself.

His boots creaked over the skulls of a million dead Jews.

His boots had creaked without conscience.

He wasn't a soldier anymore, nor was he a teacher.

He was death.

And he knew he had done wrong.

He had carried on with his job, rounding up the Jews, butchering the Jews. He didn't see their bodies, but he heard their cries when he turned off the light at night.

He knew he was worse than Rossett, because he knew where they went.

He had seen the chimneys, smelled the stench, and seen the ash fall around him like snow from the roofs of the buses on the London streets.

He was a butcher, with a clipboard instead of a knife, but a butcher all the same.

He didn't deserve Lotte and Anja, but he vowed he would get them back and change things. He would go back to Germany, maybe teach again. Build a new life, for all of them, for Germany, for the children he taught, for the future.

He'd do it with them because without them, without the hope that they brought, there was no point.

No point at all.

IT WAS COMING again, fat, slow snow, flakes as big as plums, drifting down faster as the seconds passed. Koehler slipped the car into neutral. The road was too narrow to overtake the bus in front of them, even on a day when the road wasn't deep in snow.

Rossett opened the door of the car.

"I'll get cigarettes from the kiosk. Do you want anything else?"

Koehler looked across the road and saw a tiny street kiosk with a vendor and a few commuter customers.

"Some mints?"

Rossett closed the door and crossed the pavement to the kiosk.

Koehler watched him go, then went back to staring at the back of the bus. He looked in his mirror and saw a black cab, only a couple of feet from the back of the Austin. The driver was blowing into his hands, trying to keep them warm. Some more snow pattered against the Austin's windscreen, so Koehler flicked the switch on the dashboard to sweep it away with the wipers.

The bus brake lights glared at him. The driver was riding the pedal as they waited. Koehler leaned across to the passenger side of the car, straining to see if the bus was stuck at a hidden traffic light.

He couldn't see.

He wondered if Rossett would make it back to the car before he had to move off, and gave a tiny blip of the throttle before checking the fuel gauge again.

Quarter full. He watched it drift to empty and then back up to full.

He decided they would stop and dip the tank to check how much it actually held. They couldn't afford to get halfway and then run out.

He looked up; the conductor was leaning out of the open platform at the back of the bus, holding the shiny chrome pole with one hand, staring toward the front of the vehicle.

Maybe there had been an accident?

The snow was coming more heavily; he could hear it pattering on the tin roof of the car.

Koehler opened the door, stepped out into the road, and looked at Rossett, still waiting to be served. Then he took a step to his right so he could look beyond the bus to see what was holding them up.

Four German soldiers, in long greatcoats, rifles slung over shoulders, gingerly making their way through the snow toward him.

Checkpoint.

"Shit."

One of the soldiers, a ruddy-faced, middle-aged corporal, waved an arm at Koehler and shouted.

"In there!" Bad English, but clear enough.

Koehler nodded, hoping the sensation in his stomach wasn't showing on his face. He looked at Rossett, still waiting, unable to see the soldiers on the other side of the bus.

Koehler took hold of the still-open door of the Austin and turned to look back at the queue that was forming at the checkpoint. Ten or so taxis and cars, followed by another bus, sat in the falling snow that was gusting on a freshening wind.

Nobody was beeping their horns; nobody was out of their cars.

Koehler realized he was standing out from the crowd.

The troops were ten feet away, and the corporal was staring at him, unhappy that he'd been ignored.

"I said—"

"I'm an SS major. Be careful who you are talking to," Koehler replied in German.

ROSSETT HEARD KOEHLER'S voice and looked up, then looked at the bus, and then the road ahead.

"Yes, guv?" the vendor asked him.

Rossett ignored the vendor; he was too busy wondering how he had missed the truck half blocking the road in front of the bus.

"Guv?"

Rossett looked at the vendor and then back to the checkpoint, automatically slipping his hand into the coat pocket where his Webley was waiting, cursing himself for switching off.

"What'll it be?" the vendor tried again.

The checkpoint corporal looked at the Austin and frowned as Koehler approached; it was a strange car for a major to be traveling in—battered, old, barely roadworthy.

Koehler fought the urge to look toward Rossett, not wanting to give away Rossett's position to the checkpoint crew.

On the pavement side of the bus another three soldiers appeared. Two climbed on board to check the papers of the passengers. The conductor stepped out of the way, eyes down, not looking for trouble.

"Forty Players," Rossett said to the vendor without looking at him.

"Bleedin' Nazis, everywhere this morning." The vendor was watching the soldiers as they came around the back of the bus and approached the Austin.

"I'M SORRY, SIR, I thought you were English." The corporal approached Koehler, the others in his squad hanging back, probably wishing they'd gotten on the bus.

"I need to get going. Get this traffic out of the way."

The wiper on the Austin juddered across the windscreen and the corporal looked at it, and then at Koehler.

"I'll need to see your papers, sir."

Koehler patted his chest, feeling for his wallet under his heavy woolen coat, the urge to see where Rossett was almost overpowering.

Did the soldiers know?

Was this a routine checkpoint?

Koehler patted his side pocket and felt his Mauser bumping against his body, reminding him it was there.

Two of the soldiers had stepped up onto the curb; one was staring into the bus while the other was looking back toward the checkpoint. Another was standing at the front of the Austin, and that damned corporal was waiting, hand out, blushing slightly, regretting asking to see Koehler's papers, but still waiting for them.

Rossett kept watching as he paid the vendor for the cigarettes. He studied the soldiers, all young men, fresh faced, with bolt-action rifles, old infantry Karabiners, the sort issued to soldiers in low-risk postings, slow to maneuver. He squeezed the grip on his Webley and guessed the distance between him and the nearest soldier to be approximately fifty feet. Even with their heavy coats and gloves making them slow to react, Rossett doubted he'd be able to take down more than three before the others fired on him.

He watched as Koehler undid the top button of his overcoat, trying to read his friend's body language.

"Your change, guv?" The vendor was holding out some coins.

Rossett ignored him, so the vendor followed his gaze, watching the group by the Austin, slowly realizing that something was wrong.

At the car the corporal shifted slightly, lowering his hand an inch or two but still adamant that he wanted to see this strange, nervous major's papers.

Koehler flicked away the cigarette he was still holding and then reached into his coat. He gambled, breathed, readied himself. He was praying Rossett was ready for the fight; he didn't dare look to check.

Rossett will be ready, Rossett is always ready, Koehler told himself, eyes on the corporal, hand on his Mauser.

He saw another soldier getting off the back of the bus.

A soldier with an MP40 machine pistol in his hands.

The young soldier was watching his colleague come down the steps from the top deck; he'd been covering him as he'd checked the papers of the passengers upstairs. There was probably a round in the chamber ready to go.

The young man looked at Koehler and then at the corporal, reading the standoff, drifting the gun around in a casual covering arc.

Koehler let go of the Mauser, then produced his papers, slapped them into the corporal's hand, and waited.

Rossett felt his grip loosen on the Webley.

"Major Koehler?" The corporal looked up.

"Yes?"

"Could you come with us, please, sir?"

Koehler had failed.

Rossett was on his own.

CHAPTER 18

THE TEA WAS sickly thick and dirty brown; the mug it was in was greasy and covered in fingerprints that weren't Anja's, but still, she sipped it again.

Enjoying the first kind thing anyone had done for her in what seemed like forever.

The boy who had brought the drink to her stood on the other side of the garage workshop, awkwardly watching her in dirty overalls and heavy boots that looked too big for his skinny legs. He worked his hand through his greasy, floppy black hair and tried unsuccessfully to coax the mess on his head into some sort of order.

As soon as he lowered his hand a thick wedge of hair collapsed and dropped down his forehead, hiding his right eye. The light was poor in the workshop, but Anja could see that there were three cars in various states of repair loitering in the gloom. Everything but the cars seemed to be wrapped in a layer of old oil, especially the floor, which was concrete dappled with slick and matte shades of old and new spills and splashes.

The chair Anja sat on was comfortable but, like everything else, covered in oil. At first she had worried about her coat and tried not to sit back too far. But time had passed—half an hour? maybe an hour?—the tea had arrived, and she had slowly relaxed, exhausted. She watched Harris the policeman and another man, the senior mechanic, talk about her behind the window of the office opposite.

The senior mechanic hadn't been pleased when Harris had first led her into the garage, through a small door cut into the bigger closed one.

Anja wasn't pleased to be there either. Harris had told her they were walking to a nearby police station, not a dirty, run-down, backstreet garage under a railway arch.

"Are you really a German?" The boy finally spoke, and Anja looked up from her tea. "I didn't know they had girls here. I thought it was just soldiers and such."

Anja lowered her face to the mug again without replying.

"Harris was saying you was hiding?" the boy tried again.

Anja looked at the tea, noticing how there appeared to be a tiny rainbow floating in the oil on its surface.

"Do you speak English? He said you was above an empty shop with a gun. Where did you get that from?"

"Hey!" Anja and the boy looked up at the mechanic, who had stuck his head out of the office. "Don't you bleedin' talk to her, just watch her and keep your trap shut."

The door slammed as the mechanic ducked back into the office. Anja looked at the boy, who stared back. She saw that behind the oily cheeks he was blushing.

"He's not the boss of me. I can do what I want," the boy said quietly, head tilted forward but looking at Anja from under his fringe.

"How old are you?" Anja asked in her excellent English.

"Fifteen." The boy eased back against the bench he was leaning on and folded his arms, trying to look the man he nearly was.

Anja smiled behind the mug, her mouth hidden but her eyes giving it away.

"What is your name?"

"Jack."

"I thought you were younger."

Jack flicked his hair again, picked up a wrench, and scratched himself behind the ear with it.

"We're not supposed to be talking," he finally said, flushing brighter with irritation.

The mechanic banged on the glass, pointed at Anja, and gestured for Jack to bring her to the office. She was out of the chair and on her way before the he made it to her. She opened the door and stepped into the harsh light of the small office as Jack struggled to keep up.

It was warm. A small heater sat in the corner popping and bubbling and making the room smell even oilier.

"Sit." The mechanic pointed to a leather revolving chair similar to the one she had sat on outside. Anja did as she was told, putting the mug down on the worn wooden desk.

She looked up at the mechanic expectantly.

He was wearing blue overalls that opened at the neck to show a gray collarless shirt underneath. His throat looked wrinkled, red, angry, and sore. His face seemed to be potted with a million tiny pits of oil; he looked old and tired, but Anja guessed him to be the same age as her father.

He took a rag out of his pocket, wiped his hands with it, and sat down on the edge of the desk, looking down at her as he seemed to search for words.

Anja beat him to it by turning to Harris, who was standing in the corner of the office, drinking tea from a mug that was even dirtier than hers.

"You said you were taking me to a police station."

"All in good time," Harris replied.

"I want to go now."

"In a minute," Harris said again.

She turned to the mechanic.

"Are you in charge here?"

"Yes."

"My father will pay you if you take me to him now. He will be very worried about me."

"I bet he is."

"You will be rewarded for your trouble, I promise."

"Who is your father?" the mechanic asked.

Anja shifted in her seat.

"Who he is doesn't matter. Take me to the German sector and I will be sure to have you rewarded."

"Who is your father?"

Anja ignored the question and looked at Harris.

"You have a duty to protect me. You are a police officer and you have a duty."

"I have no duty to you," said Harris, the smile gone.

Anja looked at the boy, then back at the mechanic.

"I want to go home." Her voice sounded weaker than she had expected, and she folded her hands in her lap and lowered her eyes.

The mechanic sighed deeply and ran the rag around the back of his neck before stuffing it into his pocket and looking at Harris.

"What time you off duty?"

"Eight. I've been on nights."

The mechanic looked at the clock on the wall; it was twenty to eight.

"You'd better go, come back later. I'll have to have a think about what we should do."

"It's obvious, isn't it?"

"She's only a child."

"Yeah, but"—Harris lifted a finger and almost pointed at Anja before dropping it again—"she's a German."

"I'll have to have a think."

"If the boss finds out we had her and we didn't let him know—"

"Harris, go away and then come back, like I told you."

"I'm only saying."

"Go."

Harris swigged back his tea and picked up his helmet from beside the heater. He stepped past Anja and opened the door, pushing the boy into the gap between it and the wall as he did so. He turned back to the mechanic before leaving.

"Don't do anything without me, all right?"

"Give me her identity papers."

Harris frowned, then took out the papers and handed them across to the mechanic, who tossed them onto the desk.

"I mean it—wait for me, yeah?" Harris tried again.

The mechanic nodded and Harris looked at Anja, and then closed the door behind him. Anja watched him through the window as he went, putting on his helmet and exiting the garage.

"Go lock the door," the mechanic said to Jack.

"Mr. Adams is coming for the Alvis at eight. We've been working on it all night. What was the point of that now? He'll think we've gone home."

"Go lock the door," the mechanic replied.

Jack sulked out of the office, giving Anja the same look through the window as she gave him.

The mechanic closed the door, then pulled a small wooden milking stool out from under the desk. He sat and leaned forward, elbows on his knees. He stared at Anja and then took out the rag again, holding it in both hands, as if waging a tiny tug of war between them.

"You are in a lot of trouble, girl; I'll be honest with you. You are in a lot of trouble. Do you understand?"

Anja nodded.

"I'm under a lot of pressure here. You've put me in a dangerous place. I need you to be honest with me, yes?"

"Yes."

"Harris told me you were in a house with a machine gun, is that right?"

Anja nodded.

"How did you get there?"

Anja didn't reply. She looked down at the floor and then back at the mechanic.

"What is your name?" she asked him.

"I don't matter to you. You've got bigger problems than me to worry about if you don't answer me. Unless you are quick and honest, you'll not be staying here for long, you'll be moving on somewhere you don't want to go. So, how did you get there?"

Anja looked at the floor again.

"Listen to me, child. I don't wage war on kids. I don't want to hurt you, but you need to speak to me so I can decide what to do."

Anja looked up at the mechanic; she watched the rag turn again in his hands and felt a wave building inside, pressure forming so hard her forehead suddenly seemed tight.

"They killed my mother," she whispered.

"Who?"

"The men who took us, they killed her and then shoved her in the boot of the car." A tear leaked from her left eye and ran down her cheek; she let it fall, not feeling it through her pain.

"Who were they?"

"Americans."

"How do you know they were Americans?" The mechanic sat back.

"I used to watch films, with my nanny, back in Berlin, American films." There was another tear.

"Why did they . . . why did they do what they did?"

"They want my daddy; they were using me, using us, to make him—"

"Make him?"

"Do something important."

The mechanic stared at her. A second or two passed between them and Anja sniffed, then wiped her cheek.

"Who is your father?"

"He is a major in the SS. His name is Ernst."

"Koehler?" The mechanic looked at her papers and then back at her.

Anja nodded and another tear trickled free, then fell to the floor silently.

"What did they want him to do?"

"He was fetching someone important, I don't know who, from Cambridge. I heard them talking but that is all they said."

"Where are the Americans who took you?"

"I don't know. I snatched a gun and they ran away."

"From you?"

Anja shrugged.

"I had a gun, although—"

"Although?"

"There was shooting before, outside. That's why they left the gun."

"Harris told me there was a dead man outside the flat. Was that one of them?"

"No, sir. I don't know who that was."

The mechanic looked at the floor and rubbed the back of his neck again, this time with his bare hand. Anja watched him and wondered if he ever managed to get all the oil off his skin or if it was there all the time, like a scar.

He looked at her again.

"You don't know who your dad is getting or why the Americans want them?"

"No."

The heater popped in the corner.

"My father will reward you," she tried again, but the mechanic just sighed by way of reply.

"The front gate is locked," Jack said as the office door clicked shut behind him.

The mechanic nodded slowly, barely lifting his head. He finally stood up, then picked up a battered blue hardback notebook off the desk.

He opened the cover and flipped through a few pages before lifting the heavy receiver of the phone that was sitting on a shelf next to the window, all the while looking at Anja. He dialed a number out of the book.

He stopped dialing and went back to looking at Anja, who, in turn, stared blankly back.

"What you doing?" Jack asked.

The mechanic ignored him.

Anja heard the click and the voice at the other end of the line, faint and female.

"Hello?"

"It's the garage. I need to speak to Sir James, about the service for the car."

"Hold on, please."

The mechanic looked at Anja. She thought he was sad, but it was hard to tell.

Anja heard a male voice from the phone, louder but still a long way away. "Hello?"

"Hello, sir, I need to discuss your car, that service we do for you, the special one, it is very important."

"How important?"

"Very, very important, sir. Something has come up that you really need to know about."

There was a pause, then the voice on the phone again.

"Can you call me back on the other number?"

"Yes, sir."

"Five minutes, exactly."

"Five minutes, sir." The mechanic put the phone down and Anja looked at him.

"Who was that?"

"The man who will know what to do." The mechanic searched in his pocket for loose change and pulled out a few coins. He looked at Jack. "I'm going to ring him from across the road. You watch her. Don't let her out of this office, do you hear me?"

Jack nodded and the mechanic took a heavy coat from a hook on the far wall. He nodded at Anja and then opened the door as Jack moved out of the way.

"Is he going to take her?" Jack asked quietly.

"That's not your problem."

Jack lowered his head and the mechanic stared at him a moment before nodding to Anja and leaving the office.

Anja waited until the mechanic had walked past the window before finally speaking to Jack.

"Who is 'he'?"

Jack raised his head.

"You don't want to know."

THE SUN WAS well hidden behind clouds when the mechanic exited the building onto the street outside. The garage was half buried under railway arches just off a main road, so he had to walk for two minutes until he made it to the public telephone box on the corner of Christian Street.

In another call box, five miles away, there was barely half a ring before the receiver was picked up.

"Hello?"

Pips sounded, then the mechanic pressed the connect button.

"Hello?"

"Chestnut," said the voice on the other end, and waited for the correct response.

"Crimson," the mechanic replied, slightly embarrassed to be using code words and playing spies.

"What do you want?"

"H, from Whitechapel, do you know who I mean?"

"Yes."

"He brought a girl to my place this morning."

"Lucky him."

"She is a German girl. Just a kid, SS officer's daughter. I think you need to speak to her, sir."

"Name?"

"Is it all right to say on the phone?"

"What is her name, man?"

"Koehler, Anja Koehler."

"Is it, by God?"

"She has a very interesting story. She says two Americans kidnapped her and her mother to blackmail her father."

"Americans?"

"That's what she says."

"Any names?"

"Not yet."

"We need a proper interrogation."

"She's a child, sir."

"I'll send a car; keep her warm for me."

"She's only a child, sir. Will you—"

The phone in his hand went dead and the mechanic lowered the receiver slowly onto its cradle. He paused, looking out of the window at the passing scene; he felt insulated in the phone box and allowed himself a moment before exiting.

Back into the real world.

CHAPTER 19

THE INTERVIEW ROOM was cold. They'd taken Koehler's coat, his suit jacket, his tie, his shoes, his watch, and his belt. He was sitting on a wooden chair that was slightly too small for him, at a table in the center of the bare white room, deep in the darkest bowels of Scotland Yard.

He stared at the empty seat opposite, rocking forward an inch or two as he considered swapping it for the one he was sitting on. He knew they would put him, as the suspect, in a smaller chair; it was a clumsy old trick he'd used himself a million times. They'd want to dominate the suspect, crowd him, make him feel small as they battered him with questions and God knows what else.

He looked at the white walls. It didn't look like fresh paint, which was a good sign. It meant that no blood had been splashed around recently.

He wondered when being beaten up in a cell had become a concern for him.

Koehler stood up, walked to the door, and reached for the handle; he was surprised at his embarrassment as he turned it slowly. It was locked. He frowned and paced back to the table, taking the interrogator's seat.

Fuck them.

It was another ten minutes before he heard the door unlocking behind him. He turned, looking over his shoulder to see who was coming in. A young British policeman looked into the room, holding a bunch of keys on a chain; he stared at Koehler, who stared back.

A second passed, and the bobby stepped back and nodded his head to someone just out of sight. Koehler turned back, sick of the games.

He heard footsteps, then a slim folder of papers dropped onto the table in front of him.

Koehler looked up.

"You're in my seat," said Neumann.

"It didn't have your name on it."

"Could you move, please?"

"There is a seat there in front of you." Koehler gestured with his head.

"Could you move?"

Koehler pursed his lips and looked at the seat opposite, studying it, then looked back up at Neumann.

"No."

Neumann frowned, sighed, then shuffled around the table and sat down. He reached across, dragged the paper folder over, and opened it. As he scanned the first page, he absentmindedly reached up to the back of his head with his left hand and gingerly touched it.

"How's the head?" Koehler asked.

"What?"

"How's the head? You took a nasty knock earlier at my apartment. How is it?"

Neumann stared at Koehler flatly before finally speaking.

"Two stitches."

Koehler whistled through his teeth.

"Could have been worse."

Neumann leaned back in his chair, studying Koehler, and then shut the folder in front of him, leaving his left hand on the tabletop, the other on his thigh.

"What the hell is going on here?" Neumann asked.

"You tell me," Koehler replied.

"I don't think you're the sort who would kill your wife and child."

"I'm not."

"But they vanished off the face of the earth." Neumann looked at his watch. "Nearly twenty-four hours ago."

"It's a mystery."

"Last year, it was a mystery when your secretary disappeared as well."

"That's women for you."

"And then there is the robbery where we found your wife's identity card."

"You think she did it?"

"I'll not dignify that with an answer."

"Your job to do the questions."

Neumann drummed the fingers of his left hand on the desk and tacked in the wind, trying again to make some headway.

"Then there is your friend the policeman."

"I thought you were the policeman?"

"The policeman who hit me over the head."

"I'd never seen him before."

"Rossett."

"It wasn't Rossett."

"Don't strain my patience, Major Koehler."

"Why not? You're straining mine."

"You're in a lot of trouble."

"I've been in worse."

"But this time Lotte and Anja are involved."

They stared at each other; Koehler made to speak and changed his mind. Neumann stroked his mustache with his right hand, then rested his hand back on his leg before continuing, his tone softer this time.

"Major, I don't know what the hell is happening here. Honestly, I am at a loss. One thing I do know"—he tapped his hand on the folder—"is that this will not stay my problem for long unless you help me. It is still early. In an hour or two people will be arriving at offices—bosses, our bosses, yours and mine. They will hear that I had to issue an order for your arrest, they will want to know why, and they won't want this problem to remain . . . unresolved. You understand that?"

"I do."

"Then you will also understand that these things can have a habit of spiraling out of control, like forest fires that start from just a tiny spark. Issues like this can sweep all before them."

"I am aware of that."

"Then why won't you speak to me? Maybe we can put out this fire before it burns all of us too badly."

Koehler didn't reply.

Neumann breathed out loudly and then shuffled his chair closer. He linked his hands on the tabletop and lowered his head for a moment. Koehler saw the stitches through his thinning hair.

Neumann looked up and Koehler smiled.

"I'm a policeman—" said Neumann.

"I was aware," Koehler interrupted.

"Let me continue."

"Of course. Forgive me."

"I'm a policeman." He waited a second for Koehler to interrupt again, then continued. "I've been in London for a year now. They brought me over from Berlin to deal with what my superiors call 'domestic matters.' By that they mean issues they want kept in the family—our family, the German family. Do you understand?"

"Yes."

"Good. When something happens involving our family, the Met Police ring me, and I drag March along and we see if we can sweep things up. I'm a problem solver. I make problems go away. Normally this takes a couple of hours. I'll be honest with you: it isn't very stimulating work. I normally deal with drunken soldiers and civil servants, and the occasional visiting businessman who has slapped around a whore. Sometimes I pass the matter back to the British, sometimes the army, the navy, or even, on occasion, the air force. Sometimes I deal with the matter myself. I have the tacit approval to hold people for a few days in the cells here, as a punishment." Neumann pointed at the floor, indicating where the cells were beneath them.

"Judge and jury."

"Indeed, it's a little unorthodox, but I've never had anyone complain. You see, they prefer me dealing with matters because I'm a little less ... direct than others. But you'd know all about that, wouldn't you?"

"Would I?"

"I'd assume so; you do work closely with the Gestapo, don't you?"

Koehler didn't reply.

"What I am trying to say, Major, is that there is a window here, and it's closing very quickly. You might think you are sitting opposite a dumb flatfoot from Berlin, and"—Neumann shrugged—"you might be right. But I'm the best chance you have to resolve this issue and come out of it in one piece."

"What about the person who gave you those stitches?"

"Accidents happen. You were under a great deal of pressure in a stressful situation. You were concerned for the well-being of your family. I can understand that. I've been a policeman for a long time. I've bumped my head before; this won't be the last time it happens."

"I need to get out of here."

"You need to talk to me."

"I need to get out. You have to promise you will let me out."

Neumann looked at the table and then back at Koehler. "I will not make promises I can't keep."

Koehler wiped his hand across his eyes, then rubbed with his finger and thumb so hard that when he looked at Neumann again he had to blink two or three times to be able to see him.

"Do you want my wife and child to live?" Koehler said quietly.

Neumann lifted his chin. "Of course."

"Then you have to let me go."

"It isn't that simple."

"No, really, it is." Koehler stared at Neumann, the certainty of his statement causing the policeman to open and close his mouth without speaking.

There was a knock at the door, and it opened before either Koehler or Neumann had a chance to react. March leaned halfway into the interview room, looking at Koehler and then at Neumann.

"Sir, I need to have a word," he said to Neumann.

"Not now."

"It's urgent."

"Later."

"They've found a body."

Koehler and Neumann looked at him and said in unison, "Where?"

March tilted his head toward Koehler and then looked at his boss, who gestured that he should continue.

"On the riverbank. Someone looking for scrap metal found it . . . her . . . an hour ago." March swallowed and looked at Koehler. "It matches the description of your wife."

Koehler felt the earth drop through him.

"Identification?" said Neumann.

"Nothing on her."

"Do we know how she died?"

"Nothing confirmed yet, but . . . the suggestion is she has been shot or stabbed." March looked at Koehler and despite himself said, "I'm sorry."

Koehler raised his hands to his face and rested his elbows on the table, leaning into his palms, pushing his face hard, hiding behind the pain.

"Where is the . . . deceased now?" he heard Neumann say.

"Still at the scene, sir. They are waiting for the doctor and Met detectives to finish up."

"Get the major's belongings and bring them. We're going down there."

THERE IS A stubborn silence at the scene of a death. As Koehler, Neumann, and March ducked their heads under the hole in the fence, Koehler noticed that silence, settling like the snow, all around them.

Nobody had spoken in the car. Neumann had sat in the back with Koehler, and when they'd arrived Koehler had realized that the handle on his door didn't work. He'd sat and watched March walk around the car, waiting as the big policeman had opened the door, and then stepped out.

"Should I cuff him?"

"No," Neumann had replied, and Koehler had looked across and nodded thanks.

The snow made the ground look even, but the frozen mud it concealed was anything but. All three picked their steps carefully as they made their way down to the mucky brown riverbank ahead of them. The sun was up but hidden behind the clouds when they first caught sight of the group of men at the water's edge.

Koehler slowed, putting off the moment, clinging on to hope as long as was possible. The group around the body turned to face them, as a fresh scattering of snow blew in off the river.

The tide was coming in; the Thames looked to be flowing left to right, a brown carpet, lapping at the toes of the one naked foot that emerged from under a canvas sheet on the shore. Koehler realized that they'd been expected. Nobody challenged them, and everybody was staring at him.

He looked at the sheet, trying to avoid the foot, glacier white against the dirty sand and the Thames.

Lotte's foot.

A plainclothes English detective crouched down next to the canvas, taking hold of the corner with finger and thumb, looking up at Koehler, waiting for the nod.

It came.

The sheet folded back eighteen inches, and Lotte stared into the sky, lips parted, tips of teeth showing, hair wet, yellow strands across her cheeks, lifeless.

As Koehler looked at his love, a snowflake brushed her face and then settled on her lips, unnaturally staying in place, not melting. She was cold.

Koehler crouched, reached with a fingertip, and touched the flake. It melted, and the water trickled across her lip. He gently wiped it away, then ran his finger across her cheek, moving her hair.

For the first time since they had met, her eyes didn't smile at his touch.

He lifted his head. A few of the policemen were looking out across the Thames, letting him have his moment. He blinked a flake of snow from his eyelashes and looked down again to Lotte, just as the policeman covered her face once more with the sheet.

"Major?"

"It's my wife."

The English detective nodded to one of the uniformed bobbies. "Victim identified by husband."

The policeman looked at his watch and wrote something in his notebook.

Victim, thought Koehler.

Koehler stood up, nodded to Neumann, then walked a few paces away from the group along the riverbank. He stared to the south bank of the Thames, with its cranes and its steaming ships getting ready to run, move on to the next place. A seagull swooped low across the water, fifty feet away, its wingtips tapping on the Thames, leaving two tiny wakes.

The old river didn't notice; it kept moving, in and out, time and tide; nothing else mattered, changing of the seasons, here long after all of them.

"I'm sorry," Koehler said softly.

Neumann came up behind him and stood to his left.

A horn sounded as the snow increased, casting a shroud across the far bank and making it harder to see.

"They've had men and dogs up and down the bank in both directions."

"Anja?" Koehler didn't look at Neumann as he spoke.

"No sign of her."

"The river?"

"They've boats looking, but the man who found your wife said there were a lot of tracks in the snow when he arrived, all covered now, I'm afraid, but he thought it was a few people. Maybe . . . maybe she was here?"

Koehler nodded, then lowered his head, looking at the water lapping at his feet.

"This doesn't look like resistance," said Neumann. "They prefer more of a . . . statement."

"It isn't resistance."

"Who is it, then? Help me."

Koehler lifted his head to look toward the south bank; he licked his lips and gave a slight shake of the head.

"Do you have family, Neumann?" Koehler finally spoke as a gust of wind caused him to rock slightly.

"I do."

"What would you do for them?" Koehler turned to face Neumann as he asked the question.

Over Koehler's shoulder, Neumann saw March watching from where he was standing next to the body, maybe thirty feet away.

"I'd do anything for them."

"Would you kill?"

"If I had to."

"Would you betray your country?"

Neumann paused. "Why are you asking?"

"Answer the question."

"If I had to." The words barely carried on the wind.

Koehler turned back to the river before continuing. "You said before I had a window of time."

"I did."

"I think my daughter is still alive. I need that window to save her."

"The window was to save you."

"I don't care about myself."

"Same as you don't care about your country?"

"I care about my daughter."

"And in saving her you are going to damage Germany?"

Koehler nodded.

"If I have to."

Neumann stared at him and then turned to follow his gaze across the river.

"What have you gotten yourself into, Major?"

"Hell."

CHAPTER 20

FRANK KING HAD chosen a house almost directly opposite the one where he had seen Eric being taken. He'd been pushed for time, only allowing himself one pass in the car before parking around the corner and walking down to the place he'd picked out.

He'd chosen it for several reasons, but mostly because he had seen a little old lady struggling to pick up a milk bottle from the front step as he approached.

One old lady.

One milk bottle.

No big family, at best an old man to take care of as well.

Perfect.

He'd strolled, collar up, head down, to the house and cheerily tapped on the door. When it opened he'd been fast. One hand had covered her mouth and the other had gripped her throat as he walked her backward into the living room. He'd asked her if anyone else was at home; she had shaken her head with scared eyes that had already begun to brim with tears.

She'd fooled him.

"If you are quiet, you are quite safe. Please, go sit down," he had whispered. She had taken a step backward and then punched him squarely in the mouth.

She wouldn't fool him again.

King ran his tongue across the split just inside his lip, then looked at the tough old lady sitting on the floor.

"Are you all right?"

She grunted something through the gag that sounded rude and angry.

"If you behave, you can sit on the chair."

Frank got the same reply, so he shrugged and went back to looking out of the window and stirring the cup of tea he had made himself.

Before he had chosen the old woman's home he'd checked the back alleys that crisscrossed behind the houses opposite. He had counted off the tiny brown brick buildings and sneaked a look through the half-broken back gate that led to the tiny yard. He'd seen that the windows and back door were boarded up, meaning that only the front door was available as a means of rapid entry. King needed to figure out how many people were in the house, which was why he was sitting at the window of the old lady's house.

If the situation didn't change and his information didn't improve . . . well, he didn't want to consider that. He would watch for a few hours at least. He guessed Koehler would be heading to Cambridge by now, but he knew the journey would be a tough one in this weather.

There was no panic, everything was in hand, he could give Cook a few hours of his time. He owed Eric that much, at least. Plus, King had a feeling Dulles wouldn't be happy if a dead embassy worker turned up on the news.

No, he would try his best to save the boy, for everyone concerned.

King looked at his watch, sipped his tea, and waited.

He didn't move for two hours. The quarter inch of tea at the bottom of his cup was long cold when the van came back.

King watched as the driver of the van got out of the cab, casually looked around, and then crossed the pavement to the already opening front door, where he went straight inside.

"Here we go," King said softly, and the old lady on the floor, who was by now lying on her side, grunted in agreement.

THE VAN DRIVER stood in front of Ma Price in the back room of the house, the snow on his feet barely melting in the chill.

"Sterling says the kid claims she was held by two Yanks. They were trying to make her dad do something."

"So this one upstairs is telling the truth?" Ma Price had to peer up at the driver, who was holding his cap in front of his chest.

"Looks like it."

Ma Price turned and stared at the empty fireplace as everyone else in the room remained silent, waiting for her decision, watching her back as she paced a few steps.

Not many men interrupted Ma Price when she was thinking. Not many men interrupted Ma Price ever. She was a woman to be reckoned with, respected, listened to, and most definitely not interrupted. She had once run a crime family that covered most of the East End of London, but then along came a war that had taken half of her boys away.

And then along came the occupation, which took nearly the other half.

Hitler had interrupted Ma Price, and she hadn't liked it.

She had never made a concrete decision to join the resistance; she couldn't put her finger on when it had happened. If pushed, she would guess, it would have been around the time she bought a job lot of stolen dynamite from a quarry in Cornwall. One thing had led to another, and then it had suddenly seemed obvious to her to blow up a railway line to stop a goods train.

At first she'd wanted to steal what was on board.

When the bomb went off, it turned out the cargo was humans in the wagons, humans who had hugged her and held her hand in thanks, calling her a hero as they had stumbled out into the night. Ma Price became a freedom fighter, whether she meant to or not.

She hadn't totally given up crime, of course; a woman had to make a living. She'd made some money and opened up channels with people who "knew people." The resistance liked doing business with her, and she liked doing business with them. They paid well and didn't mess her around. When they gave her a wireless and a code book, it had seemed a natural extension of their dealings together.

Over time, crime had increasingly given way to resistance warfare, and she had found the two lives weren't that far apart in their nature. They were both about power, power built on money and violence. Price had often thought that politicians were just criminals who knew what fork to use in a restaurant, and being a freedom fighter had only deepened that conviction.

She wasn't happy, though, because she had realized one important thing: her time was running out.

Back when she was a kid with no shoes except on Sunday, she had known she was different. Her life had been no more or no less miserable than everyone else's had, in the shithole tenement she lived in. She used the same outside toilet, wore the same rags, slept with the same bedbugs, coughed the same rattling cough, with the same damp half-dead lungs everyone else had.

But she was different.

People in that tenement dreamed of a better life, but Ma Price was the only one with the balls to go and get it.

She had nothing to lose. She didn't care if she died trying because if she failed, she didn't want to carry on living.

So she started grifting and grafting, ducking and diving, buying and selling, and then lifting and loaning. She got some cash, a little; she fought men; she fought women; and she was their worst enemy because she didn't care.

They had it all to lose.

She had nothing.

She earned her place; she earned respect, and she got it wherever she went.

Ma Price wasn't scared of anything and anyone then, but that was then and this was now. Ma Price was clever enough to know things never lasted forever. She'd seen people come and go over the years, some dead, some in prison, some just wiped off the face of the earth.

She'd watched the changes carefully, seen how they came and went, learned from them, and second-guessed them. She'd done that because she was different, because she had always been different.

And now, after all this time, Ma Price knew the clock was ticking down for her. All good things must come to an end, and she knew they were coming to an end sooner rather than later. She knew because she was tired; she knew because she was scared for the first time in her life, and she knew she couldn't afford to be scared.

Not now she had something to lose.

Back in the day, if the law caught you up, you'd go to prison, do your "bird," ride the ride and come out the other side. You'd maybe have a bit of money salted away, you'd maybe start again or maybe take a backseat, let someone else come up, take your place so you could walk away.

Those were the rules. Prison didn't scare her.

Rivals didn't scare her. They knew better than to attract her attention, let alone cause her concern.

The one thing that scared her, the one thing that made her think twice, the one thing that caused her to furrow her brow and bury her head?

The Nazis, because just like her, the Nazis didn't care about anything.

They didn't have rules, they didn't play by the book, they didn't worry about consequences, they had nobody to answer to and nobody to worry about.

And that scared Ma Price, because an enemy with a million men and nothing to lose can't be beaten.

Ma Price had started thinking about a future, something else, and that was when she realized all her hard work had given her something to lose, which meant it was time to get out.

Deep down, deep, deep down, when she dared to dream, Ma Price wondered if there might be a way out of England. A passage to somewhere where she could spend some of her money and finally relax, kick off her boots, stare at the sunset, breathe out.

Live.

One day, but not yet, because now, right at that minute, she was stuck in London, in a dreary house with a confused American who was presenting her with a situation she needed to figure out.

"We could just let him go." The old man in the black suit bobbed his head as he spoke, as if expecting a slap around the ear.

Somewhere nearby a train whistled and the sound of clattering tracks carried across the snow-covered rooftops. It died away as the train traveled on, leaving the room seemingly quieter than before.

Ma Price stared at the empty hearth, not moving, chin in her hand, deep in thought, until she finally looked up at the van driver.

"What else did Sterling say?"

"He says he wants us to give him the Yank upstairs."

She frowned and returned to staring at the hearth. She was worried.

She could walk away, hand over the Yank, wash her hands, and leave Sterling and the Germans to their games.

She could, but she wouldn't, because if she did, she would look weak. She wasn't worried about the boys in the room seeing that weakness; she was worried about the boys outside the room, around London, in pubs, warehouses, taxis, and cafés seeing that weakness.

It didn't do to look weak, not in her line of work.

"He's our Yank." Ma Price scratched her head. "If Sterling wants him, he can either pay for him or try to take him. Sterling has the girl, she fell into his lap. But he only knows half the story." Ma Price pointed at the ceiling. "We've got the important bit upstairs. The girl doesn't know what is going on; all she knows is she was snatched. She is the riddle, but upstairs we've got the answer. Him upstairs knows what her old dad had to do to get her back, upstairs knows what was so important, and upstairs knows what was going to happen next. Upstairs is the key to all this, we just need to figure it out. Once we get to the bottom, we'll know how much that information is worth, and I'll wager what upstairs knows is worth a hell of a lot."

"So what do we do?"

Ma Price lowered her hand and pushed past the driver.

"We go and ask him."

ERIC WAS STILL lying on the floor facing the wall when they entered; Mustache was sitting on the same chair he had taken hours earlier. He rose and gave the seat to Ma Price, then joined his colleague by the door.

"Prof?" Ma Price nodded to the old man who crossed the room and knelt down next to Eric and rested his hand on his shoulder.

"You need to roll over and speak to us now," he whispered.

Eric turned his head and looked up. His cheeks were wet with tears and he sniffed loudly before slowly rolling over and looking at Ma Price, who smiled at him.

"He started crying ten minutes ago," said Mustache.

"I hope you ain't hit him?" Ma Price replied and Mustache shook his head.

"He just started crying."

"You all right, my lovely?" Ma Price said to Eric.

Eric nodded and wiped his nose again, pushing himself up onto his elbow as he did so.

"Why are you crying?"

"I don't want to die."

"Oh, dear." Ma Price tilted her head and looked at the others in the room. She turned back to Eric and smiled sadly. "What you told us about the girl was true. We checked."

Eric nodded.

"People we know have the girl now. Seems like she scared you and your chum off, didn't she?"

Eric's elbow was hurting on the floorboards, so he moved again, pushing himself up so that his knees were tucked under his chin and wrapped by his arms. He looked at the two men leaning against the wall, who both stared back at him impassively.

"Now then, you need to tell us what you wanted her old dad to do," Ma Price continued.

"He is going to get someone from Cambridge, a scientist, and give her to us."

"What kind of scientist?"

Eric looked at Ma Price and swallowed hard.

"I don't know."

"Where in Cambridge?"

"I don't know, I wasn't told. I just know that Koehler, the girl's father, is going to get someone and then get further instructions on where to take them. When we got word that he had, we were to take his daughter and go to that address ourselves."

"What's the address?"

Eric looked at Ma Price and then the men by the wall. He knew he had to hold something back. He knew once he gave away what they wanted, he ceased to have a reason to exist. He had heard the horror stories whispered around the embassy, tales of careless or unlucky German soldiers captured by the resistance, then left hanging by piano wire from lampposts.

He'd heard about the guts ripped from stomachs, about the burning tires jammed around necks.

He wasn't a German, but he also wasn't English. These people were animals, and he didn't want savaging. These people knew about the American government's growing fraternity with the Nazis. Eric was aware that this had caused anger with the British both at home and abroad. Eric had seen KEN-NEDY IS A KRAUT LOVER daubed in white paint on one of the embassy cars, not long after the ambassador had given a long interview to the *Daily Mail* about his admiration for Nazism.

The Americans were becoming enemies, which meant Eric Cook wasn't among friends.

He buried the information they wanted down deep inside, away from them and their questions, behind the last vestige of bravado he could muster, behind his watery eyes.

He stuck out his chin.

"You release me, take me to somewhere where I am safe, and I'll tell you."

Ma Price raised an eyebrow, gave him a motherly smile, rose from the chair, and crossed the room. She rested her hand on the Prof's shoulder and lowered herself down until her face was inches from Eric's, so close he could smell a faint whiff of carbolic soap.

"You aren't getting released, my lover. I'm sorry, but you're not leaving here alive. I wish I could tell you different, but I haven't got time, so I'm not going to lie to you. Now, the only choice you've got left is the choice to make this easy or hard. So save yourself some bother and tell me the address before I have to ask you again."

Ma Price moved back a few inches and smiled at Eric.

Eric started to cry.

CHAPTER 21

THE SNOW WAS coming down hard and fast by the time Rossett made it to the café. The morning had passed at a snail's pace since he and Koehler had parted. He'd taken a taxi back to his lodgings, paying the driver to wait while he had skirted the property on foot, checking for any sign that his house was under surveillance. Ideally Rossett would have stayed clear, but he had little money and no transport, both of which were waiting for him at home.

Once inside, he had made a call to Wapping Police Station and tentatively inquired whether anyone was looking for him. The desk sergeant there had sounded bored, tired, and uninterested in Rossett. This meant that so far, he wasn't a wanted man after the previous night's incident involving Neumann and March.

Maybe Koehler had been right? Maybe they weren't interested in him?

Rossett had taken the precaution of setting up a mutually agreed rendezvous, where they could leave messages in the unlikely event that they had been split up.

That unlikely event had arisen, and in the minutes before he was due to set off to Cambridge after eating and changing into warmer clothes, he had telephoned the café. They were used to him checking in through the day; he'd used the café for years as a meeting place and message point, in an attempt to stay out of the pubs and clubs where police work was so often done. In truth he hadn't expected to hear from Koehler. In fact, he wondered if he would ever hear from him again, so when the waitress told him there was a message, he wondered if it was a trap.

"Meet Ernst at one P.M."

"That's what it says?"

"Yes, Mr. Rossett."

"Who took the message?"

"Ethel, sir."

"Is she there now?"

"Gone home, sir."

Rossett had placed the phone down and stared at the wallpaper in the hallway.

If it was a trap, why not stake out his lodgings and arrest him there?

He looked at the frosted stained-glass front door and half expected a team of storm troopers to come kicking their way into the hallway.

They didn't.

Maybe Koehler had been released?

Maybe the joint mission was back on?

He'd picked up the phone again and rung around a few police stations, checking overnight logs. He spoke to the few detectives and sergeants who would still speak to him, checking for anything out of the ordinary.

He came up blank.

He'd had a few hours before the scheduled meeting at the café, so he had driven around the dark side of the city, rolling a few old underworld informants out of bed in search of information about Lotte and Anja, but again, nothing had come to light.

All of which led him to believe Koehler was right: the kidnappers weren't locals. This was something that went beyond the usual villains and resistance operators.

He was in uncharted waters, alone and surrounded by sharks.

And he loved it.

HE'D WALKED AROUND the block four times before deciding to enter the café himself. Everything seemed normal, so he bit the bullet and went inside to get out of the cold.

The waitress spilled his tea when she put it on the table in front of him; he wiped the spill with a napkin and checked his watch: quarter past one. Koehler was late.

Nothing new there.

Rossett glanced out the window at the growling blizzard outside. He could barely see the other side of the street, it was coming down so thick and fast. A taxi driver was scraping some snow off the roof of his cab next to the window, head buried in his shoulders, sweeping armfuls into piles next to the cab. Rossett wrapped his hands around his hot tea in sympathy.

Maybe Koehler hadn't made it through the snow? He took out his cigarettes, put one in his mouth, and started to pat his pockets for matches.

"Do you mind not lighting that?"

Rossett looked up.

Neumann looked down.

Rossett stopped patting his pockets and took the cigarette out of his mouth. Holding it in his left hand, he tilted his head, checking to see if March was loitering around.

Neumann read Rossett's mind. "He's waiting in the car. May I sit?"

"I'm waiting for someone."

"I know: me."

Neumann put his hat down on the table, which was still damp from the tea spill. Rossett thought about telling him but didn't bother, and instead went back to patting his pockets looking for his matches, eyes all the while on Neumann's.

Neumann sat down after growing tired of waiting for the invite. Rossett found the matches and put the cigarette back in his mouth. He took out a match and struck it against the side of the box, letting it flare, and waiting for a reaction.

"Please, Inspector, I'd much rather you didn't. I have a chest complaint."

Rossett touched the match to the cigarette, shook out it out, and dropped it in the ashtray.

They sat in silence, Neumann leaning back from the smoke, as the bustle of the café crashed around them. Rossett took another drag and then removed the cigarette from out of his mouth, smoke drifting between them.

"Can I get you anything?" The waitress hovered.

"No, thank you," Neumann replied without looking at her.

Neumann turned to the window, then back to Rossett.

"I'd heard you were an arsehole," he finally said.

Rossett didn't reply, so Neumann continued. "We've all heard of you, even before this case. Everyone knows that you are impossible to work with."

Rossett still didn't reply.

"I have to add, I don't buy all this 'British Lion' bullshit, either. The British were desperate for a hero and you came along. You were lucky."

"You were lucky," Rossett echoed impassively.

"What?" Neumann raised an eyebrow.

"You were lucky I didn't kill you last night."

"You're lucky I don't arrest you right now."

"You're lucky you haven't tried."

The boiler behind the counter started to hiss and Neumann looked across toward it, and then back at Rossett.

"Look," Neumann tried again, shifting in his seat. "Koehler sent me." He lowered his hand from his mouth and placed it flat on the table next to his hat.

"Where is he?"

"Scotland Yard." Neumann lifted his hand, inspected his palm, and then looked at the damp patch on the table.

"Is he in custody?"

"Yes."

"Why?"

"I had him arrested."

"But you're here."

"Indeed." Neumann slid his hat away from the damp spot and then looked at Rossett.

"And you haven't tried to arrest me."

"No."

"So what do you want?"

"To pass on a message."

"What message?"

"Koehler's wife is dead."

"How?"

"Shot. Found by the Thames, east of St. Katharine Docks."

"Koehler didn't do it."

"I know."

"But you've arrested him?"

"After issuing a countrywide warrant I couldn't do much else, could I?"

Rossett didn't reply, the cigarette now at his lips.

"We don't know where his daughter is." Neumann's voice took on a gentler tone.

"Anja?"

"Anja," Neumann repeated.

"Why are you here?"

"I have a daughter." Neumann shrugged and looked at the table. "If she was hurt, or in danger, I'd do anything to help her. I think Koehler is a fool, but . . . it is his daughter, so I did as he asked."

Rossett nodded. "Koehler wanted you to come to me."

"To give you a message."

"Go on."

"It's all up to you now."

Rossett stubbed out the cigarette. "That's it?"

Neumann reached into his pocket and then passed an envelope across.

"A travel warrant. You'll need it to get past the checkpoints in London. It'll be reported stolen or missing, but that won't matter for a few days. I can't afford to be tied to this if you fail. Do you do have a car?"

"Yes."

"I can't do much to help you, you understand that?"

"You could release Koehler."

"I can't. It would leave me embarrassed, especially with his wife being found dead. We circulated his name, stating he had assaulted me in the course of an inquiry into her disappearance. He has to be charged, at the very least, with my assault, and he'll probably face some sort of fine and disciplinary action, but he'll live, don't worry."

"So he stays in jail because you're embarrassed?"

"Embarrassment is a dangerous thing. I have to hold him for an acceptable period, then I have to get my superiors to agree to his release."

"Will they?"

Neumann shrugged and Rossett nodded.

"I trust you'll be discreet?" Neumann lowered his voice.

"I will."

"It's time for you to go and be the hero." Neumann leaned back from the table.

Rossett didn't reply.

"Will you do it? Get his daughter?"

"Has he told you what is going on?"

"Enough to know it isn't going to be easy, enough for me to question if you're the man for the job. I still think Koehler is a fool. He has the whole of the German occupying forces to call on and he chooses you."

"He chose right."

The two men stared at each other in silence until Neumann nodded, picked up his hat, and stood.

"Thank you," said Rossett.

Neumann scratched his forehead and took a half step away from the table.

"Don't thank me. You're his last chance."

"Tell Koehler I'll make it, and when I have Anja, I'll deal with them all."

CHAPTER 22

ANJA TRIED TO turn herself to take some of the pressure off her left shoulder, but failed. The weight of the boots resting on her back increased the second she tried to shift, hurting her, pushing her down.

She tried to speak through the rag that had been stuffed in her mouth, and failed all over again. She felt sick, dizzy, scared, and a long way from home.

She blinked, turning her head in the sack in the hope that gravity would help her in her struggle with the gag, but it didn't.

She wanted to scream.

Her arms felt cramped and she couldn't straighten her legs. The urge to scream and twist herself free tortured her as the drone of the engine squeezed her head, filling her ears.

"Is she all right?" she heard the mechanic say in front of her, but nobody answered.

They hit a pothole, and the car made another one of the thousand turns it had seemed to make for the last however long she had been in it.

However long.

It seemed so very long, and Anja felt the panic rising inside again.

She tried to look inward, tried to see the fear and reason with it.

The fear washed close to her, like a wave on the beach she was teasing, just missing her; ebbing away, about to catch her next time.

She took some comfort from Jack and the mechanic being in the car with her. Even if the mechanic had sold her out to the men who had turned up, tied her up, stuffed her head into a bag, and then thrown her on the floor of the car, he was still worrying about her.

"Are you sure she can breathe in that?" Jack had said as the bag had gone on in the garage.

Anja thought about Jack's eyes, the last thing she had seen as the darkness was inflicted on her. He was upset and confused.

He wasn't a bad boy. He cared.

Another pothole slammed her hard; she used the bounce from the blow to turn slightly, easing her shoulder, lessening the pain, lessening the panic.

The feet pushed again.

The gag shifted.

She wanted to cry.

The brakes whined, the car slowed, and she felt herself rolling in the footwell as it lurched to a halt. The engine died. Silence, then the handbrake ratcheted and Anja forgot about the gag, the pain, and the fear.

She'd arrived.

"Get her out," someone said outside the car, and all of a sudden the doors all around her opened as one. She felt the feet pushing down one last time as the person they belonged to got out.

Anja shivered. It was cold, and the draft from the door next to her head seemed to claw its way through the bag.

Someone grabbed her and dragged her. She tried to kick with her legs to push herself free, but whoever was pulling was too quick. Another hand under her arm and then she was pulled from the car and dropped a few inches.

The ground was hard, solid, and flat, and there was no snow. She wondered if she was under a shelter or maybe inside. What little light made its way through the hood gave no clues, so she rolled onto her back, searching under it, looking down toward her feet without bending her neck, desperate for a clue as to where she was.

She didn't need to bother. Someone ripped the hood off her head and Anja closed her eyes against the sudden light. She waited. Nothing happened. She opened her eyes, blinked, and looked up.

She was in a large shed, maybe a warehouse. Above her she could see the wooden roof, about forty feet up, resting on thin steel rafters. The shingles were in poor repair, because she could see shafts of daylight shining through a few gaps in the gloom.

Daylight made her think of freedom, and she twisted her wrists, rolled onto her side, and looked behind her.

Five men, the mechanic and Jack included, stood and stared at her. One of them, a big man, well dressed in a sharp suit, held the sack that had been over her head in a hairy hand that looked like a ham.

She looked at his feet. Black boots with heavy soles, toe caps, and solid heels. Anja had him to thank for the bruises on her back.

"Get her up, please," one of the men said. He was older, his words precise, so clear you could almost hear every letter, as if there were a gap between them.

He was in charge. His kind was always in charge.

The big man walked toward Anja. She felt like a doll as he grabbed her arms and lifted; she seemed to float to her feet. He stepped back, holding one hand out to catch her in case she fell.

She didn't, she just glared at him and then at the man in charge.

"Bring her inside."

The big man took Anja's arm, but she was already following the man in charge. The big man let go and placed his hand in the small of her back. She was surprised at his gentleness and she looked at him.

He smiled sadly. "Do as you're told, there's a good girl," he whispered.

The man in charge led the group through a door with a frosted glass window-pane. It opened onto a dark corridor, with more doors and wood-paneled walls, which seemed to crowd in on Anja as they made their way along it in single file.

For every two doors that led off to the side, there was another partitioning the corridor into self-contained cells that reminded her of carriages on a train. Anja guessed they were in a block of offices that dealt with the paperwork for the warehouse.

But the warehouse was empty, and the offices were silent, and she was alone.

All the side doors were solid wood, while the corridor doors were glass. The big man almost had to turn sideways each time they passed through a glass door, until they eventually stopped, halfway down the corridor at one of the office doors.

The man in charge opened the lock with a bunch of keys, stepped back, and gestured that Anja should enter. She paused, then felt the gentle hand in the small of her back again. She turned to look at the big man, who nodded his head.

Anja went in.

There was a table, four chairs, wooden walls, and a shabby two-seater couch; hanging from the ceiling, a bright lightbulb that made the dust look dustier as it floated round the room.

The solitary decoration was a calendar on the wall that reckoned it was still October 1940.

"Take off the gag and unbind her." The man in charge again.

Anja turned to look at the big man, who gently spun her away from him. She faced the wall, looking at the picture on the calendar; it was a black-and-white picture of a duck in a lake.

Anja felt fat fingers pulling at the gag. The knot caught her hair, but she ignored the pain as the fingers tugged and the gag came loose.

She spat it out, coughing as it dragged along her tongue and fell to the floor. Suddenly her hands were free, and she turned to face the men behind her.

She wasn't afraid anymore. She was angry.

"What do you think you are doing? How dare you treat me like this? I would not have screamed. There was no call for a gag."

Nobody argued with her. Jack looked at the floor and the mechanic nodded, openly agreeing with her.

Anja felt the wind drifting out of her sails. She looked at the big man, who scratched at his nose and then lowered his eyes.

"Sorry, miss," he said before offering her a freshly ironed white handkerchief.

Anja took it, even though she didn't want it, and looked at the man in charge. He smiled, held out his hands apologetically, then gestured that she should sit.

"Tea?" he asked.

"Yes, please," Anja said.

The man in charge smiled, and then looked at the mechanic and Jack.

"There are makings next door, gentlemen, if you would be so kind?"

Anja watched as the mechanic nodded, then backed out of the room.

"Maybe a sandwich as well, boy?" The man in charge smiled at Jack, who took the hint and left the room, closing the door behind him.

"Please, sit." The man in charge removed a thin leather glove and pointed to a chair at the table.

Anja hesitated and then sat. It was better than the floor of the car. The man sat opposite and studied her face for a moment before speaking again.

"I must apologize for your manner of arrival. I was unsure how you would react to my bringing you here. I thank you for your cooperation."

Anja nodded, thinking that she hadn't had much choice when it came to cooperation.

"I'm led to believe you are Ernst Koehler's daughter. Is this correct?"

Anja nodded, then coughed to clear her throat. "Yes, I am."

"My associates tell me you were kidnapped by two men."

"Yes."

"This was to coerce your father into carrying out a task?"

"Coerce?" Anja's English was good, but it wasn't that good.

The man in charge tried again.

"Make your father do a job? He is to kidnap someone?"

Anja shrugged and watched as the man in charge pulled his other glove off, then placed his hand on his leg delicately, almost like a dancer might.

Anja wasn't good with ages, but she guessed him to be about fifty or sixty. He was pale, sickly. His face looked greasy and his eyes looked pink-rimmed and sore—angry eyes that didn't get enough sleep.

He had nice clothes, his shoes shone, and his hands were smooth like those of the men who worked in her father's office.

He looked normal except for his sore, angry eyes.

She needed to take care.

"You told my associate that the men who abducted you and your mother were American, is that correct?"

Anja swallowed and looked at the big man again over her shoulder.

"I've no wish to hurt you, child," the man in charge said softly.

"Then let me go."

"If you answer my questions I shall."

"How do I know you're not a liar?"

"I am a gentleman, my dear; as you grow older you'll learn that you can trust a gentleman to keep his word. Now, if you answer my questions, I'll do all I can to ensure that you get the opportunity to grow older. If you don't . . . you won't."

Anja felt a flutter in her chest and looked at him.

"They were Americans."

"How do you know?"

"Their accents, and they also said they worked at the embassy."

"They gave no indication to you what they wanted of your father?"

"No."

"You're sure?"

"Yes."

"Did they have names?"

"Frank and Eric."

"Frank?"

"Yes."

The man in charge frowned and leaned back slightly.

"How old were they?"

"Not very. One was maybe twenty-five, the other a little older, I think. I'm not very—"

"Frank was older?"

"Yes."

"And they said they were Americans?"

"No."

"No?"

"No. I said they had American accents, like in the movies, and they mentioned an embassy, so I *think* they were."

"But you're sure they were not English?"

"Yes."

"Absolutely sure?"

"They had good teeth."

The man in charge lifted an eyebrow and smiled, keeping his mouth closed as he did so.

"This man, Frank, did he have light-colored hair, like your father?"

"Yes."

"Thank you, Anja." The man in charge smiled again.

"Can I go home now?"

"Not yet, child; hopefully soon, though."

There was a knock at the door, and the man in charge half turned in his seat and nodded to the big man to open it. Harris the policeman stood there, out of uniform, nervously holding a flat cap across his chest. He seemed smaller, less confident.

Anja wondered if it was the lack of uniform or the man in charge who was sapping his confidence.

"I got a message to come see Sir James Sterling?" said Harris, confused, checking out the various men who were dotted around the room and in the corridor.

The man in charge visibly flinched, turned to look at Anja, and then smiled.

"I'm so terribly sorry, my dear, so very sorry." He lightly slapped his gloves against his leg, then turned to Harris. "You really are an arse."

"What?" Harris replied, looking around the room once more, searching for support this time.

Sterling gave a tiny bow toward Anja and then left the room, taking Harris with him. The door clicked shut behind him.

The big man who had removed Anja's gag smiled sadly at her.

"Make yourself comfortable, girl, this could take a while."

Anja twisted the handkerchief in her hand again, then looked back at the duck in the calendar.

She wished she were back in 1940 as well.

STERLING TOOK HIS tea without milk, strong, a decent brew. The kind of tea that put fur in your mouth before it went down, the kind of tea you could taste before you drank it. That was the reason he was frowning into the enamel mug Jack had just placed on his desk with a clunk. The mug was filled with a greasy brew; there were small gray dots of slimy stale milk turning like stars in a miserable brown galaxy.

Sterling gestured to Jack to remove the mug and its murky contents from out of his sight.

"It really is most urgent," Sterling said into the telephone that was pressed against his ear, as he watched Jack retreat with the tea. "Most urgent indeed."

"I'm afraid the ambassador is extremely busy, sir. I can maybe schedule a call for you later in the week?"

"This is a matter of utmost importance. You are aware of who I am?"

"I am, sir, but again, the ambassador is extremely . . ."

Sterling was barely listening to the secretary on the other end of the line, such was his frustration. There had been a time, back when the occupation was new, that the Americans treated senior British civil servants with respect, courtesy, even urgency. But over time the English had slid further down the order of importance, especially in light of the new diplomatic push toward cooperation with the Germans.

Now he was lucky to even get to speak to a secretary.

Sterling knew that the Americans were aware he was the senior royalist resistance commander in London. He and the Americans had worked closely on occasion over the last few years. They had once had respect for him, but now, he knew he was falling out of favor and very much in danger of becoming an embarrassment.

And that was why he had to listen to this ridiculous woman brush him off on the phone. He was walking a tightrope with the Americans. They could drop his name into conversation at any time they wanted, casually toss him to the Nazis.

He was worthless to them. He needed them, but he wanted them to need him.

"Listen to me, woman!" His shouting caused the line to fall silent.

He waited; finally the same flat voice came back. "Yes, Sir James?"

"Get off your arse, go into Kennedy's office, and tell him I have urgent information about Frank King, your military attaché to London."

Silence.

"Do it now."

Another pause.

"Please hold the line, sir."

There was a click, and Sterling took the opportunity to lower his head into his hand, squeezing his temples to ease the ache behind his eyes.

He'd not wanted to mention King on the telephone; he'd wanted to keep as much back as he could, for as long as he could, but the combination of belligerent secretary and a tension headache had caused him to snap.

His cards had fallen onto the table for all to see. He'd have to wait to see how Joseph Kennedy, U.S. Ambassador to Occupied Great Britain and the Court of St. James, decided to play against them.

"Sir James." Kennedy came on the line. "What can I do for you?"

"Is this line secure?"

"All of our lines are secure; I'd suggest the worry lies with you and yours." Kennedy sounded tired, bored almost.

"I've got the girl."

"What girl?"

"The girl Frank King kidnapped."

There was silence on the other end of the phone. A moment passed, and Sterling imagined Kennedy gesturing for an aide to listen in to the conversation.

"Frank King?" Kennedy spoke again, enunciating the words carefully.

"Yes."

"Our Frank King?"

"I wouldn't ring about anyone else called Frank King, would I?"

"No, I imagine you wouldn't."

"Do you want the girl?"

"I would imagine that if she is claiming she has been kidnapped, you'd want to get her to the authorities as soon as possible?"

"I'd much rather help a friend, Mr. Ambassador."

Jack walked back into the little office with a fresh cup of tea; he hovered by the desk, unsure of what to do as Sterling ignored him.

"And we are friends, Sir James?"

"I would hope so."

"Would it be possible that this young lady can stay with you until I can ascertain the circumstances surrounding this situation?"

"You don't know about this?"

Kennedy's pause answered Sterling's question, so he continued.

"She'll be going nowhere for the foreseeable future, Mr. Ambassador. She's aware of who I am and my role here. All that makes her returning home extremely unlikely, I'm afraid."

"Ah, that's unfortunate. Could you call me in . . . let's say two hours?"

"Certainly."

"Thank you."

Sterling lowered the handset and placed it gently back in the cradle. He tapped the fingers of his right hand on the desk absentmindedly as he processed his position in the game. A moment passed, and then he noticed the fresh cup of tea steaming on the far corner of his desk.

No milk, just how he liked it.

CHAPTER 23

YOU'RE GOING TO where?"

"Cambridge."

"Why?"

"To pick up a Jew."

"Why? Did they fall over?"

The German soldier at the checkpoint started laughing at the joke. The comedian, a corporal in the British Home Defense Troops, looked over his shoulder at the German and winked before turning back to Rossett.

Rossett sat stoically in his car, staring straight ahead, one hand half out the window, waiting to be given back his travel papers.

"Who is the Jew?" the corporal asked, unfolding the travel warrant.

"I don't know. I'm to be told when I get there."

The corporal looked at the warrant and then at Rossett's police ID card, comparing the names on the two documents, then lowered his head so that he could look into Rossett's face.

"Hey."

Rossett looked up.

"Look at me. How am I supposed to see your face if you won't look at me?" The corporal took half a pace to the side, resting his hand on the polished leather holster on his belt.

Rossett looked at the holster and then up at the corporal, staring at him with dead eyes, unimpressed with the hand-on-the-holster routine.

"You're a police inspector?"

"Yes."

"In London?"

"Yes."

"You're a long way from home."

Rossett didn't reply.

"I had a bit of trouble with the police in London before the war, down Cable Street. Do you know it?"

Rossett remembered the fascist Black Shirt marches and the riots they had sparked. It all seemed so long ago now.

"I do."

"Were you there?" The corporal tilted his head.

"No."

"All them coppers that day were a bunch of bleedin' communists and Jew lovers. You sure you weren't there?"

Rossett pursed his lips, thought about speaking, then decided the mission was more important. Instead he chose to stare out the windscreen, resting both hands on the steering wheel.

"What do you want with a Jew?" the corporal tried again.

"I don't want anything. I've been told to collect them, so I am collecting them." Rossett turned so he could look into the corporal's eyes.

"In this weather?"

"It appears so."

A gust of wind rocked the little Austin, and a few flakes of snow whistled past. The corporal squinted against the cold, and Rossett saw the German shuffle out of the wind and back into the hut, which sat next to the barrier that was blocking the road to Cambridge.

Rossett returned to looking at the corporal, who was reading the travel warrant carefully, with tiny movements of his lips as he picked his way through the German.

"I'll have to check this is valid," the corporal finally said, half turning away, enjoying his moment of power over the police.

"Why?"

The corporal stopped turning and looked at Rossett. "Because I will, that's why."

Rossett stared back, sighed, and went back to looking out of the windscreen.

He'd known there would be checkpoints on all of the main roads and many of the minor ones. Had the weather been better, Rossett would have skirted them as best he could with back roads and country lanes, but the snow, and the sensation of time ticking away, had forced him onto the main drags and into the arms of bored soldiers.

So far things had gone well.

Up till now.

This checkpoint, less than four miles outside of Cambridge, was the first manned by an Englishman, and the first manned by a pain in the arse.

Rossett wasn't certain if that was a coincidence, but he was certain he didn't want that pain in the arse telephoning London and finding out the warrant was fake.

"Hey!" Rossett called to the corporal, who was almost at the hut doorway. "I'm sorry, I've had a terrible drive over here. I didn't mean to be rude. I really need to be getting going before it gets too dark. Do you really need to check that thing?"

The corporal looked at the documents in his hand and then back at Rossett.

"Yeah."

Rossett opened the door of the Austin.

"Come on, mate, I need to get going."

"Stay in the car."

Rossett raised both palms in surrender and remained sitting in the car. The corporal stared at him a moment and then entered the little cabin, which was barely big enough for the two men stationed there to stand up in. Rossett watched him through the window of the hut, squeezing past the German, making his way to the field telephone that was hanging on the far wall, next to the tin chimney. The chimney snaked up and out through the flat roof, where an anemic snake of smoke, the same color as the clouds above, sneaked out.

Rossett climbed out of the car, watched by the German, who was now holding an enamel mug. Rossett took out his cigarettes and approached the hut, checking up and down the road the checkpoint bisected. It was empty, scrubbed of traffic by the heavy snowfall. The road, the fields, the soft rolling hills in the distance, all were wintery white. The only contrast was the hut, the sides of frosted hedgerows that skirted the fields, and the stout trunks of the English oaks, standing up to the winter and its wiles.

"Car." The soldier had moved to the doorway and was pointing as Rossett walked toward him, one hand holding the cigarettes, the other patting his pocket.

"Car, in." The German pointed, then put his mug down on a shelf just out of sight. He gripped the leather sling of his rifle, shucking it slightly off his shoulder, moving it an inch or two.

"I need a light." Rossett was eight feet away now, holding up his cigarettes for the soldier to see.

The soldier half unslung the rifle, as far as the crook of his arm. Rossett looked toward the window of the hut.

"Your car . . ."

Rossett fired once, center of the chest. The soldier dropped backward and down, landing on the seat of his pants, lifeless legs stretched out in front of him. His head lolled to the side, his back against the wall of the hut.

The English corporal ducked and half turned, one hand still holding the phone, the other dropping to the holster he knew he wouldn't be able to open. Rossett shot him in the left bicep. The bullet carried through and into his chest cavity.

The telephone hung limp from its wire, swinging slowly left and right, like the pendulum of a grandfather clock. Rossett remained in the doorway, checking for movement from the men he had just shot.

A kettle was steaming on the tiny stove.

"Hello?" A woman's voice, far away, crackled across the miles. "What's going on there? Hello?"

Rossett frowned and fired a round into the field telephone.

The Englishman shuddered at the sound of the shot and silently watched as Rossett turned off the flame under the kettle.

Rossett looked down and picked up his ID card and warrant from the floor. He lifted the Englishman's arm and inspected the wound in his side.

"Don't kill me."

"Did you give them my name?"

"Don't kill me," fainter this time.

"Did you give them my name?" Rossett shook the Englishman's shoulder.

"Don't kill me." Eyes rolling in their sockets now.

"I already have," replied Rossett, before he pulled an old, battered Browning automatic pistol from the corporal's holster.

Rossett looked at the gun. It was poorly maintained, with nicks and scratches; the grip was loose in the handle and rattled as Rossett shook it.

"Is this all they'll trust you with?" He held it up for the corporal to see.

The corporal struggled to focus on his pistol.

"It was hardly worth it, was it?"

The corporal closed his eyes.

"Did you give them my name?" Rossett rested his hand on the corporal's shoulder, a gentle shake this time, trying to bring him back.

The corporal's eyelids fluttered, too heavy to lift.

"Did you give them my name?" Rossett tried again, but it was useless. His countryman was gone.

CHAPTER 24

RUTH HARTZ HAD stared at blackboards all of her life. She couldn't remember a time when her hands hadn't felt dusty with chalk, or when she had been able to wear a dark outfit that didn't have white fingerprints on it.

She could work all day, decipher, decode, and create equations that would make most of the greatest minds in the world scratch their heads.

But right now, right at this minute, the blackboard in front of her was leaving her confused.

"Come on, Ruth, we haven't got long."

Ruth turned to Peter Winterbottom, her boss for the last two years, and shook her head.

"I don't know, I can't . . ." She looked back at the board. "What kind of fish is it?"

"A dead one," replied the catering lady, who was staring blankly back across the counter at Ruth.

"She'll have the soup." Winterbottom smiled at the catering lady, who shook her head and lifted the tin lid off the soup pan, nudging away the skin with a ladle.

"I was thinking about the fish." Ruth looked at the menu blackboard again as the dinner lady plonked a bowl of steaming soup on her tray.

"Next?" the catering lady shouted.

Ruth looked at the soup, then at Peter, and then back at the catering lady before finally lifting the tray and walking off to find a table.

The Cavendish Laboratory canteen at Cambridge University was one of the few locations in England that didn't have to suffer the rigors of the ration book. Great minds needed great food and great accommodation, and Cavendish had all three in abundance.

People who visited often said it was like the war had never happened at Cambridge University. Life had barely missed a beat as the bombs had started to fall. If it weren't for the portrait of the university's honorary chancellor, Rudolf Hess, on the wall at the far end of the dining room, one could imagine it was 1939 and all was well with the world.

Ruth stirred her soup and took a roll out of the basket on the table. She tore it in half, then looked over at her colleagues sitting on the other side of the canteen from her.

Peter held up his forkful of fish and smiled; Ruth smiled back before dunking her bread and eating it.

"How is the soup?"

Ruth looked up at the SS captain standing to her left.

"It is very good, Captain Meyer."

Meyer smiled. "You must be the only Jew who gets to eat before the SS."

"But not with my colleagues." Ruth pulled off another chunk of bread, gestured with it to the table on the other side of the canteen, and then popped it in her mouth.

"We can bend the rules, Fräulein Hartz, but I'm afraid we cannot break them. Jews and Gentiles don't mix, except when absolutely necessary. Those are my orders." Meyer smiled and touched the peak of his cap with his fingers. He turned from the table and waved to the small squad of SS soldiers waiting by the door, indicating that they could collect their own lunches from the serving hatch.

He turned back to Ruth, winked, and walked away to take his place at the head of the queue.

Ruth looked at the other table, full of scientists and mathematicians. They were chatting, some laughing, enjoying each other's company. She put down her bread and stirred the soup again, breaking the fresh skin that had formed out of nowhere.

"I don't even believe in God," she said to the soup.

Unlike the others who were working at the Cavendish Labs, Ruth was glad they only had a half-hour lunch break in the middle of the day. Being forced to sit alone meant she missed the exchange of ideas over a meal.

She wasn't worthy to join in.

As someone whose parents were Jews, Ruth had been given a set of strict instructions on her arrival at Cavendish, back in 1943, by the German administrator who ran the place.

"In the lab you will be exempted from most rules governing your unfortunate Jewish background. Outside of those doors your treatment will be the same as any other Jew working in a reserved occupation. You will eat alone and travel alone. You will live in the same building as the other scientists, but you will be housed in a separate part of the residence in secure accommodation. As a gesture, with consideration of your importance to the Reich war effort, you will be allowed to remove the star of David from your clothing while at work, but it must be worn on your outdoor clothing at all times." The administrator had looked up from the sheet he was reading and removed his spectacles. "I warn you, and take great heed of what I say, that any fraternization with non-Jews outside of work hours is strictly forbidden. You must not take advantage of your lack of obvious identification as a Jew while indoors to hoodwink unsuspecting Gentiles into fraternization. Is that understood?"

It seemed like such a long time ago that Ruth had been formally fired from her work at the Birmingham University physics department. It was almost as soon as the invasion had been completed, in the first few days of distorted normality, that she had received her notice to terminate her work in Birmingham's world-famous physics laboratory.

Her notes and research had been taken away as the lab was dismantled around her on that final day.

One minute she was the youngest doctor working under Rudolf Peierls in the physics department at one of the leading universities in the world. The next she had been placed with her parents under strict house arrest, staring at the four walls of her bedroom like a bored child.

A week went by before she was separated from her dear mother and father and put on a bus heading south for London. Once there she had been placed in a barracks with hundreds of other Jews, all of whom worked in the arts, sciences, media, or politics. Ruth hated to admit it, but that had been one of the most exciting times in her life. It was as if the previous twenty-eight years had led to immersion in a vast pool of intellect and talent. Night after night, the conversation soared in the updrafts of intellect from those gathered around the heating stove. Genius rose to the rafters with the smoke from the tin chimney.

Each morning, roused from their beds, breath hanging the cold air, they had been sifted, separated, and interviewed. New faces came and went like ingredients in a great intellectual stew, simmering with wit and wisdom. Days passed, then weeks, and then Ruth started to notice that the empty beds in the dorm were no longer being filled. People were being moved on, to God knows where.

One by one they had been interrogated and removed. First the politicians, then the actors, then the musicians, then the writers: all gone.

Suddenly the room no longer echoed to the sound of genius. Now it simply echoed.

Although she was only twenty-eight years old, Ruth was already known as one of the great theoretical and applied physicists of her generation. Her work at Birmingham had produced papers that had stirred the scientific world, marking her out as one to watch.

Unfortunately, the ones who were watching were the Nazis.

The quiet German professor in the shabby woolen suit who eventually came to London especially to meet her had been polite, nervous, even a little in awe. Sitting next to a stiff SS colonel in the tiny interrogation room, he had said, "We are assembling teams around Europe to work separately, and eventually together, on a project you will find of great interest. We have facilities and resources beyond your wildest dreams, and some of the scientists we have on board are extremely keen to work with you. It will be an honor to have you on the Cavendish team. Please, I beg you, say you will join us?"

Ruth had wondered if the quiet man in the suit understood her situation when he begged her.

He didn't have to beg.

She had no choice.

She had arrived in Cambridge accompanied by a team of guards led by two officers, Captains Meyer and Frenz.

It had taken her some time to settle down. Her notes had been sent ahead and her position in the lab explained, but try as she might, Ruth was the outsider.

The Jew.

All over Britain, posters had started to appear warning of the threat from "the Jew." In cinemas, cartoons and newsreels featured crude caricatures of grubby, greedy, dirty-faced scoundrels and louse-infected moneylenders, while national newspapers talked about "Jewish profiteering and Bolshevik subversion" on an almost daily basis.

Ruth had seen her first crudely painted star of David on a shop window as she drove from London to Cambridge. She had twisted in the seat when she saw a solitary old man, disheveled, lost, and lonely, standing on a street corner in the rain staring at the yellow paint pooling on the windowsill.

He had held out his hand as they waited at traffic lights, bony fingers brown with dirt, hovering outstretched and then pointing at the glass as Captain Meyer had looked at him from the front seat.

He didn't seem to want anything more than an explanation.

He didn't get one.

They drove away as if nothing had happened.

When Ruth arrived at the university, it seemed as if the other scientists already there didn't want to be associated with her. She wondered if it was for fear of being marked out as Jewish sympathizers by their new bosses. Ruth hated them for it, but guessed that she would probably do the same if she were in their shoes.

She couldn't blame them for not being brave.

She worked at Cavendish but lived a few miles out, in the same centuries-old hall as her colleagues, in the tiny village of Coton. She had her own plush apartment, but she never saw the others.

Rules were rules, and they even followed her home.

She had written long letters to her parents complaining about her loneliness and the pain of her betrayal. The country that had sheltered her mother and father when they had arrived battered from the horror of the Russian pogroms had now raised its own hand against them.

Ruth felt betrayed by the cowardice of a country that had spent so long pretending it was better than the rest.

Things had improved for her slightly as time went by. Her almond eyes and auburn curls made soldiers smile when she walked past. Ruth knew she was pretty; she understood facial symmetry and the theory of beauty, and she knew that she possessed it.

She just didn't care.

At least not until the night Captain Horst Meyer had stopped and chatted to her in the dining room. It was only idle chitchat, but it was like water on the lips of a dying man. A spark of humanity in an SS uniform: the irony wasn't lost on her, but she found herself playing with her hair and smiling under her fringe whenever he passed by.

He smiled back, and the spark began to flicker at the back of her mind and deep in her heart. Even though she knew she was doomed if she dreamed, she dreamed anyway.

Dreams provided release from her work, away from her burden, her consciousness of what she was doing.

Ruth was working to destroy the world. The papers she wrote were written in the blood of the millions who would die, should she and her team succeed.

She felt shame.

She was selling the lives of millions to buy time for her own.

She was angry with herself.

It was a small mercy that she didn't believe in God, because she had no wish to face his judgment.

She wrote letters to her parents that told of that guilt.

They never replied.

She guessed that the letters never left the halls she was locked up in, but she didn't care. They allowed her to confess, to share her guilt with the ones who still loved her, even if they never got to read them.

One night, almost three years into the project, Captain Meyer had knocked softly on her door. She had let him in, and he had whispered that he had received word her parents were dead. He gave her a flimsy piece of paper, headed with a swastika-clutching eagle whose head was turned, unable to look her in the eye.

She couldn't read German, but she knew what the letter meant.

"*Tote.*"

Dead.

She had cried.

Meyer had touched her arm, an unsure effort at consolation; it had seemed natural to step forward, natural for both of them.

She had cried in Meyer's arms the first night, and then lain in them the second, the third, and many nights since.

Both felt doomed, as if the bomb she was making was ticking in the same room they lay in.

Then he had told her he loved her.

Words in the darkness.

He reached for her hand under the sheets, and then held it tight through the night until he crept out of the room before the shame of the sunrise.

All they had during the day was stolen glances, half smiles, and snatched brushes of shoulders. Of a night they had each other for minutes, in darkness and whispers.

They were lovers, huddled around the only warmth of humanity left in their world.

Playing a dangerous game.

Ruth guessed that as time went on some of her colleagues had figured out what was happening; one had once winked when Meyer held open a door for Ruth as they entered the laboratory together.

Now Ruth was scared; she knew time was running out.

Whether she loved him or not, he was her anchor to self-worth, her chance to be human. For those few snatched hours she was an equal, even more: she was raised up high in the eyes of another, and she could remember what she was. She was as good as the rest; she was a human being, a person.

For all the guilt it inspired, Ruth loved her work. She had a passion for it, possibly her only true love. Her team was winning the race; they were close to the solution that the Führer was calling for.

She had attended enough conferences, enough failed experiments, enough seminars to know that the pressure was mounting for one of the four teams—two in Germany, one in France, and one in England—to crack the riddle, harness the atom, and create the weapon the Führer so desperately wanted.

Needed.

"Your work will bring peace to the world. Your work will open a new chapter for the future of mankind. With this weapon we will be able to end the Bolshevik barbarism on the Eastern Front, and halt the aggression of America. We will say 'no more' to their attempts to undermine the greatness of the Third Reich. The Führer's and the Fatherland's destiny will be sealed in the power you will unleash. The world will finally know the security that only National Socialist strength of arms provides!"

Ruth had tried to believe a weapon as terrible as the one that was about to be unleashed on the world would be a tool for good.

She had tried so hard.

She had failed.

But she had carried on working to create it.

Her life depended on it.

They were nearly there; the formulas and equations were coming together. Theories were being proven. Her work, her hours of staring at numbers, her imagination, her dreams . . . her brain was the key.

As time had passed, she had risen through the lab, climbing higher, becoming more important, more confident, and more relaxed.

She was safe while she worked; she knew that. She knew that the only thing that would put her in peril was success.

She wanted to succeed, to prove she was the best, but she knew that do so was the end.

The end of her.

She had a use; they had a need; she exploited them as they exploited her.

Ruth had played a game. Like landing a fish, she had played out the formulas and then reeled them in slowly. Give and take, ebb and flow, sometimes right, sometimes wrong.

Not too fast, not too slow.

She was running out of line. Her colleagues were getting closer. Her time wasting was letting them catch up, and they were finding their own solutions to the problems she had seen through months before.

She wasn't stupid.

She was a genius.

She knew what was coming and she was struggling to stop it.

She would be the first casualty of a working bomb.

And she could hear it ticking.

CHAPTER 25

SO YOU THINK he's killed his wife?"

"I can't say for sure that he has, sir, and, I must confess, he doesn't seem the type." Neumann stared at the top of his boss's head across the table, conscious that March was rocking from side to side as he stood next to him.

"They often don't look the type, Neumann, you should know that." Kriminalpolizei director Muller turned over Neumann's statement, then rested his hands on top of the papers, as if trying to stop them blowing away.

"I do, sir, which is why I'm here."

Muller looked up. "You do know Major Koehler is due to receive Oak Leaves for his Knight's Cross quite soon?"

"I am aware of that, sir."

Muller looked down at his hands for a moment, and Neumann took the opportunity to look at March and frown. He was staring back at his boss by the time Muller's head rose again.

"Is that why you want to release him? Are you worried about how his arrest will reflect on you?"

"Not at all, sir."

"You should be." Muller stared at Neumann. "Arresting senior SS men is a dangerous business, Neumann. It shouldn't be done lightly."

"I didn't take the decision to arrest Koehler lightly, sir."

"But you want him released with barely a charge against him?"

"In light of developments in the case, I've decided to pursue other avenues, sir. The major will still be assisting our inquiries, but he is no longer a suspect."

"In your report you mention a British police officer who assaulted you. Is he to be charged?"

"No, sir. That was an honest mistake on his part. I've accepted an apology and decided that is the end of the matter."

Muller sighed, then shook his head as he picked up the first sheet of the report, holding it up to Neumann.

"You're setting dangerous precedents here, Neumann, and not only that: you're making this whole department look incompetent."

Neumann became aware of March rocking backward and forward again.

"I'm sorry, sir; I can only follow where the investigation leads. I'm genuinely sorry if that causes embarrassment."

Muller put the sheet of paper back on the pile and then picked up a pen from his desk, which he held an inch from the page.

"You're sure Koehler isn't going to make a fuss?" He looked up again.

"He genuinely wants to help us find his daughter, sir."

"The SS are a strange breed. Neumann, you are absolutely sure of this?"

"One hundred percent, sir."

The pen wavered; Muller shook his head as he looked at the sheet. Finally, after what seemed like a lifetime, he signed with a flourish. The full stop at the end of the signature sounded like a twenty-one-gun salute to Neumann, and he had to resist the urge to punch the air.

Muller lifted the report and held it out for Neumann to take.

"Find this girl quickly, alive or dead, do you hear me?"

"Yes, sir." Neumann took the report from his boss's hand.

"And don't make a habit of letting Englishmen hit you and get away with it."

"No, sir."

"The whole country is getting out of hand; we need to be firm with these people. I don't want any of this 'genuine mistake' rubbish, do you hear me?"

"Yes, sir."

Muller nodded and then waved them away as he continued to mutter, almost to himself. "Letting them charge around, doing what they want to, only leads to trouble. Trouble means people get hurt . . . people like those poor soldiers just outside Cambridge this morning."

Neumann, who had turned from the desk, stopped and looked back at his boss.

"Cambridge, sir?"

"Two of them, in a checkpoint. It's letting the locals get off with the little things that gets them thinking they can do what they want. Next thing you know people are being killed. Little things can easily get out of hand."

"Do we know who was behind the attack, sir?" Neumann's mouth felt suddenly dry.

"Not yet. The report came in an hour or so ago. The locals are looking into it. We were notified in case whoever was responsible was heading here."

"Here?"

"It was on the main road to London, although we don't know which way they were traveling."

"They?"

Muller leaned back in his chair, irritated with the questions.

"The checkpoint was on the phone to London, checking an ID and travel warrant, when the line went dead."

Neumann's stomach dipped and went cold.

"Oh . . ." was all he could think of to say.

Muller stared, and Neumann heard the sounds of his boss's outer office behind him. He finally nodded, swallowed again, and turned to March, who was still holding the door open.

"Neumann?"

Neumann stopped and turned back to Muller.

"Find that girl, do you hear me? The department needs something to show for all this mess."

"Yes, sir, of course."

NEUMANN HAD TO fight the urge to lean against the wall as he made his way along the corridor back to his office. Once or twice he caught March looking at him, about to speak, but each time Neumann held up a hand to silence him.

Now wasn't the time.

March held open their office door as Neumann entered and slumped into the chair at his desk. He slapped down the file Muller had signed, then rested his forehead in his hands.

Finally March spoke.

"Are you all right, sir?"

"Go get Koehler."

March stared at the top of his boss's head, then exited the office wordlessly.

Neumann heard the click of the door closing, looked up to check he was alone, then lowered his face into the palms of his hands again and groaned.

His fingertips made tiny circling motions on his forehead. He sighed once more before picking up the heavy black telephone receiver and dialing the switchboard.

He waited less than two seconds before the operator came on.

"Switchboard."

"Communications room supervisor, please," Neumann said in English.

"Hold on, please."

A click, then a crackle, then a different voice came on the other end of the line.

"Communications room supervisor."

"Generalmajor Neumann here. What can you tell me about the incident today at the checkpoint in Cambridge?"

"Sounds like a bad one, sir. Two dead, a German and a Brit. Preliminary reports suggesting that it was a lone gunman."

"What else do we know?"

"Not much at this time, sir. The army are looking into it themselves. You know what they are like; they don't really trust us to follow things up fully. There is someone on his way over shortly to interview the operator the checkpoint was talking to at the time of the attack . . ."

"The operator is still here?"

"Yes, sir. She's a bit shook up, to be honest."

"Put her on the line."

"I think the army's investigator would want to speak to her first, sir."

"Get her and put her on the line now."

There was a pause, then the sound of the phone mouthpiece being muffled, and then the supervisor came back on.

"Someone is fetching her now, sir."

"Who is she?"

"A young English girl. Smith, Ellen Smith. One of the new ones coming through who are bilingual."

"How long has she been with us?"

"Couple of months, sir. I can get her file if you like?"

"Don't bother."

"Will you be handling the investigation, sir?"

"In a manner of speaking. Where is she?"

"I've sent someone up to the second floor, sir. She is in the canteen. I thought it best. She was rather —"

Neumann slammed the phone down and rushed to the door. His office was on the third floor, while the communications room was in the basement. It would be quicker and better to speak to the girl in the canteen, away from the prying ears of bosses and colleagues.

He almost ran through the outer office and small squad room and then out into the corridor. A few long strides and he was on the stairs heading down to the canteen. He charged through the double swing doors and saw Smith immediately, nervously sitting alone at a small table on the far side of the half-full canteen. Smith looked up and seemed to instinctively realize Neumann was coming for her. She stood up from the table, crossed her arms over her chest, and took a small step backward.

Neither had ever seen the other before, but each knew the other was equally concerned about Cambridge.

"Miss Smith?" Neumann said in English.

"Yes, sir."

"Please sit down." Neumann struggled to control his breathing and pointed to the chair Smith had been sitting in moments earlier.

He briefly gave thought to ordering tea but decided it would take too much time. Neumann took the seat opposite to her, realizing its back was to the door and immediately regretting it.

"I want to ask you some questions about this morning."

"Yes, sir."

"You speak German?"

"Yes, sir."

"Do you mind if . . ."

"Not at all, sir." Smith switched smoothly to German.

"You took the call?"

"Yes, sir."

"Tell me about it?"

Smith folded her hands on the table, gripping her left thumb in her right hand.

Neumann realized that she had been rehearsing this speech in her head.

"I received a call at about—" Smith broke off and looked over Neumann's shoulder.

He turned in his chair. A man in civilian clothing was approaching, slightly out of breath.

"Ellen, the boss wants you downstairs; someone wants to speak to you on the phone," he said in English.

"That was me." Neumann held up his hand.

"It's about Cambridge," the man said, resting one hand on his hip.

"I know," said Neumann.

"I ran up here for nothing?"

Neumann half turned in his seat and looked at the Englishman, who slowly took his hand off his hip, then nodded and turned away without speaking.

Neumann watched the man go and then faced Smith again, forcing a smile.

"Where were we?"

"I took a call this morning, sir, from the checkpoint."

"Yes, go on."

She smoothed a hand over her neat dark hair before touching a fingertip to her lips as she thought. Neumann felt like screaming at the girl, but instead made do with clenching one fist so tightly his knuckles hurt.

Eventually Smith spoke again.

"The English Home Defense trooper came on the line, sir; it was him who made the call."

"Do you get many calls from outside of London?"

"We get some, sir, mostly checking papers and warrants and such."

"Go on."

"He said he wanted to check the identity of a policeman, and a travel warrant."

Neumann's heart thudded.

"A warrant?"

"Yes, sir."

Neumann couldn't get the next question out, so he merely gestured that she should continue with the story.

"He said it was a travel warrant issued by Scotland Yard. He'd just given me the warrant number when I heard the . . ." Smith paused and then lowered her eyes a fraction before continuing. "The shooting start."

It was Neumann's turn to smooth his hair. The number on the travel warrant would correspond to the duplicate sheet in the book that was kept in the inquiry desk safe downstairs. Neumann knew that his signature was in that book, next to that number.

He needed to get the book.

"Did the trooper give the name of the policeman carrying the warrant?"

"No, sir."

"You're sure?"

Smith didn't answer Neumann; she was too busy looking over his shoulder again. Neumann opened his fist, placed his hand flat on the table, and irritably pushed himself in a half turn to face whoever was interrupting again.

Technically Neumann was part of the RSHA, the Reich Main Security Service, a bloated whale of an organization filled with various factions fighting for space, each standing on the other's toes and thrusting elbows into ribs with varying degrees of fierceness.

None of this had ever been Neumann's concern. He wasn't even a party member; he was a policeman, a Kriminal Polizist, a Kripo, a detective who fought crime wherever he was sent.

On the other end of the elbow was the SiPo, the security police, and as far as Neumann was concerned never the twain should meet.

What the SiPo did was their business. If they left Neumann alone, he was happy to leave them alone.

Unfortunately, today, they weren't going to leave him alone.

Two Gestapo officers were walking across the canteen toward the table where Neumann and Smith were seated.

Neumann stood up as they drew near.

"Miss Smith?" the older of the two Gestapo men asked in German.

"Yes, sir."

"You are?" the Gestapo officer looked at Neumann, the question as rude as the stare he was giving.

"I'm leaving," Neumann replied.

"Your name?"

"Generalmajor Neumann, Kripo."

"Why are you talking to Miss Smith?"

Neumann looked at Smith and then back at the Gestapo man.

"I was making inquiries about the incident at Cambridge." Neumann felt like he was standing on a cliff edge that was crumbling beneath his feet.

"Why?"

"Because I thought I might be able to help."

The Gestapo man tilted his head.

"It isn't a Kripo matter."

"I know the area," Neumann lied and felt the cliff crumble some more.

"How do you know the area?"

"I've visited."

"When?"

Neumann breathed in through his nose and inflated his chest half an inch.

"I'm not being interrogated by you," he said, with less confidence than he'd intended.

"But you are. Answer the question."

"Who are you?" Neumann tried again.

"My name is Weber. Answer the question: when did you visit Cambridge?"

"A few months ago." Another lie, another inch of cliff crumbled.

"In an official capacity?"

"No, it was for pleasure; I drove up there to look around."

"You have a record of this visit?"

"This is ridiculous." Neumann looked at the second Gestapo officer for reassurance, but didn't get any.

"Why?" Weber again.

"Why what?"

"Why is it ridiculous? I come in here and you are interrogating Miss Smith for no reason that I can yet understand." Weber's voice was level, in contrast to Neumann's, which was rising steadily.

"I was not interrogating her."

"Was he asking you questions?" Weber looked at Smith, who nodded dumbly, and then back at Neumann, his statement confirmed.

Neumann stared at Weber with an open mouth before turning to look around the canteen, where nearly everyone was looking at him, waiting for his next move.

"I don't have to stand here and take this from you." Neumann turned back to Weber, his cheeks reddening.

Weber's brow furrowed. He was visibly confused by Neumann's behavior. A second passed between them before Neumann spun on his heel and walked away.

Away from the Gestapo, and as far from the cliff edge as he could get.

Neumann didn't head back to his office; instead he took the stairs down to the ground floor, two at a time, eventually bursting out into the long corridor that ran the length of the building.

The ground floor was always the busiest part of Scotland Yard. Night and day it seemed to be always full of people, busy people, heading this way and that, opening doors, closing doors, accompanied by the chatter of conversations and typewriters and telephones.

It was place to get lost in, a place to disappear, a place where nobody had time to wonder what you were doing.

Neumann used that confusion to stop and stare at the large iron safe, which stubbornly stared back at him in the inner office behind the inquiry desk.

Two British police sergeants were seated at the front desk, both handwriting entries in identical black leather ledgers. The safe was through a doorway behind them, away from public view, only visible to those inside the station.

It held sundry items: found property that had been handed in and the paperwork that went with it, station keys, important evidence awaiting collection by the property team, the petrol issue vouchers, petty cash, and, most important, the travel warrant book.

Neumann needed that book.

He stroked his mustache and checked up and down the corridor for anyone watching him. Life went on as if he weren't there. Behind him, through an open door, a telephone was ringing unanswered. Neumann turned and looked into the office where the phone was, wiped a hand across his mouth, and entered.

The phone was making the desk vibrate as it rang, inches from where Neumann was bending over to look in a drawer for an envelope. He scrabbled through the drawer's contents and brought out a large brown envelope and a pair of old burnished scissors.

He dropped the scissors into the envelope and walked out of the office, closing the door on the ringing telephone. He waited, minutes ticking slowly by, until both desk sergeants were occupied with members of the public making inquiries at the front desk.

"I need to drop this in the evidence basket," Neumann held up the envelope as he tapped the nearest desk sergeant on the elbow.

The sergeant looked at him, then held up a hand to stop the member of the public talking.

"I'm busy. In a minute."

"Just give me the keys. I'm pressed for time, I'll pass them back."

The member of the public tutted at the delay and shifted his weight from one foot to the other, attracting the attention of the desk sergeant, who sighed, pulled out a bunch of keys, and passed them to Neumann with the desk diary.

"Make an entry in the log."

"Of course."

Neumann took the logbook through to the back office, then selected the longest key on the chain and opened the safe. He leaned in and picked up the travel warrant book. It was about six inches long and nearly an inch thick. He rolled it in his hand and then slid it into his inside suit pocket.

"Looking for something?"

Neumann looked over his shoulder at Weber, then tossed the envelope with the scissors into the safe.

"I'm putting evidence in the system."

"Hmm."

Neumann made to swing the safe door shut but Weber reached out a hand and caught it, just as the desk sergeant joined them in the little office. Neumann moved back from the safe door. Conscious of the bulge in his suit jacket, he passed the sergeant the ledger and nodded thanks before leaving the office.

Neumann didn't hear the sounds of Scotland Yard as he walked back to his office; he passed through the crowds in the corridors like a ghost, until he finally turned the handle on the door to his office and entered it.

Koehler was seated at the desk and March stood leaning against the wall, arms folded, staring at the floor.

March looked up, saw his boss's face, and unfolded his arms slowly as he pushed off the wall.

"Sir?"

Neumann flicked his head, gesturing that March should leave them alone.

The door closed as Neumann flopped into his chair.

"Did you speak to Rossett?" Koehler asked.

"Yes."

"March says I am to be released?"

"You are, on bail, pending a final decision regarding the charge of assault on me."

"Anja . . . have you heard anything?"

"No."

"So I can go?" Koehler rested his hands on the arms of the chair, ready to spring out of it.

"You never told me he was a killer."

"Who?"

"Rossett."

"What's he done?"

"Killed two men at a checkpoint outside Cambridge."

The tension seemed to leave Koehler's arms and he settled back into the chair.

"You're sure?"

Neumann nodded.

"Fuck," Koehler said softly, leaning his head back and looking at the ceiling.

"Yes." Neumann rubbed the lump on his scalp again. "I gave him the travel warrant. If they trace it to me, I'm as dead as the men at the checkpoint, and so are you."

"Do they know it was Rossett?"

"Possibly." Neumann adjusted his suit jacket, pulling it across his chest to hide the warrants from Koehler, embarrassed at his panic and the theft of the book. He inspected his fingertips. "If not now, they will if he gets caught or stopped again."

Koehler placed the palm of his hand against his mouth and breathed out through his fingers.

"I was crazy to get involved," Neumann said quietly.

Koehler looked at him, slowly lowering his hand.

"You're a detective?"

"Of course I am."

"Let's find Anja and the scientist. Maybe we can turn this around."

"Around?"

"If we find Rossett, after we find Anja, we can get the scientist and look like heroes."

"And Rossett?"

"He'll do as he is told. He trusts me."

"Can I?"

"We're in this together, Neumann; I don't think you've got much of a choice."

"No . . . I don't think I have," Neumann replied, producing the travel warrants from his jacket.

CHAPTER 26

ERIC COOK WAS covered in blood. His head hung to the side, and he traced his tongue around the gap where one of his front teeth had been knocked out, then moaned a low moan that said, I can't take any more.

Ma Price disagreed; she took another sip of tea from her cup and nodded her head to Mustache.

Mustache punched Eric hard on the left side of his face with a ripping downward right hook that caused Eric's remaining teeth to clatter together and his jaw to feel like it had been dislodged.

His ears rang, the room spun, and then came the pain.

His head hung to the side as the agony ebbed and the room steadied.

His eyes were puffed up so badly he could barely see through them. The sound of his breath snorting through his broken nose was the only noise in the room. Mustache stepped back, took a quick look at his knuckles to check for damage, then waited for the nod from Ma Price to continue.

"Ask him," Ma Price said to the Prof.

"Tell her the address where the German is to take the scientist. Please, I promise this'll be over quickly if you do."

Eric half lifted his head and through one puffy eye managed to look at the old man.

"Tell her to release me and I will." Eric barely managed to speak the words, lisping them through the gap in his teeth, before his head dropped again.

The bedroom door opened before the Prof could pass the message, and the other heavy stuck in his head.

"It's ready," he said to Price, who in turn indicated that he should help Mustache get Eric out of his seat.

They carried Eric into the front room, followed by the others. Eric squinted against the bright light beaming through the high windows, dazzling him after the boarded-up blackness in the back room.

Blinking, looked around as he was half carried, half dragged in.

The room was almost empty except for an electricity cable that hung from the ceiling light to a wooden box, which sat next to a tin bath full of water.

Eric stiffened and tried to stop them from taking him farther into the room, but his body had been weakened by the battering it had taken for the last hour, and he barely managed to slow them a fraction.

They dropped him into the bath. Water slopped out over the sides onto the floorboards as he struggled not to go under. Eric gasped as the cold soaked through his clothes, chilling him into snatched half breaths. Mustache pushed down on Eric's head as the other man dragged his feet up into the air.

Eric found new strength; even though his hands were tied, he thrashed his body and kicked his feet in a desperate attempt to keep his head out of the water.

It was no good; he was helpless, gagging and choking as water filled his mouth and eyes.

It seemed he was under forever.

The cold faded, the pain faded, the light that dappled down to his half-closed eyes faded. He was succumbing to the darkness when he vaguely felt his hair being gripped, and then he was pulled upward. He weakly tried to lift his hands as his face cleared the water and he began to cough and retch.

It was like he was dreaming—the noise, the blurred vision, the light, and the cold air.

That was the moment he knew it was his last day on earth.

He knew he was going to die.

He knew he had nearly died just then.

He wished he had.

He looked at Mustache.

These people cared nothing for him; they weren't human.

Eric wanted to cry but barely had the breath. A sudden sense of hopelessness enveloped him almost as much as the water had.

He was going to die.

This was it, all his life, leading to this moment, all so pointless.

Ma Price appeared at his side and sadly shook her head.

"Why are you doing this to yourself, my love? Tell us what the address is." She gently touched the back of his head, as if holding a newborn baby.

The room seemed to spin.

"Please . . . a minute . . . please?" Eric whispered. Ma Price stepped back and nodded to Mustache, who immediately pushed down again on Eric's head, sending him back under the water.

Eric thrashed.

Water slapped onto the bare floorboards, enough to soak all around, but not enough to empty the bath that was becoming his tomb.

The darkness was coming again as Eric was yanked back into the cold air, coughing and crying.

"We're going to fry you in that bath now, burn you with electricity. I don't want to have to do it. It's up to you. Please don't make me." Ma Price shook her head. "We can keep it going all day and all night, until you tell us the address."

Eric sobbed and gasped in reply, unable to string together words.

THE BOY NEEDS to think. You're going to kill him before he has a chance to tell you anything," the Prof said to Ma Price. "Do we need the address that much?"

Ma Price stared at Eric sadly and then turned to the Prof, beckoning him closer. "Whoever Koehler is getting for the Yanks obviously matters a lot. So much so that they have gone to all this trouble. Imagine how hard that must have been to organize? Kidnapping an SS major's daughter, spiriting someone from Cambridge, getting them out of the country? Think about it."

"I understand, but—"

"You don't understand, that's the problem. If you understood, you would know that all the trouble they've gone to makes whoever they are kidnapping very important. And people pay lots of money for things that are very important. People pay a bleedin' lot. Once we have the address, then we have whoever was kidnapped, and then we have the money. Understand?"

"Yes."

"We can name a price, or, if we want to, we can negotiate something else from the Yanks. We can get out of 'ere, maybe, out of the country, get to safety, yes?"

"But . . . this . . ." Prof gestured to the bath and the bloody swollen mess that was lying in it. "This is barbaric. Aside from the fact that you'll kill him before he has a chance to speak, it is downright barbaric. If the Americans think we have done this to one of their people they will never help us, never."

"They'll never know, because we'll never tell them."

"We're human beings; we shouldn't be doing . . . this." The Prof gestured to Eric, who was shaking uncontrollably.

Ma Price stared at the Prof and then looked at Eric, head hung over the side of the bath; his face now swollen beyond recognition. She looked at the floor and then at Mustache.

"Give him five minutes."

She left the room followed by the second henchman. The Prof crossed to Eric and struggled down to his knees to speak to him.

"You have five minutes' rest. You'll not get another chance: tell her what she needs to know and end this suffering."

Eric's head jerked slightly, seemingly almost a reflex at the sound of the Prof's voice speaking so gently. He visibly struggled to open his eyes.

"Please . . . take me out of the water. I'm so cold," Eric whispered, his voice barely audible behind the chattering of his remaining teeth and gasps of breath.

"He wants to get out of the bath. Can you help him?" the Prof asked Mustache, who looked at the closed door and then nodded.

"Come on then, five minutes." Mustache gripped Eric under the arms, bodily lifting him out of the bath with a grunt.

Mustache tried to support Eric while attempting to avoid the water that was dripping off him. He waited as Eric struggled to lift first one leg out of the bath and then the other.

Water drained off his sodden clothes onto the floor. Eric struggled to remain upright under his own steam, his knees locking and unlocking under him seemingly at random until he managed to finally stand, head hanging, on his own two feet.

Mustache took another step back to prevent himself from getting soaked.

That was when Eric went for the window.

Mustache was blocked by the Prof as Eric staggered toward the far side of the room.

HE DIDN'T WANT to escape, he wanted to die.

He figured that to fall through the glass, and then the twenty feet to the road below, would be a better way to die than at the hands of these English barbarians.

He felt a hand grab his shoulder. Eric spun, still moving forward, twisting as he went, desperate for the release that the window offered, out into the light.

He broke free and took another step, spiraling, his legs unsteady. The next step would pitch him into the glass. Eric prayed that when he hit it he would have enough momentum to smash through.

He was falling before he struck the window. Plunging downward, his head shattered the pane and he spun end over end out into the street, splinters of glass all around him as he went.

Despite the thick layer of snow, he hit the cobbles hard. What little air his lungs still held was jolted out, but he felt no real pain.

He rolled onto his back and looked up into the gray sky above. His face felt warm and wet, and he blinked through the slits of his eyelids.

He was disappointed he hadn't died, but he knew didn't have long to go. He felt strangely calm as he realized blood was leaking into his mouth from somewhere.

He'd be gone soon.

They couldn't hurt him now.

FRANK KING WAS idly spinning his empty teacup in its saucer when he heard the crash. He looked out through the net curtains, where he saw Eric lying in the street with tiny shards of glass falling all around him like flakes of diamond snow from the sky.

It took a moment for what he was looking at to sink in.

King looked up at the broken window and saw a big man with a mustache staring down at Eric in the street below. King stood up, pulled his pistol out of his pocket, and crossed the tiny room to the front door. He turned the handle and then stopped.

Crouching slightly, he stepped back to the edge of the window, trying to see through the curtains without disturbing them.

The snow around Eric was staining crimson. King's heart thudded in his chest, and he fought the urge to rush outside to help.

He swallowed, waited, and watched, knuckles white as they gripped the pistol, the old lady on the floor behind him forgotten for now.

He didn't wait long.

The front door of the house opposite flew open and the man with the mustache, a second heavy, and a fat woman charged out into the street.

MUSTACHE HAD WATCHED Eric go out of the window and barely believed his eyes. He hadn't thought the American capable of standing unaided, let alone running to the window and jumping through.

He had been shouting for help before the Yank had hit the ground, and he was halfway down the stairs when he saw Ma Price and the other man coming out of the kitchen at a run.

Mustache had had to pull the sticky front door two or three times to get it open, and as he'd run onto the street, he could see the American lying still, staring at the sky.

KING WATCHED THE three of them running to Eric; he worked the slide on the gun, waiting for the right moment.

As he saw the first big man crouching down, King went to the front door and twisted the handle.

One . . . two . . . three . . .

He burst out into the street lifting his pistol as he ran, shooting the man with the mustache twice as he looked up with open mouth and wide eyes.

Two in the chest.

Mustache tried to rise and then stumbled backward, ending up sitting in the snow, looking down into his lap.

The woman slipped as she stumbled back toward the door. King ignored her and shot the second man high on the left side of his chest, and then once again, hitting him just above his right hip as he spun.

Sending him down, sprawling in the snow.

Something caught King's attention off to his right; he spun dropping to one knee. Three children were running as fast as they could in the opposite direction up the street, away from the shooting and the blood-soaked snow.

King processed them and turned back to his main threat.

The house opposite.

The woman was being bundled through the door by another man, older, tall and spindly, in a dusty old black suit.

King stared down the sights, took a breath, and then lifted the pistol. They weren't a threat. The old man turned and stumbled into the hallway, kicking the door shut behind him, only for it to bounce half open again.

The second man King had shot rolled onto his back and fired his revolver. The boom of the shot caused King to flinch before he redirected his aim and fired once.

The revolver dropped into the snow.

The second man was dead.

Mustache slowly keeled sideways onto the ground from his sitting position, just as the door opposite King finally slammed shut. King adjusted his aim and pointed his pistol at the door, then realized that the slide was back.

He was empty.

He released the magazine and in one quick movement inserted another and dropped the slide.

A second and a half and he was ready to go again.

Silence.

Nothing moved.

King was panting as he stared down the pistol sights at the front door. He looked quickly left and right, up and down the street. Several houses down, somebody poked out a head and then ducked back in, but all else was quiet.

He rose up from his knee, which was wet from the snow. He moved quickly, half crouching, with the Mauser still pointing at the house opposite. He snatched up the heavy revolver that was lying on the ground next to the second man, dropping it into his overcoat pocket as a reserve. He moved back toward Mustache, his gun still trained on the door, and quickly patted him down in a search of a weapon.

Nothing.

Mustache was watching him with strong, steady eyes, giving no sign of the pain he was in, struggling to control his breathing.

Frank stared back at Mustache and then went to Eric. He looked down at his friend, the young inexperienced clerk who did nothing but talk about girls, and saw the faintest flicker of life on his lips.

King dropped to his knees, one eye on the door opposite.

"Eric?"

Eric opened his bloodshot eyes and searched the sky for King.

"Frank?"

"Yes."

"I told her nothing, Frank." Eric's voice barely carried the few inches between them.

"Her?"

"The woman, I told her nothing." Eric paused. His mouth moved but no sound came out.

"Eric?" King leaned forward slightly.

"I'm so glad you came for me."

King looked down at Eric and stroked his hair, and Eric died.

The blood around him had painted the snow, framing him with butterfly wings that sparkled with broken glass.

King gently touched Eric's cheek.

He'd gotten a dumb kid killed.

Shit.

He breathed, he looked at Eric, and then in the distance he heard a policeman's whistle.

He took another look at Eric and then the house.

The whistle sounded again, ghostly, seeming to come from the gray cloud above.

King wanted to go into the house to make them pay.

He gritted his teeth and let out a low moan.

The whistle sounded again, and then he heard another from the other direction, coming to assist.

He had to go.

He started to jog away, looking once over his shoulder at Eric, and then running faster.

MA PRICE AND the Prof crouched behind the front door. She held a Browning Hi Power pistol as she pressed the wound on the Prof's shoulder, trying to slow the bleeding.

"I think it went through Kenny and hit me." The Prof's voice was high. Shock was setting in.

Ma Price listened to the police whistles. They sounded close.

"I feel faint . . ." The Prof shivered.

"I'm going to go check to see if he's gone," Price whispered, and the Prof nodded.

He choked back another shiver, slid down the door, and lay with his head resting on the back of his hand.

Ma Price made her way as quickly as she could up the stairs and into the front bedroom. She hung back as far as she could from the window, standing on tiptoes to look out into the street, the Browning pointing up at the ceiling, next to her ear.

By the time she could see out of the broken window, she was certain whoever had been shooting at them was long gone.

The whistles again, closer. Time was ticking. Below, down in the snow, lay three men, surrounded by blood that looked like ink dropped into water.

She saw Mustache kick a leg, trying to push himself up and failing, no doubt aware of the approaching whistles and trying to get away.

The shooter was nowhere to be seen. Curious neighbors were coming out of their houses now. Ma Price cursed and quickly headed downstairs. She ran as fast as her chunky legs could carry her into the back room of the house, grabbed her coat and bag, and then went back to the hallway.

The Prof looked terrible.

He was shaking as he held his hand against the hole in his shoulder. He held the bony, bloody hand up and gestured that she should help him up from behind the door. Ma Price obliged. Taking a grip with two hands she dragged him clear, then helped him sit at the foot of the stairs.

The Prof coughed, his head drooped forward, and some blood spattered his grimy white shirt.

"Give me a minute."

"We ain't got a minute."

"I just need to catch my breath."

"You need to get up; I can't leave you here for the police to find."

"Give me a minute."

Another whistle, so close that they both looked at the door, as if it was about to crash open.

The Prof looked at Price and raised his blood-soaked hand to her. "Help me up." He wafted with his hand again, less than convincingly.

Price sadly shook her head and shot him dead before he could realize what was happening.

"I'm sorry, Prof," she said as he slid off the step onto the floor.

Ma Price tugged at the door handle to free it of the jamb and stepped out into the street, slipping her pistol into her coat. The bystanders had scattered slightly at the sound of the final shot. Ma Price ignored them and took in the scene in the street. Nobody was moving now. She stared at Mustache, trying to see if he was dead. Ma Price didn't like loose ends.

She looked at the few onlookers still floating around but keeping their distance and avoiding eye contact. She held her ground, letting them know she wasn't scared, that she knew who they were, where they lived; letting them know she could snuff them out now or later.

It was up to them.

Another whistle.

Ma Price walked away.

Not too fast, always in control.

CHAPTER 27

SOMEONE, A LONG time ago in a country even farther away, had once told Allen Dulles that no matter where you were in the world, the air you breathed in an American embassy tasted of freedom.

That person had wafted his cigar and leaned forward in his seat; spilling some whiskey on his leg, he had looked deep into Dulles's eyes and pushed home the point.

"We are the future, we are the hope for the world, and we'll make it a better place so that one day everyone will know the taste of good old American free air."

Dulles had watched the cigar jabbing the American air and nodded.

He'd nodded because back then, he had believed it to be true.

Right now?

Right now, he wasn't so sure.

He drew on his own cigar, looked at his own glass of whiskey, and shook his head.

Dulles got out of the chair and walked to the window of his Mayfair apartment. Somewhere out there was King, somewhere out there was Dulles's future, and somewhere out there was America's future.

He sighed again, turned away from the window, then stopped, paused, and then turned back, looking down into the street below.

Two long, fat, beetle-black American cars were double-parked outside the apartment block. Dulles had guessed they'd be coming, but he hadn't thought it would be so soon.

He opened the front door of the apartment and waited, listening to the echoing steps of the men trotting up the stairs. He recognized Captain Bryan from the embassy security team leading the way, all square jawed and certain. Dulles had known Bryan's father back in New York; he was an asshole as well.

At the back of the group came Kennedy, taking his time, methodically working his way up till he got to the top.

Kennedy all over.

"Allen."

"Joe."

"May we come in?"

"Please." Dulles stepped back and let the five of them into the small hallway.

Before Dulles closed the door he looked down the stairs, feeling a strange loneliness that he wasn't expecting. The click of the latch sounded louder than he remembered it ever sounding before.

The air tasted the same, though.

Cigars and whiskey, the smell of freedom.

Only Kennedy and Dulles entered the sitting room; the rest of the men took up station in the kitchen with instructions to help themselves to whatever they wanted.

Kennedy took the offered Scotch from Dulles, then sat at one end of the floral and gilt settee nearest the window. Dulles placed his cigar in an ashtray and took his seat on the armchair in the center of the room, directly opposite Kennedy.

"You were expecting us, Allen?"

"I saw your cars out the window."

"So you weren't expecting us?"

Dulles smiled. "You're sharp, Joe."

Kennedy smiled back.

Dulles swirled his Scotch, listening to the ice rattle in the glass. The two men sat quietly for a minute, listening to the clock on the mantelpiece.

Finally Kennedy broke the silence.

"You've been a good advisor to me, Allen. I've enjoyed your counsel. We've worked well together."

"You haven't listened to me, though."

"Oh, no, I've listened, Allen. I really have. You're a smart man, and I'd be a fool not to."

"But?"

"You can be smart and still be wrong." Kennedy sipped his whiskey.

"So can you, Joe."

Kennedy chuckled. "I'm not smart, Allen, not like you. I see things simply. I play the game in front of me. I don't try to change the rules as I go along."

"It isn't a game, Joe."

"See? That's where you are wrong again." Kennedy chuckled and shook his head. "It is a game, that's exactly what it is."

"People are dying."

Kennedy raised a hand and nodded. "You're right, you're right. Although people have always died, people always will, it's what they do."

"People are being crushed."

"They always have been. It's up to them to do something about it if they don't like it."

"It isn't a game for them."

"Chess wouldn't work without pawns."

"Jesus, Joe."

Kennedy put his glass on the arm of the settee, then shifted slightly in his seat, pulling his jacket from under him.

"Why did you get into politics, Allen?"

"I'm a diplomat."

"Ah, don't give me that shit; seriously, I don't want to hear it. There is no such thing as a diplomat. A diplomat is just a politician who is scared to voice his own opinion."

"Speak for yourself, Joe."

Kennedy shook his head and looked back out the window. The light from the window bounced off his glasses, making his eyes hard to see.

"You're not seeing the bigger picture, Allen, which is the sad thing for me; you're just not getting it."

"Getting it?"

"The world is changing. Politics, diplomacy, people, all of it, the whole thing is changing."

"I see that, Joe."

"No, you don't. You think you do, but you don't. President Lindbergh? He gets it, I get it, Washington gets it, and the American people get it, but you don't. You and the people behind you, you just don't get it. The fascists have won, and they did us a favor on the way to victory, when they saw off Stalin with his communists and his Jews. Okay, we've got Hitler to deal with now, and I'll grant you he is a . . . a curious man, but he wants to be our friend. He needs America. We're brothers. And this is the thing I want you to remember, the thing you don't understand: we need him."

"America needs Hitler?"

"You're damn right we do." Kennedy leaned forward and lifted a finger toward Dulles. "He's showing us how to get things done. He's showing us how to deal with those who don't work for what is best for the country."

"Like who?"

"The communists, the colored, and the kikes. The bastards working behind the scenes, those who want to undo what has taken us generations to get right. He's shown us how to deal with them."

"By locking them up and throwing away the key? By killing them?"

"Yes!" Kennedy held out the palms of his hands, and for a moment Dulles thought he was going to knock the Scotch onto the floor. "It's for the good of the country, for the good of the people. Hitler and Lindbergh know what is for the best."

"Taking away freedom?"

"Oh, come on, Allen." Kennedy sat back again, picking up his drink. "Freedom? What is it, really? You think those Brits out there feel any worse off under Mosley than they did under Chamberlain?" Kennedy was pointing with the Scotch toward the window, and Dulles looked out, even though he knew what was there.

"The rich are still rich and the poor are still poor. Only difference is there is nobody trying to spoil that balance."

"They were free under Chamberlain."

"You sure about that?"

"They could vote him out if they didn't like him."

"And vote another one in to take his place. You've seen them. They're all the same. How many of those guys swept the streets before they got elected?"

Dulles didn't reply.

"Yeah . . . that many. At least with Hitler and Mosley at the helm they know where they stand."

"What about us then, Joe? Would you have the same for America? President for Life Lindbergh?"

"I can think of worst things. America would be working, people would have their place, they'd have their lives, and their future would be secure. The country would be secure, run by people who knew what they were doing."

Dulles shook his head as Kennedy continued, lowering his voice slightly. "You've been to Germany; you've seen how it is there. The new Berlin is taking shape. People are happy, now that things are settling down."

"You really believe that, Joe?"

"I've seen it!"

"What about the rest of Europe and Africa? Does that look happy to you?"

"You have to give things time. People will find a level as they adjust." Kennedy waved his hand toward the window. "Once they know their place, they'll settle into it."

"You're wrong, Joe. People will never settle into it."

"They will, they already are. Oh, sure, you're going to have your troublemakers, I understand that, but if enough people get the message . . ." Kennedy removed his glasses and gestured at Dulles with them. "If we can show them what we want, push it till they see the truth, till they understand that we know best . . . they'll do what they have to and thank us for our work. We just need everyone at the top to be on board. Which, I'm afraid, brings me to you."

Kennedy polished his glasses with his tie and then put them back on. He picked up his Scotch, sipped it, and carefully placed it back on the arm of the couch.

"I've spoken to Washington. As you can imagine, they are very unhappy; they want you home on the next flight. You've opened a can of worms over here, made it very difficult for us, so I need you to tell me what the situation is, so I can try to close this down and patch things up."

Dulles looked at the carpet and gave a slight shake of his head; he chewed his bottom lip and then turned back to Kennedy.

"I'm not saying anything."

"The operation is dead in the water, Allen."

"America needs that scientist."

"But not the trouble she will cause."

"We can't fall behind."

"We aren't under threat." Kennedy raised his voice for the first time. "Don't you see that? Germany is our friend; you're making them our enemy. You are the enemy, you and the people behind you. Lindbergh wants the Germans, needs the Germans as an ally, and allies don't steal secrets from each other."

"I'm sorry, Joe, I truly am, but I'm not telling you anything."

"You're going to leave Frank King spinning in the wind?"

"Frank's a good man. He'll find a way."

"A way to what? He can't go home; he can't come back into the embassy. What is he going to do with this scientist, build a goddamned bomb in a hotel room and threaten Hitler with it?"

"He can go to Canada," Dulles said quietly.

Kennedy chuckled. "You think the government in exile will help him? The British resistance blew you out of the water; it was them who told me what was going on."

"Canada will see her importance."

"You're a fool, Allen."

"I believe in democracy, Joe. I believe in the Constitution."

"Like I said . . . you're a fool."

"WHO IS SPEAKING, please?"

"Just connect me to Allen Dulles."

"May I ask what the call is in connection with, and who is speaking?"

King looked out the window of the call box, and then back at pile of damp phone books on the shelf in front of him.

He'd been calling Dulles's private numbers for over a year, and not once had someone ever asked him what the call was in connection with. King either spoke directly to Dulles or was put through to his private flat if he wasn't in his office.

Something was wrong.

"Who is this?" King asked, trying to keep his voice steady.

"Finch, embassy security. Who am I speaking to, and what is your call in connection with?"

Frank King slammed the phone receiver down, then picked it up and then slammed it down again. He rested his forehead in his hands and then drew them slowly down his face as if scraping thick paint from his skin.

Embassy security asking questions at Allen Dulles's apartment meant Allen Dulles was answering questions somewhere else.

Frank King was alone.

He turned ninety degrees and rested his back against the windows of the phone box, his hands now hanging by their fingertips from his jaw as the cold glass pressed against the crown of his head.

He was finished.

He sighed, dropped his hands, and shook his head.

No.

He was never finished.

He took a deep breath, filled his lungs, held it, then took some more change for the phone out of his pocket.

He listened for the tone and then dialed the guard room number at the embassy. It rang once. He breathed out, steadied himself, breathed in, and smiled.

"Guard room."

King recognized the voice as belonging to an old salt of a marine sergeant named Bob Fisher.

"Fisher? It's Frank King, I'm trying to get hold of Allen Dulles but I can't get an answer on his line. Do you know where he is?" King kept on smiling, letting his expression lighten his voice.

There was a pause.

"People are looking for you, sir."

"Yeah . . . I know that, I need to speak to Dulles to sort things out."

"Umm, I haven't seen or heard of him today, sir."

"You don't sound too certain there, Bob."

"People have left messages for you, sir. Pretty urgent messages."

The smile slipped a little on King's face. "What people?"

"Umm, pretty much everyone, sir, from the ambassador's office down."

"What about?"

"I don't know, sir. I was told to let you know about the messages and that's all."

"Hey, come on, Bob. Nothing happens in that place without you knowing what's going on." King had made a career on developing relationships, all the way down and all the way up the chain of command. He was everyone's pal, everyone's buddy in the bar, and he hoped all those drinks he'd bought would start paying off.

They did.

Fisher lowered his voice. "It's a rumor sir, just a rumor, but I heard Mr. Dulles is under house arrest."

"What?" The smile was now most definitely gone.

"It's just what I heard; they took a squad over there an hour ago."

"They?"

"The ambassador, Captain Bryan, and some men, they all went over to his apartment."

"Why?"

"I've no idea, sir, and you never heard that from me, okay?"

"They want to speak to me?"

"Bryan telephoned down here himself, sir, said if you were to call, we were to tell you to come in right away." Fisher was whispering now.

King turned his head an inch and looked out the window of the call box at the people passing by.

"Dulles is at his apartment?"

"You never heard this from me, sir."

"Is Dulles at his apartment?"

"Yes, sir."

"With the ambassador?"

"I think so."

"Who is in his office?"

"They posted some men on the door, sir."

King ran his free hand over the top of his hair, then rested it on the shelf in the call box.

"Okay, thanks, Bob."

"Are you coming in, sir? Shall I tell them you're on your way?"

"I gotta go, Bob. Stay safe." King put down the phone and stared at it. A million thoughts bottlenecked in his brain. He felt a fluttering in his chest, which lifted and then sunk to his stomach.

He breathed out, turned his head, and watched a shopkeeper shoveling snow away from the front door of his business. More snow was falling, settling quickly on the freshly exposed walk, making the shopkeeper struggle in a losing battle.

Frank King knew how he felt.

King used the last of his change to call Dulles's private number again. It rang once.

"Hello?"

"Put the ambassador on."

"Who is this?"

"Put him on the goddamn phone, Bryan!" King shouted and then looked up at the shopkeeper, who had paused at the sound coming from the callbox. King did a half turn, presenting his back to the shopkeeper and lowering his head.

"Who is this?" Kennedy sounded calm and in control. Frank realized it was only the second time they had spoken directly in all the time he had been at the embassy.

"Sir, this is Frank King."

"Hello, Frank. Where are you?"

"I'm in a call box in London, sir."

"Whereabouts?"

"In London, sir."

There was a pause, and for some reason King imagined Kennedy smiling.

"What can I do for you, Frank?"

"Sir, I think I'm involved in something that has gotten out of hand."

"I heard something along those lines, Frank."

"I've been working on a . . . a project for Mr. Dulles, and, uh, I may have drifted out of the loop, sir."

"You have, Frank."

"I'm wondering what I can do about that, sir."

Kennedy paused before answering.

"You and Mr. Dulles have broken the law, Frank. You two have been plotting with God knows who to destabilize the relationship between the United States, Great Britain, and Germany. I don't know who put Dulles up to this, but they have left you seriously out on a limb. You understand that?"

"I was following orders, sir."

"You were conspiring, Frank. You knew what you were doing was wrong. Some people would say you were acting against your government's best interest, and that's treason, so don't take me for a fool."

"No, sir."

"You're a good guy, Frank. I have some sympathy for what you were doing, son, but you were doing it the wrong way. There is a lot at stake here, do you understand?"

"I was—"

Kennedy interrupted. "You need to come in so we can sort this out."

"I . . . I don't know if I can do that, sir."

"You can't stay out there forever, Frank."

"Sir, I need some guarantees. I don't deserve to . . ."

"Frank, you are embarrassing me, and you are not in a position to ask for anything. You gentlemen have left us exposed here at a time when our country cannot afford it. Do you understand?"

"I do, sir."

"You could get shot for this."

"Sir, I was . . ."

"Where are you up to with this whole scheme?"

"The matter is still in hand, sir," King lied.

"It is not, so don't try to bullshit me. The British resistance have the kid you kidnapped, they've told me themselves. You lost her, didn't you?"

"As I said, sir, the matter is in hand." King clenched a fist and slowly drove it into his own forehead as he struggled to keep his voice steady.

The line popped and hissed while King waited for Kennedy's next move. Finally the ambassador spoke.

"I am aware of the scientist and what you were doing; Mr. Dulles has explained the reasons for this clusterfuck. I am also aware of her importance to Germany. It might surprise you, but I have some . . . sympathy with what you were trying to do." Kennedy paused again, and when he continued his voice was lower, softer. "The way I see it, you have no choices, son. Come in now, and you get shipped home with Dulles to face the music. You forget what you've been mixed up in, try to save your career, yours and the kid, what's his name . . . Cook?"

King touched the back of his knuckles to his mouth and lowered his head before replying.

"Cook's dead, sir."

"How?" Kennedy finally asked.

"Brit resistance, sir."

"Were you there?"

"Things got out of hand."

"How many?"

"A few, sir. I'm sorry."

"Come in, Frank, before you totally fuck up the whole U.S.-German relationship single-handedly."

"What about Koehler's daughter?"

"Forget her; she's not your problem."

"The British, they'll kill her."

"Like you killed her mother?"

"That was an accident."

"No, Frank, that was two idiots with guns, and you were one of them. Forget the girl and come in."

"There is the scientist, sir, she's very important to America. She can help us . . ."

"King, you have no idea what is at stake here!" Kennedy was shouting now. "We've got a government in America that wants to get closer to the Germans, not upset them. Dulles was wrong to lead you down this route." Kennedy subsided slightly. "Jesus, son, trade is at stake here, not just your career; we're talking billions of dollars, and you could blow it out of the water."

"They could blow us out the water if we leave them the scientist."

"Forget that, it isn't your problem."

"If they have a superbomb and we don't, they'll walk all over us, sir."

"Get your ass in here now. That is a direct fucking order. You're going home, do you hear me?"

"Yes, sir."

"Okay," Kennedy took a deep breath. "All right, go to the embassy and wait for me there." He hung up.

King slowly placed the receiver in the cradle and then pushed open the door of the call box. He stood in the falling snow a moment, then climbed back into the car he'd stolen earlier.

He thought about Eric Cook.

He closed his eyes and lifted his head slightly, breathing out through his mouth, letting his chin drop to his chest.

"Poor kid," he said softly. "Poor kid didn't deserve that."

King thought of Cook's face, eyes fluttering, his blood in the snow. King shook his head. He needed to think clearly. He couldn't afford to dwell on the past, not now. Maybe later, maybe never, but not now.

He wanted a cigarette badly.

He looked at the shopkeeper, who was watching him back.

King started the car, checked over his shoulder, then pulled away from the curb. London was still quiet, heavy clouds pushing down with each gust of wind seeming to shake another shower of snow down from the sky.

He shivered, drifting across the city, not heading for the embassy, not just yet. He had a feeling he was experiencing his last hours of freedom, at least for some time to come. He drove on, not knowing where he was going, lost in thought.

Once Dulles's backers in Washington knew the plot was blown they'd disappear into the shadows from where they had come, leaving him and Dulles to carry the can in the courtroom.

Kennedy was right. They were an embarrassment.

Maybe he and Dulles wouldn't make it to a courtroom.

It would be easier for the government if they didn't; maybe they'd end up in one of the camps he'd heard were being built in the Midwest.

He stopped at some lights and looked around. The bright white snow was losing its luster. London was slowly turning back to the same old gray, grimy shithole the occupation had turned it into a few years before.

The only color he could see was red.

A red traffic light and a sodden red swastika flag, waving on a four-story building.

King wondered what Washington would look like if the Nazis had a bomb. Would the same bloodred flag hang low over the White House?

The lights changed and he pulled away slowly, no direction in his mind. He drifted to a halt at another set of lights less than one hundred yards down the road, and looked around for a tobacconist.

Then he saw her: a young woman, stopped on the street corner by two Germans and a British HDT foot patrol. The woman was presenting papers. Her head was down; she was looking at the heavy boots on her feet. Men's boots, too big for the spindly bare legs that sprouted from the top of them.

She was holding a shawl over her shoulders, and one of the Germans grabbed it and dragged it from her, half turning her before she let go. The German dropped the shawl into the gutter and the young woman stared at it, too scared to look up. The German jabbed at the star of David on her chest, the mark that had been covered by the shawl she had been using to shelter from the snow.

She finally said something, and the HDT hit her. A backhanded slap, hard across the mouth. She fell, down into the gutter, next to the shawl, and her papers fluttered to the ground next to her.

Frank King felt the blow that knocked her down.

He opened the car door. He heard someone beeping their horn because the lights had changed, but he ignored them. He walked toward the HDT with his hand in his pocket, his knuckles brushing his pistol.

The Germans watched him approaching. One of them unshipped the MP40 he was carrying from his shoulder, as the other held out his hand.

"Stop!" the German shouted.

Frank King leaned down to the girl in the gutter. "Are you all right?"

She didn't answer.

"Get away. This is nothing to do with you," the HDT man said to King, who ignored him.

"Papers." The German with the MP40 held out his hand.

King looked at him.

"Papers!" the German shouted this time.

King took his hand out of his pocket, brushing the pistol again. He wanted to kill them all. He held out his ID, watching the flicker of uncertainty that often clouded the eyes of bullies who no longer were in charge.

"This is nothing to do with you." The HDT sounded less confident now.

"Can you get up?" King asked the girl on the ground, stretching out his hand.

"Please leave me," she said quietly. She looked away. She didn't want his help.

A car horn sounded again, and King lowered his hand.

He figured that she was too scared to stand up in case they knocked her down again once he was gone. He couldn't always be there for her; by helping now he was making it worse, unless he helped forever.

And he couldn't.

He was just one man. What good could one man do?

He straightened up and looked at the men in front of him.

"You must be proud," he said quietly.

"She was hiding what she is. It is against the law," said the HDT man, handing back King's ID.

"She was trying to keep warm."

"She was breaking the law."

Another horn. The lights had changed again. Frank looked at the girl, who slowly turned to face him. The whites of her eyes were yellowish and looked too big for her face.

"Please," she mouthed, and King saw her teeth were the same color as her eyes.

He felt useless, and turned away without looking at the men. His car seemed much farther away than it had been a moment before; the sound of the snow crunching under his feet seemed louder.

He slammed the car door and stared at the red light. It changed, and so did Frank King.

He'd get the scientist.

Kennedy was wrong. America did need her.

One man might not be able to make a difference, but one man had to try.

CHAPTER 28

THE BREEZE WAS picking up. Rossett's cheeks burned as the cold air brushed his face above the raised collar of his greatcoat. In his immediate vicinity were a pub, a boarded-up post office, eight or nine small cottages, a telephone box, and four roads heading off in different directions.

He was at a crossroads.

The problem was, he didn't know which way to go. Back in the run-up to the invasion the government, desperately clutching at straws, had called on the public to remove signposts to confuse any German invader who had forgotten to bring his map.

Rossett wasn't a German invader, but he had forgotten to bring a map.

He looked back down the road he had driven up. The thin tire tracks his Austin had plowed were the only sign anyone was still on the face of the earth. In the distance were beautifully white snow-covered fields dotted with lifeless trees and low black hedgerows.

Movement caught his eye in the hamlet. Rossett turned his head and watched a farm laborer, with a long double-barreled shotgun broken over his arm, emerge from the pub, pulling an old British army overcoat across his stomach and chest. He kept his head down, doing his best to avoid looking at the stranger watching him from across the road. Rossett lifted his hand in greeting. The other man ducked his head in a miserable attempt to ignore him, pulling the coat tighter still over his bulky frame and adjusting the shotgun.

Rossett watched as the man, staying close to the building line, walked along the row of cottages before opening the door of the final one and going inside. The door slammed so hard, Rossett heard it from fifty yards away.

He looked around the village, checked that the roads around were still empty, and then walked slowly to the same cottage.

The door shook in its frame as he knocked on it with his fist. He turned and checked the Austin.

A strong gust of wind caused him to lower his face and shield his eyes as it whipped snow across the road toward him. He turned back to the door as he heard the handle turning.

A tiny sparrow of an old lady stood before him. The skin hung off her face as if it had been stretched and left there to dry. She was wearing a blue woolen cardigan with a two-inch frayed hole on its left breast. As soon as she saw who had knocked, she instinctively reached up to cover the hole before taking a step backward deferentially.

Rossett twitched a smile; aware that he was crowding the old woman, he dipped his head slightly and looked into the tiny sitting room behind her.

"Hello."

She didn't speak.

"The gentleman who has just arrived, I'd like to speak to him?"

The old lady fiddled with her cardigan.

Rossett showed her his police warrant card.

She stepped off to the side.

Rossett ducked his head and entered the cottage, seeming to fill the tiny space as he waited for the old lady to close the door and join him.

He took off his hat as she shuffled past him, taking up station at the crackling log fire. There was another door in the wall opposite him, made of rough wood, with inch-wide gaps at the bottom and top.

Rossett pointed to it.

"There?"

The old lady nodded, still clutching the hole in her cardigan.

Rossett crossed the room in two steps and lifted the simple latch on the door. He found himself entering a kitchen barely bigger than the living room. The man was standing at the sink, back to him, washing a dead bald bird under the solitary banging cold water tap that hung over the middle of the white enamel sink.

"Who was it?" the man asked without looking around.

"Me," Rossett replied.

The man spun quickly for his size. He was still wearing his coat, but now it hung open over high-waisted woolen trousers belted with string. His purple jumper, too short to cover his belly, was full of holes. Through it Rossett could see some gray material that he guessed was a pair of long johns.

Times were most definitely hard.

The man dropped the bird in his hand onto the floor, where it landed with a sad thud. He looked down at it, then back up at Rossett, with a jaw as slack as that of the bird below him.

"Hello."

"Hullo, sir," the man replied dumbly, with a thick country accent.

"What is your name?" Rossett held up his warrant card, then dropped it back into his pocket.

"Reg."

"Reg?"

"Yes, sir."

"Have you been poaching, Reg?"

Reg looked at the two rabbits and the three unplucked birds on the counter next to the sink, then nodded.

Rossett heard the sniff of a worried mother behind him.

"Where did you get the birds and the rabbits?"

"Out on Hargreaves Farm. He breeds them for the game season, *sir*." Rossett realized that the man was a simpleton.

"He don't mean nothing, sir. We needs them for food," the old lady said behind Rossett, who half turned and nodded.

"Where is the shotgun?"

Reg lifted a fat finger and pointed to the wall over Rossett's left shoulder. Rossett followed the finger and saw the long-barreled shotgun resting on two hooks above a wooden chest of drawers.

"The shells?"

"In the drawer, *sir*."

Rossett backed toward the shotgun and took it down; he opened the breech and saw that it was empty, and looked at Reg before pointing at the cupboard.

Reg read the signal.

"Top drawer there, sir."

Rossett opened the drawer and saw two boxes of shells, one of bird shot, the other of buckshot, for larger game.

He slipped the lid off the buckshot and loaded two cartridges, clicking the shotgun shut with a solid crack.

Reg looked like large game.

The gun was agricultural but well maintained. It was the side-by-side configuration, with the barrels next to each other. Rossett held it with one hand for a moment, testing its balance.

"How much do you want for this gun?"

Reg tilted his head and looked at his mother before looking back at Rossett.

"Wha'?"

"How much do you want for the gun?"

"I needs it."

Rossett frowned and looked at the old lady, ending negotiations with Reg.

"How much?"

The old lady's eyes narrowed. She looked at the battered shotgun.

"Forty pounds."

"Remember, I have hold of it, and it is loaded," Rossett said quietly.

"Thirty," she said.

"Try again."

"Twenty-five?"

The old lady ran a thin pink tongue across her bottom lip as Rossett frowned.

"Twenty."

"Done." Rossett knew the money would buy enough food for both her and Reg for the winter.

"Do you have a toolshed, Reg?"

"Yes, *sir*."

"Show me."

Reg wiped his hands on his stomach and licked his lips, looking at his mother, who had taken Rossett's place in the doorway. She nodded vigorously that he should do as he was told, so the big man lolloped across the kitchen to the back door of the cottage and went outside.

Rossett picked up the two boxes of ammunition and followed. At the door he turned back to look at Reg's mother.

"We keep this quiet?"

"As long as you give me the money we do." Her eyes shone.

Outside Rossett found Reg standing next to a battered wooden shed that seemed about to collapse under the weight of the snow on its roof. The big man didn't appear to be able to look up to meet Rossett's eyes.

"Open it."

Reg did as he was told and held out a wavering hand as if inviting Rossett to enter. Rossett stepped into the shed, smelling the wood that was stacked against the far wall.

"Do you have a hacksaw?"

"Yes, sir."

Rossett blinked.

"Where is it?"

Reg got the message. He dragged out a heavy toolbox from beneath the narrow workbench, opened the lid, and rummaged among the rusted tools before pulling out an old hacksaw and handing it to Rossett.

Rossett stroked the blade with his thumb and was relieved to feel the teeth were sharp. He unlocked the shotgun, removed the two cartridges, locked it, and laid it on the bench. He measured the barrel with the blade and then made to start cutting.

Reg coughed behind him and Rossett turned to look at him.

"You don't own it yet, sir," the big man mumbled, still looking at the floor.

Rossett sighed, laid down the hacksaw, and took out his wallet, from which he produced two ten-pound notes; he waved Reg away with the money before starting to cut the barrel. It took a solid ten minutes of work, and he could feel the sweat under his clothes when the end of the barrel finally detached and clattered onto the floor.

Rossett stepped back from the bench, balancing the shotgun in his hand, feeling how the weight had changed. He took down an old wood saw from a nail and scythed through the stock of the gun, removing so much that he was barely left with a pistol grip. He looked in the toolbox and found an old wood drill, with which he bored a hole in the stock.

He cut through a length of twine and tied the string through the hole. He removed his coat and jacket and then hung the shotgun over his shoulder so that it sat under his arm against his body. He adjusted the string so that the end of the barrel slipped into his trouser pocket an inch, holding it in place and stopping it from swinging free.

Rossett put on his jacket and coat then and then practiced drawing the shotgun a couple of times.

Once he was satisfied with the action, he emptied the box of shells into various pockets.

He tried the draw one final time and then turned to the door.

Reg was watching him, hands in pockets, head tilted, taking in what he had just seen.

"You ain't going poachin'," Reg said.

"You don't need to worry about where I'm going."

Reg smiled, nodded, and held out a hand, which Rossett shook.

"Good luck," said Reg, still smiling.

CHAPTER 29

ANJA HAD BEEN doing a lot of thinking for the last few hours. Time had ticked slowly in the little room where she had been stowed. She'd sat, hands tucked into her armpits for warmth, on an old office chair, trying to ignore the stare of the man sitting opposite her, breathing heavily through his nose even though his mouth was open.

All day she had tried not to think about her mother.

All day she had failed.

She had fought to push the sound of her mother's voice, the sound of the shot, and the sound of the sordid splash of the river to the back of her mind as far as it would go.

But the memories wouldn't stay there.

A minute later, or in the blink of an eye, she felt her mother's fingers on her face, heard the shot, saw the light going out, and felt alone all over again.

She shook her head.

She couldn't afford this, not now; there would be a time to grieve, but now wasn't it.

Anja had studied the cast-iron-framed window and its dirty glass. The glass had a fine wire mesh running through it, and she doubted she could smash it and break through quickly enough to get away. Even if she did, she had no idea of what lay beyond. For all she knew she would be trapped in another room, or even find herself dropping into Sterling's lap.

Whoever he was.

She thought about Sterling.

She knew that hearing his name had been a bad thing; she had read it in the faces of those around her when the policeman had blurted it out.

She knew what they were going to do with her.

They were going to kill her; they couldn't afford to do anything else.

Unless she did something about it first.

Anja looked at the big man at the door, who stared back at her with slow blinks and a dull expression.

She smiled at him.

He blinked again.

She went back to looking at the window, trying to decide if the man at the door would be harder to get through than the glass in the frame.

There was a knock, the door opened, and Jack entered. He looked at Anja and then at the heavy.

"Sterling wants to see you in the yard at the back," Jack said.

"Me?" said the mouth-breather.

"Yeah."

"What about her?"

"I'm to wait with her."

The mouth-breather looked at Jack, then at Anja, and then at Jack again before slowly unfolding his arms, uncertain.

"What does he want?"

"You."

"In the yard?"

"Yes."

"Why?"

"Because that's where he is."

The mouth-breather frowned and stood up; he clenched one fist as he considered what Jack had said.

"He wants me now?" he finally said.

"Oh, for God's sake . . . yes, he wants to see you now," Jack said impatiently.

The mouth-breather looked at Anja again.

"Will she be all right?"

"She's not going anywhere."

"With you I mean. Will she be all right with you?"

"Yeah, she's just a girl," Jack replied, stepping back from the door and holding it open wider.

The mouth-breather scratched his top lip and then nodded.

"I won't be long. Shout if you need me, yeah?"

"Yeah."

The mouth-breather left the room, and Jack shut the door behind him.

He quickly turned and rested his ear against it.

"Just a girl?" Anja said. Jack waved his hand at her to be quiet.

A second passed and it suddenly struck Anja what was going on. She leaned forward and the chair wobbled under her.

"What are you doing?"

Jack waved his hand once more, then opened the door an inch or two and looked out before turning back to Anja.

"I think they are going to kill you. We need—"

Anja was already out of her seat and crossing the room. She reached the door and dragged Jack to one side before sticking her head out into the corridor.

"Are you coming?" She turned to look at Jack, and he bit his lip and flicked his head to shift the hair out of his eyes.

"I don't know."

Anja was already off down the corridor on tiptoes, moving quickly on the scuffed and dusty concrete floor through the succession of glass doors that she had come through earlier.

She reached the final door and pulled it open an inch as Jack appeared next to her. Anja looked at him and he nodded.

He was coming.

She was about to step through when Jack placed a hand on her arm and pointed to his chest that he should go first. Anja frowned, shook free her arm, and set off quickly out of the office block and into the high-roofed warehouse, where the cars still sat some fifty feet away.

Jack followed her.

Anja looked over her shoulder at Jack and then pointed at the doors to the warehouse. He nodded and then indicated he was heading toward the cars. Anja ran across and pulled one of the doors open wide enough for a car to get through, then ran back to Jack, who was leaning through the driver's window of one of the two cars. He emerged with some keys, held them up, and waved her over to the second car.

Anja heard the engine start and the passenger door opened just before she reached it. She leaned forward to look in; Jack smiled at her and revved the engine. His white teeth shone from his oily face, and he flicked his head again to shake off his fringe.

"You can drive this?"

"If I can fix 'em I can bleedin' well drive 'em! Come on, let's get out of here!"

Anja smiled and jumped in as Jack enthusiastically revved the engine.

The car stalled with a sudden jolt, and silence filled the warehouse.

They looked at each other and Jack's smile disappeared. He started the car again and Anja looked over her shoulder through the back window.

Jack revved, the car jolted forward, the car stalled.

"Jack, please," Anja said turning to look at him.

Jack flicked his hair again and looked down at his feet as he fired the engine, revved it fiercely, and then stalled again.

The door of the office block behind them opened and the mouth-breather emerged. He stared at the cars, unsure, before shouting back over his shoulder to the offices. Anja heard him call for help before he started to run toward them.

"Please, Jack," Anja said, looking at the door of the car, trying to figure out how to lock it.

The car started once more and Jack looked at his feet again, revving the engine hard as the mouth-breather sped up to a sprint.

"Please!"

The car revved, seemed to dip, half stall and then revved again.

"Handbrake!" Anja shouted, realizing the problem.

His hands lifted off the wheel as he looked around for the lever; he fumbled down the side of his seat.

The mouth-breather made it to the rear door of the car on Anja's side.

She heard the door handle rattling and she looked up into the dull eyes she'd been staring at all afternoon. The man pulled back his arm, balling a ham of a fist, making ready to punch through her window.

Anja closed her eyes.

The car shot forward, wheels spinning and screaming on the smooth concrete before they gripped with a squeal, then the car shot forward toward the exit.

The mouth-breather shouted.

Anja opened her eyes, already spinning in her seat to watch the mouth-breather through the back window. He reached around behind him, then brought a heavy pistol to bear.

The shot echoed around the warehouse.

The back window shattered in an explosion of glass. The gun boomed again and both Jack and Anja ducked low as they heard the round hit the bodywork.

The engine was screaming in first gear as they made their way toward the exit. Jack's foot was hard down on the accelerator.

Anja had slipped down into the footwell, and she looked up to see Jack crouching, barely able to see over the steering wheel as he wrestled with it in both hands.

Another shot, then another. The car jerked left, bounced up hard into the air and then down again. There was a crash of scraping metal and then they jerked right, this time less violently. Anja braced herself with a hand under the dashboard as they hit a curb. Finally Jack remembered second gear and shifted with a crunch.

Anja heard another shot, and then she realized they were outside the warehouse.

Jack whooped and looked down at her.

"Did you see that? Did you? Oh wow! Ha ha!"

Anja smiled, then found herself laughing as Jack selected another gear and the car picked up speed. She pulled herself up and looked behind her.

The back window was shot through; it was almost completely shattered, giving her a clear view of the road.

The snow was thick on the road, and all around them were high, dark buildings that looked like more warehouses. She turned to look out the front window and saw there were two bullet holes in it.

Jack fumbled with some switches and eventually the headlamps came on. There were no other vehicles around and the warehouses looked empty. Jack slowed slightly, skidded in the snow around a corner, pushing and pulling the big steering wheel, then accelerated again.

"Where are we?" Anja shouted over the noise of the engine and the wind blowing through the broken windows, glancing at Jack and then craning to look up at the buildings as they went past.

"We're out east." He looked at Anja and noted her confused face. "The East End of London. Miles from anywhere, really. I need to get you to the center, near to the ring of steel where you'll be safe, see if we can find some Germans and hand you over."

"Thank you," Anja said. Jack looked across and smiled.

"It ain't nothing. I couldn't leave you, could I?"

Anja smiled back and ran her hand through her hair. She opened the window, lifting her head to the onrushing wind.

Enjoying the freedom and the fresh air, letting it intoxicate her.

She closed her eyes and laughed, shaking her head, feeling the chill on her cheeks. She opened her eyes and looked at Jack, shouting over the wind, "What are you going to do?"

"Get you to safety, like I said."

"No, after that. What are you going to do?"

Jack glanced at her and then back to the road.

"I'll think of something. I don't know, something will turn up." He smiled at her again, a little less brightly than before.

Anja frowned, turned her head to the wind again for a second, then closed the window halfway.

"My father will help you. He's a good man, he'll help you."

Jack nodded, wanting to believe Anja.

They drove in silence for a few minutes, slight shock setting in.

It was Jack who noticed the wobble in the car's steering, moments before Anja did. She looked at him and saw that the steering wheel was shaking in his hands.

"What is it?"

"I don't know, it's like . . . I don't know," Jack replied as the shaking grew worse and he had to slow the car to compensate.

A sudden loud rhythmic banging began. It felt as if it was coming up under

Anja's feet. The wheel was dodging right and left in Jack's hands, at least four inches either way.

He pulled into the curb, and as the car drew to a halt Anja saw that Jack was unable to stop the wheel turning. The whole car seemed to weave before hitting the pavement and finally bouncing up onto it.

Jack was out of the car in a flash.

Anja pulled the handle on her door to get out but found that it wouldn't move. She scooted across to the driver's side and followed Jack out onto the street, then around to the damaged side of the car.

She didn't have to be a mechanic to see the problem.

The front passenger side wheel was leaning into the wheel arch drunkenly, at well over a twenty-degree angle.

The wheel arch and front door were gouged, a deep two-inch-wide scar that had exposed the silver metal underneath.

Anja instinctively looked back to where they had just come from, then crouched down with Jack to inspect the damage more closely.

"I'll jack up the car and have a look," Jack said uncertainly.

"We haven't time," replied Anja, already looking back down the road for any cars that might be following.

"I think the front spring has snapped; it must have happened when I hit the wall."

"What wall?" Anja looked at Jack, who pointed at the gouge in the side of the car.

"That wall."

She nodded, then stood up.

"Let's find a telephone and call the police."

Jack looked up at her.

"You met the police this morning. They are what got you into this in the first place. We can't trust them. Anyway, there won't be a phone round here for miles. Let's see how far we get on this wheel. I think I know a place that will help us."

Anja looked at the car uncertainly and then nodded.

She didn't have much choice.

THEY BARELY MANAGED to extract another mile out of the car before the wheel gave up the ghost. It slammed up into the arch with a crash and a lurch and they skidded to a halt on a deserted street just south of Stratford.

There was no point in inspecting the car when they got out. They abandoned it in the middle of the road and took off holding hands, running along a side street that was silent and lit by dirty yellow streetlamps.

"Do you know where we are?" Anja said as they slowed to a walk. She was looking at the darkened houses that sat squat and orange bricked on either side of the narrow street. All drawn curtains and smoking chimneys.

Jack didn't answer but kept walking, a half step in front of Anja, leading her forward by her hand.

"Maybe we should knock at a house and ask for help?" Anja tried again.

"Just keep walking."

"Where are we going?

Jack stopped. "It don't matter where we are going, all right? We're just putting distance between us and them."

"But they don't have a car. We took their keys."

"How long do you think it would take for my boss to get that other car going? He's been a mechanic all his bleedin' life; he could start that old thing with a spoon. He'll try to take his time, but sooner or later they'll be after us."

Anja turned and looked down the street they had walked along. She saw tracks in the snow, dark shadows, a record of every step.

Their tracks.

The only tracks in the street.

She looked at the far end of the road and saw the car abandoned with its headlamps still shining, like a stranded black lighthouse.

"They can follow our footprints from the car," she said softly. Jack followed her gaze and then looked back at her, gently pulling her hand toward him.

"We need to get going."

Anja glanced at the houses all around as they started to move again. The houses seemed warm, safe, inviting, full of happy families and hot food.

"We can knock on a front door; someone will take us in."

"Which one do you fancy?" Jack lifted a finger and pointed at one of the houses with welcoming lights behind thick curtains. "That one?"

Anja followed his finger and then nodded.

"Yes."

"Problem is, that one might have a mum and dad who lost a son when the Germans invaded France. What about that one?" He pointed at another house but didn't wait for an answer. "Then again, that one might have a dad who had his leg blown off in the Great War. What about that one? Oh, hang on, that one might have two boys who have been sent to work in Europe on one of the grain farms. What about that one, where their son has been conscripted and sent out to fight in the east? Or that one, or that one, or that one?"

Jack stopped suddenly and looked at Anja. "We can't knock at any of these houses, or any house anywhere, because they all bleedin' hate you. So keep moving until we can figure out where we are."

Jack turned and stalked off. Anja realized he had let go of her hand. Her head dropped and she felt the weight of the tears she'd been holding back.

She had to hold on.

She looked back at the car, shook her head, and followed Jack.

She caught up quickly as he marched, hands buried in his pockets, silently ignoring her. Their breath misted the air between them and the streetlamps. They didn't speak for at least five minutes as street after street of the same tiny terraced houses went by.

The air smelled of smoke, and a few restless flakes of snow started to drift down out of the blackness, causing both Anja and Jack to look up into the night sky as they walked.

"The snow would be good, it'll cover our tracks," Anja said, and although Jack didn't reply, he did take her hand again.

They reached a main road with darkened shops and a set of traffic lights that changed every few seconds, even though there wasn't a car in sight.

Jack looked up at the building behind him.

Anja followed his gaze and read the sign out loud.

"Romford Road. Do you know it?"

"I think so; my old man is from round here."

"Your old man?"

"My dad."

"Can we go there?"

"He's dead . . . the war."

"I'm sorry."

Anja stared at the dirty streetlamps and the sooty houses. The smoke coming from their chimneys made the falling snow look dirty. She looked at Jack with his oily hands, greasy hair, and dirty neck, and realized that he could only have come from a place like this.

Jack ran his hand through his thick hair and stared off down the road.

"I think . . ." He looked left and right again, hand still on head. "We go this way." The hand on his head suddenly shifted position and pointed.

"You think or you know?"

"Do you know?" Jack asked.

"No."

"Well then, this way." Jack set off, tugging Anja behind him.

They walked for fifteen minutes before Jack saw the pub he was looking for. The Rising Sun stood on the corner of a row of shops and a side street. It looked rough, tough, and decidedly uninviting.

"That's it."

"That?" Anja didn't sound convinced.

"Yeah, I know people there. They'll help us. We're going to be all right." Jack turned and smiled at Anja for the first time in what seemed like an age.

Anja forgot the cold, forgot the hunger, forgot the day she had suffered, and found herself smiling back. Maybe she was going home after all.

"You have to wait here by these shops. Stand in the doorway of this one and wait for me, I'll not be long."

Anja looked at the darkened shop and then back at Jack, the smile fading.

"Can't I come with you?"

"No. You'll stand out a mile. People don't know you. You stay here. I promise, I'll not be long."

Anja nodded uncertainly.

"It'll be all right, I promise. Just wait in the shadows."

Jack was off before she could reply. He pulled open the door of the pub and Anja watched as the light from inside shone on him. He looked every inch a fifteen-year-old boy entering a man's world. The noise of the bar leaked out with the light, then faded as the door swung back into place.

She heard the sound of a piano but couldn't recognize the music it was play-ing. It sounded rough, bouncy, a little out of tune, messy, too fast for her liking.

A lot like London itself.

She leaned forward out of the doorway, looked at the pub, and then turned her head the other way to look down the main road.

In the distance she could see headlamps coming toward her slowly, very slowly. Flecked with falling snow, they bobbed and weaved, as the car slithered from rut to rut.

She looked back at the pub, a quiver of panic in her chest, then back at the car, the first she'd seen since they'd left their own crippled vehicle earlier.

She stepped back into the shadows of the doorway as far as she could go, her back against the cold wooden door. It seemed an age before she could make out the sound of the engine, coming closer, traveling slowly, taking its time.

She tried to breathe shallow breaths, in case the steam from her mouth gave her away.

The car drew nearer; it seemed slower. Anja couldn't breathe.

Not now, not when she was so close.

The car went past.

It was a tiny little saloon, with a toad of an old man frantically rubbing at his misted windscreen with the back of his hand.

Anja breathed again. She almost laughed at her own nerves until Jack sud-denly appeared in front of her, causing her to jump with fright.

"You okay?"

"You scared me!" she cried, feeling an urge to throw her arms around him.

He flashed his bright smile at her and flicked his fringe.

"Come with me, we're sorted." He held out his hand and pointed at the pub.

Anja took Jack's hand, feeling its warmth. She followed him to the pub where, at a side door, a girl, maybe two or three years younger than Anja, was waiting for them. She pulled open the door, having to lean back to get the le-verage, and then went inside followed by Jack and Anja. As they walked down a corridor Anja could hear the piano and voices singing along to a song she couldn't understand.

"Why are they singing?" she whispered to Jack.

"Because they're drunk, it's what they do," he replied over his shoulder as the little girl opened another door that led to a flight of stairs. They thumped up the wooden staircase, which took them to a warm kitchen where a large man in an apron was waiting, hands on hips.

"This is Mr. Edwards. He's the manager, and he's going to help us."

Edwards gestured that they should sit at the kitchen table.

"You hungry?"

Anja nodded, scared to speak in case her accent should embarrass them all.

"Yes," replied Jack for her. "We've not eaten all day. I'm starving."

Edwards placed two bowls in front of them, into which he ladled a thick steaming stew from a pot that was burned black up the sides.

He placed the pot back on the stove, then put some rough-cut bread onto the table, along with two spoons and two white enamel mugs full of water.

"Eat." He pointed at Anja's bowl.

"Thank you," she replied softly, picking up the spoon and looking at Jack for confirmation that she was doing the right thing.

She was.

Jack was already tucking into the soup and ripping a chunk of bread with his oily hands. He paused, smiled at Anja, and offered her the bread.

She looked at his hands with their grime-filled lines, smiled back, and took the bread.

"I'll make a call, get someone we can trust down with a car," Edwards said as he wiped his hands on the apron.

"Could we use your telephone to call my father, sir?" said Anja.

"No offense, but I don't want it getting out I'm helping you. I can't risk having Germans turn up here; it wouldn't be good for me. Do you understand?"

"Yes. I'm sorry. Thank you."

Edwards nodded and then spoke to Jack. "I'll make the call, then go back in the bar. If I don't they'll start wondering where I've gone."

"Thanks, Mr. Edwards," Jack replied with a full mouth.

Edwards nodded and then looked at the young girl.

"Get them anything they want and stay with them."

The child nodded and took a seat opposite Anja, staring at her as she ate.

Anja smiled at the girl.

The girl didn't smile back.

CHAPTER 30

ROSSETT WAS HALF frozen as he made his way along an old stone wall to the south of Coton. He was about two hundred yards from the village boundary when he stopped to get his bearings. Behind him, across five hundred yards of open ground, was his car, parked in a small copse of trees well out of sight of the road. To his right was the village, which lay slightly below him in a shallow valley, barely sheltered from the wind, which was gusting in hard from the cold north, making his cheeks ache and his throat dry.

The late afternoon sun had long since sunk tiredly over to his right. He had moved across the fields, occasionally lying flat, at other times at a half crouch, taking his time, careful to see all and not be seen in return. When he finally had to cross a shallow stream, then fight his way through the two feet of soft snow that had drifted up against the boundary wall, he was frozen to the bone and soaking wet.

He lifted his head and did a quick 360-degree scan of the surrounding countryside. Everything was covered in snow, shading down to a soft pink in the dusk, the only contrasts some scattered trees, the stone wall he was hiding behind, and the village itself. Where two machine gun emplacements guarded the entrances of the lane that ran through its center.

Rossett had driven past the emplacement closest to the Cambridge road earlier. He'd then spent an hour getting lost in hidden country lanes before finally finding the other way into the village, and the other forbidding emplacement.

Coton was a typical English village, larger than the one he'd visited earlier when he had picked up the shotgun, but essentially the same: a single road dotted with thatched cottages on either side. The village widened slightly in the center, with a medieval church and graveyard.

He ducked down again, cupping his hands to his mouth and blowing some warmth into them. He looked around the field to his rear. There was a bit of cover from a few squat, fat-trunked trees that looked as old as the church, their winter-scrubbed branches scratching against the pink clouds in the sky. Rossett plotted an escape route.

He'd just have to hope there was enough light to see in case he had to get out quickly.

He counted about fifteen or twenty thatched cottages, slightly set apart from a larger whitewashed, three-story building on the edge of a courtyard beyond the church.

The biggest building in the village by far, so big it was about the size of all the other cottages put together, it had to be St. Catherine's Hall.

Rossett made his way along the wall to where it intersected an untidy hedgerow, behind which was a drainage ditch of muddy water sheltered from the snow.

It occurred to him that this was the first time he'd visited the English countryside in years. He paused a moment and looked at the view around him. It was beautiful, edges softened, pink with the reflecting light off the heavy clouds. A gust of wind scratched Rossett's face and he took a moment to savor the air, emptying his lungs of the smog of dark and damp London.

He thought of Great Britain before the war, the freedom to travel to places like this, no checkpoints, no papers, nobody watching and monitoring your movements.

He wished he'd treasured it more, especially now it was gone.

The wind whipped again.

He shivered, looked up, and focused on the now.

He was a soldier again, on a mission.

He carefully scanned his surroundings again, then hopped over the wall.

He stared at each house in turn, checking windows, checking if smoke was coming from chimneys. Looking for back doors, seeing which had curtains, which had light, who had transport, who had animals.

The place looked deserted.

It all came easy—hunting, fighting, killing. All the old instincts, all the old senses, lit up, ready for action.

He felt alive.

He slid back into the hedgerow, ducked down into the ditch, then started to slowly make his way toward the village. He was sheltered from the wind by the bushes; free of its buffeting, he could hear it raging above his head. He stopped again, listened, then crept to the edge of the bushes, finding that he was now less than twenty yards from the nearest house.

From his new position he could see that in the courtyard of the hall there were a couple of Opel staff cars and one larger, statelier Mercedes, the sort normally reserved for senior officers or VIPs.

Rossett could hear the flapping and slapping of the canvas of the Opel Blitz truck that was parked a short way down the lane. He couldn't see any foot patrols but didn't for a minute assume they weren't there.

He couldn't afford to.

The Mercedes meant there were officers about, and he'd spent enough time in the army to know that where there were officers, there were always privates trying to look busy. He slipped back into the bushes and flicked the powdery snow off his coat, then adjusted the shotgun, which was still hanging from his shoulder, out of sight. Even with his coat unbuttoned, the gun would be unseen until it was needed.

Rossett hoped it wouldn't be needed.

He puffed out his cheeks before taking another look behind him. Then he made his way out of the hedgerow toward the back of the nearest house.

Each footstep through the snow made Rossett wince as though he had stepped on a mine. He'd forgotten the treachery of snow to the creeping soldier. It seemed that no matter how softly he placed his feet, driving in with his toes, balancing midstep, the snow seemed to crunch like dry celery.

He kept moving toward the house, now ten yards away. He had no plan, no tactics, and not much hope.

He thought about his friend Koehler, and about Koehler's love for Anja and Lotte. Rossett remembered his wife and son, the love lost, never found again.

The memories flooded through his consciousness. Now wasn't the time, he needed to focus. He reached the back wall of the cottage and realized his breathing was labored. He dug deep for oxygen and shook his head.

He swallowed, puffed out his cheeks silently, and rested his head against the cold stone wall of the cottage.

He wouldn't let Koehler down. Rossett had nothing to lose, while his friend had everything. He'd do his best so that Koehler would keep the love that he himself had lost.

Rossett would right the wrong.

It was what he did.

He swallowed again, the moment passing, as he listened to the wind, which was howling now, blowing fast flurries of snow across the fields behind him.

Rossett moved so that he was at the edge of the building line, right next to the narrow lane. He dropped to one knee and checked the lane, then dodged back again.

It was empty; the whole village seemed empty.

He considered the situation.

He knew the scientists were here.

He knew they would be under guard and that the soldiers guarding them would also be living in the village.

If he were in charge, he'd keep everyone in the big hall. The best way to look after prisoners is to keep them where you can see them, and the hall looked big enough for a couple of platoons of men plus whomever they chose to guard.

He'd head for the hall and check it out.

Rossett crouched and looked around the corner of the house toward the western end of the lane. In the distance, at least 150 yards away, he saw one of the gun emplacements.

The soldiers there had lit a fire in a brazier; one of them was standing warming his hands facing toward Rossett, who pulled back quickly out of sight, not trusting the whipping snow to hide him.

He looked toward the church, fifty yards to his right on the same side of the road, surrounded by a low stone wall topped with snow.

He'd use the graveyard as cover.

Rossett ducked back to the field and then ran, bent at the waist, as quickly and as quietly as he could toward the church. It was an almost straight dash except for one low hedgerow, which he jumped over without breaking stride before he reached the graveyard boundary wall.

Once he had caught his breath, Rossett rolled over the top of the wall, landing with a soft crunch onto the snow on the other side. He lay still, the wind howling as he scanned for movement.

There was nothing, just pink, gray, and black, all sharp shapes and shadows, confusing his eyes as the snow flicked this way and that. Rossett squinted, taking time to let his heart rate drop after the run.

He rose to his haunches and checked the shotgun was still secure under his coat. He picked up a few handfuls of snow to smooth the gap he had disturbed on the top of the wall, then drew his Webley, his thumb on the hammer.

He moved through the headstones slowly, eyes flitting from the church to the road and then to the small vestry that lay a short distance to his right, just on the edge of the graveyard. Off on the other side of the village a dog started to bark at the night, its voice carrying on the wind. Rossett kept moving, listening, looking, living on his nerves.

He skirted the church around the back and found himself facing a small copse of trees. Somewhere behind him he heard music that sounded like it was coming from a radio. He turned his head, blinking against another flurry of snow, and saw a sliver of light angle to nothing as the front door closed at the vestry.

Rossett checked behind him, then dodged to a larger headstone, one that provided enough cover to allow him to stand upright.

He tried to see if whoever had opened the door had been coming or going. He tilted his head to listen.

All he could hear was the wind and the damn dog in the distance.

He dodged back behind the headstone, checking the lane and the village behind him, considering his next move.

He could see lights in the hall, but he could also see a sentry, wrapped up against the cold, standing at the front door under a solitary outside lamp that was swinging in the wind.

And then . . . there . . . on the edge of his senses, a smell. He lifted his nose like an animal. Pipe tobacco: it hadn't been there before.

Rossett dropped down to a crouch, shoulder to the stone. He leaned out slightly to try to see the person who was smoking the pipe, but nothing moved, no shadows. There was nothing but the smell of tobacco.

Rossett shifted again to look to the other side of the stone, this time toward the church. All he could see were the black outlines of grave markers standing to attention like frozen stone soldiers in the snow.

He could just make out the dark wooden doors of the church chancellery against the stone blocks of the walls.

He squinted.

A shadow, almost lost in the shade of the door.

Did it move?

Rossett opened his eyes wide, and there, in front of him, someone was looking back, dressed in black, difficult to see against the doors but there, watching.

Rossett didn't move. His heart pounded. The urge to advance flooded every part of his body, but he didn't move.

Maybe the figure hadn't seen him. Maybe it was just someone enjoying an evening smoke in the fresh air. Maybe it was someone checking the church was locked.

Maybe.

"Hey." The figure spoke in English, hushed, but loud enough to carry across the forty feet to Rossett. "Hey, I'm here."

Rossett thumbed the hammer on the Webley and set off across the graveyard at a sprint. Like a snow leopard, head down, Webley held low, he moved in for the kill.

He stopped.

An old man, at least seventy years old, stood with his back against the church doors, hands open in front of his chest, gesturing for Rossett to slow down.

The man gripped an old briar pipe in his teeth and watched as Rossett dropped to his knee, some six feet short of him, staring down the barrel of his pistol.

"You'll wake up the entire village."

Rossett lowered the gun an inch or two, but remained staring at the old man, who smiled in the half-light and lowered his hands a little.

"What are you doing out here creeping around?" the old man whispered. "I've been waiting for you."

Rossett didn't reply,

"I didn't get a call, so I've been sitting by the window watching." The old man's voice was weakening in the face of Rossett's silence and his Webley.

"I'm a friend . . ." the man finally said, lowering his hands.

Rossett lifted the Webley and released the hammer with his thumb. A flurry of snow passed between them and the old man blinked, turning his head so that his lank, surprisingly long gray hair whipped around his face like long grass on a rocky outcrop.

The wind passed and the old man looked at Rossett again.

"I'm a friend."

Rossett nodded.

The old man smiled.

"Come in here, quickly." He turned and pushed at the church doors, opening one just wide enough to slip through. He was halfway inside when he looked at Rossett, gesturing that he should follow. "We haven't got all night."

Rossett looked around, rose up off his knee, then followed the old man into the church.

It was pitch black inside once the heavy wooden door closed behind him. The sound of the wind was still there, but now it seemed distant, up in the roof, away in the darkness. Rossett felt momentarily confused by the blackness and he rested one hand against the wooden door at his back. He thumbed the hammer on the pistol again and raised it next to his head, searching for a target.

A second passed, and a match flared and lit a candle to Rossett's left, causing him to spin and face the light. The old man had moved quickly and quietly, always a dangerous combination.

The candle barely illuminated the inside of the building, and Rossett watched as the man smiled at him, then dipped a finger in a stone bowl containing holy water and fleetingly blessed himself.

Rossett lowered the Webley again. This time the sound of the hammer subsiding echoed around the empty church. The wind moaned in the rafters; Rossett looked up to where the shadows cast by the candlelight were dancing, and then back at the old man.

"I'm Frank James; I wasn't sure with the weather if you'd be coming."

James tugged at the collar of his overcoat and undid the top button, revealing an Anglican dog collar under the coat.

Rossett raised an eyebrow.

"I've been wandering round the house all night, looking through every window trying to spot you. I was about to give up, to be honest." James was still whispering, even though there was now two inches of old English oak between them and the outside world.

"You're the vicar?" Rossett finally said.

The candlelight played shadows across James's face, and he tilted his head forward an inch so that Rossett couldn't see his eyes.

"I'm your contact."

"How did you know I was coming?"

"I got a call a couple of days ago."

"From who?"

"I don't know his name; you know how these things work."

"I don't. Tell me."

James shifted a few inches.

"We never know the names of people along the chain, in case we get captured."

"We?" Rossett stepped forward and took the candle out of the vicar's hand. His steps echoed around the church as he walked down the center aisle. He held the candle high, so that it could throw its meager light into the darkened corners.

Another gust of wind moaned through the old building as Rossett turned to face James once more, candle still held high, its flame flickering and dancing in the draft.

"The resistance," James said quietly, staring at the flame as if hypnotized by it.

Rossett walked back down the aisle toward him.

"I'm not the resistance," he said quietly. "The resistance killed my wife and son. I'm not the resistance."

"I thought . . . I thought you were here for Ruth Hartz?"

"I am, but don't call me resistance."

"I'm sorry."

Rossett pointed to a pew.

"Sit."

James took a seat, shuffling down so that there was room for Rossett next to him. Rossett ignored the space and sat one pew in front, balancing the candle on the prayer book shelf before looking at James.

"Tell me what you know about Hartz." Rossett rested the hand holding the Webley on the back of the pew, in plain sight.

"She is in the hall, or, as we call it, the big house."

"Where in the house?"

"Second floor. There's a long corridor that runs the length of the building on each level except the first. She is at the very far end, to the right of the entrance. She has an apartment there."

"Can I reach the window from outside?"

"Not without being seen. It's too far to climb. You'd need a ladder, and there is always a sentry outside."

Rossett nodded.

"Other entrances?"

"All locked from inside."

"How do you know this?"

"I'm a regular guest there; most of the village has been evacuated except for the few who work at the hall for the Germans. They allowed me to stay because I provide pastoral care to some of the scientists."

"Pastoral care?"

"Some of them . . . struggle with the work they do."

"Why?"

James frowned slightly. "They are giving the future to Hitler. If they give him what he wants, they will give him the world. That power and the understanding of it . . . can weigh heavy."

"I don't understand."

"The bomb . . . it'll end all bombs, the people working on it know that. They appreciate that more than anyone does. Some of them struggle with that knowledge."

"But they keep on working?"

"They want to stay alive; you'd be surprised what people will do to stay alive."

Rossett lifted his face to look up as another gust of wind called out in the darkness above. He thought about what he had done to stay alive in recent years, as the moaning faded away.

"I wouldn't be surprised," he finally said, looking back at James.

"I can see that," James said softly.

"Why haven't resistance raided the village?"

"There's never been enough around here to pull off something like that. You have to understand, there was never much of a population here before the war. And since then most of the young people have been sent either to Europe or up north to work in factories or mines. There is also the consideration that any action against the Germans carries terrible repercussions for the local population. The Germans can be truly brutal at times."

Rossett nodded, remembering the dead men at the checkpoint, then wondering what further blood would be spilled as a result.

"What about explosives?"

"Anyone coming in or out of the village is searched thoroughly, even those known to them."

Rossett nodded slowly, considering his options.

"What about hitting them on the road to Cambridge with an ambush?"

"They travel in numbers, and these aren't just a bunch of conscripts, either. The men stationed here are SS, the best, all experienced and all highly motivated. You'd need three platoons to take them down in the open, and you could be certain they wouldn't allow the scientists to be taken alive."

The candle flickered and then caught again.

"Do you know Hartz?" Rossett asked.

"Not well, but well enough."

"Will she be cooperative?"

"She is aware moves are afoot to get her out."

"How?"

"She just does. We have ways."

"Will she be cooperative?" Rossett asked again.

James shifted in his seat then nodded. "She will, but . . . she'll be worried. She won't trust you. Ruth knows her value to the Germans, but she also knows her danger to the Americans if her escape is in doubt. If you and she were to be cornered, she'll be wary of you."

"Why?"

"If it looks like you can't get her out, she'll be expecting you to kill her."

"I'll get her out."

"You're very confident."

"I'm very good."

"That I don't doubt."

ROSSETT LOOKED IN the mirror.

A vicar who needed a drink and a shave looked back at him.

"I'm not sure about this," said Rossett, tugging his index finger around the black shirt collar in an attempt to find some more room.

Rossett and James had retreated back to the vestry. In the few minutes they had spent together Rossett had told James the outline of the situation in which he found himself. James had listened quietly as they stood in the warm living room, steam rising off Rossett's shoes and trousers in front of the fire.

James initially offered food and drink, but Rossett wanted to get moving. He knew he was in the center of the wasp's nest and had no wish to stay there longer than he had to.

"I go there every night for my supper. It's a tradition. I say grace, we eat, share a bottle of wine, and then I return here. I've done it for eighteen months now," Reverend James said as he rummaged in a drawer looking for his spare dog collar.

"They'll see I'm not you a mile off."

"I'm coming with you."

Rossett turned from the mirror and looked at him.

"You can't do that."

"Here, I've found one!" James held up a clerical collar for Rossett to see before crossing the bedroom, slipping it around Rossett's neck, and folding the shirt collar down. "It could do with starching, but it'll have to do, I'm afraid."

James stepped back, admiring his work.

"If you help me they will kill you."

James smiled and gave a slight nod before stepping forward and dusting Rossett's shoulders.

"I'm afraid it's the only way," he said as he turned to pick up Rossett's suit jacket. "The only way to get you in is to walk you in as my guest."

"You make it sound so easy."

"Security inside the cordon is considerably lighter than outside. I've taken colleagues to dinner there many times before, and it is accepted that I'm alone here; so the archdiocese often sends me company for a few days. The sentry will have no reason to think you're anything other than just my guest and won't think of challenging you; he'll assume you were checked out at the emplacements on your way into the village."

"When I've gone, when Hartz is gone, they'll come looking for you."

"I'll be long gone by then. I'll do my best to get to safety somewhere."

"Somewhere?"

James smiled and tapped his own dog collar. "I'm in the biggest gang in the world. I'm certain of shelter if I knock on the right doors. I just need to put some distance between myself and here as quickly as I can."

Rossett shook his head, not sure who James was trying to reassure more, Rossett or himself.

James seemed to read Rossett's mind. He smiled and nodded before continuing.

"I was in the Great War, 1914 to '18, out in France. Absolute hell on earth, words can't describe . . . they really can't. All of it, every last bit of blood, all of it was for nothing. It was an absolute waste. Millions dead on both sides and in between, and yet here we are, whispering in case we're overheard by Nazis through the window. I'm an English vicar who doesn't have a flock, in a church nobody wants." James lowered his eyes. "When we declared war to save Poland it all seemed so unreal, I don't think anyone thought we'd be stupid enough to actually fight." He shook his head. "Do you know the last time that church was full was when it was a field hospital? There were Germans on one side and English on the other. I prayed over the bodies of thirty men in one day, thirty men. Madness."

James sighed and held out Rossett's jacket. Instead of taking it, Rossett bent and picked up the shotgun from the floor and slung it via the string back over his shoulder. He turned and allowed James to help him slip the jacket onto his shoulders before facing him again.

"You've no chance of escape," said Rossett.

"The Lord is my shepherd."

"I'll not be able to help you."

"He's sent you for Hartz, and for the daughter of your friend, not for me." Reverend James gripped Rossett's biceps and smiled. "You'll be all right, he'll look after you."

Rossett looked at the floor.

"I'm a very bad sort, Vicar, the baddest sort there is."

"You loved your family, you love your friend, and you're risking your life for innocents caught up in this madness. You're not a bad man, my son."

"You can't imagine what I've done."

"Oh, I can, but whatever you have done, whatever has gone before, you can always try to make amends by trying to be better. The only way to overcome evil is to try to do good."

"By more killing?"

"By saving lives, millions of lives."

Rossett frowned.

"You'll succeed, and the Lord will provide for me, whatever he has planned."

"The Lord doesn't drive a getaway car."

"There are many ways to escape. I'll take whatever he decides best and pray for you."

Rossett nodded and looked at himself in the mirror. "Pray for those who are about to die," he said. "Don't worry about me."

CHAPTER 31

FIVE MINUTES LATER Rossett and James were wandering down the lane that threaded through the thatched cottages and overgrown gardens of Coton. The hiss and rustle of the trees filled the air as the wind whipped at their coats and hair.

The lane bent around the top of the village and Rossett saw the hall clearly for the first time. It was a three-story, L-shaped white building arranged around a courtyard. In the courtyard itself were the Opels and the Mercedes staff car he had seen earlier. The Blitz truck with a canvas back also hadn't moved from where it was parked at the end of the lane.

Reverend James rested a hand on Rossett's arm, then stopped and removed his pipe from his pocket and began to fill it with tobacco. He idly turned to face Rossett as he worked on the pipe and spoke softly.

"Do you see the center of the hall, by the lamp with the sentry?"

Rossett looked over James's shoulder at the hall, some one hundred feet away.

"Yes."

"The door in the middle of the center building, that's where we are going."

Rossett saw that the sentry had an StG 44 assault rifle over his shoulder; the man was kicking at the snow with the toe of his boot, moving about to keep warm.

"You go through that door and there is an entrance lobby," James continued. "Directly in front of you is the staircase. It rises one flight to a landing, off which is a corridor in either direction. On that first floor are the German quarters, left and right off the landing, officers to the left, enlisted to the right."

Rossett looked at the building and saw that lights were on in a few of the windows of the hall, and that smoke was rising from a number of chimneys along the roof.

"If you continue up the stairs, the building has the same arrangement on the second floor. Except all of the rooms are full of scientists and occasionally guests. Some English, some German. You go toward the right-hand end of the building as we are looking at it now. At the far end of the corridor, as far as you can go before it turns ninety degrees again to the right, are the rooms of Ruth Hartz."

Rossett ran his eyes along the windows until he reached the end two or three windows, then nodded.

James struck a match, which lit his face as he held it to his pipe.

Plumes of smoky breath mixed with the night air.

"Is there another way out?"

"Hmm." James nodded as he tried another match on the pipe, cupping it in his hand to fend off the wind. He sucked and the match flared. "Turn right out of her apartment door, and there is a back stairway that takes you down to the kitchen on the ground floor. Nobody uses it, though; it may well be locked. There are lots of other stairs. The place is a medieval rabbit warren. That'll work in your favor, though. I doubt there will be more than thirty men in the village, excluding scientists. It'll be a nightmare to search quickly."

Rossett nodded. "Vehicles?"

"Just what you will find in the courtyard and at the checkpoints."

"No private cars?"

James shook his head. "Another thing, don't rely on any of the scientists to help you. They have a pretty good life here. They can come and go as they please, and the Germans see to it they get everything they could wish for. While some of them are unhappy with the work they do, they've a lot to lose if they are caught helping someone like you. There are also some who don't see themselves as prisoners; for them, this is where they live while they do their jobs, nothing more."

"They wouldn't help Hartz?"

James shrugged and took his pipe out of his mouth, "She is a Jew, kept mostly separate from her colleagues unless she is working. She is persona non grata due to her religion, I'm afraid. Jews aren't very popular with the SS."

Rossett felt himself flush and was glad that James started to move again. He looked at his watch and glanced over his shoulder at the far gun emplacement. All seemed quiet, so he trotted a couple of paces, catching up with James.

They entered the floodlit courtyard and the sentry watched them as they approached. The light above the sentry was swinging in the wind. Shadows appeared and disappeared as the light moved left and right, catching stray flakes of snow.

Rossett casually looked around the building's windows, checking for movement. Everything seemed still as they drew close.

"*Gutten Abend*, Reverend."

"Good evening, Ritter. You got the short straw tonight?" James was smiling, holding his pipe up toward the wind as he spoke.

"I always get the short straw, sir, you know that." The sentry smiled at James and reached behind him to open the door for the two vicars in front of him.

"Oh, bugger, I've forgotten my tobacco."

Rossett turned to see Reverend James patting his pockets.

"I'll just pop back to the vestry to pick it up. You go in without me, I'll not be long."

Rossett nodded and stepped into the hallway of the building as James stood on the threshold.

"They're expecting you, old man. Just go up." James smiled and pulled the door closed, leaving Rossett alone inside. The sound of the wind was almost gone as Rossett started up the red-carpeted staircase directly ahead of him.

He unbuttoned his coat and checked the shotgun was still hidden as he took hold of the Webley in his other pocket. His footsteps padded through the thick carpet, keeping time with the grandfather clock ticking in the hallway below.

The dark wood paneling and the bloodred carpet seemed to press in on Rossett. He moved up twelve steps to a turning, then another twelve to the first floor.

Each landing was lit by a large chandelier that hung from the ceiling like a crystal stalactite. Fine cobwebs laced the lights, and on all the walls hung paintings darkened by years of grime, in dirty gold frames frosted with dust.

The whole building seemed like England itself: old, falling into disrepair, and full of Germans who didn't care.

Rossett didn't pause on the first-floor landing. He knew that floor belonged to the officers and men. He made sure he moved quickly, but not too quickly, stepping in time with the clock down below.

The second-floor landing was identical to the first. Even the large landscape painting in the heavy gold frame looked the same as the one he had passed on the landing below.

This corridor on this floor was narrower. Small windows to his left every ten feet or so looked out onto darkened fields, pink in the glow of the snow and slashed with dark hedgerows. The corridor ran along the back of the building, and Rossett tried to imagine where his car was in relation to his current position.

He realized it was a long way away.

Maybe getting in was the easy bit, he mused as he tapped politely on the door he believed to be Ruth's, before taking a few more steps along the corridor to take a look around the corner.

It was almost exactly as James had described, the same layout of rooms and windows. The only difference seemed to be the one dark wood door on the left-hand side of the corridor, with FIRE ESCAPE written on it in gold lettering.

Rossett heard Hartz's door open and walked back to face the person who had opened it.

"Miss Hartz?" Rossett smiled at Ruth, who was half hidden behind a door that was open barely six inches.

She nodded, blinking her oval eyes at him as an auburn lock of hair dropped forward as low as her cheek. She chased it away with a flick of her hand.

"Yes, Reverend?"

"May I come in?"

"Now?"

"Yes."

Rossett smiled, pushed the door open, and took a step forward.

Hartz surprised Rossett by pushing the door back against him with her shoulder. He had to shove almost full force to get her to move out of the way. Ruth stepped back, letting the door swing wide.

"What do you think you are doing? You can't just—"

Hartz stopped speaking as Rossett raised a finger to her lips and then used his heel to close the door behind him. He looked over her shoulder at the living room of the apartment she had been given. It was surprisingly large and well furnished. A solid, overstuffed couch dominated the floor in front of a blazing coal fire.

A fire so hot it possibly accounted for Hartz wearing a fine silk negligee, the sort you wore for show, not for sleeping in.

The problem was, Rossett knew the warmth of the fire wasn't why she was wearing a fine silk negligee.

The extra glass of red wine on the floor alongside hers was the reason she was wearing the fine silk negligee.

Or rather, the person who had just been drinking it was.

Rossett looked at the doorway off to his right and pointed to it.

"Who is in there?" he whispered, finger still on Ruth's lips.

She shook her head as Rossett lifted the finger half an inch.

"Nobody," she said softly.

Rossett looked at the door again, then lowered his hand and half slipped the Webley out of his pocket.

Ruth caught sight of the pistol and then calmly looked into Rossett's eyes.

"I'm here to help you. Call him out before this situation gets out of hand."

He gestured that Ruth should go before him and open the door; he took a pace to the side and put his left hand on her shoulder.

He leaned forward so that his cheek was next to her ear.

"Do it."

He was so close, Rossett felt her hair brush his cheek. He could almost hear the blood pumping through Ruth's veins as he pulled back the hammer on the Webley.

Its solid double crack was loud in the quiet room.

She didn't speak until he gently squeezed her shoulder as encouragement.

"It's okay." Her voice seemed to catch in her throat, so she tried again, louder this time. "Please come out."

Rossett held the Webley behind Hartz's back, staring along a dark corridor with three doors leading off on its left-hand side.

A shadow emerged from the end room; it paused before slowly making its way toward them.

Rossett stepped out from behind Ruth, moving her aside, gun out, finger still on the trigger.

The man, half dressed, frowned when he saw the dog collar and the pistol; he stopped walking, but kept his hands out where Rossett could see them.

"Who the hell are you?" Rossett said.

"Captain Horst Meyer, SS," the man said.

"Horst knows why you are here," Ruth said. "I told him someone was coming for me and he wants to help."

Rossett risked a glance at her and then went back to staring at Meyer.

"Please." Ruth touched Rossett's arm. "He can help us."

Rossett narrowed his eyes and then released the hammer on the Webley as he lowered it to his side.

"Put your trousers on."

Meyer looked at Rossett but didn't move.

"Anytime today would be nice," Rossett added before turning away and pointing to the couch.

Ruth followed his direction and took a seat on the edge.

"We thought you might not be coming. We hadn't been given an exact date, and with the weather . . ."

As if on cue the wind sounded in the chimney and the old wooden window frame rattled in sympathy. Rossett watched as Meyer hopped around in the doorway, pulling at his SS britches.

Rossett leaned down, picked up one of the wineglasses, and took a drink, eyes still on the corridor where Meyer was getting dressed.

"Where is the bottle?" he asked Ruth, and she leaned around the far side of the couch and produced a half-empty bottle of red.

He took the bottle and drank straight out of it before looking at the label.

He turned to the doorway as Meyer finally reappeared, pulling his suspenders over his undershirt and holding his shirt in his hand.

Meyer stopped, unsure of Rossett, who gestured to the couch with the bottle.

"Sit."

Meyer did as he was told, and Rossett noted how he adopted almost the exact same posture as Ruth, both sitting close, shoulders touching.

"What is going on here?"

"We're lovers." Ruth looked up at Rossett.

"I love her," Meyer said, looking at Ruth.

"He can't come." Rossett broke up the party.

"I can help." Meyer looked up, still holding the shirt in his hands.

"I wasn't talking to you," Rossett said.

"He's helped me here," Ruth interjected.

"I don't care if he does your washing, he's not coming."

"But I love her . . ."

Rossett ripped the dog collar from around his throat.

"What happens when you get to London? What happens when the Americans won't take you?"

Ruth looked at Meyer. "But he'll help us get there."

"And then what if the Yanks say no? He can't just come back here and say it was all a big mistake. For someone who is supposed to be intelligent, you're being rather stupid."

"I want to be with Ruth," Meyer said again, quieter than before.

Ruth looked at him and then back at Rossett.

"He can help us get away from here."

"You said that," replied Rossett. "But then what?"

Meyer sighed and looked at the floor. "I love her. I'm sorry. I love her. I know it is against orders, but . . . what can I do?" His halting English cracked against his emotions as he took hold of Ruth's hand and looked up at Rossett.

Rossett took a step backward, rubbed his forehead, and then took another drink from the wine bottle. He shook his head and then passed Meyer the bottle.

"Captain, we've got a serious problem."

CHAPTER 32

THE BURNED-OUT CAR had been removed by the time King got to the flat on Stuffield Street where he and Eric had originally held Anja.

The snow that had fallen since he had been there last had covered their tracks. The world looked fresh and white, as if nothing had happened and everything was as it should be. The only evidence of troubles past was a few fresh divots in the brickwork of the building behind the phone box.

That, plus Eric Cook was dead, Anja was lost, and Frank King was now on his own trying to save his career and his country a long way from home.

King had driven up and down the street five or six times in the hours since he had spoken to Kennedy. His caution was as much down to his reluctance to commit to his new course of action as it was to fear of ambush.

He'd long since decided that the resistance would have moved on from the scene as soon as the shooting had stopped. They wouldn't want to be around when the police turned up to clear up the mess that was left behind.

He pulled into the street for the seventh time and drifted into the curb next to the red telephone box outside the flat. He waited, feeling the gear stick vibrate in his hand as the little engine chuckled away in front of him. His eyes flicked left and right, up to the mirror, back to the windscreen, taking in every inch of the silent street and the falling snow.

A stray dog crossed the road ten yards ahead. It stopped halfway, caught in the halfhearted glow of the streetlamp, then lifted its nose to the air, smelling the fumes from the exhaust and then looking at him.

King and the dog shared a moment, both alone on the streets, both struggling to stay alive against the odds, both wary one might give the other away if they moved.

The dog's eyes shone yellow.

Then it breathed out, turned its head, and loped away up the street and out of sight into the darkness and the falling snow.

King switched off the engine. He eased down the window an inch and looked toward the alleyway from which he had been ambushed earlier. It was pitch black, same as before. He shifted in his seat, which creaked and squeaked as he moved. He looked at the phone box with its milky light.

King knew he was exposed. Even though the little battered British car was less conspicuous than the Opel, he knew he stood out a mile.

He told himself that if anyone did appear, anyone at all, he just had to start the engine and pull away.

Not much of a plan, but the best one he had.

He lit another cigarette, flicked the match out of the window, checked his watch, and then looked at the phone box again.

It was his only link to Koehler, now that the operation was blown, now that Dulles was being held by Kennedy; it was all he had left as a way of making contact.

Frank King had planned for this. He was alone, but he wasn't stupid. His original idea had been for Anja and Ruth to be exchanged at an American safe house. King hadn't been stupid enough to share the location with anyone but Eric Cook, but since Cook had been interrogated, King couldn't trust that location.

He knew that once Koehler got the envelope he'd ring the number in it.

He knew that the phone in the safe house wouldn't be answered.

He knew Koehler, in his desperation to find his daughter, would phone the first number he had been given.

The one in the phone box he was parked next to.

Whitechapel 6168.

King drew on his cigarette again, listening to the snow landing on the roof of the car. He breathed the smoke out through his nose, enjoying it, relaxing slightly.

He could make this work.

He looked up at the flat and considered waiting inside, then decided against it. He didn't want to be trapped in a building with only one way in and out.

He put the cigarette back to his lips.

Then the phone in the box started to ring.

King froze a moment, mouth open, cigarette held an inch from it, as the sound of the ringing seemed to rattle the box rhythmically.

Ring ring, ring ring, ring ring.

He fumbled with the door handle, almost falling out of the little car as he checked the street.

Ring ring.

It was too early; he hadn't expected a call until daylight at the earliest. Something must have gone wrong.

He pulled the heavy door open and grabbed the receiver.

"Hello?"

"Hello?" a voice crackled on the other end of the line.

King paused. The voice sounded wrong, setting off an alarm bell in his head.

"Who is this?" King asked.

"Who are you?"

King was confused. He looked at his car.

"Who do you want?"

"Tell me your name."

King slammed the phone down and went to step out of the box. He reached for the pistol in his pocket as he turned, pushing with his free hand against the door, hearing the heavy spring strain as he did so.

A pistol whipped him across the left temple, knocking him to the floor of the phone box in a half-conscious heap.

King's ears rang and his head reeled with the force of the blow; he raised his hands to protect himself, dimly aware that he had dropped his own weapon.

His coat rode up against his throat as he was dragged out of the box. King felt ice-cold snow on his face and realized he was lying facedown in it. He tried to get onto all fours, but someone whipped away his hands with a sweeping leg. King fell forward again, this time catching a mouthful of snow for his troubles.

He squeezed his eyes tight. His head hurt, a sharp pain that made him even more confused.

He spat and attempted to roll sideways to look at who was attacking him.

He stopped, senses clearing when he heard the sharp click of the hammer on the pistol that was pressing into his left cheek, just under his fluttering eye.

"Where is my daughter?" Ernst Koehler asked quietly.

King didn't answer. He tried to open his eye fully, but the pressure of the pistol on his cheek made it difficult.

"Where is my daughter?" Koehler asked again.

King swallowed, tasting blood in his mouth and wondering where it was coming from. "Please." King finally found his voice. "Don't . . . please."

The pistol whipped across his temple again, higher this time. King felt the muzzle drive into the side of his skull behind his left ear.

He blinked; he felt like he was going to be sick. He finally opened his eyes and saw that he was facing his car; he squeezed out another blink and tried to lift a hand to protect himself but found he couldn't.

"Where is my fucking daughter?" Koehler's voice was closer now, almost next to his ear.

King wondered if he was about to die.

The pressure of the pistol eased, and then Koehler jabbed it back down harder than before.

"Where is she?"

King closed his eyes tightly and then opened them again, trying to clear his jumbled brain. He could feel pressure on his chest and he struggled to take a breath. He spat—more blood—twisted half an inch, and pushed with his head against the pistol, struggling to look up at Koehler.

He took a breath and gambled.

"Kill me, and you'll never see her again." King's lips felt heavy and loose. He swallowed, felt the pressure of the pistol ease, and turned to look Koehler in the face.

This time the blow caught him on the top of his head, hard, fast, like a hammer on a nail, driving him down back into the snow and jarring his teeth together so hard the noise echoed in his ears.

He felt himself being lifted by the back of his coat and tried to resist but was too groggy. He looked at the phone box, confused by it; he knew he'd been in it, he knew he needed it, but he couldn't remember why.

He closed his eyes and tried to focus.

It occurred to him that there were two men, one either side of him, holding an arm each. He knew he was moving fast, so fast that in his confused state he barely had time to tuck his head into his shoulders before it was used to barge open a door—and King realized it was the front door of the same house, the house in which Koehler's wife had died.

Koehler kicked the door shut behind him with his heel, locking the other man outside after they had thrown King onto the bottom of the stairs inside.

King groaned as Koehler drove a knee into his back and shoved the barrel of the pistol into the side of his head again.

"I —" King started to speak but was cut off by the pressure of the gun.

"Shut up. Listen to me. You've seconds to live unless you listen well. I know you killed my wife, I know you took my daughter, and you cannot imagine how I want you to suffer for those crimes. Do you understand me?"

King managed to nod under the pressure of the gun.

"You've one chance to make it easy, one chance and one chance only. Where is my daughter?"

King licked his lips and shifted his legs slightly to get more comfortable. The gun pressure increased. The barrel felt warm on his skin.

King composed the words and then licked his lips again.

"I need a drink."

Koehler gripped the hair on the top of King's head, yanked it back, and then drove his head forward, slamming his forehead into the stairs.

King waited for another blow, but instead he felt the pistol resting on the back of his skull again.

"Last chance," Koehler said softly, not even bothering to ask the question this time.

King swallowed again, stretched his jaw, and then rolled his head an inch to the side.

"You know so much . . ." He barely managed to speak, such was the force pressing down on him. "But you don't know what I know. You aren't going to pull that trigger, you idiot, so let me up so we can talk."

Koehler lifted his knee and then roughly searched King's coat pockets and around his waistband. King felt Koehler grab his shoulder and spin him around so that he was lying on his back looking up.

"Where is she?"

King reached up and dabbed at the wound on his scalp.

"I'm sorry about your wife." King lowered his hand. "That was an accident."

Koehler reared, spinning the pistol and holding it like a hammer, ready to strike down into King's face. King closed his eyes instinctively as he listened to the sharp, hard breaths coming from Koehler's nose.

King opened his eyes.

Koehler gritted his teeth, pistol still held high. Seconds passed, and then Koehler lifted his face to look up the stairs before lowering the gun.

King started to speak and then thought better of it.

Koehler looked at him, the anger still there but sinking an inch beneath the surface, like a face looking back at him through ice in a frozen lake.

"Please," Koehler spoke again, his voice suddenly sounding weak. "I want my daughter."

"I don't have her," replied King.

"Where is she?"

"Resistance took her."

Koehler's brow furrowed as he looked down at King, who spoke again quickly.

"But I can help you get her back."

Koehler tilted his head, his knees still either side of King, his weight still holding the other man down.

"You need me," King said quietly.

Koehler blinked three times, thumbed the hammer on the pistol, and placed it on King's forehead.

"I don't," he whispered as his finger squeezed the trigger.

"I know where she'll be."

The finger stopped.

"I know where they have to take her. I'll take you there. You need me . . ."

The finger tightened.

Frank King looked into the eyes of death.

Death blinked, and the pistol lifted off his brow.

"We can all come out of this with what we want. You don't know me, but I am a good guy, trying to do something good."

"You killed my wife."

"I'm so sorry."

"You took my daughter."

"If there'd been another way . . ."

"I'm going to kill you eventually."

"Let me finish this. Let me get your daughter back to you and finish this."

Koehler pushed himself up and leaned back against the door, the pistol held at his side where King could see it.

King adjusted himself on the stairs and touched his head again. "The scientist, do you have her?"

"No."

"We need her."

"We'll have her soon."

"How?"

"Rossett will get her."

"You sent Rossett? We chose you because you were the best in the country and you sent him?"

"I'm the best German in the country."

"So you sent Rossett?"

"He is the best anyone in the country."

King nodded, not quite understanding the answer but accepting it anyway.

"My partner and I were ambushed by the resistance here, in the flat. It isn't safe to stay." King gestured with his hands to the front door behind Koehler. "We can talk in the car?"

Koehler lowered his eyes a fraction as he considered what King had said, then nodded. He leaned off the door and reached behind his back to pull it open with his damaged hand.

"Try anything, anything at all, and I'll kill you, understand?"

"We both want the same thing."

"I doubt that," replied Koehler.

CHAPTER 33

ANJA WAS TIRED.

She couldn't remember being this tired ever before in her life.

Try as she might, though, sleep wouldn't come to rescue her heavy eyes and her aching head.

The fire danced in the hearth as Jack snored next to her on the couch. Classical music, the type her father liked, drifted in and out from a radio behind them.

The fire popped on some damp coal.

Anja looked at Jack's hair; it smelled of oil and was so black it made her think of little Schwarz the cat. She hoped her father had fed him. She missed the kitten, and she missed her father.

She missed her mother the most, though.

Anja looked up to the ceiling, blinking hard, holding the tears back, just for now. She'd cry as soon as she was safe in her father's arms.

Her shoulder ached, so she shifted slightly, and Jack murmured. She smiled, and didn't know why.

She looked at the clock: five past midnight.

The pub downstairs had been quiet for over an hour, yet Jack's friend, the man who ran it, hadn't come up to check if they were all right.

Maybe he didn't want to disturb them?

Anja looked at the young girl asleep in the chair opposite and wondered why she hadn't spoken since Anja and Jack had arrived.

It was rude to stare, and yet that was all the girl had done.

English people are rude, she thought, looking at the fire. Except Jack, her Jack. He was nice.

The fire crackled again and then Anja heard voices on the stairs, getting louder as they came closer.

The girl opposite snapped awake and lifted her head, looking at the door behind Anja.

She rubbed a pink knuckle at her left eye and unfolded her legs from under her, then looked at Anja.

Anja smiled, but the girl didn't smile back.

So very rude.

The voices stopped outside the door. Anja shook Jack and turned her head to look over the back of the couch.

The door opened.

A woman smiled at her.

"Hello, my love. Do you speak English?"

"Yes."

"My name is Ma Price."

Anja nodded as Jack lifted his head, blinking himself awake through squinting eyes.

He paused, looked at Anja, then at Ma Price.

Anja didn't understand why Jack stood up so suddenly and backed over to the far wall. She watched him and then turned to Ma Price, who pulled the black woolen shawl she was wearing around her arms tighter. So tight it dug in to the flesh like string around a joint of fatty meat.

"Now then, Jack, you've grown. I've not seen you for years. What have you been up to tonight?" Price's voice was light, friendly.

"Nothing, Ma, I was, I was just . . ."

Jack looked at Anja and then the floor, giving up on trying to find an answer.

"Are you taking me home?" Anja asked.

"Sort of, my dear." Ma Price reached out a hand to Anja, who looked at Jack and then stood up.

"Jack has to come as well."

"Oh, don't you worry. He's most definitely coming with us."

Anja looked at Jack and smiled, but he ignored her.

Something was wrong.

Anja looked at the lady.

"Who are you?"

"As I said, you can call me Ma Price."

"Not your name. I want to know who you are, why you are here."

A big man, almost as wide and as tall as the doorway, appeared behind Ma Price. He lowered his head slightly to look at Anja as he pulled a tweed flat cap off his head and rolled it in his hands.

"Get your coat, we haven't got all night." Ma Price smiled.

Anja looked at the pub manager and realized he looked embarrassed by what was taking place.

Everyone in the room knew something she didn't.

"Who are you?"

"Get yer fuckin' coat, Kraut, and stop asking questions!" Ma Price erupted and Anja flinched backward with fright.

The big man eased Ma Price aside and entered the room like a glacier. He picked up Anja's coat and tossed it to her without speaking. It landed high on her chest and momentarily blocked her vision as she caught it.

"Now." The big man's voice seemed to rumble in his chest.

Anja silently put the coat on, looking once again at Jack and then the young girl, who was staring into the fire as if oblivious.

Ma Price held out a hand and clapped her fingers into her palm, beckoning Anja toward her. Anja walked around the couch and joined her at the door. The big man gripped Jack's arm, pulled him across the room, and thrust his coat into his chest but didn't release his arm so that he could put it on.

Anja followed Ma Price out of the room, past the pub manager, who didn't meet her eyes, then down the stairs toward another big man who stood at the bottom in a coat that was slightly too small for him. His hands hung at his sides. He looked like a gorilla standing on its back legs, and his high forehead wrinkled as Anja looked into his eyes.

He smiled, and Anja saw he had a front tooth missing.

She checked over her shoulder at Jack, who was following, still in the first big man's grip.

They passed a doorway that led into the bar. There were still some drinkers in there, staring into half-empty pints, looking for their futures in the flat beer at the bottom of their dirty glasses.

Anja looked at the back of Price's head, then at the big man in front of her. A sudden fear gripped her, as if she was slipping away from civilization. She looked back into the bar and then grabbed the doorframe, not wanting to leave, holding on for her life.

"Help me, please! Someone, please help?"

Nobody reacted. It was as if they were frozen in time or she were shouting in a vacuum.

"Call the police!" Desperate this time, her voice rising with the panic in her throat. "Please!"

The man with the missing tooth grabbed her hand, yanking it away from the doorframe. Anja tried to resist, but he was too quick; he caught her wrist and lifted with his other arm around her waist. Anja's legs kicked clear of the floor and she screamed, as if she were falling from a cliff and needed someone to pull her back.

"Help me! Please, somebody!"

One man in the bar lifted his head and looked at her with anxious eyes. He opened his mouth, then gave a slight shake of his head and looked down again.

Finally her tears came. She was scared. She knew she was slipping away from society, into the darkness.

She twisted and rolled, panic giving her strength, but no matter how hard she pulled against the man, she couldn't stop him.

Anja gasped at air, gripped his coat, and twisted again. Facing him, she pushed against his chest with a balled fist.

It was no good.

The fight left her.

She hung limp.

"Please don't do this. Please, I just want to go home to my daddy."

Anja looked into his eyes for a sign that he understood how scared she was, for some warmth, a tiny flicker of hope that might make her feel better.

There was nothing.

She was lost.

CHAPTER 34

ROSSETT COULD BARELY drag himself away from checking through the curtain, looking at the courtyard as he spoke to Ruth Hartz and Horst Meyer over his shoulder.

" . . . Once I get you to London, I hand you over to the Americans and they get you to freedom."

"In America?" Hartz said.

Rossett looked at her.

"I doubt they will be taking you to Berlin, so yes, I'm guessing in America."

"When do we go?"

"The early hours, when people are asleep, so we can sneak out. Your boyfriend should get us past the sentries."

"Where do you hand us over?" Ruth asked.

"I don't know."

"You don't know?"

Rossett dropped the corner of the curtain and turned toward her.

"I pick up the address when I get to London."

"From where?"

Rossett looked at Horst Meyer and then shook his head.

"You, and especially him, don't need to know that yet."

"But what if you get killed?"

"I won't."

"But you might. This is dangerous. You might be shot."

"I won't," Rossett repeated with a certainty that made Ruth look at Meyer and then drop her hands.

Once Rossett saw that they understood, he turned back to the window and eased back the curtain again. He rested his cheek against the cold glass so that he could see the sentry at the front of the building.

"I'm not happy about him coming," Rossett said without turning to them, his breath misting the window slightly.

"He can help us," replied Ruth.

"I love her," Meyer added.

Rossett looked at them in the reflection and saw that Meyer had taken Ruth's hand again.

Rossett turned to face them.

"I'll not let you risk the operation. One wrong step, one sideways look, you're dead."

Meyer didn't flinch.

Rossett shook his head and then looked into Ruth's eyes. They looked watery in the low light. In them he was just able to make out the reflection of the fire dancing in the hearth on the other side of the room.

They were beautiful, and for a moment he understood Meyer's certainty.

Rossett frowned.

"He'll kill you. He answers to Hitler. He's young, and he's committed to the cause. If you let him he'll kill you."

"He's kept me alive so far."

"You're alive because they need you."

"I wouldn't hurt her." Meyer sounded defensive.

Rossett ignored him, turning back to the window and resuming his vigil.

"You can't trust these people," he said quietly.

"You don't know that," Ruth replied.

"I do, because I was one of them," said Rossett, feeling the cold glass, enjoying the ache that it was causing in his cheek.

AN HOUR HAD passed and Rossett hadn't moved.

The snow was still falling, sometimes faster, sometimes slower, but always falling and drifting in the blustering wind that howled in the darkness.

Meyer and Ruth had sat silently holding hands, staring into the fire as it died away down to orange and gray embers. It flickered and flared as the wind gusted under the window frame, but the new flame never quite caught, dying as the night moved on into the morning.

Rossett looked up into the night sky and then back at the sentry before wiping the condensation from the glass with the side of his hand.

The sentry came to attention, staring straight ahead, suddenly stiff.

An officer appeared, shucking his coat up around his ears as he ventured outdoors from the warm hall behind him.

The officer stopped and chatted to the sentry, who relaxed slightly. Rossett could see their lips moving.

He looked at Ruth and Meyer, who were both staring back at him.

"There's an officer outside."

Meyer looked at the clock on the mantelpiece.

"It'll be the duty officer, doing rounds."

Rossett nodded and looked back out of the window as a snow-covered Kübelwagen scout car drove into the courtyard, its tiny headlamps turning the falling snowflakes black as they cut through them.

He watched as the driver alighted, saluted, and passed the officer a dispatch folder.

Rossett turned away from the window and called to Hartz and Meyer.

"Get your coats."

"Are we leaving now?" Meyer asked.

Rossett ignored him and adjusted the knot on the string securing his shotgun, allowing the weapon to descend from under his arm so that he could grip the handle.

Rossett heard Meyer and Ruth get up from the couch and leave the room.

He rested his cheek on the glass again, watching as the officer outside started to walk across the courtyard toward the village.

Rossett squinted at the officer through the falling snow and the condensation.

The officer stopped.

Rossett frowned.

The officer turned back to the sentry.

Rossett looked toward the bedroom and then back to the window.

The officer looked up.

KARL BAYER, THE sentry outside the St. Catherine's Hall, was freezing his balls off.

He'd been stamping his feet trying to keep warm for four hours on sentry duty but slowly, over the last thirty minutes or so, as the temperature dropped even lower, he'd given up even doing that.

He was hungry, he was tired, he could barely feel his feet, and he wanted to piss.

"Fucking England, fucking Coton, fucking scientists who need guarding, fucking sentry duty, and fucking snow," Bayer muttered.

He blew into his gloves to try and get some warmth into his hands, then heard the door to the hall open behind him.

He half turned and saw it was an officer emerging. He faced front and snapped to attention, kicking the snow off his boots as he did so.

"Hello, Bayer, is everything all right?"

The officer of the watch, Captain Heitel, appeared in front of Bayer, giving him a quick inspection.

"Yes, sir."

"Cold tonight."

"Yes, sir."

"Warmer than Russia, though. We shouldn't complain, should we?" Heitel was from an old-school Prussian family, the sort who managed to make friendly chitchat sound like a threat.

"No, sir, we shouldn't," Bayer stared straight ahead but relaxed his shoulders slightly.

"Have you had a break?" Heitel pulled back the sleeve of his coat and looked at his watch.

"No, sir. I don't know what has happened to Keller; he was supposed to be here half an hour ago so I could get a coffee."

"Really?" Heitel looked at his watch again and then across the courtyard to the village. "Have you seen him on foot patrol?"

"I've not seen him since I came out on duty tonight, sir." Bayer wondered if he should drop his colleague further in the shit. A second passed, and he did. "He's never on time, sir, especially in this weather."

Heitel shook his head, walked across to the first window on the ground floor, and started to bang on the glass impatiently. He stepped back as a side window swung open and an off-duty private's head popped out.

"Go get me Staff Sergeant Munsch."

The head disappeared, and Heitel turned to Bayer.

"I'll sort you out a relief. Stand by."

Staff Sergeant Munsch's big, bald, heavily scarred head popped out of the window.

"Sir?"

"Why has this man been left out here without relief?"

Munsch looked at the back of Bayer; who in turn rolled his eyes to look up at the sky, glad that the staff sergeant couldn't look into his face.

Keller wasn't the only one in the shit.

Munsch wouldn't be happy, and Bayer had a feeling it was his arse that would be getting kicked after the officer walked away.

"Keller is relieving him, sir."

"And where is he?"

Munsch looked toward the village and then back at Heitel.

"I thought . . ."

"Get this man some relief and then get Keller in front of my desk first thing tomorrow. This isn't good enough, Staff Sergeant. We might be in the middle of nowhere, but that doesn't mean things can fall apart at the sight of the first drop of snow."

"No, sir. Of course, sir."

"While you are here, is the telephone working in your office?"

"I don't know, sir; it hasn't rung tonight, but—"

"Get someone to check it. The lines upstairs are dead. It'll be this bloody snow." Heitel looked up into the sky and then back at Munsch, who was still standing, head half out the window. "Well, go on, man!"

Heitel's shout caused Munsch to flinch.

"You heard the officer!" Munsch shouted at someone in the room behind him.

Bayer realized he would have been better off just keeping his mouth shut and freezing to death.

It was going to be a long night.

The sound of a car engine carried on the night air, and all three looked across the courtyard. Twenty seconds later a snow-covered Kübelwagen slithered into sight and drove toward them, eventually coming to a halt next to the other parked vehicles.

Bayer prayed it was Keller.

It wasn't.

An army corporal climbed out of the Kübelwagen and saluted smartly, holding a brown leather folder in his other hand.

Heitel returned the salute.

"Message from Cambridge command, sir." The driver held out the folder. "Phone lines are down because of the snow. We've been trying to raise you on the radio, but nobody is answering."

Heitel turned to look at Munsch, who frowned and dodged slightly back from the window.

"And?"

The driver offered the folder again. Heitel sighed and took it from him. It opened like a book and he took out a single flimsy sheet of typed paper that folded across his hand in the wind.

He turned slightly, so that he could read it under the light above the main door. He skimmed over the opening couple of lines about who had issued the order, then read the rest out loud for the benefit of Munsch:

"Detective Inspector John Henry Rossett is believed to be in Cambridge. He is wanted on suspicion of the murder of two men at a checkpoint. Rossett is suspected of being a resistance operative and is highly dangerous. There is reason to connect him to the death of an SS officer's wife in London." Heitel looked up at the dispatch driver and then back at the sheet. "Arrest or shoot on sight. He is six feet tall, well built, thirty-eight years of age, extremely dangerous with extensive military training. Notify London, et cetera." Heitel folded the order and passed the folder back to the driver.

He passed Munsch the sheet of paper through the window before speaking to the driver.

"Is there any reason to believe this man has any interest in Coton?"

"Not that I am aware of, sir. It was just that with you being cut off tonight and having the people from the university here, the duty officer in Cambridge thought it best that you know."

"Give him my thanks, and go and get yourself a warm drink before you head back."

"Thank you, sir." The driver saluted before nodding to Bayer and going into the hall.

Even the fucking driver gets a drink, thought Bayer, his morale falling faster than the snow, which was coming down heavily again.

Heitel turned to Munsch. "Make sure Bayer here is relieved before I get back."

"Yes, sir. Of course, sir."

Heitel nodded, tapped Bayer on the arm, and then set off across the courtyard on his way to inspect the gun emplacements.

He'd gotten thirty feet from the door before Bayer shouted his name.

"Captain Heitel, sir?"

Heitel turned.

"There was a man here before, with Reverend James. I didn't recognize him and, well, it's probably nothing, but . . . well, the reverend let him into the building and never came back, and he sort of matched that description. You don't think it could be . . ." Bayer trailed off.

"Where did he go?"

Bayer hesitated and then falteringly pointed with his thumb at the hall behind him.

Heitel looked at the hall as if seeing it for the first time.

He paused, looked over his shoulder toward the gun emplacement in the distance, and then back at Bayer.

"Sound the alarm."

ROSSETT JERKED BACK from the window as the captain in the courtyard looked up at the building. Instinctively he gripped the stock of the shotgun and then looked toward the corridor that led to the bedroom.

Meyer and Ruth appeared, Meyer in uniform, minus greatcoat, and Ruth in a long black woolen overcoat, black cap, sturdy black boots, and a black scarf at her throat.

All in black, except for the yellow star of David stitched onto the right breast of her overcoat.

Rossett could barely look at the star. Shame flushed his cheeks and his head lowered involuntarily.

"We need to get going; I think they know I'm here. Meyer, you go first. Distract anyone looking for me. We need transport—anything with fuel will do. Where is your coat?"

Meyer looked down at his tunic.

"In my room."

"Your sidearm?"

"I have it."

"Okay, you need a coat and maybe a rifle, if you can get one."

"We'll need to go to the officers' quarters to get them."

"Well, that's not going to happen, is it?" Rossett grabbed a tartan blanket off the back of the couch and threw it to Ruth.

"Fold this and carry it. He'll need it later."

Ruth nodded and Rossett crossed the room. He tried to smile reassuringly, failed, and then opened the door.

He looked out into the corridor.

Empty and silent.

Rossett gestured that Meyer should take the lead. Meyer smiled nervously at Ruth, tugged at the bottom of his tunic, and put on his cap before leaving, closely followed by Ruth, with Rossett bringing up the rear.

Meyer turned to walk toward the stairs that led to the front entrance, but Rossett grabbed his arm and shook his head.

"We can't go out the front. If they know I'm here, that's where they'll be forming up."

Meyer looked toward the stairs and shrugged.

"What, then?"

"The fire exit."

Rossett pulled Meyer past him in the direction of the fire exit he'd seen earlier.

"Where does this lead?" Rossett asked, still holding Meyer's arm.

"The kitchens, I think?" Meyer looked at Ruth for approval and she nodded.

"I think so. Nobody ever uses it."

"Go." Rossett gestured that Meyer should lead the way.

They had barely reached the door when they heard the shouts from downstairs, echoing in the corridor behind them.

"Munsch." Meyer looked at Rossett.

"Who?"

"Staff sergeant, rousing the men. He'll be trouble."

"Keep moving." Rossett looked over his shoulder toward where the sound was coming from, aware it was getting louder.

They hit the stairs at a run. The escape appeared to be a fairly modern addition to the hall. There was no sign of the wood paneling or portraits. In their place were only bare concrete walls and harsh electric lightbulbs. They clattered down the wooden staircase, making more noise than an SS brass band on Hitler's birthday.

All three automatically slowed as they neared the bottom of the stairs. Meyer looked over his shoulder at Rossett, who nodded. Meyer instinctively took hold of Ruth's hand and reached for the door handle.

"Hey!" Rossett called, and they looked around. "Let go of her hand. You aren't going on a picnic. She's a Jew and you are an SS officer, remember?"

Meyer looked down at his hand and let go. Ruth frowned at Rossett and took her place close behind Meyer as he opened the door.

She looked over her shoulder at Rossett.

"You are very rude."

"You have no idea," replied Rossett before pushing her out the door.

The kitchen was a blinding cube of white tiles. On one wall a big cast-iron range sat like a dirty black bruise. A steaming pot of coffee sat waiting for the night shift to enjoy.

In the center of the room was a ten-by-six-foot oak table, and at that table sat the dispatch driver, hands cupped around a mug as he stared at the three new arrivals who had just tumbled into the room.

The driver placed the mug on the table and stood to attention, sliding his chair away with the back of his legs as he did so.

"Who are you?" Meyer asked.

"Kraus, sir. I'm a messenger from Cambridge command."

"Was that you in the Kübelwagen?" Rossett said.

"Yes, sir."

"What was the dispatch you brought?"

Kraus looked at Meyer and then Rossett, reluctant to disclose the details of the confidential order to an Englishman.

"Speak," Meyer added.

Kraus shifted and then looked at Rossett. "A message from London, sir. There is some lunatic British policeman who has murdered two soldiers at a checkpoint on the London road, and by all accounts an SS officer's wife. The phone lines are down and my CO thought Coton should be made aware."

Meyer looked at Rossett.

"Murdered two soldiers?"

Rossett raised his eyebrows, almost apologetically.

"We need to get going, Meyer."

Kraus looked at Meyer and then at Rossett. The driver frowned at the realization that an Englishman who matched the description of the lunatic policeman was standing in front of him. And that next to the Englishman was a confused SS major, who looked like he had just fouled his pants and was about to cry.

Kraus looked toward the door.

Rossett produced the shotgun from under his coat in a smooth movement that took everyone by surprise.

The sound of the hammers on the shotgun whip-cracked off the tiles in the kitchen.

"You killed two Germans?" Meyer said.

"No," replied Rossett. "One German and a Brit, and we haven't got time for this right now."

"You killed a woman?" said Ruth.

"Oh, for . . . no."

Kraus visibly swallowed, then raised his hands slowly, palms out, unarmed and unwilling to fight.

"You said a woman was dead?" Ruth spoke to Kraus, who nodded.

"I was in the radio room when the message came through. All I heard was that an SS major's wife had been found dead, and that the policeman—" Kraus paused, and then folded the fingers on his left hand before pointing at Rossett. "And that he was wanted for it."

Rossett felt his heart deflate, stutter, and start again. The barrel of the shotgun dipped a few inches. Kraus lifted his chin and tried to take a step backward, only to be stopped by the chair behind him.

"What else did you hear?" Rossett's words barely carried across the room.

"I don't know much, I'm sorry . . ."

"What did you hear?" The barrel of the shotgun rose again, as the words came out stronger this time.

Kraus frowned. "Nothing, sir, I swear."

"Did you hear anything about a young girl?"

"You killed a young girl?" Ruth's turn to take a step backward.

"No." Rossett jabbed the shotgun toward Kraus. "Did you hear anything about a child?"

"No, sir."

Rossett paused, his mind racing, staring at Kraus while behind him Ruth looked at Meyer, who gave a tiny shake of his head.

"We need to get going," Rossett finally said.

Ruth stared at him.

"Please?" Rossett tried again.

The door to the kitchen, twelve feet from Rossett, swung open and a young private entered. MP40 slung over his shoulder, he stopped, took in the scene, and started to unsling his machine pistol.

Rossett fired before the MP40 cleared the private's shoulder.

The private slammed backward into the wall, his helmet ringing against the tiles and dropping forward to cover his eyes as he slid down onto the floor. He patted at the wounds on his chest lightly as if to confirm that they were there, then looked up at Rossett.

Rossett swung the shotgun toward Kraus, who lifted his hands high above his head and closed his eyes. Rossett moved quickly around the table, through the drifting smoke of the shot, toward the private, who had stopped patting his chest and had rolled down onto his side.

The private's helmet dropped to the floor, rattling on the tiles like a spun coin coming to rest.

He was dead.

"Are you mad?" Meyer grabbed hold of Ruth and pulled her behind him.

Rossett crouched down, testing for a pulse on the soldier's neck while watching Kraus, who was still by the table.

"This is crazy," Meyer said, apparently to nobody but himself.

Rossett ignored Meyer and pulled the MP40 from the private's shoulder, half dragging him away from the wall in the process.

The kitchen door opened again. Rossett dropped the MP40 he was holding in his left hand and gripped the barrel of the one that was coming through the door, as it was nervously poked in by the soldier holding it. The soldier tried to jerk the weapon free from Rossett but failed.

"Shoot him!" Kraus screamed. He charged toward Rossett, who swung the shotgun up under his arm and fired the second barrel at Kraus. The young German took the force of the blast in his upper legs from less than six feet.

Kraus managed one step before dropping to the floor holding his buckshot-shredded thighs. He landed at the base of the door, the weight of his body pushing it back against the soldier with whom Rossett was wrestling.

Rossett let go of the shotgun, which was still fastened to him by the string, and then wrenched the MP40 forward and down. He dragged the soldier holding the gun into the kitchen, shifting Kraus as the soldier squeezed through the gap. Rossett rose from his haunches, coming up behind the soldier while still holding the gun barrel with his left hand.

Rossett gripped the stock of the MP40 and, using the soldier's hand as a pivot, spun the weapon up and into the jaw of the young man. Teeth crunched as the metal body of the machine gun slammed home, but still the soldier held on to the barrel as it spun once more in his grasp, and slammed home again.

The second blow did it. The soldier finally let go and dropped to the floor, spitting blood.

Rossett rammed the MP40 into the back of the soldier's head, a solid blow that sent him into unconsciousness. He stood up from the soldier panting, spinning the MP40 and automatically flicking his hand across the bolt to check that it was ready to fire.

Violence thrummed through his veins like electricity down cables. His teeth were gritted tight and he was breathing fast. He looked up to Ruth and Meyer, who both remained standing by the table, in shock at what they had just witnessed.

Kraus moaned and clawed at the smooth floor tiles to move backward away from Rossett. His trousers were tattered and blood soaked, and he was ghostly pale with shock, his eyes fixed on the gun in Rossett's hands.

Rossett finally found his voice. "Let's go."

Meyer looked at the two men on the floor, then clumsily reached with both hands to his holster and drew his pistol, taking a half step to the left and working the slide.

Rossett brought the MP40 to bear but didn't fire for fear of hitting Ruth.

Meyer froze, frowned, lowered the gun, and then sank to his knees, sliding off the knife Ruth Hartz had just slipped into his back.

Ruth Hartz was a killer.

She stood stiffly, eyes on Rossett, holding the bloody knife in her left hand, shaking a fraction until it dropped to the floor.

The door next to where Rossett was crouching started to open. Kraus's and the dead soldier's weight held it closed after the first inch or two of movement. Rossett spun to face whoever was trying to get in.

There was confused shouting on the other side, then a vicious burst of machine gun fire peppered the door, flicking timber across the floor and riddling a shuddering Kraus with bullets.

Rossett hit the deck as wood chips rained on his head from the splintering timber.

Ruth ducked down, dodging right, and hid behind the table as Rossett rolled on the floor. He positioned himself with both feet against Kraus, who was now slumped dead at the bottom of the door. Rossett lay on his back with his legs straight, looking at the ceiling with the machine gun across his chest and his feet pressing against the base of the door via Kraus.

Another shove, and then another half magazine rattled through into the kitchen, slamming and shattering the tiles on the far wall.

The shooting outside stopped.

Rossett sat up, bringing the MP40 to bear. He fired a two-second burst through the door and heard the shout of an injured man on the other side. Rossett dodged his head left and right to try to see through the holes the rounds had made, but there wasn't enough light to make out what was going on on the other side.

He waited, listened, blinking as the cordite stung his eyes, and then heard what he wanted to hear, the sound of someone being dragged down the hall to safety.

He'd stopped them for now.

Rossett fired again. There was another shout and he rolled to his left. Rossett quickly got to his feet on the hinge side of the door, standing so his back was up against the wall. He looked at Ruth, who was peeking over the tabletop at him, and then flinched as two or three magazines were emptied into the door from outside.

Rossett waited for the shooting to stop, then returned fire with the remaining rounds in his clip as he stepped across the door. He picked up the other MP40 from the floor as he dropped the empty one, still smoking, onto the tiles.

He dashed across the room, grabbed Ruth's arm, and dragged her up from behind the table as another volley of gunfire came into the kitchen, flicking yet more wood across the floor and finally punching a hole the size of a man's head in the shattered timber.

Rossett and Ruth were in the fire escape by the time whoever was shooting had emptied their magazine. Rossett led her up the first flight of stairs at a run, toward a two-foot-square frosted-glass window.

He used the MP40 to smash the glass and clear the bottom of the frame, then stuck his head through the window to look outside. There was a twelve-foot drop to the snow below, then forty feet of open ground rising to the bank of trees that ran along the side of the hall.

"Through here." Rossett grabbed Ruth, who reached up to the frame. He gripped her rising foot with his left hand and hoisted her through the window, almost launching her outside.

He heard more shots from the kitchen, slung the MP40 over his shoulder, then reached up to the frame. He felt some pieces of broken glass dig into his palms, and the shotgun under his greatcoat rattled and caught as he was halfway out the window. For a moment he was stuck fast. He wriggled, looked for Ruth below, and saw she was already halfway to the trees.

He twisted as he flung himself forward, hearing his coat rip as he went. The thick snow broke most of his fall, but it wasn't deep enough to stop the shotgun butt from slamming into his ribs, punching the air from his lungs as he landed.

He gasped and rolled onto his back, breath coming in quick, shallow snatches. He dug the shotgun out from under him and opened the breech, quickly ejecting the two spent shells.

His right hand fumbled in his inside pocket as he stared at the window above. He'd barely managed to insert the shells when a head appeared.

The gun clacked, clicked, and fired in less than a second at the unlucky soldier who had been the first to follow them through the window.

Rossett saw the frame erupt in a shower of glass and wood from the blast. The soldier cried out and disappeared back inside.

Rossett rolled, then rose, still half winded, before starting to run for the trees. He looked for Ruth ahead of him but she was gone, already deep in cover, and no doubt still running for her life.

Rossett covered thirty feet before turning and firing again at the window. He missed, as he guessed he would, but he knew that whoever was on the other side wouldn't fancy sticking a head out, not until they were sure the shotgun was long gone.

He dropped the shotgun, letting it swing under his coat. He unslung the MP40 off his shoulder as he ran into the cover of the trees. Finally, behind him, he heard the wild firing of a machine gun through the window. Some snow was dislodged from the branches above by the high and wide rounds; it floated down gently.

Rossett's breath was just coming back when he ran full force into a low branch that he hadn't seen in the darkness. It hit him in the throat; he felt his legs flicking forward as the momentum of his body pivoted, spinning him heels over head onto the damp ground.

He reached for his throat, the breath punched out of him again. He looked up into the trees above, thick bare branches wafting in the gusting wind against the pink sky. Another rattle of machine gun fire sounded behind him, this time lower, chipping the bark off the trees to his right. Rossett gasped for air and reached his other hand to his throat, arching his back for a breath that wouldn't come, suddenly missing along with half of his senses.

Out of the darkness came Ruth.

"Come on." She held out her hand.

Another burst of gunfire.

"Get up!" she was screaming at him.

For the briefest of moments Rossett saw her beauty again, pale, whiter than the snow, her long fingers reaching for him, beckoning him on.

He snatched a sliver of air.

He blinked, tried again, more oxygen filling his desperate lungs.

Ruth dragged at his arm and Rossett heard shouts behind him. He couldn't speak. She pulled him, lifting him slightly off the ground, so that he started to turn in the mud under the trees where the snow hadn't been able to settle fully.

He nodded and rose, with her help. Another breath sneaked past his battered Adam's apple and he managed to swallow.

More shots, closer again, more bark flying and dancing in the darkness, followed by shouts that sounded ever closer.

Rossett stood, wobbled, snatched another breath, and pushed Ruth forward, waving his hand to let her know he was all right. He took a few steps before turning and working the bolt of the MP40. He dodged his head left, just able to make out the shadowy shape of the three or four men who had dropped through the window in pursuit. They were moving slowly, spaced a few feet apart in a line, not wanting to rush into the dark wood.

Rossett fired his entire magazine at the line, and the pursuers dived down for cover. Panicked shouts sounded behind him as he threw the machine gun and started to run forward again, this time slightly slower, chin down, one arm raised to protect his face.

His lungs had finally filled by the time he saw Ruth ahead. She was moving carefully and quickly, a black panther in the night. Through the half-light he could see flashes of her face as she stole glances back over her shoulder.

They broke the tree line on the other side of the small wood at almost the same time, maybe twenty feet apart. Ruth looked at Rossett and pointed to the hedgerow that ran along the left side of the field, and they ran toward it, plowing through the powdery snow that splashed up around their high-stepping legs in clouds.

In half a minute they plunged into the ditch next to the hedge, smashing through the ice and into the drainage water.

Rossett realized for the first time that it was still snowing; heavy white flakes were blowing in across the field. They ran along the ditch, smashing and cracking through the ice and mud, brambles and hedgerow catching on their clothes. Rossett looked over his shoulder and saw that the snowfall had already nearly obscured the wood behind them.

It gave them cover; it gave them a chance.

As he ran he reloaded the shotgun, mentally counting off the eight shells he had left, including the two in the gun, plus his pistol, which was fully loaded.

Minus the two rounds he would save till last.

CHAPTER 35

THEY RAN FOR at least fifteen minutes.

Zigzagging across the fields, following the hedgerows and ditches, ducking and diving, keeping to the cover they provided as best as they could. Rossett had seen vehicle lights in the distance at one point, far off to his left. Ruth hadn't waited for his instructions; she had turned sharply to put distance between them and their pursuers.

Rossett was impressed, but he was more impressed by her fitness.

The cold night air clawed at his throat and burned his lungs. It wasn't just the injury on his stomach that was slowing him down. Rossett was quickly realizing he had spent too much of the last few months smoking and drinking. His pace had gradually slowed as the last few minutes passed, and his legs had grown heavy and uncertain in the deep snow.

He needed to stop, he had nothing left.

They dropped into another ditch under another hedgerow. Ruth splashed to the other side, ready to climb out and continue, as Rossett, gasping for air, slid down the mud-covered bank. He threw his head back, mouth wide, trying to fill his lungs as he held up a hand, beckoning Ruth back toward him.

"Stop." Rossett gasped a breath and looked up into the falling snow. "For God's sake . . . wait." Breathless, rubbing at his bruised throat with his left hand. "Give me a minute."

Ruth was eight feet in front of him, halfway up the bank of the ditch, feet out of the water. She watched Rossett struggle to breathe and then looked across the field they had just crossed. Satisfied they weren't immediately in danger, she made her way to him, careful to keep her boots clear of the sucking mud at the bottom of the ditch.

"You're bleeding," she said as she reached out and touched Rossett's forehead, tilting his head back so she could see the gash just above his hairline from where he had run into some gorse.

She touched the wound. The blood looked black in the night. Rossett flinched and pushed her hand away.

"I need a minute."

Ruth frowned, picked up some fresh snow, and put it to her lips as she watched him.

Rossett saw her big brown eyes blink as she studied him. He touched his head wound himself and then smoothed his hair down across it.

He realized Ruth wasn't out of breath and he suddenly felt old.

His turn to frown.

Ruth made her way along the hedgerow, eventually standing up to look into the next field. Rossett shifted position, finally taking his soaking feet out of the water, then slowly following Ruth as his breath returned to something approaching normal.

Ruth looked at him as he reached her. "Do you know where we are?"

"I was going to ask you the same thing."

"Didn't you have a vehicle?"

"I did, but God knows where it is now. We came out the other side of the building. I'm lost."

He turned and looked back, squinting against the wind and the snow that was almost blowing in sideways now.

"Great." Ruth looked around them and then up at the sky as another gust of wind shook the hedge at their backs.

"If we can find a farm we'll find transport." Rossett leaned forward, lifting his head out of the ditch and into the wind, which ruffled his hair and lifted one side of the collar on his coat, slapping it against his cheek.

"And then what?"

"We head back to London." Rossett slid back down and checked the illuminated hands of his watch. "I call Koehler there and we follow his instructions."

"Koehler?"

"My friend, the reason I'm doing this."

"I thought you were working for the Americans?"

"You think too much."

"It's my job."

Rossett looked at Ruth, her face out of the shadows now, hair whipping across her pale skin like flames of black fire.

"Leave it to me for now, okay?" said Rossett.

"Because you're doing such a good job?"

"We just need transport." Rossett adjusted his feet, which were sliding down into the water. "Let's get moving. We can't afford to let the Germans get too organized or they will start shutting roads and box us in."

Rossett pushed past Ruth up the bank and out into the open field. He turned, offered her his hand, and pulled her up as well.

"Did you kill the woman?" said Ruth, facing straight ahead, eyes on the other side of the field.

"I've killed lots of people, but not that one."

"The others, have they deserved it?"

"I've done what I've done; this isn't the time to question it."

The wind almost carried Rossett's words away before Ruth could hear them.

"I had to stab Horst."

Rossett held out his hand to her.

"Now isn't the time."

"You have to understand, I can't let anyone get in my way."

"I'll remember that." Rossett beckoned with his hand again.

"No, you have to understand: nothing can be allowed to stop me getting away from here, from them, nothing . . . and no one."

Rossett stared at her, and then nodded.

"It's okay."

"If Horst had stopped us, if I was forced to carry on working for the Germans . . . so many others are at risk, this is so much more than one man's life."

Rossett could see that the words were meant just as much for her own ears as for his. He gently touched her arm.

"Leave the killing to me."

"You have no idea, do you?" Ruth's hair covered her face, so she hooked some in her fingers, pulling it away so she could look into Rossett's eyes. "If you had any sense you'd pull your pistol out of your coat and shoot me where I stand. I can kill millions; I can wipe mankind off the face of the planet. You're talking to the most dangerous human being on earth and you have no idea . . . I am death."

Rossett looked to where they were heading and then back at Ruth.

"I don't care about millions, I don't care about you, and I don't care about the Americans. I care about a scared young girl who is relying on me to save her from danger. It's her, that girl, her fear, her need, it is that that makes *me* the most dangerous person on the planet. So until she is safe, you stop thinking and do as I say. Okay?"

"You really just don't understand, do you?"

Ruth dropped her eyes and then started walking.

THEY COVERED MILES, trudging through foot-deep snow and leaning into the wind. In the silence between them Rossett drifted like the snow, thinking of Ruth's hair and the way she had hooked it away. It reminded him of his wife.

The same wayward hair.

The same angry eyes.

Years apart, angry women talking to him about killing.

He lifted his face and looked toward the next low wall on the edge of the field, and stumbled in the snow before catching his own fall and carrying on.

His wife hadn't wanted him to join the army.

She'd thought he was crazy to quit the police and take up arms against an as-yet-undeclared enemy.

Rossett wished he'd listened to her.

War had damaged him, mentally as well as physically; he still bore both sets of scars, although the physical ones had faded slightly.

Ruth turned her head to look at him as they walked. He realized he was holding his hand against the scar on his stomach through his coat.

"Are you all right?" she asked.

No, he thought.

"Yes," he said.

Ruth nodded, half a pace ahead. She went back to staring at the snow as she dug out her steps and carried on.

Rossett felt empty, exhausted, but he kept going.

Same as ever.

Anja.

He thought about the girl he hardly knew. They'd met once, in Koehler's office. She was awkward with Rossett, his usual lack of words unsettling her.

He couldn't tell her he was jealous of her father; he couldn't tell her that her existence made him jealous.

Koehler loved Anja. Anja loved her father.

Rossett loved his son. His son was dead.

He wouldn't let Koehler know that pain; he wouldn't wish it on any man.

So he'd said nothing, smiled, and left the room.

"Do you smell that?"

Rossett looked up, back in the real world.

"What?" he asked.

"Smoke. I can smell smoke."

They both stopped.

Rossett lifted his face to the wind.

"Wood smoke," he repeated, turning to his right, toward the wind and the driving snow. "This way."

They walked a quarter of a mile before they saw the farmhouse in a shallow dip. They couldn't see any lights through the driving blizzard. Rossett reached forward to stop Ruth once they drew to within one hundred yards. He crouched down and beckoned her closer so he could whisper.

"There might be dogs, so we need to be careful. They'll pick up our scents. We need the wind in our face. Farmers have shotguns and short tempers."

"They aren't the only ones with shotguns and short tempers." Ruth smiled, for the first time since he'd met her.

He saw his wife again, there, a glimpse, just at the edges of Ruth's face in the darkness.

Rossett started moving forward again.

They reached the stone wall that surrounded the farm and looked over at the farmyard beyond. A small flatbed van was parked close to the farmhouse, snow a third of the way up its wheels, and covering its roof and bonnet.

The smell of the smoke was being carried away on the wind, and no light shone from any of the windows. Rossett dropped back down behind the wall and Ruth joined him, shoulder to shoulder.

"We steal the van?"

Rossett shook his head.

"We'd have to dig it out, and as soon as we started it they'd be out after us. In this snow we'd never get away."

"We could push it clear of the house?"

"Too much snow, we'll never move it."

"What, then?"

"We need to get in the house, incapacitate whoever is in there." Rossett turned and looked over the wall again.

"Incapacitate?"

Rossett looked at Ruth and frowned. He didn't want to say "kill" out loud.

"Most young people are off working on the Continent. At best there is a farmer and his wife on their own. At worst there'll be a farmer, a wife, maybe one or two young people kept back for essential labor. If we can get in quickly, get them secured, that'll give us time to get away."

"We could sit out the storm there?"

"We keep moving."

Rossett produced the Mauser he had taken from the checkpoint guard earlier that day. He held it up for Ruth to see.

"Have you used one of these?"

She shook her head, so Rossett worked the slide on the pistol, then pointed at the safety catch.

"Slide that forward and pull the trigger, that's all you have to do."

Ruth nodded and held out her hand. Rossett placed the pistol on her palm and closed her hand around it.

"We don't want to hurt these people," he said, still holding her hand. "Do you understand? They aren't soldiers, they are just normal people. I don't want any more deaths. There's been enough bloodshed. Keep the pistol out of sight and let me do the talking. Okay?"

"Yes."

Rossett nodded, then released the gun into Ruth's possession. He stood and hopped over the wall to land in the drifted snow on the other side. He turned to help her across, and as he held out his hand she paused.

"You said you had to make a call when we got to London?"

"Or on the way, but yes, I have to make a call," Rossett replied, still holding his hand out to her.

"Maybe you should give me the number, just in case."

Rossett gestured that she should take his hand and climb over. Ruth did as he wanted and Rossett reached up to her. Holding her arm, he helped her down. When she was standing next to him, calf deep in the drifted snow, Rossett leaned in close.

"You'll just have to hope nothing happens to me like what happened to your boyfriend. Now put that pistol into your pocket, you're making me nervous."

Ruth did as he asked and followed Rossett across the farmyard. Behind the house, dark, brooding outbuildings loomed through the falling snow.

A whiff of decay hung over the farm.

Ruth squeezed the grip of the pistol in her pocket.

A dog started to bark in the farmhouse, some sixth sense alerting it to the presence of strangers, sounding the alarm for those inside. Rossett paused. There was still no light shining from any of the windows, and other than the dog the only sound was the crunch of the snow under their feet.

He headed for the front door and banged heavily on it with the side of his fist. He stepped back and unbuttoned his coat, letting it hang open so that he could access the shotgun if he needed it.

The sound of the dog's barking grew louder until the scrabbling of paws on the inside of the door indicated that someone was coming. Rossett took another step back, unwilling to get this far and then be taken down by an angry dog. He looked over his shoulder and realized for the first time that there were no other animals to be seen or heard—no chickens, no sheep, no pigs, nothing.

It was as if the farm was dead.

"What the bloody hell do you want?"

The farm wasn't dead.

A head was poking out of a darkened upstairs window; Rossett instinctively grabbed hold of Ruth and dragged her with him as he stepped into the doorframe for cover.

"Oi! I asked you what you want?"

The dog was now barking louder, scrabbling furiously on the other side of the door as Rossett leaned forward, looking cautiously up toward the window.

"We're lost, we need help."

"Why you wandering round this time of night?"

"Because we are fucking lost and we need help!" Rossett shouted, then felt Ruth's hand on his arm.

She stepped forward. "Our car has broken down. We really are in trouble."

The farmer above thought for a moment and then the window slammed shut.

THE CANDLE WAS barely brighter than the dying fire in the hearth. They'd had to wait two minutes at the door before the old man had finally managed to make it downstairs and pull back the heavy bolt that was barring it.

A grizzled old sheepdog, with a gray muzzle and a bald right paw, sat squinting at them through cataracts. The farmer inched his way round the room lighting more candles that seemed to waver nervously in the constant draft that blew through the house.

"Police, you say?" The farmer and the dog squinted at Rossett.

"I need your truck."

"You can have it. Bleedin' thing hasn't started in months."

"It's broken down?"

"Totally buggered," the farmer replied as he leaned in close to Ruth, studying the yellow star on her coat and then looking up into her face.

"She's a Jew." The farmer looked at Rossett, who was putting his police warrant card back into his suit pocket. "We don't get many of them round here," said the farmer, turning to look at Ruth again.

"Do you have any other form of transport?" Rossett was already buttoning up his coat.

"Oh, aye, I've got a horse, but he's pretty much buggered as well." The farmer shuffled across the room in untied boots. He tossed a piece of wood onto the embers behind Rossett, then stabbed at the fire with a poker, speaking without looking up.

"Bleedin' 'orse just eats and shits. You ask him to pull something and he ain't interested. He's useless, he is."

Smoke billowed from the fire and Rossett took a few steps away from it. The dog retook his place.

"How far is the nearest main road?"

"Main road?"

"Yes."

"Well, that depends."

"On what?"

"On what you mean by main road. See, round here we don't have many roads you could call 'main.'"

Rossett considered shooting the old man.

"Just tell me where the nearest road is that will have cars on it."

A lonely flame crept up the back of the fresh log. The old man scratched at his chest through his vest, with a finger that was more knuckle than anything.

He looked at the ceiling deep in thought.

"Road, you say . . ."

Rossett looked at Ruth and then back at the farmer, who was still scratching and staring.

"It is a simple question. Answer it."

"Well, the old St. Neots Road is a few miles north of here. And the London Road is a few miles west, but they aren't busy roads, not by any measure. Not since the Germans showed up, that is."

"Who else around here has a truck?"

"A truck?"

"Do you have to repeat everything I say?"

The old man frowned at Rossett's rudeness and turned back to poke the fire again. He agitated a few sparks, one of which landed on the dog and filled the room with the smell of singed fur.

The dog didn't move; it was probably used to it.

"A truck?" the old man said to himself before starting to scratch his chest again.

"I haven't got all night."

"Neither 'ave I. I've got to feed the bleedin' pigs at six o'clock. Then I've got to milk them cows in the lower barn, then I've got to drive over to Caxton to pick up . . ."

"Drive?" Rossett held up his hand to stop the farmer, who paused in his scratching and squinted at the finger.

"Aye, I've got to drive up to Caxton to—"

"What in?"

"What?"

"What in? What are you driving in?"

"My car, what do you think?"

Rossett opened his hand, touched the side of his face in exasperation, and then looked at Ruth before turning back to the farmer.

"You said you didn't have a car."

"No, I never."

"I asked you . . . it doesn't matter. I'm commandeering your car. Where is it?"

"My car? You can't take my car; I've got to go over to Caxton in the morning after I—"

Rossett pulled his Webley and pointed it at the farmer.

"Give me the fucking keys."

CHAPTER 36

H**OW THE ENGLISH** drink this swill amazes me." King stirred the strong tea in the mug with a spoon and shook his head. "It's like watery mud."

He set the mug down and dropped the teaspoon next to it on the table with a rattle; then turned sideways in his seat and looked around the café. He scanned the various taxi drivers and night-shift workers who were dotted around the steamy, noisy room, eating, drinking, or reading newspapers.

King looked at his watch, then gingerly felt the lumps and scratches on his head where Koehler had hit him earlier.

"Shithole." King shook his head and looked at Koehler sitting opposite him across the table. "How long do we wait here?"

"Until Rossett calls," Koehler replied flatly.

"Why here?"

"Because this is his place. It's where he chose."

"So we just sit?"

"Till he calls."

King breathed out noisily before looking up at the ceiling of the café, and then back at Koehler.

"You come here a lot?"

Koehler didn't reply.

"The waitress knew you; I could tell when you ordered the tea at the counter."

Koehler took a drink and then put the mug back down on the table. He looked at King, pointedly ignoring the question.

King sighed once more and then gingerly touched his head again.

He looked at his fingertips and then held them up for Koehler to see.

"I've stopped bleeding."

"For now."

King smirked. "You don't say much, do you?"

Koehler didn't reply.

"I know that you are . . . well, I know that you're angry with me. Jesus, I can understand why. But you have to realize I want to help you get your daughter back. I can't make what I've done right, but I can at least help you get . . ." King broke off, not wanting to say Anja's name for some reason he couldn't quite understand. "Get your daughter back."

Koehler picked up the battered pack of cigarettes and shook one out; he closed the box and tapped the cigarette on the tabletop before lighting it.

He turned back to King, watching him over the top of the mug and through the smoke.

King waited for an answer that didn't come, and eventually he sighed and tried again.

"I'm sorry, okay? I'll keep saying it, I'm sorry . . . I really mean it, I'm sorry."

Koehler picked a strand of tobacco off his tongue, looked at it, then rolled it in his fingers before dropping it into the foil ashtray between them. He sucked on the cigarette and King heard it crackle as the tip glowed, then turned to ash.

Koehler leaned forward, blowing smoke through his nose; he took the cigarette out of his mouth and used it to beckon King closer.

"You killed my fucking wife and kidnapped my daughter, you bastard. You're a murderer, you are scum, and when the time is right I'm going to kill you."

Koehler sat back in his chair and put the cigarette into his mouth once more. He picked up the mug of tea with his other hand, still staring at King, who stared back at him.

It took King ten seconds to blink; he lowered his head, paused, and then looked up again at Koehler.

"You know, I'm sorry about your wife, I really am. I'm going to keep on saying it because I genuinely regret what happened." King looked at the table again, shifted slightly, and then looked up. "Thing is, while I can understand your anger, I can't understand your indignation."

Koehler raised one eyebrow a fraction as King continued.

"You see"—King squeezed the bridge of his nose and then lowered his hand to the table—"you're a fucking Nazi. You're in the SS. Your job, your life, your whole existence is built on killing people. Husbands, sons, daughters, and, if you'll forgive me for saying it, wives. You guys kill 'em, you kill 'em all. I didn't mean for your wife to get hurt, but I won't accept you taking the moral high ground over me. Someone who is part of a machine built by death has no right to complain when death visits him."

"She was an innocent woman out shopping with her child."

King shook his head and looked out at the street outside. Five or six black taxis were parked opposite, and he could see his face reflected in the window looking back.

"Do you see that?" King gestured toward his reflection but Koehler missed the point and looked at the taxis outside. "My reflection in the glass, can you see it?" King tried again.

Koehler looked at the window, and then back at King.

"I can look at myself. Can you?" King looked away from the window and back to Koehler.

Koehler tapped the cigarette over the ashtray.

King nodded, then carried on speaking, his voice low, barely audible over the noise of the café.

"I didn't kill your wife; she shot herself when she was struggling with Eric, my partner. I concede, with genuine regret, that my actions led to that struggle, and for that I am sorry. But I did what I had to do. I was following orders, orders that I believe to be in the best interests of my country, and the battle against fascism . . . the battle against you. Okay, I admit it, I am a bad man. I have done things for my country that I am ashamed of." King held up his hands in surrender, then folded his fingers into his palms and leaned forward, unfurling his left index finger and pointing it at Koehler. "But—this is important, and you need to remember this—I'm a long way behind you when it comes to killing. I'm an amateur compared to you. I know your reputation; I know how many lives you've taken, how many people you've disappeared . . . I'm an amateur, pure and simple."

"I am a soldier," Koehler said through the smoke.

King smiled and shook his head.

"No. No, really, you are a monster, you are a reaper of souls, you are dripping in blood. You are the man who loads the trains, Ernst; you are the man who stopped being a soldier to be the collector of the Jews. All in the name of a madman. You are the man who rounds up the innocents and then sends them away. How many is it? One hundred? One thousand? Ten thousand? Do you even know? You are evil. What you do is evil." King folded his finger back into his fist and leaned back an inch, staring at Koehler with cold gray eyes. "I think, deep down, deep, deep down, you know that. I think there's even a small chance that you struggle with it. But whatever inner wars you may fight, you keep dealing death. So don't fucking complain when it bites you on the ass."

The waitress came over and King sat fully back and smiled at her.

"Can I get you gentlemen anything to eat?"

"I'd love a bacon sandwich." King smiled again and raised his eyebrows at Koehler. "Do you want anything?"

"Sir?" The waitress looked at Koehler, who waved her away.

King smiled at Koehler, who stared back across the table, through the ribbon of smoke that was rising from the cigarette, still held in his clenched fist on the table.

"You see, Koehler, whatever I do, however badly I behave, and whatever carnage I leave behind, I'm just an amateur compared to you, and I always will be."

King picked up his tea, took a sip, and pulled a face.

He never even saw Koehler whipping his right hand out and across the table. Koehler caught hold of the lapel of King's raincoat and dragged him over the table, knocking King's mug onto the floor, where it smashed as the teaspoon clattered behind it. Koehler dragged King closer as the American pushed back in a futile attempt to fight him off.

King could smell the cigarette on Koehler's breath.

For a moment the café was utterly silent, except for the hiss of the water boiler behind the counter.

Koehler stared into King's eyes as he held the other man, inches from his face.

Nobody moved in the café, and seconds passed before King whispered softly to Koehler.

"You know I'm right. You are the devil. You just don't want to admit it."

Koehler's cheek fluttered, another moment passed, and then he released his grip on King and shoved him backward across the table, so hard King almost tipped out of his seat and onto the floor.

Koehler ran a hand through his hair and then looked toward the other people seated around them. Everyone quickly looked away.

King adjusted his raincoat, then leaned down to pick up a few pieces of the broken mug as a nervous hum of conversation resumed in the café. King placed the broken crockery on the edge of the table and adjusted his coat again.

"Ernst, we all tell ourselves we don't have a choice. We behave the way we do because we think it's all we can do. You aren't alone." King spoke more quietly this time, in a less challenging tone; he touched the lump on his head again and then placed his hand palm down on the table. "If I could go back and stop this, I would."

King lifted his hand an inch, staring at it, before nodding to himself and placing it back down.

"I had a choice today. I took the easy option. I hid and waited instead of charging in and fighting for someone else. Someone I dragged into this, someone who didn't deserve to die. I hid. I hid while they killed him."

He looked up at Koehler and then continued.

"Choices, eh? Life is easy when you don't have them. When there is someone telling you what to do, you always have someone else to blame when it goes wrong. 'I was just following orders' works every time. Do you know that's why we picked you?"

Koehler looked at him silently.

"We looked for someone who would fight, take the hard options. We needed someone who could get down and dirty, someone who could think on the move. Someone not like me. I follow orders, and we needed a *street fighter*. We hoped we were getting two when we picked you. We hoped Rossett would get on board, and we thought we'd have the dream team. You and him, doing our dirty work." King chuckled sadly. "Eric and I thought we were doing the easy bit."

The waitress appeared nervously next to them. She placed the bacon sandwich down on the table before collecting the broken bits of mug.

"I'm sorry about that," King said. "I can't stand tea."

The waitress looked at Koehler and then back at King.

"Would you like a coffee?"

"I would *love* a coffee. That would be so kind of you."

She smiled, nodded, and left the table. King watched her go, then turned back to Koehler and took half the sandwich before sliding the plate with the other half across the table toward him.

Koehler slid the plate back.

"Why do you want the Jew in Cambridge so badly?" Koehler looked out the window as he spoke.

"Because we can't afford to let you guys have her."

"So *you* having the bomb is better than *us* having the bomb?"

"You'll get your bomb, Ernst, don't worry about that. It'll maybe take a little longer, but the result will be the same."

"If we have time."

"America wouldn't attack first."

"Your government isn't that much different from mine."

"We're still a democracy."

"For now. Lindbergh is eating away at your precious liberty in the name of security."

"If we have the bomb we'll be secure, then there won't be a threat."

Koehler gave a slight shake of his head and then looked at King.

"Weapons don't make you secure; they just make the other man get a bigger weapon. Be careful, because one day you might find yourself looking at your reflection, realizing you're not that much different from me. And if that day comes, there is no going back. Once you start, you are rolling down the hill to hell, and it's almost impossible to stop."

King shook his head and put the sandwich down on the plate untasted.

"We'll get your daughter back. I'll make it right," King said without looking up from the sandwich.

"I'll get her back."

King rested his elbows on the table as his head dropped forward wearily.

He didn't move for minutes. When he finally lifted his head he found that Koehler was still staring at him, and there was a mug of steaming coffee on the table.

"The resistance jumped us at the flat. As we were trying to see them off, your daughter managed to get hold of Eric's gun and left us with no choice but to run. She outfoxed the pair of us."

"You left her to the resistance?"

"She had a gun; we didn't have a choice. We were pinned down on both sides. We had to withdraw." King slid the plate away from him, toward the ashtray, and pointed to Koehler's cigarettes. "May I?"

Koehler nodded. King lit up and then exhaled with his eyes closed. He seemed to meditate for a moment.

"I left Eric to get us some transport, and the resistance took him. I followed them to a house and I waited to see what would happen."

"And what happened?"

King shrugged. "They killed him. I fucked up and they killed him. I was waiting to see how things played out, and they were killing him fifty feet away from me while I couldn't make up my mind."

Koehler didn't reply.

"He was just a clerk, a dumb kid looking for some excitement," King said quietly.

"You know he is dead?"

"I killed two of them. Eric tried to escape, and they chased him. He was pretty badly injured . . . very badly injured." King took another drag. "They tortured him for information. He told me that he hadn't told them anything. He was brave. He wasn't a soldier, but he was brave."

Koehler swilled the cold tea in his cup, staring into it as King drifted off to the memory of Eric dying in the snow.

After a moment Koehler looked up.

"You killed two of them?"

"Yes, I shot them."

"Was that all there was?"

"No. There was an old man, very tall, and a fat woman. She was vicious, a handful, I think she made them torture him. She got away, I think," King looked at Koehler and smiled sadly. "I always seem to have problems with women."

Koehler frowned. "Was that a joke?"

"I'm sorry, bad taste."

Koehler stared across the table and then spoke again.

"Does this woman have Anja?"

"I don't think so. I mean, I never saw her there."

"How old was she?"

"I don't know, forty, maybe fifty?"

"Vicious?"

"Oh, God, yes. She—well, the injuries to Eric . . ." King shook his head. "I should have killed her."

"Anything else about her?"

"Other than fat, short, with black hair?"

"Yes."

"No. Why?"

"Maybe we can trace her. I have a friend who might know her, or he may be able to make inquiries with the local police."

King nodded.

"I'd ask the embassy for help, but . . ."

"But?"

"They've cut me loose."

Koehler's eyes narrowed.

"Loose?"

"For now. Once we have the scientist they'll deal with me again."

"You?"

"I can help you, Koehler, I told you. Once we have the scientist, the embassy will bring pressure to bear on whoever has your daughter. They'll help you get her back."

"Once they have the scientist, they won't care about Anja."

"We won't give the scientist to them until we have Anja. I promise you, we'll get her back. I promise."

"You took her, and now you want to bring her back?"

"I never thought, not for a minute, that Anja and your wife would be hurt, I swear to you."

Koehler frowned and then sighed deeply. This time it was his turn to look at the table.

"I'll do all I can for you. Once we've got the scientist and Anja, I'll be able to help you further," King tried again.

"To do what?"

"I can get you out of here."

"Here?"

"London, Germany. I know you aren't happy with what you're doing, the way things are turning out in Germany. I can get you to America with Anja. You can start again, in a free country; you can leave all this behind you."

"You just concentrate on my daughter, King. That's the only thing you need to worry about."

"You think after this your life will go back to normal?"

"My wife is dead, so no, I don't."

King shook his head and then leaned forward. "Aside from that, do you think you will go back to business as usual? I know about what happened last year with you and Rossett. I know all about it. I deal in gossip, Koehler. I'm a spy, and it's my job. I know you barely hung on last year, after the mess Rossett made with that Jewish kid and your secretary."

Koehler looked at the cigarette packet on the table but didn't pick it up.

"You're tied into this, Koehler. Sure, you're sitting here now, but whatever havoc Rossett is causing in Cambridge, and if I know Rossett that'll be a lot, it's going to end up landing at your feet eventually. I can get you away from that."

"And what do you get out of it?"

"I get to make some attempt at making up for . . . for what has happened."

"And you get to live?"

King tilted one hand above the table and dipped his head slightly.

"Maybe."

"Maybe not," Koehler replied and picked up the cigarettes. "Now be quiet."

KOEHLER HELD UP his mug to the waitress. He looked back at King, who was now looking out of the window as he smoked. Koehler followed his gaze out toward the taxis and then saw himself looking back, reflected in the glass and the night beyond it.

King had been right. Koehler couldn't look into his own eyes sometimes. For a while, not long ago, he thought he might one day be able to. When he'd sat with Hahn and asked for a transfer he thought that by at least trying, by at least making an effort to distance himself from what he was doing, he might be able to excuse himself from what he had done.

Now, as the night went on, he realized that when he looked into his reflection too many people stared back at him.

And whatever he did, they always would.

Condensation ran down the inside of the glass, cut his face in half, then trickled down his mirrored cheek.

He turned to King.

"If you think I am dangerous, just wait until Rossett gets back to London."

King looked up.

"You think he will make it?"

"Oh, yes."

King nodded.

"Nothing more than I deserve."

"Maybe."

"What about you?"

"What?"

"What do you deserve?"

Koehler looked out of the window, through his reflection, and didn't reply. There was nothing to say.

CHAPTER 37

THE AMERICANS WERE late.

Sterling twisted in his seat so he could look out through the back window of his Alvis saloon car, and then turned back to his driver.

"Five more minutes, then we go."

The driver nodded and checked his watch.

Sterling had said the same thing twice in the last twenty minutes.

They weren't going anywhere.

The snow had stopped and this part of London looked beautiful, as good as it had looked in the last few years.

Clean and fresh, as if the population had painted the town white for a special occasion.

Normally Sterling would have enjoyed the view, but not tonight, not after losing Anja.

Sir James Sterling was a man who was normally in control. He was the kind of man who pulled strings, smoothed paths, greased palms, and made the wheels of government go round in a manner that suited him.

He was a manipulator, a plotter, a survivor, an acquaintance to many but a friend to none.

He liked being in control.

And tonight, he wasn't.

Tonight things had spun out from under him. The girl had escaped. The girl who knew his name, the girl who was a German officer's daughter, the girl who could have him shot, was out there somewhere.

He wasn't in control.

He might already be a dead man.

He had money.

The Germans had steered clear of Switzerland, with its chocolate, its mountains, and, most important, its banks.

Switzerland was the money cog the wheel of the world rotated round, and as long as it toed the Nazi line, it was safe from the Nazi jackboot.

So that was where Sterling had his money.

He guessed he would be able to get out of the country; his resistance contacts would see to that. A small boat to neutral Ireland, and then it would be easy enough for a man with his connections to acquire a false passport for a flight out of the country. Even if that route was barred to him, he was senior enough to enlist what was left of the Royal Navy and obtain a berth on one of the rusting subs that still sulked around the Atlantic monitoring shipping. Once in Canada he could get his hands on his money and take up a position with the government in exile.

He'd survive.

He just didn't want to run away to do it. He didn't want to be the little man abroad; he wanted to be Sir James Sterling, senior British civil servant by day, leader of the royalist resistance by night.

He wanted to be in control, fighting for his country.

He looked at his watch, twisted in his seat, and then settled once more.

But then, beggars can't be choosers.

"Five more minutes," he said, as much to himself as to the driver.

The driver spoke for the first time since they'd left the warehouse.

"They're here, sir."

Sterling spun again to look out the back. Behind them, approaching slowly with its headlamps switched off, was one of the American embassy's fleet of Chrysler saloons.

It pulled in behind Sterling's car, gliding to a halt some fifteen feet away, its nose pointing out from the curb a few inches to ensure a swift departure if required. The low rumble of its engine switched off and the street suddenly fell silent. Sterling heard the bolt easing back on the Thompson his driver had brought along.

Sterling stared at the Chrysler out the back window, waiting for someone to get out.

Twenty seconds passed, then he finally blinked and turned to his driver.

"I'm going to them. If they leave with me inside, you make sure you follow, understand?"

"Yes, sir."

"I don't care where they take me; you come and get me."

"Yes, sir."

Sterling looked back at the Chrysler again, and then shook his head before getting out the Alvis. He stood on the sidewalk, squinting toward the Americans, trying to see how many people were inside. He lifted a hand, trying to look past the reflection of the streetlamp on the windscreen as he walked forward. His feet crunched in the snow, the cold forgotten as he bent slightly, trying to make out a friendly face.

The back door of the car opened silently as Sterling drew near. He looked toward his own car and then leaned into the Chrysler, one hand on the door, the other on the roof of the car.

"Get in." Kennedy was sitting in the shadows.

Sterling climbed in the back of the Chrysler. Aside from the driver there was one other man in the front, turned in his seat, looking at him with the kind of confidence Sterling found the Americans so often seemed to have.

Sterling frowned at the man, irritated by his impudence, then pulled the door closed behind him. The Chrysler started up and Sterling rested his hand on the door handle.

"We're better off moving. The Germans won't stop a car with diplomatic plates," Kennedy said as they eased away from the curb.

Behind them Sterling's own car followed; Sterling nervously watched it through the back window.

Once they had edged out of the side street Kennedy spoke.

"You were right about Frank King being involved in the kidnapping of the girl."

"I was," Sterling replied as if it had never been in doubt.

"He's become quite a problem for us."

"Us?"

"My government . . . me."

"So he wasn't operating under orders?"

"He's made a considerable error of judgment." Kennedy was looking out his side window as he spoke to Sterling, unable to look at him as he admitted a failing under his command.

"I take it your calling this meeting has something to do with rectifying that mistake?"

For the first time since Sterling had gotten into the car, Kennedy turned to him. "It does."

"You're going to have to tell me what is going on before I can help you."

Kennedy nodded and looked out the window again; he then surprised Sterling by sighing heavily.

"There are factions in the U.S. government who are unhappy with the thawing of our relationship with the Germans."

"There are more than factions in the British government who are unhappy about it."

"I am not one of the unhappy ones." Kennedy looked at Sterling, his face heavy with rolling shadows from the streetlamps outside. "I have sympathy for your situation, of course, I genuinely do, but I'm also a realist, a realist who has an amount of respect for what the Nazis are doing here and in the rest of Europe."

"Killing people?"

"Killing communists and bringing order."

"Thank you for your honesty, Mr. Ambassador," Sterling said flatly, not meaning it.

"If you want me to be truly honest, Sir James, I think Great Britain is dead in the water and that my country has no choice but to accept that and get on with building relationships."

"We have a strong resistance."

"You have nothing. Really, believe me, you have nothing. You people are a gnat on the ass of an elephant. Let's not pretend that ambushing the odd truck on a back road or blowing up trash cans in train stations is going to change anything, because it isn't, and you know it."

Kennedy turned back to the window but kept on speaking.

"I met Churchill, before I came out here, back in the USA. He asked to come and see me. Do you know what he said after he sat down with a Scotch in my office?"

"No."

"He said, 'Get me some decent tea from Fortnum and Mason.'" Kennedy looked at Sterling. "Tea . . . tea is all he was interested in."

"I'm sure he had more to say than that."

"Oh, sure, he did." Kennedy turned back to the window. "He talked about noble fights, British history, his war record, weapons, explosives, U.S. support, and a vocal ambassador in London standing up for the oppressed British people and what is right. But—and this is the crux of it—he knew one thing." Kennedy lifted a finger. "Despite all the bluster, all the pacing back and forth, he knew there was only one thing he had a chance of getting: that tea from Fortnum and Mason."

"Even though your government has 'factions'?"

Kennedy chuckled to himself. "I said 'factions,' but what I should have said was 'fools.' Fools who think they can stop the inevitable, fools who still think Germany is our enemy."

"They aren't fools for trying to stop the Germans from becoming too powerful."

"You're talking about this superbomb?"

"I am."

Kennedy studied Sterling before continuing.

"That bomb won't be aimed at us; it'll be aimed at the Japs and the commies. Hitler knows that in Lindbergh we've got a president who understands what he is trying to do. We aren't Hitler's enemy. He knows that. He might be crazy, but he isn't stupid."

"And what if the next president isn't as accommodating to Hitler?"

"Germany needs us, and we need them; any politician worth his salt knows that. In ten years' time it won't be bombs that keep us from going to war, it'll be money. Lots of money. Already Germany is investing billions in the USA. We're building a . . . a special new sort of relationship here. Lots of people are getting rich on both sides of the Atlantic, and rich people like getting richer. War is bad for business, and rich people are influential. Rich people make good politicians on both sides of the Atlantic. The USA is safe from superbombs and doesn't need one for itself. Frank King and the people he is working for just haven't realized that yet."

"So?"

"So we need to stop them from risking the new U.S. and German relationship. Matters are thawing, we don't need them to cause an incident and freeze the whole situation all over again. There is a lot riding on this."

"A lot of money."

"Damn right. That money means jobs, industry, and that's all that matters now." Kennedy nodded to himself as much as to Sterling, who spoke again.

"It would be in my country's interest to . . . destabilize this special relationship. I'm surprised you think I'll help you in this matter." Sterling noticed the eyes of the driver watching him in the mirror.

"You may think that, Sir James, and you may be right. But let me assure you, if it is not in the interests of the British government in exile to help me in the matter, it most certainly is in yours. You've had dealings with us over the years, back when my government's policies were somewhat different than they are now. Through this we have learned an awful lot about you and your organization. You can rest assured your cooperation in this matter will ensure our future discretion."

Sterling didn't reply, so Kennedy continued.

"That cooperation would also ensure that we would do our best to support you, or your organization, in the short term."

"How?"

"Money."

"How much?"

"Twenty thousand dollars."

"And weapons?"

"No weapons. Just the money, in a Swiss account, in your name."

"What form would you expect my support to take?"

"You make all this go away."

"How?"

"You make this an English problem and nothing to do with America."

"What about King?"

"Like I said, you make it go away."

"What about his sponsors?"

"Once the mission fails, they'll skulk off to plot something new, but that won't be my problem. My problem is this problem, and that makes it your problem."

"How would you explain the disappearance of King?"

"King and his sponsor in this country are due to return to the USA with fresh passports in a few hours' time. Once we find two people who look sufficiently enough like them."

"Would it be possible for you to arrange one of those fresh passports for someone else?"

"Who?"

"Me."

Kennedy stared at Sterling a moment, then nodded.

"I'm sure something could be arranged."

Sterling smiled and scratched behind his ear.

"The Germans won't like this; the death of the scientist will result in severe repercussions."

"So be it. This has to be a visibly British operation. Anything that links it to the U.S. will ensure there is no compensation for your work . . . or for you."

"The rich get richer?" Sterling looked at Kennedy.

"The rich get richer," Kennedy replied, signaling that the driver should pull over to let Sterling get out.

CHAPTER 38

THEY'D BEEN DRIVING for twenty minutes and Rossett still hadn't managed to get out of second gear.

Not that Rossett really wanted to get out of second gear.

The Austin Seven they had taken from the farmer was nearly twenty years old, smelled of pigs and piss, falling apart, prone to stalling, and bereft of brakes.

If the German army didn't kill them, the Austin probably would.

"Does this thing go any faster?" Ruth shouted over the rattle of the engine.

Rossett dipped the clutch and revved the engine once more, a desperate attempt to coax life from another wheezing cough and stutter.

"I hope not."

"They'll be setting up roadblocks. We need to speed up."

Rossett tried for third, snatching at the gear stick and dipping the clutch again. The car slithered to the edge of the road on some drifted snow. He swung the steering wheel as branches from roadside trees clattered against the windscreen and the passenger window.

Rossett changed his mind about third and returned the stick to second, wheel still slewed to the right, car still sliding to the left.

The tires gripped, the car lurched, and the center of the road came back into view as Ruth braced herself with one hand on the dashboard and the other on the roof.

"Are you sure you can drive?" she shouted, lowering her arm slowly.

"I can. I'm not sure if the car can, though."

"The Germans will be waiting for us; the roads will be crawling with them."

"They haven't got communication with the outside world back at Coton. The lines are down. We should be all right for now."

"What if they have radios?"

"They never used them earlier, hence the dispatch driver. We're safe."

"And when we get to London?"

"London is a big city; there are lots of ways in, too many to cover with road-blocks. We'll get around them under cover of the weather and darkness. This snow is our best friend tonight."

"Unless we end up a tree."

"Unless we end up a tree," Rossett agreed as the car bucked again.

The snow had stopped, but there was still the occasional flurry that dropped from overhanging branches along the narrow lanes they were using. The solitary windscreen wiper on the Austin didn't work, so eventually, after about an hour, Rossett finally admitted defeat and stopped the car to clear the drift that had built up on the front window.

As soon as the car slithered to a stop the engine died.

Ruth got out of the passenger side and walked a few paces ahead of the car. She stopped, listened to the silent night, and then walked back to watch Rossett scoop the snow off the roof, bonnet, and windscreen.

"We're going to need another car. We'll never make it in this."

"I know," Rossett replied, stepping back from the car and clapping his hands together to warm them up. He looked up and down the lane. "The problem is finding one. I want to stay off the main roads and out of towns as best I can."

"We should stop the next car we see and take it."

"Take it?"

Ruth shrugged and then went back to the Austin and got in. Rossett watched her go and then joined her in the car. He battled for two minutes to get the little engine to fire up. Eventually, after a cough, a splutter, and an almighty backfire, they were off again along the back roads of Cambridgeshire on the way to London.

They traveled in silence for half an hour before Ruth spoke again.

"I loved him."

"What?"

"Horst. I loved him."

He looked at her and searched for something to say, didn't find anything, so instead wiped the windscreen with the back of his hand, smudging the condensation of their breath.

"I had to kill him, I want you to know. I had to do it."

"It doesn't matter. Forget it. Now isn't the time to think about it," Rossett replied.

"I'm too important, too important for him to try to stop me. I wanted him to come with us, but when he went for his gun . . ."

Rossett looked at Ruth and then back at the road.

"Shush now."

"If I stayed in Cambridge, if I did what they wanted, if I succeeded in my work . . ." Ruth drifted off and looked out of the window, chewing one of the fingers on her glove.

"What are you doing there? Is it a weapon?"

Ruth nodded.

"A bomb?"

Ruth nodded.

"Why aren't you in Germany?"

"There are teams of us, working separately, but on the same project—some in France, some in Germany, and some in Cambridge. We are all looking for the solutions to the same problems, but we're looking for them in different ways."

"Wouldn't it be better to get everyone in one place?"

"It's politics, funding, people trying to gain influence and prestige. We're pawns in a game. Besides, the work we are doing in Cambridge, the German scientists think we're wrong. Their calculations and our calculations are different. We meet occasionally to discuss it, but they think that we're second-class citizens, and they begrudge our involvement."

"It's just a bomb. Why can't you make the bomb, then blow it up to see if it works?"

Ruth shook her head and didn't answer, as Rossett finally managed to find third gear.

"Aren't there other people there who know what you know? Why are you so important?" he tried again.

"I know they're wrong, everyone: the French, the Germans, even my team. I've figured out what everyone is doing wrong. I know the secret. That's why the Americans want me."

"You have a high opinion of yourself."

"You wouldn't understand."

"Try me?"

Ruth shook her head. "What I know, what I have figured out, is the key to the bomb. I know the amounts of the atoms and the heavy water." She tapped her left temple with a gloved finger. "I've got the formula in my head. I'm the fuse. I know how it goes together, I know every part, every material, every weight and every measure . . . I'm the component that they need."

"Just you?"

"My brain, everything in it . . ." Ruth shook her head. "What I know, it's the most terrible war machine you could ever imagine."

Rossett looked at her.

"You're right about one thing."

"What?"

"I don't understand."

Ruth smiled as she cupped her hands to her mouth.

"So you build a bomb for the Americans instead of the Germans?" Rossett said, seesawing the steering wheel with tiny movements, trying to keep the car straight.

Ruth shrugged. "The Germans won't take long to learn what I know. They have my notes and most of my calculations; they'll have their bomb soon enough, don't worry about that."

"So why bother?"

"The Americans want me to build them a bomb quickly, to balance the scales. It's a race, and the world needs the right team to win, or both teams to draw."

"How do you know what the Americans want?"

"They've got messages to me. There is someone at Cambridge, I don't know who, but they have left messages for me. They told me you, or someone like you, was coming for me one day."

"But why you?"

"I'm the best, the brightest. Whoever left the notes must have told the Americans. One day I found a note under my door when I returned from the lab. They told me to leave a reply, in the ladies' toilets at the hall. I managed to copy some of my papers and pass them on by leaving them hidden in prearranged places. I told them we were getting close, that I couldn't hold off any longer with my calculations; making mistakes on purpose was getting too dangerous. Then one day, last week, I was told you were coming to get me."

"And here I am."

"Who are you?" Ruth looked at Rossett, her face half in shadow and half lit by the reflected headlamps bouncing off the snow.

"Me?" Rossett looked at her and then back at the road.

"Yes."

"I'm nobody."

"I don't want to know your name . . . I just want to know who you are."

Rossett turned again, and this time the glance lingered longer.

"Please?" Ruth tried again.

"I'm just somebody helping a friend."

"You'd do all this to help somebody out?"

"A friend."

"That makes you a good friend to have."

"You'd think so, but you'd be wrong."

"Why?"

"Because I'm not a good man to know."

"Why?"

"Because people die—too many people die."

"We live in wicked times."

"Yeah."

"People dying isn't your fault."

"You haven't known me very long, have you?"

Ruth smiled at Rossett, and he surprised himself by twitching his own smile as he looked at the road.

They drove a while longer in silence before Ruth spoke quietly again.

"You aren't a bad man."

"Thank you."

"When you knocked on my door tonight I wondered if you were coming to kill me."

Rossett looked at her and then back at the road, jerking the steering wheel again to straighten the car.

"The only way I'll kill you tonight is by crashing this car."

CHAPTER 39

I'M TELLING YOU, guv, the kid was definitely German."

Neumann looked at the little man in front of him and then at the desk sergeant, who was standing in the corner of the interview room in Bethnal Green Police Station.

"You can vouch for this man?"

"I know him, sir. Arthur Trellis. He's been a rat, a common criminal and informer, for as long as I've been on the manor."

"The manor?"

"This area, sir, Bethnal Green."

Trellis shrugged at the description. He twisted his cap, looking up at Neumann from his seat at the wooden interview room table.

"Honest, guv; she was German, I swear," Trellis tried again.

"You say she was dragged out of the pub?" Neumann finally spoke to him.

"Yes, guv, shouting for help she was."

"And you didn't help her?" March asked from behind his boss.

Trellis shifted in his chair so that he could address March directly.

"They'd have bleedin' killed me! What am I to them? They'd swat me like a fly." Trellis waved his hand in front of his face.

"What have you done since you called us?" Neumann asked the sergeant.

"I sent a car round to get the pub manager, sir. They'll not be long."

Neumann nodded, glanced at March, and turned back to Trellis.

"Who took her?"

Trellis lowered his head.

"I don't know them, guv. I ain't never seen them before. All I know is some-one took a German girl out the pub and I thought you fellas should know. I'm doing my duty, that's all."

Neumann nodded to March and stepped out of his way. March took a pace forward then kicked the chair out from under Trellis and into the corner of the room. Trellis landed heavily on his backside and looked up at March just as the German policeman hit him hard above the right eye with a small leather sap.

The English sergeant in the corner rubbed his hands together nervously.

"He isn't a suspect, sir, he's a witness," the sergeant said quietly.

March held a finger to his lips, all the while watching Trellis, who was moving on the floor as if he were underwater. March stepped in again, this time grabbing Trellis's shoulder and pushing him onto his back.

Neumann saw that Trellis's eye was split open. He was blinking and gri-macing, trying to shake off the concussion the blow had blown through his brain. March dropped and straddled Trellis so that he was sitting on his stom-ach; he slapped Trellis lightly once or twice and then shook him by his lapels.

Finally Trellis managed to speak.

"Stop, please, I—"

March rested a finger on Trellis's lips and looked up at Neumann.

"Who took her?" Neumann asked, civility to March's ferocity.

"I don't know!"

The sound of Trellis's nose breaking made everyone but March pull a face. March pulled back his right fist and made to punch the little man again.

"Who took her?" Neumann asked.

Trellis moaned, eyes closed. He gurgled, then twisted his head and spat a gob of blood onto the wooden floor of the interview room. The desk sergeant frowned and looked at the door as March inspected his knuckles, then wiped them on Trellis's jacket before gripping the lapels again. He lifted him slightly and then dropped him so that his head banged against the floor.

"Please, sir, please, I can't, sir, I don't—"

Trellis stopped speaking as March put his pistol into his mouth and cocked it. The little man looked up at the gun and then into March's eyes.

March stared back, waiting for the word from Neumann.

"Who took her?" Neumann said quietly.

"Mumph." Trellis struggled to speak, so March withdrew the blood-spattered pistol from his mouth, resting the barrel on the tip of Trellis's damaged nose.

"Ma Price, sir." Trellis gabbled the words with a newly nasal voice. "Her and her geezers, she took 'em, sir. Please, sir, I don't know where she took 'em, I'd tell you if I did. I swear, I thought I was doing the right thing coming 'ere. Please, guv, please!"

March looked up at Neumann, who in turn looked at the sergeant.

"Do you know this person?" Neumann asked.

"Ma Price, sir?"

"Yes."

"Oh, yes, sir. She's a proper villain, a nasty piece of work."

There was a knock at the door. A young constable looked in, and then down at March and Trellis. He visibly swallowed and turned to the sergeant.

"We've got the pub landlord."

"Bring him in," said Neumann.

The young bobby nodded nervously and then beckoned the landlord with his head.

Edwards the landlord edged into the room as the young bobby stepped aside. He looked down at Trellis on the floor, then up at Neumann, who smiled as the bobby closed the door behind him.

"Where did Ma Price take the girl?" said Neumann to Edwards.

"Ma who?" Edwards replied.

March looked up at Neumann, who nodded.

March whipped his pistol across Trellis's face in a sharp sudden strike.

A spatter of blood flicked across the floor and the landlord looked at the semiconscious Trellis, then at Neumann.

"Here, you can't—"

"Where is this Ma Price?"

"Who? I don't know who you're talking about?"

Neumann nodded to March.

March got up and stood in front of Edwards, close, far too close for comfort.

The landlord moved backward, and March moved with him, ending up inches from his face when the landlord finally came to a stop, his back against the wall.

"I . . . you can't . . . get him away . . ." Edwards looked at Neumann.

"What can't I do?" Neumann shrugged and gestured to March.

March wiped his bloody right hand down the front of the Edwards's shirt. He then casually placed the pistol against his right temple, all the while staring straight into his eyes.

"Answer the question of the Generalmajor. A young German girl's life is at risk and we don't have much time," March said calmly.

"Where did Ma Price take the girl?" Neumann tried again.

Edwards felt the pistol dig a fraction deeper into his temple. He looked into March's eyes and his lips started to tremble as his bladder let go and piss ran down his leg onto the wooden floor.

Neumann looked at Edwards's stained trousers and shook his head.

"Last time, and then I tell him to pull the trigger: where did Ma Price take the girl?"

The landlord could barely speak; his teeth were clenched so tightly together it looked like they might break behind his drawn-back lips. He shivered and then managed to turn his eyes toward Neumann without moving his head.

"Please . . ."

"Think hard now."

"I have a family . . ."

The pistol pressed harder, and Edwards felt his neck strain under the pressure.

"I only have a telephone number, sir. I only have a number to speak to her. I pay protection to her. She is a crook, she'll kill me. Please don't shoot, sir, it's all I know. I'll tell you everything I know, I'll give you the number, sir, please . . ." Tears ran down Edwards's face as he babbled to Neumann.

March looked at Neumann, frowned, and nodded.

"Okay."

March stepped back, lifting the pistol up and away from Edwards, who dropped to his knees, almost as if the gun had been holding him up.

He knelt, sobbing, as March put the gun back in his holster and then inspected his hands for blood before leaning down to him casually.

"What is the number?" March took hold of Edwards's hair and pulled it back so he could look into his eyes.

"Spitalfields 2127, sir. All I know is that the German girl was called Anja. A local lad brought her to us; I didn't have a choice, sir." Edwards sobbed. "I didn't have a choice, she took them both away. I didn't have a choice, sir . . . you've got to believe me."

At the mention of Anja's name March and Neumann looked at each other.

"Get me your reverse telephone directory," Neumann said to the desk sergeant, who nodded and stepped over Trellis in his hurry to get out of the room as quickly as he could.

"Please don't tell her I told you, sir." Edwards was still sobbing on his knees as he looked up at Neumann, hands held together in supplication.

Neumann smiled and nodded once.

"Thank you for helping with our inquiries."

CHAPTER 40

ANJA AND JACK had held hands for over an hour.

They hadn't spoken, they hadn't acknowledged they were holding hands, they hadn't squeezed them tighter to reassure each other, and they hadn't cried or shown they were scared.

But they hadn't let go, either.

They'd clung to each other as if they were adrift in a storm, each holding the other up. Every time there was a noise on the other side of the door, they flinched, their eyes chasing shadows and imaginary flashes of light in the darkness.

Jack had never been so scared in his life.

He was glad he wasn't alone.

Anja was scared, but she was also very angry.

She was sick of being locked in rooms, being dragged by adults who should have known better, being hungry and cold, not being in control of her own life.

She wanted to scream at the injustice.

But instead, she lay on the floor and held Jack's hand.

There was a noise outside the door. Anja and Jack both watched the gap underneath it for signs of movement. Boots broke the light, walking past, left to right. Heavy cludding boots that caused the floor to vibrate under them, like a giant in a fairy tale.

Jack finally squeezed.

"You all right?" His whisper sounded loud in the darkness and Anja looked at him in the gloom. She nodded, knowing that Jack was more scared than she.

"How long have we been 'ere, do you reckon?" he whispered again.

"An hour maybe? I don't know."

Anja looked around the room to see if it had changed in that hour. It hadn't. There was still no window, no plaster on the walls, no carpet on the floor, and no furniture.

There was just the same bright light, beaming through the inch at the bottom of the door like a torch through a letterbox.

They lay in the light, away from the darkness in the corners of the room and the corners of their mind.

The boots were coming back.

Clump, clump, clump, into view at the bottom of the door; then stopping, toecaps peering at them like rats through the gap. Something metal dragged through a rusty lock and then the door opened inward, forcing them backward into illuminating corners.

Jack was squeezing Anja's hand so tightly she thought it might break. She looked down and saw his fingers wrapped over hers like string making rope. She looked up at the man in the doorway, who pointed at Jack.

"Up."

Jack didn't move.

"Get up, collaborator," the man said again, and this time he flicked the finger to show which way was up. "Now."

Jack looked at Anja and she shook her head. Her heart beat faster and she suddenly knew she didn't want to be alone again, not now, not ever.

"I demand to see whoever is in charge," Anja said, moving an inch forward, positioning herself in front of Jack slightly.

"Get your arse up now." The man in the doorway took a step into the room, ignoring Anja as if he hadn't noticed she was there, let alone heard her speak.

Jack slid up the wall, pushing with his feet, his back scraping against bare brick every inch of the way. He finally released Anja's hand as she tried to pull him back to the ground.

Anja grabbed his leg, wrapping both arms around it, hugging it to her body as she looked at the big man by the door.

"Ma Price wants a word," the man said.

"No," Anja said, squeezing Jack's leg harder.

Anja felt Jack's fingers in her hair, brushing her scalp. She looked up and the same fingers touched her cheek.

"I'll not be long, promise." Jack looked about to cry. His fringe, that thick, black, floppy, oily fringe, dropped forward again, shadowing his eyes.

Anja wanted to reach up to scoop it away.

He smiled at her.

The man in the doorway reached across the gap and took hold of Jack's arm, then pulled him from Anja. She grabbed for the man's hand, ripping his arm as she screamed and pulled and tried to hold on.

The man reached down and pushed her away, shaking her off and shoving her back into the corner. She fell heavily. Looking up, she met Jack's eyes; he was still smiling.

And then he was gone.

The door was slamming shut by the time Anja had gotten to her feet.

Too late.

Time passed in silence, moments passing slowly, the only thing to keep her company, an unwanted friend.

She cried silently, wiping the tears away before they made it past her eyelashes.

Then it started.

Anja listened to Jack's screams.

They lasted nearly ten minutes, but it seemed much longer.

High-pitched, panicked, desperate screams.

Lonely screams.

Anja screamed back. She banged on the door and shouted his name. Thin tears became fat, rolling angry and fast, filled with salt and vengeance.

She banged, kicked, screamed; banged, kicked, and screamed again.

Making herself heard.

So Jack would know he wasn't alone.

She hoped he was thinking of her when his screams stopped.

She didn't want him to think he was alone.

She could smell something burning in the silence that followed; she pretended that they were cooking, even though she knew they weren't.

Sometimes it was better to pretend.

CHAPTER 41

MR. KOEHLER?"

Koehler switched on, lifted his head, and shook off a snooze. The weird state of half awake, half asleep he'd last known when he was sitting in a foxhole in Russia.

King was still sitting opposite. Like a drunk he was trying to force his eyes open and lick a sticky tongue across his lips.

"Mr. Koehler?"

Koehler was awake now, back in the café, switched on and ready.

He looked at the waitress, who was standing behind the counter, holding up a telephone receiver and shaking it in his direction.

"Stay here, don't move," Koehler said to King.

"What?" King was still rubbing his eyes.

Koehler got up from the table and picked his way through the café. He looked at his Rolex: 3:30 A.M.

He took the phone out of the girl's hand.

"Two teas."

"Your friend is drinking coffee, Mr. Koehler."

"Two teas, on the table, thank you."

The girl stared at Koehler from behind the counter a moment, and then turned away, shaking her head as she went.

He watched her go, then lifted the phone to his ear and turned so that he could keep an eye on King in the booth. King, in turn, was watching Koehler on the phone and stretching his legs under the table.

"Koehler."

"Ernst, it's me." Rossett sounded far away on the crackling phone line.

"John. Are you okay?"

"I wasn't sure if you'd be there, after you getting arrested."

"Neumann, the policeman at the flat, he arrested me; he thought I'd killed Lotte."

"You got away?"

Koehler took a deep breath, dipped his head, and then turned sideways on to King, so that he was facing the wall at the end of the counter, but still able to watch him out of the corner of his eye.

"John." Koehler paused, then lowered his voice. "Lotte is dead. God knows where Anja is. I've got one of the men who took them, but this whole thing has gone to shit."

After a pause, Rossett replied, "I'm sorry."

"We can still get Anja."

"She's alive?"

"That's what the American says, and I think he is right. There is nothing for the resistance to gain by killing her yet."

"American?"

"Long story. All that matters is Anja escaped from them, and now we think the resistance have her."

"She's kidnapped?"

"Maybe. We need to reach out to them, but I don't know how yet." Koehler looked around the café again, catching the eye of one of the waitresses, who smiled. He went back to staring at the wall, using the phone handset to shield his mouth. "Did you get the scientist?"

"Yes."

"Well then, we still have a chance to get Anja. They'll want the Jew. We need to get her to them."

"I'll get her there."

"Do you know anyone who can help us?"

"Maybe. Do we know what faction has Anja?"

"Not yet. Neumann is helping with that."

"Neumann?"

"He knows what is going on. I had to tell him. I had to get out to save Anja . . . I gambled he would understand."

"And he did?"

"I'm out."

"For now."

"For long enough, that's all that matters."

"What is your plan?"

"We need the American alive. Without him the British can't do much with the scientist except kill her. I say we keep him with us, we find out who has Anja, then we arrange a handover and we get my daughter."

"Simple as that?"

"I can't afford to risk Anja."

"Have you thought about what happens after?"

"No."

"We see what plays out?"

"It's the only way."

"If the weather stays as it is and doesn't get worse, I'll be back in London by eight in the morning, I reckon."

"Should we wait in the café?"

"It's worked so far."

Koehler looked at King again, who was now fully awake, staring back at him.

Koehler blinked, lowered his eyes, then turned his back on the café to face the wall.

"Thank you, John."

"Thank me when you've got your daughter back."

ROSSETT PICKED HIS way through the snow on the grass verge next to the telephone box as he headed back to the car.

He could see headlamps in the distance.

Headlamps that were getting closer.

The hamlet of Colliers End straddled the main A10 road that led from Cambridge to London. Rossett had originally hoped to crisscross the lattice of lanes and side roads that laced the open countryside between the two cities, but the heavy snowfall of the last few days had made most of the roads impassable to the little Austin, with its tiny wheels and poor ground clearance.

He'd given up several miles back and resorted to the main drag, such as it was, to get them to their destination.

In truth the A10 itself was barely wider than the lanes they had been using. On a normal night it wouldn't see much traffic due to the scarceness of private cars and the danger of moving military vehicles through the countryside in darkness. Roadside explosives and occasional ambushes had made military convoys scarce in most parts of the country, but that night the added ingredient of heavy snow had turned the A10 into a ghost road. It was deserted except for Rossett and Ruth, and their spluttering, slipping, and sliding car.

Until now.

Rossett could hear the engine of the other vehicle now, low, almost a rumble, steady behind the bright headlamps.

Ruth climbed out of the Austin.

"Can you see who it is?" she asked, watching the lights approach.

"No."

"We should open the bonnet; maybe they'll stop to help us."

"And then?"

"We take their car."

There was that word again, *take*. Rossett looked at Ruth as she moved around the front of the Austin and lifted one flap of the bonnet to expose the engine.

She looked at him.

"Are you ready?"

Rossett nodded.

Ruth walked toward the headlamps, raising her hands and waving to the oncoming car to stop. Rossett moved to the verge and turned slightly, so that he could shield himself as he checked the load in his pistol. He unbuttoned his coat, making way for the shotgun. He took out his police warrant card and then followed Ruth, lifting his hands to his shoulders, palm out, showing them to be empty except for the warrant card, its gold-embossed badge glinting in the headlamps ahead of him.

A black Mercedes.

"Shit," he heard himself say out loud, and then wondered if the word had shown on his face.

Rossett looked left and right at the cottages on either side of the road, then back at Ruth. The car was less than fifty yards away. It was too late.

Rossett followed Ruth toward the Mercedes, hands still up, taking slow steps, the gap between him and Ruth growing as she moved toward the other vehicle.

"Ruth, wait," he called, aware that he was disturbing whoever might live in the cottages, but less concerned about them than the occupants of the Mercedes.

Ruth looked over her shoulder at him, still waving her right arm at the car, less than twenty yards and slowing.

The Mercedes stopped next to her; he could see her silhouette in the headlamps as she gave a little wave to whoever was in the car.

She stepped beyond the beam and he lost her.

He half lowered his hand and walked forward slowly until his head broke the beam itself. He saw her, leaning into the driver's window. Rossett stopped, flicked his head to the warrant card, and waved it at the driver.

"Police," he mouthed.

The driver said something to a passenger, then gestured that Rossett should approach the car.

He high-stepped through the thick snow on the verge, hands still palms out, slightly lower than before.

". . . we're heading to London. Our car has broken down and we need help."

Rossett leaned in so he could fully hear the conversation.

Ruth was talking to an officer in the rear of the car, while the driver watched Rossett, one hand on the wheel, the other on his MP40.

The barrel of the machine pistol was resting on the driver's forearm, aimed squarely at Rossett's chest. In the passenger seat, another soldier, slightly older, was leaning forward to inspect Rossett, another MP40 at the ready.

Rossett nodded to the two men in the front of the car. The driver studied the warrant card and then seemed to relax slightly, but still watched him with the wary eyes of a soldier in an occupied land.

Ruth turned to Rossett.

"Darling, I was just telling the general that we've broken down." She flashed a dazzling smile, suddenly beautiful in the darkness; a tumble of hair dropped over her cheek and Rossett wondered if she was able to do it on cue.

To his right, a window lit up in one of the cottages. He looked at it and then saw that the soldier in the passenger seat was also checking it out, and bringing his MP40 to bear.

Ready, experienced, head screwed on, addressing the potential threat.

One to watch.

Rossett leaned forward and smiled at the driver, seeing that he was wearing an SS dress uniform. He was young, but not too young, Rottenführer tabs on his collar and an Iron Cross on his chest.

A decorated corporal driving; that meant someone senior to him, and more experienced, was in the passenger seat holding the MP40.

Rossett wished he had a grenade to drop through the window. "Excuse me, darling." Rossett eased Ruth away from the window, then regretted it when he saw a youngish Brigadeführer in the backseat.

A Brigadeführer who was much happier to talk to a beautiful woman than a disheveled policeman.

The Brigadeführer frowned.

This was getting worse.

Rossett touched his temple with the hand holding his warrant card, a half-hearted salute.

"Sir, apologies for delaying you. I'm sure we can manage. Please, don't allow us to detain you any longer."

The front passenger door on the other side of the car opened as more lights lit the upstairs windows of the cottages opposite, no doubt awakened by the sound of the Mercedes rumbling outside. Rossett looked over the roof and saw the front-seat passenger get out.

An SS sergeant, covering the windows with his MP40.

Rossett looked back into the car.

"Really, it'll be best if you keep moving."

"We can't just leave you here on a night like this, Constable." The Brigadeführer smiled.

Rossett ignored the wrong rank and tried again.

"Honestly, sir, I've telephoned for help." Rossett pointed up the road to the call box. "They are minutes away, coming from Cambridge, it's quite all right."

"I insist." The Brigadeführer tapped the driver on the shoulder. "Hans, take a look at the constable's car."

The driver looked at Rossett and put his hand on the handle of the car door, waiting for Rossett to take a step back so he could get out.

Rossett paused, smiled, and stepped back.

He looked at Ruth, who had walked toward the rear of the Mercedes, then ducked his head again to the officer.

"Thank you, sir. That is very kind of you." Rossett saluted to the closed rear window, then straightened, looking again at Ruth and giving a microscopic shake of the head.

No . . . let them go.

Ruth smiled at him.

Rossett's heart sank.

The driver climbed out, carrying his MP40 and working the bolt slowly, eyes on the cottages.

"The car *ist kaputte*?" the driver said, still not looking at Rossett as they walked to the Austin.

"Yeah, we borrowed the car to get back to London, it's very old. I should have waited till tomorrow for the train." Rossett was speaking loudly, as if to a child. He was following the driver as they made their way toward the Austin. He looked over his shoulder at the Mercedes and Ruth, who was walking fifteen feet behind him.

The front-seat passenger of the Mercedes still had eyes on the surrounding houses for signs of trouble. He was turning his head and scanning both sides of the road while occasionally checking on the driver, who still had his own MP40 in his hands.

These men knew they were in bandit country, and Rossett wondered why they hadn't had some sort of escort.

"Jesus." The driver shook his head when he saw the old Austin.

"We were at a dinner. It belongs to the host. I received a call to return to London urgently, so . . ." Rossett shrugged. "It was all they had."

The driver leaned into the engine of the Austin, looked at Rossett again, then slung his MP40 over his shoulder and rested one hand on the wing of the car. He pulled and pushed at the spark plug cables.

"It just . . . die . . . stop?"

"Yeah." Rossett was watching the Mercedes; the Brigadeführer had climbed out and was speaking to the sergeant across the roof of the car as he put on his cap.

Ruth was standing some twenty feet from Rossett and some thirty from the Mercedes, collar up, hands in her pockets, watching the Mercedes also.

"It . . ." The driver paused, looking for the word in English before continuing. "It go bang?"

"No, just spluttering for a while, losing power."

Rossett glanced at the driver and then back at Ruth, lit up by the headlamps of the Mercedes still.

"Gasoline?"

"I think so, I . . ." Rossett broke off; the Brigadeführer and the sergeant were walking toward them. The sergeant had crossed to the far side of the road, walking along the building line. The Brigadeführer was coming up behind Ruth, keeping her between himself and Rossett.

From where Rossett was standing it looked like he was being outflanked. He looked at the sergeant, who was watching him as he approached on the other side of the road.

Eyes on him, not the buildings.

Changed priorities.

Eyes on the immediate threat.

"Constable?" The Brigadeführer had reached Ruth; he stopped, smiled politely at her, and then turned to Rossett.

"Sir?"

"Why are you calling a Jew 'darling'?"

Rossett looked at the star of David on Ruth's coat.

Even in the darkness, he could see it.

Mocking him for the deeds he'd done, for the sins he'd sinned, and the crimes he'd committed.

Time seemed to stand still.

Then he woke up.

He slammed the bonnet down on the driver's head and shoulders, then dropped to his knees on the other side of the car, using it as cover between him and the sergeant across the road.

The Brigadeführer gripped Ruth around the throat, dragging her backward, using her as a shield as he shook his pistol out from his holster.

Rossett pulled his own pistol free of his overcoat. Once the front sight unhooked from the edge of his pocket, he reached around the front wing of the Austin and pressed it against the hip of the driver, who was lifting the bonnet off his head, dazed and trying to get out of the engine bay.

Rossett pulled the trigger and a round shattered the hip of the driver, who cried out and dropped to the ground, sliding out from under the bonnet like mail onto a doormat.

Rossett spun away and darted up the side of the Austin toward the rear of the car.

No shots came from the Brigadeführer.

Rossett caught sight of Ruth, struggling in the Brigadeführer's arms, her feet kicking high and her hands pushing at his face.

Rossett dropped flat to the road at the back of the Austin, looking underneath it toward the front.

The driver was down on his side, fighting with the sling of his MP40, trying to get his weapon from out beneath his broken body.

"No!" Rossett shouted at the driver, who paused, realizing Rossett had a clear shot at him.

A second passed between them.

"Throw it away." Rossett was staring down the sight of his Webley.

The driver blinked, clearly in a lot of pain, and in the darkness Rossett saw him licking his lips.

Rossett gestured with his pistol that the driver should throw his gun and he nodded, slowly easing the sling off his shoulder, flinching as he moved to free the weapon from over his head.

Up the road Rossett could hear Ruth shouting, but his eyes stayed on the driver, who eventually, with considerable difficulty, tossed the gun a few feet from himself, into the middle of the road, where it landed with a muffled crump in the snow.

The driver rolled onto his back, eyes no longer on Rossett, resigned to his fate.

Rossett, still flat on his belly in the snow, looked for the sergeant. He twisted his head, dodging quickly left and right, trying to see through the shadows and shade the cottages were scattering in the darkness.

His night vision was completely gone now, blown apart by the headlamps of the Mercedes, which still burned brightly to his left, leaving him in the spotlight. He lifted himself out of the snow, onto his haunches, crouching at the rear of the Austin. He risked a quick glance around the side of the car, toward the cottages, where he had last seen the sergeant.

He saw him.

Instincts, somewhere on the edge of his senses, caused him to duck back as the sergeant let go a short burst.

Snow kicked up and the thin metal of the car drummed as the lead hit home.

There was another burst, slightly longer, and the windscreen and the front passenger-side window shattered.

Rossett looked back down the road to Coton and saw the shadow of the Austin, cast by the Mercedes headlamps, in the white snow. It was a solid block of black, and Rossett thanked God for the driver lying in front of the car, blocking the light from shining underneath and giving away the position of his feet.

Rossett looked at the phone box, where he had been earlier, where he had made promises to Koehler. It stared at him, judging him, waiting for him to make good on what he had said.

The sergeant across the street fired again, just a couple of rounds this time, wary of exhausting his clip of ammunition.

Rossett edged closer to the corner of the car, one hand resting on the cold metal, feeling the gritty paintwork against the palm of his hand. He paused, holding the Webley cocked next to his ear, feeling the weight of the shotgun under his coat digging into his shoulder.

Rossett listened.

Silence.

Not even Ruth was making a noise.

The quiet unnerved him. It smacked of someone taking aim or lying in wait.

He poked his head out and then back in.

Nobody fired.

"Shit."

He was being outflanked again.

It was what he would do.

He looked at the cottages on the opposite side of the road. He figured the sergeant would have pinned him down and then made his way around the cottages. His intention would be to come around to Rossett's rear, thereby not only outflanking him but removing the risk of shooting his colleague, who was lying injured in front of the Austin.

Rossett rose up and came out from behind the car.

The MP40 in the snow was gone.

He half turned and saw the driver, lying on his side, hand on the grip, finger on the trigger, reaching for the magazine to steady his shot.

Rossett continued the turn, moving into a fast forward roll as the driver pulled the trigger before he had chance to take hold of the magazine. The MP40 bucked, kicking up snow with its muzzle blast, seven feet away from Rossett, arcing as the recoil of the gun twisted it in the driver's hand.

Rossett fired the Webley while he was still in midair, spinning, his legs higher than his shoulders now, his gun hand coming under his body and twisting him.

He missed.

The MP40 followed him in his tumble, higher, then arcing around, silhouetted in the headlamps.

Rossett fired again, a fraction before his shoulder hit the snow, twisting then rising to a crouch with the Webley outstretched.

Rising to a silent MP40.

The driver was dead.

Rossett turned and started running, heading for the other side of the road. He hit the end cottage, some forty feet away from the Austin. Rossett crouched, squinting at the night and the shadows, looking for movement.

Nothing.

He slipped the Webley back into his pocket, brought out the shotgun, and risked a glance at the Mercedes. He couldn't see anything beyond its headlamps, and he wondered if the car had a radio on board.

He looked back toward the cottages, opening his eyes as wide as he could, straining against the darkness as he started to edge into it.

One half step at a time.

Almost in the crouch, shotgun held low in both hands.

Rossett reached the rear of the first cottage. The darkness was almost total except for the soft glow of the snow. Off to his right he could hear a distant cluck of nervous chickens in a coop, disturbed by the shooting, fretting as they huddled for warmth. He listened to the birds, trying to read their voices, listening for sounds of sudden alarm.

They babbled among themselves like a distant brook.

The sergeant wasn't over there; he was ahead of Rossett, hiding behind the cottages, either moving toward him or lying in wait.

Rossett glanced back over his shoulder and started to move, each crunch of the snow under his feet sounding like gravel on sheets of glass.

Six slow steps and he stopped, left shoulder to the back door of one of the cottages, using the doorframe as half cover.

He listened.

The chickens were still there, same sounds as before, just a tiny bit farther away.

He moved forward again, stopping at the edge of the cottage, eight feet from the next.

His night vision was improving now. Shapes and shadows were becoming lawn furniture, sheds, outhouses, and privies.

Everything could provide cover to someone lying in wait. Rossett considered breaking off from his slow advance and concentrating on reaching Ruth.

His priority.

He looked down the alley between cottages toward the road.

He could see the Austin and the dead driver lying in front of it.

He was no closer to the Mercedes than he'd been at the start of the shooting. He took his hand off the muzzle of the shotgun, wiping his nose, which was running because of the cold.

Then he heard a shot cracking through the frozen air.

He dipped his head, then realized the shot wasn't aimed at him. It was off to his left, off by the Mercedes in the road at the front of the houses.

Rossett started to run, keeping low, eyes checking left and right for the missing sergeant.

Another shot, then another, then a burst from an MP40 followed by another shot.

Ruth.

Rossett ran behind the cottages until he could see the Mercedes through a gap in between them. He dodged his head trying to see through the windows of the Mercedes but couldn't. He crossed the gap to the other side. Hiding behind the wall, he tried again.

Still no sight of anyone.

He rose and ran along the back of two more cottages, before heading for the front of them so he could see the road. He was halfway down the side when he saw Ruth standing over the sergeant, who was lying in the road, on his back, MP40 some six feet away, hands held in front of his chest in surrender.

Rossett called Ruth's name and then jogged forward to join her. He looked down at the sergeant, who ignored him, too busy staring at Ruth and the pistol she was holding.

"The officer?" Rossett looked toward the Mercedes.

"He's dead. I shot him and then this one here."

Rossett looked down at the sergeant and noticed for the first time that he was hit in the chest. Rossett knelt and inspected the wound. When he touched it the German didn't make a sound.

Rossett looked up at Ruth and then down the lane at the Austin.

"Jesus," he said softly as he looked back over his shoulder at the cottages to his right.

All through the hamlet curtains were twitching. Rossett stood up from the German and wiped his hand across the back of his nose again. He breathed deeply, catching his breath after running in the snow.

"Wait here," he finally said to Ruth before walking off to the nearest house, the one where he had seen the light in the bedroom window earlier.

He hammered on the front door and waited, looking back toward Ruth and the sergeant, who hadn't moved. The sergeant still had his hands half raised as he lay flat on his back, staring at the Mauser held over him as the blood leaked silently from his chest.

Rossett stepped back from the door, looked up at the window, then stepped forward and hammered again, for longer this time.

"Open the door!" He stepped back again, looking at Ruth and then back up at the window.

A moment passed, then a bolt slid and the door opened a few inches.

Rossett took another pace backward and held up his shotgun.

The man was large, good farm stock, with a black beard, blacker in the shadows inside the cottage behind him.

"Come outside." Rossett took another step back to allow the man room, gesturing with the shotgun.

The man stepped out into the snow and a woman took his place at the door. The man was wearing long johns, and on his feet were a pair of untied heavy boots. His arms hung at his side and he lowered his face so as not to look directly into Rossett's eyes, or at the shotgun.

"Do you have a car?"

"We can use the Mercedes," Ruth said behind Rossett.

He ignored her and asked the man again, this time quietly as he lowered the shotgun to his side. "We need your help. I'm sorry for bringing this to you . . . Do you have a car?"

"No, sir."

"Who does in this village?"

"Nobody, sir. There are a couple of bicycles, but nobody has a car." The man still didn't look up.

"Where is the nearest vehicle?"

The man shrugged and looked over his shoulder at his wife.

"Dr. Evans has one, but he's nearly four miles away, sir," the wife said from behind the door, her face half in shadows, speaking for her husband.

"We can take the Mercedes!" Ruth again, this time shouting.

"Who has a phone around here?"

"Nobody, sir. There is the box." The woman's arm snaked out of the shadows and pointed up the lane toward the phone box.

"We can use . . ." Ruth took a few steps toward Rossett, looking at him as she kept the pistol trained on the sergeant.

"I know!" Rossett spun and looked at Ruth, a fleck of spittle on his lips. He took a deep breath, his voice straining to remain level. "I'm trying to decide what to do with him." Rossett pointed at the sergeant on the ground.

Ruth looked at the German, then pulled the trigger on the Mauser.

She shot him in the chest and he bucked once in the snow. His two hands fluttered and then dropped to his side with soft whumps.

Rossett stared at the sergeant and then at Ruth, who in turn pointed at the Mercedes.

"We can take the Mercedes."

"Are you mad?"

"We don't have time for this." Ruth lowered her hand.

Rossett crossed quickly to the sergeant and dropped down next to him.

The sergeant's eyes were rolling as he gasped short, sharp breaths. The heel on his left boot scratched deeper into the snow, moving backward and forward rhythmically, creating a tiny drift.

Rossett touched the man's face and then looked up to Ruth, who stared down at him, pistol now at her side.

"He wasn't a threat." Rossett pressed on the fresh wound of the sergeant, whose leg had stopped moving.

"We don't have time."

"They could have helped him!" Rossett was shouting now.

"He isn't our problem. We cannot be stopped. We don't have time."

"He might have a family, children!" Rossett pulled at the sergeant's tunic, trying to open it.

"I'm trying to keep them alive, don't you understand? I'm trying to save millions! Not just one man, not just one daughter. I'm trying to save the whole world!" Ruth shouted at Rossett.

The only sound was the choking last breaths of a man dying a long way from home, in the snow, on a road in Cambridgeshire.

Ruth lowered the pistol to her side. She looked at the farm laborer and his wife, then down at Rossett, who was still kneeling at her feet, one hand in the blood on the sergeant's chest.

"We can use the Mercedes," she said quietly as she turned toward the car.

CHAPTER 42

STERLING HATED USING public call boxes. They smelled of urine, they were always damp, and worst of all, they were used by poor people.

He wiped the handset with his handkerchief, studied it, and peered at the receiver before lifting it to his ear and dialing a number, his finger still wrapped in the handkerchief.

"Yes?" Ma Price picked up straightaway.

Sterling held the handset a fraction away from his head.

"Is the girl dead?"

"Sterling?"

"Don't use my name." Sterling sighed and half turned in the box, as if anyone outside might have heard Ma Price on the other end of the line. "Just answer the question, is the girl dead?"

"No."

"Listen to me very carefully. I want you to keep her safe and secure, extremely secure."

"The way you did?"

Sterling ignored Price and carried on.

"That child is worth her weight in gold, do you understand? Do not harm her, and don't let anyone else harm her. No matter what, she is to be kept alive. It is critical you understand that. She is to be kept alive at all costs."

"What's going on?"

"Just lock her up in the tightest room you can find, keep her safe, and wait for me to call you."

"Sterling . . ."

"Don't use my name!"

"Sterling." Ma Price ignored him, keeping her voice flat and low. "If you want me to look after this girl, you'd better tell me why. I'm risking my life here. If I was found with her I'd be dead by the morning. So you'd better be honest with me. What is going on?"

Sterling shook his head, and then leaned in close to the shelf in the phone box.

"We need her for leverage. Kennedy is trying to shut this down, this whole thing, as if it never happened. We need the girl to get the scientist from Koehler. If we have the scientist, we can use her to influence Washington to help us again."

"How important is one scientist?"

Sterling paused.

"You have no idea what this woman can do for us. We can win the war."

"The war is over."

"The next war."

Sterling ended the call before Ma Price had a chance to ask another question.

Across the city in a Spitalfields warehouse, Price looked at the dead phone in her hands, then dropped it back into its cradle. Ma Price stood up, the chair creaking as it was released from her weight.

She left the office, fastening the top button on her coat, her boots thumping as she walked across the deserted, freezing cold warehouse. On the far side, she pulled back a heavy wooden sliding door that led to the back of the warehouse and the steps down to the basement.

The temperature dropped even lower as she descended. Her breath mingled with the smoke in the air as she turned the final corner, deep in the bowels of the building, and walked toward the room in which Anja was being held.

Bare stone walls crowded in as the corridor seemed to narrow to where two men sat, watching Ma Price approach. One stood, producing a key and unlocking the door.

"Get some soup for the girl, and put the light on," Price said as she stood in the doorway looking down at Anja. The light flicked on and she entered, pushing the door closed behind her.

ANJA BLINKED, HOLDING a hand over her eyes, looking up from the floor where she was sitting in the corner.

"Your old man, what does he do for a living?" Ma Price asked, halfway across the room, with hands on hips.

"Pardon?" Anja replied, confused by Ma Price's thick Cockney accent.

"Your dad, what's his job?"

"Where is Jack?"

"Answer the question."

"You answer the question. Where is Jack?"

Ma Price sighed. "He's gone."

"Where?"

"Home."

"I don't believe you."

"I don't care."

They stared at each other.

"I want to speak to him." Anja lowered her hand and lifted her chin.

"You can't. He's gone, forget him."

"I won't. I want to speak to him."

"You can speak to him when this is over. I'll let him know you want to, but only if you behave."

Anja sat up straight, leaning her back against the wall as Ma Price settled her weight onto one leg.

"What does your father do?" Price tried again.

"Did you kill Jack?"

"No."

"I heard him screaming."

"He had to be taught a lesson."

"Is he hurt badly?"

"Yes."

"Why?"

Ma Price stared at Anja, weighing her up. She chewed her lip and shifted her weight again, this time only an inch.

"He helped you."

Anja blinked.

"You didn't have to do that. He hadn't done anything wrong."

"He helped you."

"He didn't deserve to be hurt."

Ma Price put her hands in her pockets and dipped her head, looking at the floor a moment, and then back up to Anja.

"No, he probably didn't. But he has been, and that's all that matters."

Anja shook her head. "You people kill and hurt others so easily, all of you . . . I hear my father talking about bombs, shootings: Why?"

"Because we want our country back."

"What Jack did won't change who is in charge."

"He helped a German."

"I'm just a girl."

Ma Price's eyes wandered a moment while she processed Anja's reply, then she looked at Anja again and nodded.

"You're right."

"All this . . . all of it is for nothing."

"We didn't start it, we just want the country back."

"You don't care about the country or the people. You just want power." There was no challenge in Anja's voice, just a certain sadness.

She pulled her knees up to her chest, wrapping her arms around them and resting her chin.

Ma Price wandered to the side of the room and leaned against the wall. Hands still in her pockets, she stared into the distance a moment and then rolled, so that her back was against the wall and she was looking at the floor in the center of the room.

"It is about power. You're right. All of it, the whole thing . . . it's all about power. When I was your age, I wanted power. I wasn't pretty like you, I didn't have schooling or none of that stuff. I had nothing, bugger all. I barely had clean knickers to see me through the month." Ma Price chuckled to herself and Anja looked up at her. "I wanted power for myself, over myself." She looked at Anja. "Do you understand me?"

"Yes."

Ma Price nodded and went back to looking at the floor.

"I don't give a toss about the country. I don't give a toss about Americans or scientists or even you. Honestly, I don't give a toss about any of it. I just want to keep hold of the power I worked so hard for, the power I gave meself." Ma Price looked at Anja. "That young lad?"

"Jack?"

"What he did, helping you?"

"Yes?"

"I couldn't let it happen. Once I know what he's done, once I know others know I know, then that affects my power. Not the country's, not America's, not Germany's . . . mine. And that is what is most important."

"I don't understand."

"I hope you never have to."

Ma Price pushed herself off the wall and then resumed her position in the center of the room.

"I don't want to hurt you, I really don't. All I want is enough to get away from this, away from London, away from the person I've made myself into, so I can start again."

Anja nodded, so Ma Price continued.

"Do you know something? I've never seen the sea."

Anja smiled.

Ma Price smiled, too.

"I've seen the river, every bleedin' day I see the river. But I've never seen the sea. I've never seen if it really is blue like they say, instead of the dirty brown of the Thames."

Anja stopped smiling.

"It is," she said softly. "It's beautiful."

Ma Price smiled at her warmly, then the smile faded into sadness.

"That is what my power is going to get me—that second chance to start again, by the sea, on my own, away from here, happy." Her voice barely carried, so light was the whisper.

Anja nodded. "I understand."

"You have to understand, child, in this room, right here, me and you. I'll tell you, I don't want to harm you, and I mean it, I really don't, same as I didn't want to harm Jack, and all the 'undreds of others over the years. But out there"—Price flicked her head to the door without looking at it—"I'll do what

I have to do to keep that power, and to keep that dream alive as long as I can. If you help me, if you do what I need you to do, I'll make sure you get to your old fella and you live happy ever after . . . but only if you do what I ask. Do you understand me?"

"Yes."

Ma Price nodded, smiled, then was stern.

"What does your old dad do?"

"He is an officer in the SS."

"What rank?"

"Major."

"What is his job in London?"

"He works in the office of Jewish affairs."

Ma Price processed the information.

"How long has he been in London?"

"Why?"

"Answer the question."

"Years. I don't know, maybe three?"

"And he's just worked with the Jews?"

Anja shrugged. "Yes, I think, with his friend Mr. Rossett. They are clearing the Jews so Londoners don't have to live with them." Anja's statement was simple, years of indoctrination having taken its toll on her sense of morality.

"Rossett?" Ma Price tilted her head.

"Yes."

"Shit."

"What?"

"Nothing."

Anja watched as Ma Price scratched her head, then took a couple of paces back and forth across the room, before finally stopping again by the door.

"Does your old man have money?" Ma Price looked at Anja.

"I don't know . . . a little. We have a house in Berlin, and—"

Ma Price waved her hand and turned away, pacing again until she stopped by the door, facing it.

"If he can't buy you back, I'm going to need the scientist."

"My father loves me."

"Shush."

Anja fell silent as Ma Price held up a fat finger.

"I'm going to need you to get the scientist off him."

"My father won't harm Germany."

Ma Price turned to her and smiled sadly.

"He's lost his wife; he isn't going to lose his daughter."

Anja dropped her chin to her knees and frowned at the mention of her mother. She felt her mother's dying fingers again and touched her cheek. She fought with the memory, consciously trying to push it back into the box, in the depths of her mind where she had been keeping it.

"He'll have to give me the scientist to get you back," Ma Price said to the floor before pulling the door open and nodding to the man standing outside.

"Bring her and don't hurt her. I swear, if you so much as harm a hair on that girl's head I'll kill you, understand?"

He nodded.

"And if you lose her, I'll kill you even more."

The man looked at Anja, then at Ma Price, and shrugged.

Ma Price nodded and left the room. The man gestured for Anja to stand up, then took her firmly by the arm. They followed Ma Price up to the office.

Once they were in Price's office, Anja was seated in the corner and given a bowl of soup. She ate quickly, in quick mouth-singeing gulps, conscious it might be taken from her at any moment, watching the others watching her, over the top of the bowl.

"We need more men. Get on the blower and get me six of the lads down here sharpish. Then break out the Thompsons and whatever else you might need. I want everyone armed, understand?"

"Who we expecting, Rommel?"

"Rossett."

"Rossett?" The heavy looked at his companion and then back at Price. "Jesus."

"Yes, so spread the word and warn people, all right?"

"Yes, Ma." He left the office.

The second guard took the empty bowl from Anja.

"Wait outside the door; don't move unless I tell you." Ma Price spoke without looking at him and he left, closing the door behind him.

Ma Price flicked through an address book she had taken out of her desk as Anja watched from her chair. Through a window Anja saw the first guard pulling open the floor-to-ceiling wooden sliding door on the far side of the warehouse. She caught a glimpse of the street outside before he closed it again behind him.

Anja knew that if more men were coming to the warehouse her chances of escape would diminish on their arrival. If she was going to escape, she was going to have to do it soon.

Ma Price was still thumbing through the book, pausing occasionally, apparently lost in thought. The shadow of the man at the door was rippled by the frosted glass on which was painted OFF CE.

Anja wondered what had happened to the *i*, and then looked at Ma Price again.

She noticed a fountain pen on the desk.

An inky, old, sharp pen.

The kind of pen you could use to stab.

Anja looked at the door once more, and then back at the pen.

Six feet away, too far to reach without moving from her chair, but close, maybe close enough to give her a chance.

Ma Price picked up the receiver of the phone, placed it on the table, and then started to dial with the same hand as she held the address book up to read the number, squinting her eyes and pursing her lips.

The book was blocking Anja.

Anja took her chance.

Out of her seat like a cat, fast, silent, crossing the ground like a shot, she reached for the pen.

Ma Price grabbed her wrist, so tightly that as she twisted her arm Anja thought her skin might rip. The big woman barely moved in her seat as she pinioned Anja so that her right shoulder hit the desk and her head landed next to the pen.

Anja looked at the pen, her face contorted with the pain in her arm and back.

She tried to reach with her other hand, but stopped and screamed as Price twisted again, then flicked the pen out of reach with the book she was holding in her other hand. The door opened behind Anja, but Price shook her head at whoever was coming in. She put down the book and picked up the phone receiver, holding it to her ear with one hand while holding Anja with the other.

Anja tried to move, so Ma Price twisted her arm a fraction tighter and shook her head.

"Be still now, love."

Anja did as she was told.

The phone picked up.

"'ullo?"

"Fraser?"

"Yeah, who's this?"

"Ma Price."

A pause.

"How did you get this number?"

"I need to speak to your old chum Rossett."

"Who? Do you know what time it is?"

"Don't piss me about, Fraser; I need to speak to him."

This time the pause was longer.

"How would I know where he is? We haven't spoken in years."

Ma Price sighed.

"I know you're the only friend he has left in the police, and I also know you shared a cigarette outside the nick and that you're about the only copper who still speaks to him. Now don't mess me around. Where is he? And don't you dare lie to me. I bought you that house, so don't you dare lie, because I can take it away just as easy. Where is Rossett?"

"I don't know where he is. I don't even know where he lives nowadays."

"How long have I known you, Bill Fraser?"

"Uh, I don't know, Ma. A few years . . . since the occupation."

"Long enough for you to know what I do to people who let me down?"

"Yeah . . . long enough."

"Well then, you know you'd better find out where he is, Bill, because I want to talk to him, and he'll want to talk to me. If you don't find him, he'll want to kill you as much as I will."

"What if he asks what it's about?"

Ma Price paused, mulling her options, until eventually she continued.

"If I say this involves a man whose name begins with S, and who is right posh, a peer of the realm no less, do you know who I mean?"

"I do."

"Well, me and him have got mixed up in something with the Yanks, and Rossett's boss's daughter."

"His daughter?"

"So you give him my number, and you tell him I've got Anja Koehler, nothing else . . . You just say I've got the girl, I want to do a deal, and he's got what we want."

Ma Price put down the phone and looked at Anja, who was still pinned beneath her meaty fist.

"This is power, my girl . . . this." She twisted Anja's arm again. "And so is that." She nodded to the phone. "I can do whatever I want."

CHAPTER 43

ROSSETT WAS DRYING out for the first time in what seemed like days. The Mercedes was warm, comfortable, fast, and easy to drive.

He'd disabled the phone box in the hamlet and spent ten minutes explaining, with the help of one of the MP40s, that it was in everyone in the village's best interest to dump the bodies of the dead Germans in a slurry pit and then keep their mouths shut. Nobody had spoken during this lecture; the fifteen or so locals had mostly hung their heads and held their winter coats around them silently as a solitary dog sniffed uncertainly at the dead sergeant on the ground.

As he and Ruth had driven away, Rossett had watched the villagers, arms hanging limp at their sides, watching them fade away into the night.

Death had come to their village and danced through, and yet they seemed dulled, lost, beaten. Not scared, not worried, just beaten and alone.

Like Britain itself.

During the invasion people had fought like lions, raging against the Germans with petrol bombs and stones in some cities. But now it seemed like the fight had left them, just like Churchill and the old king.

A distant memory, resignation in its place.

Sometimes Rossett felt that he was waking up just as Great Britain was falling asleep.

"Are you angry with me?" Ruth broke the silence between them, causing Rossett to snap back into the real world and look at her.

"What?"

"I think you are angry."

Rossett looked at her again and then went back to driving without replying.

"I understand if you are, but you don't understand. I had to do it," Ruth tried again.

"You had to?"

"Yes."

"Same as you had to stab your boyfriend?" Rossett replied, still staring straight ahead.

"Yes." A little quieter this time, but just as determined.

Rossett shook his head.

"You're crazy."

"No."

"You kill so easily."

"So do you."

"I kill when I need to."

"You find it easy?" The challenge left her voice.

Rossett looked at her again and then went back to driving. Ten seconds passed before he answered her.

"I used to."

"But not now?"

"No."

"Why?"

"Because . . ." Rossett squinted through the windscreen, as if the words he was looking for were just beyond the reach of the headlamps. "I'm trying to be a better man."

"But you still kill. I've seen you."

"I have to stay alive."

"Why are you so special that you have to live, and the people you kill can die?"

Rossett looked at Ruth again, the light from the dashboard casting shadows on his face.

"Don't play games with me."

"I'm not. It's a genuine question: why should you live and the others die?"

"Because I have to save Anja."

"Why?"

"She's a child."

"She's one child."

Rossett looked at her and then back out the windscreen.

Ruth waited for his response, but none came, so she tried once more.

"Did you fight in the war?"

"Yes."

"For how long?"

"Start to finish. I was in France, then England."

"You were captured?"

"Yes."

"Then when you were released you became a policeman?"

"I was a policeman before the war, then a soldier, then a policeman again . . . then . . ."

"What?"

"Then I worked for the Germans." Rossett looked at her.

"What did you do?"

He looked away.

"I rounded up Jews."

Ruth touched the star of David on her coat subconsciously.

"I'm sorry," he said quietly.

"Do you still . . . do you still do that?"

"No."

"Why not?"

"Like I said, I'm trying to be a better man."

"Why did you change?"

"I woke up."

Ruth shook her head and played with a loose thread from the star on her coat.

"No."

"No what?" He looked at her again.

"People who do bad things aren't asleep."

"My wife and boy died."

"I'm sorry."

"It . . . it changed me. The war, my family . . . it changed me. I lost myself, lost my way."

Ruth turned to look at Rossett as he continued.

"Last year, I woke up, I saw what I'd become, what I was doing . . . I'm trying to be better."

"Are you better?"

"I'm trying." Rossett looked at Ruth and nodded before saying it again. "I'm trying."

They drove a few more miles before Ruth spoke again.

"The men I killed, at the village . . . Horst . . . I had to."

"Forget it."

"Look at this." Ruth pulled at the front of her coat, twisting it so that the star of David was visible to Rossett, who glanced at it and then looked back at the road. "This means I had to kill them, do you understand?"

Rossett didn't reply.

"This thing, this little bit of felt, held on with this shitty thread . . . this means they had to die. I loved Horst. You might not believe it, but I did. But he had to die because of this. The men in the village? I made their widows cry, all because of this." Ruth looked down in the gloom at the star and then back at Rossett, still holding it toward him. "As long as there are people in power who make others wear this—English, German, Nazis, as long as someone makes someone else wear this . . . people have to die because we can't afford to let them win."

Still Rossett stared straight ahead.

"If your friend's daughter dies, she dies; it isn't my fault, even if it is me who pulls the trigger. Do you understand? I need to live, I need to get away, I need to keep working to stop this. That is all you need to remember. I need to live to stop this." She gestured with the star. "If you want to be a better man, if you really want to be a better man, you'll make that happen."

Ruth let go of the star of David. She turned in her seat to look out of the side window at the passing hedgerows, which gave occasional glimpses of the snow-covered fields beyond.

Rossett watched her a moment, then turned back to the windscreen as the snow started to fall again.

THEY DIDN'T SPEAK for an hour until Rossett gently nudged her leg and held up a penknife.

"Use this to cut off the star."

"What?"

"Take off the star." Rossett gestured with the penknife in his hand, offering it to Ruth. "You can't walk around London with that thing on your coat. Cut it off."

Ruth took the penknife and began to pick at the thread. It came away easily; her mother had sewn it on in a hurry, fretting that the cotton was a different shade of yellow from the badge itself on that final day that they had parted forever.

Ruth held the star in her hand. It seemed so light and yet it felt so heavy whenever she put on the coat. She opened the window and thought about throwing it away, but then changed her mind and slipped it into her pocket along with the thread.

She wanted to remember her mother, how upset she had been. Ruth never wanted to forget.

CHAPTER 44

HE SAYS HE wants to speak to Mr. Rossett. Seeing as you're his boss, I thought . . ." The waitress offered the phone to Koehler, who looked at his watch, wondering why a friend of Rossett's would be ringing a café at six thirty in the morning.

"Did he give a name?"

"No, sir."

"Thank you."

Koehler nodded, waiting for the waitress to move away. It took her a moment to get the message. She paused, then realized and walked off down the counter.

Koehler adopted the same position as before, one eye on King, as he held the phone to his ear.

"Hello?"

"John?"

"Who's this?"

"Who's that?"

"Major Ernst Koehler."

There was a pause.

"Major Koehler, sir."

"Who is this?"

"I'm a friend of Jo . . . Mr. Rossett's."

"Rossett doesn't have any friends. Who is this?"

"It don't matter who I am, sir."

"I'm going to hang up unless you give me a name. How can I trust someone who claims to be a friend but who won't give me a name?"

"I can't, sir."

"Good-bye." Koehler put down the phone.

He stood stock still, staring at the receiver, his hand hovering just above it, willing it to ring again.

Seconds passed. Koehler felt a flutter of panic, his attempt to wrestle back control seeming to fail.

The phone rang.

He picked it up, holding it to his ear but not speaking.

The line crackled.

"Bill Fraser. My name is Bill Fraser. I used to work with John. I'm trying to help you."

"How?"

"I need to give you a message, about your daughter, sir."

"You have my daughter?"

"No, sir! Good God, no, sir. I'm a . . . I wouldn't be involved in something like that, sir, no way, not at all."

"You are involved in something like that."

"I'm trying to help you, sir. I've been asked to get a message to you and him."

"What is it?"

"Do you know who Ma Price is, sir?"

"I've heard of her."

"She has told me to tell John, and I suppose you, that she has your daughter, sir. She wants to speak, so this can all come to an end. Have you got a pen?"

Koehler patted his pocket and then gestured to the waitress for some paper. She ripped a sheet off her pad and approached him to hand it over.

"Go." Koehler spoke to the waitress and Fraser at the same time with the same command.

"Spitalfields 2127."

"Anything else?"

"That's all she said."

"How well do you know this woman?"

"Hardly, sir. I hardly know her at all."

"Do you know where she is based, where she does business?"

"No, sir."

"I'm not the kind of person you want to lie to."

"I know that, sir. I'm trying to help."

"You have, Bill, and I'll remember that."

Fraser hung up.

Koehler listened to the purr on the line and then put down the phone. He glanced at King, then turned back to the phone, picking it up and dialing, not bothering to ask for permission from the waitress this time.

It rang once.

"Hello?"

"Price?"

"Is this Inspector Rossett?"

"It's Koehler."

"Ah."

"You've got my daughter?"

"I have."

"Give her to me."

"It isn't that easy, Mr. Koehler."

"Do you know who I am? Do you know what I do?"

"I do," Ma Price answered matter-of-factly.

"No, you don't. You think you do, but you don't. You have no idea of what I can do to you. You couldn't imagine it. I'm a dangerous man, dangerous to those who have done me no harm, so imagine what I can do to those who have. I'll bring the weight of the world down on you, I'll crush you and everyone around you, I'll kill your family, I'll kill your friends, I'll wage war on you . . . and that will be only the beginning." Koehler tilted his head forward, his knuckles white on the receiver.

The line popped and crackled in his ear.

Ma Price answered evenly.

"Do you feel better now?"

Koehler lifted his head an inch.

"What?"

"Do you feel better?"

"Are you laughing at me?"

"No."

"Did you hear me?"

"Yes."

"And you ask me do I feel better?"

"Look, we haven't got time for this. Are you going to listen?"

"Give me my daughter," Koehler heard himself say.

"Listen to me, my darling. You keep your temper now, and listen to me. Do you know me?"

"I've heard of you."

"Good, then you'll know I'll kill her if I have to."

"If you so much as—"

"Listen to me, please, and don't interrupt." Ma Price waited for Koehler to respond.

"Speak."

"All right, as I was saying, if I have to, you can be in no doubt I'll kill her, okay?"

"Yes."

"Good. Now you need to know that I won't, not unless you make me do it, understand?"

"Yes."

"I like the girl; she is very brave, very strong."

"What do you want?"

"I want the scientist."

"You can have her."

"Good, that keeps it simple. I trust you realize that if you involve anyone else but me, you, and old Mr. Rossett it will make this agreement invalid?"

Koehler looked at King and then back at the wall.

"I have the American you need to get the scientist out."

"Do you now?"

"I do. Just so you know, we both have something the other needs. You harm Anja and I'll gut this American and post him to you in pieces. Then, when you have all of him? I'll come for you."

"We both know where we stand, then?"

"We do."

"When you have the scientist, you call this number."

"Yes."

"When you ring we can sort something out."

"I want to speak to Anja."

"When you have the scientist."

"Now."

"Say hello to your father, Anja," Koehler heard her say away from the phone.

"Daddy!" Koehler's heart jumped in his chest at the sound of her voice, but Ma Price immediately came back on the line.

"Don't cause problems, Mr. Koehler, there's a good fellow."

Ma Price hung up. Koehler cradled the receiver and turned to look at the waitress.

"Two teas, two breakfasts."

"You hungry now?"

Koehler ignored her and picked his way across the café to sit down opposite King.

"Are you hungry?" said King, looking at the waitress, who pulled a face at Koehler's back.

"Never go into battle on an empty stomach," replied Koehler.

CHAPTER 45

NEUMANN AND MARCH sat in their car on Dock Street, Spitalfields, and stared at the warehouse opposite. The storm had stopped; the streets around them were slowly coming to life, with dockers and warehousemen swaddled in coats and scarves making their way to work through the snow that had fallen overnight.

March looked at his watch, then shifted, causing the car to rock a little.

"Will you sit still?" said Neumann.

"I'm sorry."

"It's like you've never sat in a car watching somewhere."

March scratched the back of his head and then dropped his hand back into his lap. He breathed out through his nose loudly, and Neumann looked at him again.

"What?"

"Nothing."

"What is it? You are getting on my nerves."

"Nothing, I'm sorry."

"Jesus . . . just sit still."

"I'm sorry."

Neumann shook his head and resumed the position he'd held for the last three hours, a Zen-like stare watching the warehouse opposite.

"It's just . . ." March interrupted Neumann's concentration again, and his boss swiveled in his seat.

"What? Fucking hell, what?"

"I'm not happy, sir."

"You're not happy?"

"No."

"Why?"

"We should have backup, sir."

"You're scared?"

"No!" March reared slightly in his seat.

"So what?"

March sighed, folding his arms as he stared at the warehouse.

"This . . . unorthodox."

"What is?"

"This . . . what we are doing right now. It isn't right. We're off the books, nobody knows we are here, and I'm not sure I understand why."

"You don't need to know."

"I disagree."

"You do?"

"Yes."

"Why?"

"If I am to risk ending up in a concentration camp, you should have at least the courtesy and respect to explain to me why."

Neumann shook his head and turned again to look out the window, resting his hand on the steering wheel of the car with his elbow on the top of the door.

He tapped his thumb on the steering wheel for a moment and then looked at March.

"Not knowing why we are here will keep you safe." The edge was gone from his voice.

"I deserve better than that, sir."

Neumann turned to March.

"How long have we worked together, March?"

"Two years?"

"Do you trust me?"

"Well, yes . . . but this . . . what you are doing, it's . . ."

"It's what?"

"You are helping a murder suspect. A man who should be in jail right now . . . except, well, you let him go. You make inquiries about the case and then you make no record of the information received, nor do you allow me to, and then you use that information to stake out this warehouse . . . and I think I deserve to know why."

Neumann nodded and looked back at the warehouse as he tapped his thumb again.

"I have a family, sir," March said. "I'm worried, that's all."

Neumann lifted his hand and rubbed his tired eyes. He lowered his hand and then blinked away the blurred vision it had left.

"You're right. I'm sorry."

"I just need to know, sir. I'll follow you . . . but I just need to know."

Neumann looked at March and then tapped him on the leg.

"Give me a cigarette."

March produced his cigarettes, waited for Neumann to take one, and then lit it for him.

"I've let my heart rule my head," Neumann said, smoke tumbling out with the words. "But there is one thing I am certain of. It is that Koehler didn't kill his wife."

"You know?"

"I'm getting sentimental, I've broken the rules." Neumann looked at his cigarette and then put it back into his mouth. He took a drag and then held it to the gap at the top of the window, letting the smoke out into the cold. "The people opposite, in the warehouse we are watching? I think they've got Koehler's daughter."

"Ma Price is in there?"

"Yes."

"Why we don't just get a squad and raid the warehouse?" March looked at the warehouse and then back at his boss.

"Because they will kill the child."

"We can surround them, wait them out?"

"No, we can't. You see, they've got nothing to come out for. Why surrender if you are going to die anyway?" Neumann turned to March.

"They might not . . . they . . ."

"Don't be such an idiot, March. Do you think the people who dared to kidnap a German child are going to be allowed to live?"

March shifted in his seat and then looked at the warehouse again.

"Koehler wants his daughter back; I want him to have her back," Neumann said, taking another drag.

"So how does he get her?"

"That's the part you don't want to know."

"Tell me."

"Koehler is involved in the kidnapping of . . . well, let's just say he is involved in a kidnapping. He hands them over, he gets his daughter back."

"Kidnapping? What—"

"He's being blackmailed. The one thing he can't afford to lose is at risk, so he's delivering a certain scientist so that he can get his daughter back."

March looked at his boss and then back out of the windscreen.

"I'm not happy with this, sir."

"Neither am I. I've made a mistake, March, and I'm trying to figure out a way back."

"We should tell somebody what is going on."

"You said you didn't want to end up in a concentration camp?"

March looked at Neumann and then shook his head.

"I don't."

"Well, then, you'd best not tell anyone."

"But we can't just . . . we can't just . . ."

Neumann held up his hand, stopping a floundering March from continuing.

"We've one chance, one way to make this work."

"What?"

Neumann scratched his temple with the hand holding the cigarette, then looked at his junior officer.

"You can get out of this car now. All I ask is that you go home, end your shift, and give me one day to see if I can sort this out. I'll make no mention of you if it goes wrong. I'll make sure you aren't involved."

"I'm not going to do that, sir. I just want to know what is going on."

Neumann nodded, looking at the junior officer, letting him know how much he appreciated his loyalty without actually saying it.

He took another pull on his cigarette.

"When Koehler gets his daughter, we catch the scientist before she is handed over. The plan is we hang back, we wait for the handover, and then we move in. That way Koehler gets the kid, then he helps us recapture the scientist, and we all get to look like heroes."

"But Koehler won't go for that. He'll end up in jail himself—he'll probably be shot for being involved in the kidnap of the scientist."

"He won't."

"Why?"

"Because he has a plan."

"Which is?"

"We're going to blame the Englishman. We're going to blame Rossett."

IT WAS AN hour before the black taxi pulled up at the warehouse. During that time the docks had started to come to life, and the road was now full of horse-drawn carts, wagons, and cars.

Neumann and March hadn't spoken for the entire time. Neither moved when the taxi arrived. It came to a stop, but no one got out.

A few minutes after the taxi, a box van pulled up, drawing to a halt just ahead of it. The van reversed slowly so that the taxi's nose was a couple of feet from the van's back doors.

Three men climbed out from the back of the taxi and stood on the pavement.

Neumann and March didn't move an inch as one of the men on the pavement looked across at their car for a moment. Neumann thanked God that cars weren't as rare in the docks district as they were in other parts of the city.

He twisted in his seat, pulled his Mauser out of his pocket, and checked the clip. March did the same. Neumann had heard stories of Germans being kidnapped and tortured; he didn't intend to be one of them.

The door of the warehouse opened. The men by the taxi stepped out of the way as another unmarked box van pulled out of the warehouse and double-parked next to the first.

Neumann watched as a fat woman, wrapped up against the cold like a Russian babushka, waddled out of the warehouse and climbed into the taxi. Two of the men took up station on either side of the warehouse door as the third held open the door of the taxi. Anja Koehler, dressed in black and looking tired, pale, but not the least bit scared, emerged from the warehouse. Her left arm was held tightly by a fourth man, who seemed twice as big as the others.

Anja was pushed into the taxi, where she took a seat next to Ma Price. The big man who had escorted her squeezed in on the other side of her as someone else shut the door. Neumann watched as Anja looked over her shoulder in the back of the cab, almost directly toward them.

She seemed to stare.

Neumann and March breathed out.

"We could go and get her now," said March. "She is right there."

"There's too many of them."

He watched as the back door of one of the vans opened up and the men who had got out of the taxi climbed up and in, closing the door behind them.

The first van pulled away, closely followed by the taxi, then the second van.

Neumann started the car and watched the convoy head to the top of the road, then turned to March.

"Last chance."

"Last chance for both of us."

The convoy turned right, away from the river, heading toward the maze that was London.

Neumann looked at March and back at the last van, which was making the turn.

"Drive," said March.

CHAPTER 46

NOBODY SPOKE AT the table.

In the early morning clatter and bang of a twenty-four-hour café, their table was a silent void that dripped with words unsaid.

Koehler sat opposite King, who was squeezed against the window by Rossett, who sat across from Ruth.

Ruth and Rossett had turned up moments earlier, after parking the Mercedes five minutes away from the café. Rossett had left the shotgun in the car and changed back into the white shirt he'd been carrying in his coat pocket. They had telephoned ahead to check all was clear. As they sat at the table, still buttoned up against the cold, Ruth's cheeks glowed red. Her hands wrapped around the mug of tea in front of her on the table.

She broke the silence, looking at King.

"It's good to meet you at last."

"Don't speak to him," Koehler said quietly.

"You must be the Nazi."

Ruth tilted her head as Koehler looked at her.

"I must be the man whose wife died because of him, and because of you."

Ruth nodded. "I'm sorry for your loss."

"Don't be. Just do as I say when I say it."

"You're not in a position to order me around, Major," Ruth replied.

"Oh, I am; believe me, I really am."

They stared at each other.

Rossett tapped his index finger against a teaspoon, causing it to ring like a tiny gavel on the tabletop.

"When and where are we meeting Ma Price?" he asked.

Koehler stared at Ruth a moment longer, then checked his watch and looked at Rossett.

"Finsbury Circus, in one hour. Do you know it?"

"Yeah, it's a good spot. Lots of ways in, lots of ways out."

"You can trust this man Fraser to not lead us into a trap?" Koehler was speaking to Rossett but still looking at Ruth.

"I think so. We've known each other a long time."

"You're friends?" Ruth asked.

Rossett shrugged but didn't reply.

"It'll be difficult for them to ambush us there," Koehler said to Rossett, as if Ruth hadn't spoken. "It's wide open in the park, and this time of the morning there will be lots of traffic. It's a good spot for both sides for the same reasons."

King spoke up for the first time since Rossett had arrived.

"If you would let me make some calls, I can maybe help here. I can put a lot of pressure on this Price woman, make this work out right for all of us. I can get some money down here, whatever she wants."

Koehler turned to King.

"Be quiet."

"Listen to me, I know—"

"No, King, you listen. You have to be quiet. Seriously, you have to be very quiet. I want to blow your brains out. I want to put my hand in my pocket, pull out my gun, and kill you. If you think because we've sat here all night and talked, that we are now friends and I've forgotten what you have done . . . you are wrong. You're walking a tightrope made out of piano wire, so be quiet, and be thankful that you still have a use, because I swear, the second that use expires, I'll make you pay for what you've done."

King sat back in his chair and placed both hands flat on the table.

Koehler turned to Rossett.

"How should we play this?"

"Who is this Price?" Ruth interrupted.

"She has my daughter," Koehler replied.

"Am I to understand you are handing me over to her instead of him?" Ruth pointed at King.

"Yes."

"That isn't possible."

"It is, because it is what is going to happen. Once I have my daughter, you can do what you want with whom you want, but until then, you do as I say."

Ruth looked at Rossett.

"You know how important this is, how important I am. Tell him I have to get out with King as soon as possible, and with no complications."

Rossett looked at Koehler, who nodded that he should answer.

"You are important, but he is my friend. My priorities lie with helping my friend. I'm sorry. Once we have Anja, then I'll help you, but until then . . ."

"Price will arrange a deal with him." Koehler pointed at King. "Assuming he is still alive."

King looked at Ruth but didn't speak.

Ruth looked first at Rossett, and then back to Koehler.

"You can't risk me. I know it is your daughter, I truly understand how important this is to you, but—"

"I'm afraid you don't get a say."

"I need to explain—"

Koehler dropped his hand onto Ruth's arm, holding it so tightly that she stopped speaking and looked down, and then up into his face as he moved closer.

"Be quiet," Koehler whispered.

"Ernst." Rossett stared across the table at Koehler. "Let go of her arm."

Koehler looked at his hand, then at Ruth. He lifted his arm and shook his head.

"My daughter, she is all I have now, all I want. Nothing, none of you, is going to get in the way of that."

"We need a taxi," said Rossett, and everyone at the table looked at him.

"You want to go by cab?" Koehler sounded surprised.

"I'm going to steal one." Rossett nodded to the ten or so taxis parked outside the café, on both sides of the street. "This place is a shift changeover spot. Night drivers pass the cab on to the day man; some cabs stay here all day and all night if the driver isn't working. I'll find one with a cold bonnet and it won't be missed, plus it'll help us keep a low profile. There isn't a better way to blend in than being a black cab in London."

Koehler looked at the taxis outside. "Can you get one quickly?"

"Most of them are push-button starts. We can pick one away from the window. None of these drivers will realize what I'm doing."

Koehler nodded.

"Ernst, remember." Rossett flicked his head at King. "If something goes wrong, we need him."

"How long have we got?" Koehler asked.

Rossett looked at his watch. "Forty-five minutes."

"Let's go steal a taxi."

Koehler stood up, gently taking hold of Ruth's arm and helping her to her feet.

She looked at him once they were both standing, and he leaned in close to whisper in her ear.

"Don't try anything, don't try to get away, and don't risk my daughter's life. If I have to, I will blow off both of your kneecaps to keep you with me, do you understand?"

Ruth nodded, all the while watching Frank King, who was pulling his overcoat on behind Koehler. King returned Ruth's gaze and smiled, barely a millimeter's worth of movement.

But Ruth read it.

The smile said, Don't worry, I got this.

Ruth didn't have the heart to let him know she had "this" herself.

THEY WALKED TOWARD the farthest taxi in the rank; Koehler glanced back at Rossett and King, who were coming out of the café after paying the bill. Rossett walked a few paces behind King, and everyone except Rossett passed the cab and stopped a couple of doors down. Rossett casually stepped into the street and jumped into the driver's seat.

His head dipped beneath the steering wheel.

Koehler looked up and down the street and then fixed his eyes on King, who was standing between him and the taxi.

King turned to look at him, almost as if he had felt the weight of Koehler's gaze upon his back. King's face was white, like the snow on the streets, his eyes partially bloodshot. He looked tired and dispirited.

Koehler squeezed the grip of the pistol in his pocket.

The pistol felt light in Koehler's hand. It wanted to slide out, slip free, do its job.

King looked down at the pocket, as if reading Koehler's mind.

The world was silent.

King looked into Koehler's eyes.

Koehler's thumb circled the hammer.

King's eyes.

Watching, waiting, almost willing.

The pistol rose, lighter than air, as if it had a mind of its own.

Rossett grasped Koehler's arm.

So close to Koehler that from a distance it might have looked as if they were embracing.

"Anja," Rossett said.

Koehler looked at him, and the pistol felt heavy and mindless again.

"I . . ."

"We need him if things go wrong with Price, if we lose Anja today, or even Ruth. He gives them a reason to keep in touch with us. He is their ticket out."

"I'm sorry."

"Remember Anja." Rossett eased his hold on Koehler.

"Yes."

"Come on." Rossett stepped away and Koehler let go of the gun, feeling it drop back the few inches to the bottom of his pocket.

Koehler climbed into the taxi first, followed by Ruth. Rossett shoved King firmly, causing him to stumble toward the cab.

"Get in."

King did as he was told, sitting at the other end of the bench seat from Koehler, with Ruth in between.

Rossett revved the engine and edged out into the traffic.

FINSBURY CIRCUS WAS a long way from being under a big top. There were no clowns, no acrobats, and definitely no elephants.

Instead, there was traffic, a lot of traffic, slowly rotating around a small park set in the center of a wide circle of gray granite five-story Georgian houses. A grim, heavy gray sky seemed to box the circus in from above.

Finsbury Circus was a roundabout. Traffic entered from three streets positioned at the east, south, and west of the park. Vehicles rotated in both directions, stop-starting until they reached their exit or parked next to the narrow sidewalks. The park in the middle was maybe an eighth of a mile in diameter and was surrounded by a wrought-iron railing with gates equally spaced around its perimeter. The gates were positioned like quarter-hour marks on a clock, although they were slightly offset so as not to open onto the busy street junctions. Pathways in the park met in its center, like spokes on a wheel.

Rossett chose to approach via Moorgate Road, which entered the circus from the west. He'd spent the ten-minute drive constantly checking the rearview mirror, but he'd barely paid attention to the traffic behind. His eyes had been on Koehler, who was staring silently at the passing streets, head rolling with each bump and bang of a passing pothole, lost in thoughts that Rossett didn't want to know.

"Ernst!" Rossett shouted through the partition that separated the driver from the passengers.

Koehler looked at him.

"Two minutes!" Rossett shouted, wanting to say more, but reluctant to share his concerns about Koehler with King and Ruth.

Koehler nodded and leaned forward to pick up one of the MP40s they had collected from the Mercedes on their way to the park. He checked the magazine, then slotted it back in and worked the bolt before repeating the exercise with the second gun.

Once finished, Koehler returned to staring out of the window, this time with both machine pistols on his lap, his hands folded over them.

"One minute," Rossett said. "I'm going to turn into the circus and then do a couple of laps so we can see the lay of the land, okay?"

"The lay of the land?" Ruth leaned forward.

"All these houses and apartments give great cover for anyone looking to ambush us. If there is any doubt, we can pull out and leave before we're separated from the vehicle," King said to Ruth.

"Nobody is leaving," Koehler said softly, face still turned to the window.

Rossett watched the exchange in the mirror, experiencing a sense of dread that he'd not felt since the early days of the war in France. Back then he'd sometimes been surrounded by people who either weren't ready for a fight or were too ready to fight.

Either attitude could be lethal, especially when it was coupled with people you couldn't trust.

No wonder Rossett preferred working alone.

He slowed the cab and then turned into Finsbury Circus.

The circus was quieter than usual, mainly due to the snow and the early hour. What cars and buses there were moved slowly, picking their way through rutted roads with occasional slips and slides. Rossett scanned the area for any sign of Ma Price and her men, but everything looked normal, the same as it always was.

Rossett checked his watch. Eight fifty, not much time to do a proper reconnaissance.

During his army training, an old sergeant had once screamed, "Piss-poor preparation equals piss-poor performance!"

As Rossett picked his way through the traffic of the circus, making two complete circuits, he understood exactly what that old sergeant had meant.

He pulled over just across the road from the bandstand entrance of the park. No sooner had the cab stopped than Koehler had his door open.

Koehler stepped out onto the curb, facing the cab, keeping his body close to it; he passed an MP40 through the driver's window to Rossett.

"You all right?" Rossett asked Koehler.

"Yes," Koehler replied, his eyes scanning the area.

"She'll have someone watching, ready to give a signal that we're here," said Rossett.

"Yes."

"I'd sooner you didn't take Ruth, but I'll have my hands full with King. I'll go around once more and then come in the gate to your left; I'll be able to watch your flank and rear from there."

"Good," replied Koehler, still looking toward the park.

"Price will probably come through the main gate, the one at the top of the park. It's the widest, and gives her the best chance of escape. We'll call that the west gate, yeah?"

"Yes."

"This gate, where you are going in, this is south. I'll come in the east. That way I can cover your flank and rear if you need to get out in a hurry."

"Okay."

"As you move toward Price, I'll take up a position in the center of the park. From there I can see all the entrances."

"Great."

Rossett leaned out of the window slightly so he could speak quietly to Koehler over the throb of the old diesel engine up front.

"Ernst, remember, Anja will be there. Focus on her. Get her back before you worry about King, okay?"

"Anja comes first." Koehler nodded, still looking toward the park.

"Just remember that you and Anja need to get out of this together. She needs you to keep a clear mind."

For the first time since they had stopped, Koehler looked at Rossett.

"Thank you, John."

"You don't need to thank me."

"I do. You're a good friend, and you've done more than I could ever ask for."

"It's okay."

Koehler held up a finger, silencing Rossett.

"I don't deserve a friend like you. You're a good man. Whatever happens today, however things turn out . . . I'm sorry . . . I . . ." Koehler looked toward the park and then back at his friend. "Anja, I have to make sure she is okay."

"I know."

"It's important that we have a future together, you understand that?"

"Of course I do."

Koehler looked at the ground and then back at Rossett.

"Thank you."

Rossett went to speak, but Koehler stepped back from the window with the MP40 concealed under his coat. He beckoned to Ruth with a finger and she climbed out of the car, pausing on the pavement, listening to the sounds of a busy city for the first time in a long time.

Rossett watched her; she met his gaze, smiled, a little sadly, and then took a step forward, taking the place Koehler had been moments before.

"Thank you," she said softly, placing her hand on Rossett's arm.

"Everyone is thanking me today."

"You've done a lot."

"There is a lot left to do."

Ruth smiled and looked over her shoulder at Koehler, then back at Rossett.

"Be careful."

"I always am."

"You should remember something after today."

"What?"

"You don't have to keep trying; you're already a better man."

"You look after that war machine of yours." Rossett tapped his head.

"Take care, John Rossett."

"Take care, Ruth Hartz."

Ruth stepped away from the window, leaving her hand resting on his arm a moment before finally letting go.

Rossett checked over his shoulder, first the traffic, then Frank King, and then he pulled away from the curb.

ROSSETT TOOK HIS time, slowly watching pedestrians and buildings as he drove around the park and eased the cab into the curb at the east gate.

Rossett killed the engine and swiveled in his seat to look through the partition at King, who was still staring out the window.

"I'll make you a deal."

King turned to look at Rossett. "Which is?"

"You don't mess this up, the handover, you play it straight. If it goes as planned, and we get Anja back, I'll let you go."

"Let me go?"

"I'll stop Koehler from killing you."

King's mouth twitched and then he nodded.

"He's told you he is going to kill me?"

"No."

"So how do you know he will?"

"Because I know Koehler."

"You sure?"

"Sure enough."

"And you think you can stop him."

"I can stop anyone."

King sat back in his seat, lifting his chin and then nodding.

"Why do you care if I get away? Koehler is your boss."

"Because Ruth needs you, and because it is the right thing to do."

"So the man who catches Jews for a living expects me to believe he is suddenly doing the right thing?"

"Yes."

"Why should I?"

Rossett sighed.

"You'll just have to trust me."

King smiled and shook his head.

"I guess I don't have a choice, do I?"

"No."

"Can I have a gun?"

"No."

King shook his head and then reached for the door handle. "You know, John, you might be a good cop, but you really need to work on your negotiating skills."

Rossett shook off his overcoat and draped it over the MP40 so that he could carry the gun one handed while still concealing it. He tucked his Webley into the back of his trousers, under his suit jacket, then joined King on the pavement.

"Warm enough?" King smiled as Rossett pulled at the collar of his jacket, aware that he looked out of place, carrying an overcoat instead of wearing it in the freezing cold.

Rossett gestured that King should lead the way into the park. As they passed through the gate, flanked by high privet hedges and rusted railings, King spoke.

"You might want to think about your position in this, John."

Rossett didn't reply, so King continued.

"When this is over, you might be an embarrassment to Koehler."

The only sound from Rossett was the crunch of snow under his feet.

"Being an embarrassment to Koehler makes you a danger. You'll be a threat to his future with his daughter. I'll guess Ernst is wondering how well you'd stand up to a Gestapo interrogation."

"Quiet," Rossett finally said.

"If you were to help me, I could get you out of London. You should think about that."

No reply.

"Just think about it, that's all, and remember, Koehler knows one thing for certain: dead men don't tell tales."

"You know I said I'll stop Koehler from killing you?" Rossett caught up with King, taking up position at his left shoulder.

"Yeah?"

"I might just kill you myself to get some peace and quiet."

THE PATH ON which Rossett and King were walking was buried in snow. Koehler and Ruth were to their left. A small clump of bushes sat in the center of the park, which was almost empty except for two old ladies walking together toward them, dragging a reluctant tiny dog, its belly brushing the snow.

"I think we can handle them," said King.

Rossett shook his head and kept walking, checking out the old bandstand hidden behind a bank of trees, with more low bushes at its base. It was slightly ahead of Koehler and Ruth where they stood some one hundred yards away.

The bare branches of the trees were bold and black against the gray sky, while the bushes were frosted by a thick layer of snow that pushed down their outlying branches and broke up their shadows, exposing their darkened insides and making the branches look like exposed ribs on a half-butchered carcass.

"Keep your eyes open," Rossett said, as they walked toward the center of the park. They stopped next to the snow-covered bowling green. At the far end of the green, to their rear, there was a small, weathered wooden clubhouse that was shuttered up for the winter.

The wind was picking up again, less strong than the storm the night before, but still able to whip occasional flurries of snow across the open areas of the park in dancing white whirls.

Rossett saw another woman, pushing a pram with difficulty through the snow, slowly making her way toward them. The hood of the pram was up and Rossett couldn't see if there was baby inside. It was an ideal way to carry weapons into a public area. He looked at King and saw that he, too, was watching her approach.

Rossett could see Koehler and Ruth standing ahead and to the left of the bandstand. It was smaller than Rossett remembered. Its low roof had kept the snow off the stage, and the bright blue paint on its pillars seemed like the only color left in the world. Ruth turned and looked at Rossett as the wind whipped between them again. She held out one hand in a "there's nobody here" manner that made Rossett groan.

If he and King had had any cover, it had just been blown.

"I hope she's better at making bombs than she is at keeping a low profile," King said quietly.

"Watch the pram."

"I can hear the baby crying."

The old women with the dog strolled past. One nodded at Rossett, who ignored her.

The old lady shook her head.

"Anyone else worry you?" Rossett asked King.

"Other than Koehler? No."

"Ma Price wouldn't come here without laying the ground first."

"Maybe she isn't coming?"

Rossett chewed his lip and turned a slow 360 degrees, checking all the entrances and the dead ground between him and them.

"Maybe she isn't," he said.

All he could see were old women and dogs with frostbitten bellies. Even the clubhouse had thick padlocks on its windows and doors.

"Rossett," King said, and Rossett spun to face him. King nodded his head toward Koehler, who was talking to a small boy at the north entrance.

"MISTER?"

Koehler and Ruth turned in unison as the boy walked out of the bushes on their right.

The child was maybe ten years old, and dressed poorly for the winter. He was wearing a tattered old lightweight brown raincoat, tied in the middle with string and torn at the top of the right sleeve, where a purple woolen shoulder poked out. Just below the bottom of the coat, the boy's shorts ended above dirty knees, and he was wearing boots that looked two sizes too big.

Despite this, he strode toward Koehler with a confidence well beyond his years.

The boy stopped short, close enough for Koehler to see that his hands were dirty and that he had a thick smudge of something that looked like mud across his cheek.

"Is you the German?"

Koehler looked toward Rossett and then nodded.

The boy smiled, showing he had a front tooth missing. He raised his right arm.

"'eil 'itler!"

Koehler almost reflexively raised his own arm, but then realized the boy was laughing at him.

Koehler felt a flush.

"Who sent you?"

"Some geezer gave me a shilling and told me to tell you to look up there when you got 'ere." The boy raised his hand and pointed to one of the buildings just outside the park entrance, just to the left.

Koehler could barely understand the thick Cockney accent, but followed the boy's gesture. He saw windows, all the same, dark against the granite building. He squinted into the wind, and then he saw it.

One window not quite the same, on the fifth floor, a quarter raised. A ghostly face, just in the shadows of the room, a face looking out from maybe two hundred feet away.

"Can you see it?" The boy looked at Koehler.

"Yes."

Sniper.

Shit.

"Is that it?" Koehler asked the boy, who shrugged.

"Not unless you want to give me a shilling as well?"

"Get lost," Koehler said, already turning to look at Rossett and King, who had walked halfway toward them along the path. Rossett stopped some fifty yards away, then looked up toward the window and then back to Koehler. Their eyes met, and Koehler gave a tiny shake of his head. He turned to Ruth, who was staring up at the window.

"He's gone," she said.

"He hasn't. We know he's there, so he's moved back into the room so he can't be seen from the street. He's a sniper. He probably broke into a flat so as to keep us covered."

"But why tell us?"

"So we know that if we try anything, we're in his sights."

"What do we do?"

"We wait. She is just letting us know we are covered. If she weren't coming, she wouldn't have bothered."

Off to his right Koehler saw three men in overalls approaching from the north gate. One was pushing a wheelbarrow full of garden tools across the snow.

Garden tools, in the snow?

It was starting.

He looked toward the bandstand; it would provide cover from the sniper if needed, but it would expose them to the men in the park with the wheelbarrow, who were loitering around the same distance from him as Rossett, but across toward the north.

Koehler looked at Rossett, who nodded back toward him.

Rossett had them covered, which meant that Koehler could concentrate on the black taxi that had stopped at the west gate.

The taxi from which he could see Anja staring back at him.

Koehler's heart thudded.

"It's them."

Ruth looked at him and then the cab. She saw a fat woman climbing out unsteadily onto the pavement before turning back to pull a young girl out behind her.

"Is that your daughter?"

"Yes."

The big man who had also been sitting on the backseat unfolded from the cab, a leather bag slung over his shoulder.

"These people are dangerous. Be very careful. If anything happens, drop to the snow and stay there." Koehler didn't look at Ruth as he spoke; instead he kept eyes on Ma Price and Anja walking toward them.

Anja was crying, wiping her cheek with the palm of her hand, fighting back sobs that sounded like half laughs.

"Daddy!"

Koehler heard her calling to him, and he took a step forward, his heart dragging him closer, before his brain made him stop.

The big man adjusted his bag and put his hand inside.

Ma Price still had Anja's arm, and Koehler could see her whispering to the girl as Anja wiped her cheek again and nodded.

"Major Koehler?"

Koehler nodded as Ma Price smiled at him from twenty feet away. "And you must be our scientist?"

"Yes."

"Right, then, that was easy enough." Ma Price smiled at Koehler. "Off you go, my love, back to your old dad."

Ma Price let go of Anja's arm.

Anja ran toward her father and slammed into him like a magnet to metal. Koehler stroked her hair as she buried her face in his chest. Her arms reached fully around his waist, squeezing and holding on to him as if they would never let go again.

"You are to come with me. I'm going to take you to the American," Ma Price said to Ruth, holding out her hand as she spoke.

Ruth blinked and rocked a little as a fresh gust of wind battered her body for a second or two.

"The American is here."

Ma Price followed Ruth's glance toward Rossett and King.

"Not him, lovely. He doesn't matter anymore. You can forget about him." Ma Price gestured to Ruth to follow her.

Koehler took a half step backward, still wrapped in Anja's arms.

"We need to move, child," he whispered in German.

Anja looked up at him as he took another step away from Price and Ruth.

Ruth glanced at Koehler and then looked back toward Price, a slow frown spreading across her face.

"But the man over there, he has organized all this." An element of doubt hung around the edge of Ruth's voice.

Ma Price frowned. "We need to get moving. He isn't important now." She held out her hand to Ruth.

Ruth looked over her shoulder toward King, unsure what to do next.

ROSSETT LOOKED AT the workmen to the side of him, and then back to Koehler and Price, then the sniper, and then Koehler and Price again.

Things were moving fast. He knew they'd arrived at the tip of the needle and that they could fall either way if they weren't careful.

He shut down everything else but the group in front of him. They were what mattered. He tried to read Koehler's body language, looking for signs of alarm, any signal that the handover wasn't going according to plan.

He tunneled his senses, blocking out the sound of the traffic, the cold, other people in the park, a distant dog yapping, the red London bus whose roof he could see above the hedges.

All of it slipped away.

He shut down everything that wasn't a threat to Anja and Koehler and focused on them alone, his mission, his need to make sure father and daughter were united, to close the circle, have what he couldn't have.

He forgot about King.

THE KNIFE SLAMMED into the front of Rossett's shoulder through his suit jacket, so hard that King felt it punch through the muscle and scrape across bone.

Reflex caused Rossett to dip to the left, then swivel to face the threat. King half dragged the blade out of Rossett's shoulder before Rossett drove a solid punch into King's forearm, hitting a nerve and forcing him to release the knife.

King stumbled, went to cradle his arm, and then reached for the knife again.

Rossett grabbed King's wrist and pulled it toward and then past him as he pivoted in the snow, dropping the MP40 as he tried to wrestle King around and drop him to the ground.

King didn't resist. He allowed himself to be pulled forward, and then, using the whipcrack of momentum Rossett had generated, he swept his other arm up, using his elbow to strike Rossett hard on the left cheekbone.

Rossett let go and dropped to one knee.

King stumbled a few steps and then turned, advancing on the MP40 Rossett had dropped. Rossett was stunned but still dangerous. He reached around behind him, woozily drawing his Webley, struggling to free it from his belt.

King realized he wasn't going to make the MP40, and instead stepped in and punched Rossett hard on the right temple, a solid blow that stunned the Englishman. Finally, like a fallen bull elephant, Rossett hit the snow, face-down, driving the knife halfway back into the wound again.

King had picked the knife off the counter when Rossett was settling the bill, before they had left the café. It wasn't much of a knife, but at the time, he didn't have much of a plan to go with it.

He'd never intended to leave his fate in the hands of Rossett. All along he'd doubted that Rossett could stop Koehler from killing him. Frank King was a spy and a soldier, and he was never going to leave his life in the hands of some flatfoot copper from London.

He'd been waiting for the moment, and that moment was when he saw Ruth turn toward him, looking for him, wanting his help, unsure. He knew he had to do something, something for Ruth, something for his country, something for the world; he had to take back control and stop being a passenger.

King picked up the MP40 and unfolded the stock of the gun. He worked the bolt, put the stock in his shoulder, and looked down the sights, first at Price, then at the big man with the leather bag just to Koehler's right. King dropped to one knee and leaned into the weapon, ready for the recoil, then took a deep breath.

Just to the left of the sights he could see Koehler half turning toward him, holding Anja close to his chest while flicking back his coat to reveal his own machine gun slung across his body.

King fired two rounds, a second apart, and the big man to Koehler's right shook and then dropped his head as he lifted his hand out of the leather bag to his chest.

Bang.

The big man dropped on the third shot, crumpled in the snow as the round hit home, center mass.

King rose and moved forward and to the side at a low crouch, MP40 still pushed into his shoulder, advancing on Ma Price, who was pointing at him and dragging Ruth toward the gate. Koehler had hit the ground, throwing himself over Anja. King could see that Koehler was pulling his own weapon free, but not bringing it to bear for fear of drawing fire toward Anja.

King stopped, leaned into the stock, took another breath, focused on the sights, and fired two shots at the back of Ma Price as she ran. She was pushing Ruth ahead of her toward the gate and the taxi that was waiting in the street beyond it. In the taxi King saw the driver pointing a pistol at him, so he moved forward again, adjusting his aim past Ma Price, and fired another shot.

The driver reacted as the round hit his door, and King fired again.

The driver winced and the pistol disappeared from sight as he leaned forward.

King heard shots coming in from the sniper but ignored them; he kept moving forward. Koehler, in his peripheral vision, was still facedown, protecting Anja.

King adjusted slightly to make Ma Price the target.

Snow kicked up around him, but he didn't flinch. He kept his sights on Price, who was now at the taxi door. His finger tensed but he didn't fire. He could see Ruth, pushing back against Price, trying to get back out of the taxi, too close for him to take the shot.

King moved forward again, feeling the air part as another sniper round fizzed past and flicked up more snow. Ma Price shoved Ruth while looking over her shoulder at him. He moved toward her like a machine, ignoring danger, remorseless death. Ma Price spun and struck Ruth high and hard on the temple with her fist. Ruth disappeared backward into the taxi, sprawling onto the floor.

King fired.

Bang.

The round hit Ma Price high on the left shoulder, and he watched as she spun and dropped sideways into the taxi, which was already moving away from the curb. King fired twice more. The first shot shattered the side window, and the second punched a hole in the black metal above the fuel cap. The back wheels on the cab spun in the snow and then caught.

King started to run.

Snow was flicking up around him as he sprinted, high-stepping, toward the north gate. He knew the taxi would be trapped in morning traffic and that to exit the circus it would have to pass the north gate. If he could catch it there, he could cut it off.

He was aware of the workmen with the wheelbarrow firing Thompsons on full auto at him, useless vague noise, spewing their fire high and wide from one hundred yards away.

King ran hard, head down, cold air rasping his throat, feet kicking up snow as he sprinted for the gate.

He heard Rossett's Webley boom behind him.

He didn't look back.

The Webley boomed again, but King just kept running for the gate, running to catch a taxi.

ROSSETT PULLED THE knife out of his shoulder and tossed it into the snow. The pain burned deep as he lifted the Webley and fired once more, another loose shot at the men with the Thompsons.

He missed, and turned to look at King making for the other exit. Rossett half lifted the pistol, then let it drop again.

He couldn't make the shot, whether because of the pain in his shoulder or because he was tired of killing, he didn't know.

He'd never know.

He looked toward the west gate and saw Koehler. His friend was lying in the snow, head up, watching King run away. It took Rossett a moment to focus until he realized Koehler was smothering Anja, who was barely visible except for a spray of blond hair fanning out from under his shoulder.

The child was safe.

Rossett wobbled and thought about lying down in the snow, letting it go, letting someone else do the fighting while he looked up into the heavy clouds above.

He thought about it.

But he knew he wasn't going to do it.

He had to help Ruth, make sure she was safe, be a better man.

He breathed deep, forced himself to go again, struggled to his feet, and fired another shot at the men with the Thompsons. Who were by now lifting an injured comrade out of the snow before they started half walking, half running across the park in an unruly retreat.

Rossett shook off the punches he'd just received, watched the retreating men, and lifted the pistol. Scanned the park in a 360 spin and then started to jog after King toward the north gate. His head was throbbing, and he felt unsteady, still groggy after being half knocked out. His vision seemed focused in places and dreamlike in others. He shook his head as he ran, the pain in his shoulder slowly increasing in intensity as his feet crunched through the snow. Ahead, he could see King at the park gate, heading out onto the road.

KING WAS NOW gasping for breath as he ran. He burst through the gates and into the street, slipped, skidded, and landed hard before scrabbling to his feet again. He looked back into the park and saw Rossett in the distance jogging, unsure in his steps, heading toward him.

King was starting to regret using the knife.

He turned and started to look for the taxi, taking short, sharp gulps of breath as he scanned the oncoming vehicles. Traffic parted as it approached the madman with the machine gun in the middle of the street.

Passersby were watching now as he started to move through the slow-moving vehicles, MP40 held high, King leaning into the shoulder stock. Cars passed him in either direction, missing him by inches as they pushed their way through the rush hour. Horns blared and people on the sidewalks shouted, but King ignored them all as he hunted his target.

He found it.

The taxi was trapped by the traffic that engulfed it like a slow-flowing river. King could see the driver hunched forward, one hand on top of the wheel.

The driver lifted his head and saw him.

The cab slowed as the cars on either side bunched around, then it accelerated, scraping down the side of another car, aiming for King.

King opened fire.

The windscreen shattered; he watched through the sights as the driver bucked in his seat, then lifted his free hand in a futile attempt to stop the rounds from hitting him.

He failed.

The cab lurched right as King stopped shooting. For a moment he thought he was about to be run down, but the taxi continued, skidding across the road, back end sliding in the compacted snow, then hitting another car at a forty-five-degree angle.

Both vehicles crashed to a sudden halt.

Silence.

Just for a second, as the world stopped and watched.

Then screaming.

Bedlam broke out as people on the pavement ran in all directions, left, then right, away from the madman with the gun.

King walked the twenty feet toward the taxi slowly, machine gun still at his shoulder. It appeared the back of the cab was empty, and for a moment he felt a wave of panic that he'd hit the wrong taxi. He leaned in, lowering one hand to the back door, the other still holding the MP40, and pulled open the door. Ma Price, blood leaking out the collar of her coat, was lying under Ruth, who had been thrown off the backseat and on top of her in the collision.

Both women looked up. King stared down at them as they lay on the glass from the broken windows that seemed to fill the entire floor of the taxi.

Ma Price tried to lift her pistol but saw the MP40 leveled at her.

"No," King said, and Price paused, then let the gun fall from her hand onto the floor. "Let's go, we haven't got long," he said to Ruth, all the time his eyes on Ma Price, who smiled at him with bloodstained teeth.

"Where you gonna go?" Price asked. "Your own government want you dead."

"Ruth, please, quickly."

Ruth looked at Price, then pushed herself from the floor of the cab; she picked up Price's pistol and turned to King, who held out one hand to pull her free.

There was a shot.

King staggered as his coat seemed to puff with air and then deflate around him.

There was another shot and King turned, falling sideways into the cab, ending up sitting with his feet in the road, his body filling the doorway, his back to Ruth.

Another shot and he bucked again and the MP40 dropped into his lap.

"Run," he whispered, as his shoulder slowly slouched against the door-frame of the taxi.

ROSSETT WAS HALFWAY out of the park when he saw the two German police-men, Neumann and March, advancing on the taxi. He could see King sitting in the open doorway of the cab, MP40 useless in his lap, hands lying on it, palms up, as the American struggled to lift his head.

Rossett scanned the pavement for Ruth, but she was nowhere to be seen among the people who were either running or diving for cover. He saw move-ment in the taxi, a bobbing head in the shadows behind King, pushing at the door on the other side of the cab, trying to escape.

March and Neumann were still moving forward, in half crouches, pistols raised ready to fire again.

"No!" Rossett shouted. "There are people in the taxi, you'll hit them!"

Neumann kept his aim on the taxi, but March swiveled his pistol toward Rossett.

Rossett raised his hands; he was only forty feet away at the park gate, well within striking range of the Mauser. He realized he was holding his Webley and let it fall to the snow at his feet, half lowering one hand due to the pain from the wound in his shoulder.

"I'm a British policeman!" Rossett shouted at March.

"*Erlegen!*" He heard the single word shouted in German.

Rossett knew what it meant; he'd heard it many times before.

"*Shoot!*"

Rossett turned and saw the one man he could still call his friend, the one man he had risked everything for. That man was screaming at March to shoot him.

Rossett's hands lowered another inch.

"*Ihn zu toten!*" Koehler shouted, pointing at Rossett while looking at March. "*Kill him!*"

Rossett looked at March, saw him lick a thin tongue across his lips and adjust a shoulder.

Rossett dropped to his knees, one hand taking hold of the Webley in the snow, so fast that March fired into the air where he'd been a quarter second before.

Rossett managed a fast, fluid draw off the ground, the Webley cold in his hand as he whipped it up, flinging a flurry of snow as it came to bear and fired.

March staggered right and then dropped, a bullet in his hip.

THE ECHO OF the Webley filled the street. Neumann half turned, looking at his subordinate and then at Rossett.

King, still slumped in the doorway of the taxi, managed to find the strength to half turn the MP40 and press the trigger.

Neumann hit the ground as the MP40 kicked drunkenly in King's lap, aimlessly scattering bullets high into the walls of the buildings on the far side of the circus and sending the few remaining bystanders running for cover.

Neumann heard the click of the MP40's bolt as the magazine came up empty, then rolled onto his side and looked at King as the machine gun slid from his hands into the snow.

Neumann rolled again, now looking for Rossett.

He was gone.

RUTH WAS KICKING at the door, trying to burst her way out of the back of the taxi. The crash had twisted the chassis half an inch, and no matter how hard she pulled the handle or kicked at the door, she couldn't get it to open.

She had lain flat as King emptied his magazine. The stink of cordite in the cab clung to her throat as she pulled another deep breath, and braced to kick the door again.

"Go on girl, you can do it," Ma Price muttered behind her, one hand on her shoulder, blood leaking through her fingers. "Give it a good old boot."

Ruth gritted her teeth, squeezed her eyes tight, and, lying flat on the floor, her back pressed into the broken glass, slammed both feet at the buckled door.

It moved an inch. She could see daylight around its edge.

She kicked again. Another inch.

Then a hand from outside pulled at the top of the door, yanking with each of her quickening kicks.

Rossett appeared in the gap. He looked at her, then at Ma Price.

He didn't speak, he just held out a hand for Ruth to take.

She took it.

She didn't look back as she followed Rossett, both ducking and running through the parked, mostly abandoned traffic that had backed up behind the crash.

As they ran toward the west end of the circus, they passed a few people standing with frozen faces, staring. She became aware of police cars and whistles approaching, echoing off the walls of the buildings.

After fifty yards of flat-out running, she slowed, aware that Rossett was struggling to keep up. She held out her hand, pulling him closer. The crowd thickened around them, people moving and pushing to a point where they were reduced to a walking pace, with just occasional glances back over their shoulders.

Nobody seemed to be following them in the mass of spectators.

They turned off Finsbury Circus, away from the scene of the shooting, heading toward Moorgate tube station, just a minute's walk from the west side of the park.

The street was jammed with traffic unable to move in either direction. A bus had been caught in the middle of turning off the main road, and it blocked both lanes. Car horns were blasting, unaware of what had just taken place a few hundred yards away.

It was bedlam.

Rossett wanted to descend into the maze of the London Underground, away from the mayhem. He looked at Ruth; her hair had tumbled across her face in the crash. She looked back at him.

"Are you okay?" he asked her now that they were out of the crowds of pedestrians on the edge of the circus and able to move more freely.

"Are you?"

Rossett didn't reply.

"I heard Koehler shouting," Ruth said, fixing her hair as they stopped at the entrance of the tube station, just inside the doorway, pausing to check that they weren't being followed. "I thought he was your friend?"

Rossett frowned and felt her arm slipping through his. He turned to her and she nodded, scooping some hair away. Rossett tried to smile reassuringly but failed, so he looked back as a police car blared its way through the snarled traffic, trying to get to the scene of the shooting.

"We should go." Ruth tugged on Rossett's arm.

He nodded, looked at her, started to speak, and then nodded again. They turned, heading toward the Underground in more ways than one.

CHAPTER 47

NEUMANN WAS PUSHING down on March's hip with a woolen scarf that an old lady on the pavement had handed him.

Koehler dropped to his knees alongside them.

"I said shoot." Koehler hissed out the words, looking first at March on the ground and then at Neumann.

"I tried." March was shaking and speaking through gritted teeth as Neumann applied pressure to his wound.

"Where were you?" Koehler looked at Neumann.

"I was trying to shoot the girl, like you told me to."

"We're fucked now, absolutely fucked. If she tells anyone what we've been doing . . ." Koehler leaned back on his haunches and looked at the crowd that had gathered around them, watching Neumann's first aid efforts.

Koehler stared at their faces and wondered how many could understand what he was saying in German.

"Where were you?" Neumann asked, now having to use two hands to push on March's wound.

"I was with my daughter." Koehler pointed to Anja, who was standing with an English bobby, hands held to her mouth, watery eyes on her father, thirty feet away.

"You got her back. You should be happy." Neumann adjusted his hands, checking to see how much blood was soaking through the scarf.

"I would be, except that because of you two messing things up, I'll probably be in a cell in half an hour."

The sound of an ambulance siren pushing its way through the crowd drowned out the last part of Koehler's sentence. He looked across as it nudged its way to a stop. A medic jumped out of the passenger seat, running toward them with a small leather doctor's bag before dropping into the snow next to March.

"Let me have a look at him."

Neumann struggled to his feet as the ambulance man lifted the scarf. Koehler's eyes found Anja again; he smiled reassuringly.

He turned back to Neumann, and they both stood over March and the medic as he worked.

"You'll have to tell them you were just trying to save your daughter." Neumann started to put his hands in his pockets, but stopped when he noticed the blood on them.

"You think that'll help me?"

Neumann leaned down, picking up two handfuls of snow. He massaged it into a ball, enjoying the cold. He wiped his bloodstained fingers on the ball and then broke it, before wiping his fingers through the now bloodstained powder and then dropping it again.

"You think the Gestapo will just say 'Oh well, you had your reasons, don't worry about it'?" Koehler tried again, leaning in closer to Neumann, watching him try to clean his hands. "Well, do you?"

Neumann flicked the melt water off his fingers, then wiped his hands on the front of his coat and across his backside before inspecting them again.

He held them up for Koehler to see.

"I just washed my hands of this." Neumann walked away from Koehler, wandering across to the taxi to take a look at King, who was still sitting in the doorway.

Now quite thoroughly dead.

Neumann crouched down in front of King, looking into the American's open but unseeing eyes.

Behind him he could hear another ambulance arriving. He turned as the crowd parted once more to allow it to slowly make its way toward Ma Price. Who was lying in the road on the other side of the cab, being helped by two British bobbies.

Neumann became aware of Koehler at his shoulder.

"We need to find the scientist," Koehler said, voice raised just enough for Neumann to hear over the siren of the ambulance.

Neumann looked at him.

"You do what you have to do, just leave me out of it."

"You're already in it."

"Do you think?"

"You're in it because I say you are in it."

They stared at each other until finally Neumann spoke, more quietly now, the siren having fallen silent.

"I was just doing my job."

"I'll tell them you knew what was going on. That you were involved in springing the scientist from the start."

"They'll never believe it."

"They don't have to believe it, they just have to suspect it. These are dangerous days, Neumann. You know what suspicion can do to a man."

"Why would you do that? I've helped you; I've done all I can to make this work for you."

"Because I need to fix the final loose ends. If I don't, if this isn't put to bed, Anja will lose me just the same as she lost her mother. She'll be alone, and I won't let my daughter be left on her own, not for anybody."

Neumann swallowed, then looked over his shoulder at March, who was still being treated on the pavement. Neumann rubbed his index finger across his mustache and then slipped his hand into his pocket as he turned back to Koehler.

"Why would you do this to me?"

"I can't have any loose ends, Neumann."

"Rossett?"

"I'll deal with Rossett."

"And me?" Neumann tilted his head.

"Your involvement buys your silence. I know that. And if it doesn't . . . don't doubt me, Neumann, I'll do whatever I have to do to stay with my child. You need to know that. I'll drop you, your partner, my friend, whoever it takes to make it right."

Neumann shook his head; he turned to look at March as he wiped the back of his hand across his own mouth.

"How are we meant to find Hartz now? They'll be miles away. We don't know their plans."

"We don't know the plan . . . but she does." Koehler pointed at Ma Price, who was being carried to the back of the ambulance on a stretcher.

She was watching Koehler, staring at his outstretched finger, and as he turned to look at her she smiled.

"GET OUT," KOEHLER said to the bobby, who was sitting in the back of the ambulance, getting ready to escort Ma Price to the hospital.

"But my sarge said I was . . ." The bobby broke off as Neumann flashed his police ID.

"Please." Neumann wearily gestured with his thumb to the open door. "Just go."

The bobby picked up his helmet, nodded to Neumann, and then climbed out of the ambulance, closing the back doors behind him.

The medic who was working on Ma Price called through the gap between the front seats to the driver.

"Get going, Charlie. St. Bart's Hospital."

"Get up front," Koehler said to the medic.

"I can't leave her, she's my patient."

"Go sit up front," Koehler said again.

"But—"

"Do it," Koehler said flatly.

"Go on, my love, I'll be all right." Ma Price spoke for the first time as the ambulance started to move. "Go on; let me speak to the gentlemen."

The medic looked at Neumann and then Koehler, then reluctantly squeezed through the gap to the front passenger seat. He sat side on, keeping an eye on Ma Price. Koehler gestured that he should face front, and the man sighed and acquiesced, folding his arms like a chastened schoolboy.

The siren of the ambulance started up again.

Koehler leaned in close to Price, keeping his voice low.

"How were you getting the scientist out of the country?"

Ma Price smiled at him but didn't reply. The ambulance juddered, stopped, and then started to push through the traffic jam again, more slowly than before.

"Tell me how she is getting out and I can help you," Koehler tried again.

"I never took your daughter. You know that, don't you?" Price replied, staring straight into Koehler's eyes.

"I know."

"I found her, and I never harmed her. I fed her and kept her warm."

"I believe you. Tell me what was going to happen to the scientist. I can help you if you do."

Ma Price lowered her voice to a whisper, forcing Koehler to move in closer.

"We both know it isn't me who needs helping, it's you."

Koehler sat back slightly; he glanced at Neumann and then leaned in again.

"I can make you tell me," Koehler whispered.

Price smiled at him.

"No, you can't, not by the time we get to the hospital. And if you think I'm wrong, you're not the man I heard you were."

They stared deep into each other's eyes. Seconds passed before Price broke the silence.

"You tell these fellas to pull over once we're well clear of the circus. You get your mate there to fetch me a taxi, then we'll talk."

"I can't do that."

"Well, I can't talk, then, so you figure it out."

Koehler slumped back into the jump seat the bobby had recently vacated. He rubbed a weary hand across his face, feeling the last few days crash in on him as he struggled to make sense of things.

His Anja, his love, the only thing he had left . . . he couldn't lose her, and she couldn't lose him. He remembered her face as he had shoved her into the arms of a young policeman, ordering that she should be taken to SS Group Command and left there until he returned.

He'd left her again, minutes after telling her he would never leave her again.

He'd lied.

He shook his head.

It felt heavy pushing into his hand.

The ambulance rocked slightly as it threaded through the last of the jam. He felt it picking up speed, the siren still sounding, making it hard for him to think.

He opened his eyes. Price and Neumann were watching him. He blinked slowly, then nodded.

"Okay."

"Okay what?" said Neumann.

"You get what you want." Koehler ignored Neumann.

"What does she want? What does she get?" Neumann raised his voice, this time in German.

"Thank you, Major, and you'll get what you want," said Ma Price, all smiles.

"What are you doing, Koehler? What the hell are you doing?" Neumann, still in German.

The ambulance was traveling at speed now, the siren switching off and on intermittently as traffic dictated. Koehler leaned forward and took position behind the front seats, resting his hands on their backs as he looked through the windscreen.

He waited half a minute, then said, "Pull over."

"What?" The driver looked at his colleague, who in turn looked at Koehler.

"Pull over."

"Here?"

"Here."

"But . . . but she's been shot. We need to get her to hospital."

"Stop the ambulance here."

Koehler was still looking out the windscreen, but now his Mauser was in his right hand, resting on the back of the driver's seat, inches from the driver's head.

"Stop," the medic said to the driver, who eased to the side of the road.

"Thank you," Koehler said quietly.

"We need to get her to the hospital."

"Get her some dressings and whatever else you have here to help her." Koehler turned back to Ma Price.

"Ernst, what the hell are you doing?" Neumann was out of his seat now, still speaking in German.

"Saving our lives," Koehler replied in English, as he helped Ma Price into a sitting position on the side of the stretcher. "Go stop a taxi."

Ma Price's head was bowed slightly, one hand pressing against the fresh bandage on her shoulder.

"Please, Erhard, go get her a taxi," in German this time, softly.

Neumann swept a hand across the top of his head and then spun, almost kicking the back doors of the ambulance open.

The cold air off the street rushed in, and Ma Price visibly shivered as she gingerly lowered her feet onto the floor. She stood, one hand on his arm, head still bowed. A second passed, and then she looked up and smiled at him.

"I knew you'd see sense, Mr. Koehler."

"You lie to me, I'll find you and then I'll kill you."

"Help me out the back."

"Don't doubt me, woman."

"Yes, yes, now help me out the back. We ain't got much time."

With the medic's help, Koehler led Ma Price down the two steps and out onto the pavement.

He gestured to the ambulance man.

"Give her your coat."

"I have to pay for this."

"You'll pay for it if you don't."

The ambulance man reluctantly slipped out of his overcoat, and then gently placed it across Ma Price's shoulders.

"You'll get it back," she said as she took a few steps unaided away from the ambulance, toward where Neumann was standing next to a black taxi.

Passersby were watching but not stopping as Koehler followed Ma Price. His hand hovered an inch from her, ready to catch her in case she fell. She shuffled through the snow to the taxi as Neumann opened the back door.

"She's been shot, Ernst," Neumann said in German as Koehler helped push Ma Price up into the back of the cab. "We shouldn't be doing this."

"I've been shot before, I'll most likely be shot again," Ma Price surprised them by replying in excellent German. She sank into the seat with a sigh, helped down by Koehler, who sat next to her.

Ma Price puffed out her cheeks, catching her breath, watching the driver, who was staring back in his mirror, a look of concern on his face.

"Oooh, it does sting a bit, mind," she finally said, looking at Koehler. "Open the window and get out."

Koehler looked at Neumann, who was still by the door, then gestured that he should move back and make space.

Once Koehler was outside, leaning his head through the open window, Ma Price spoke again.

"We could do with some privacy?"

Koehler banged on the glass partition, causing the driver to turn and look at him.

"Get out."

"You what?"

"Get out of the taxi, we need privacy."

The driver rolled his eyes, cursing himself and his bad luck for stopping by an ambulance. He climbed out of the cab and stood next to Neumann on the pavement.

"So?" Koehler leaned back in through the window.

"The Yanks, Kennedy especially, they don't want the scientist anymore. Don't ask me why, I don't know. I'll wager it's because they don't want to upset you lot." Price took a deep breath and put her hand to her shoulder again, this time under the overcoat. "I was told to kill her, Ruth Hartz, but I wasn't going to."

"Why not?"

"Because she was worth more to me alive than she was dead."

"You were going to sell her?"

"I wanted to. I was going to buy my way out with her, out of this shithole."

"Who was going to buy her?"

Ma Price smiled sadly, considering her words carefully.

"Nobody must know I told you this."

"Nobody ever will."

"If it got out that I told you this, I'd be dead before dinnertime."

"Nobody will know, I swear . . . on my daughter's life, I swear."

"Sir James Sterling wants Ruth. He thinks he can get her to Canada. He thinks she can build a bomb for Britain. Or, at the very least, convince the Yanks she's worth working with."

"James Sterling?"

"Yes."

"The civil servant?"

"Yes."

"He was a fascist before the war. He marched with Mosley." Koehler tried to compute the information.

"I know."

"He is in the resistance?"

"He *is* the resistance. You get him, you get the girl, and plenty more as well."

"How do I know this isn't just you getting rid of Sterling?"

"I don't think you want to kill Sterling, although I don't care if you do. I'll wager you'd just as soon do a deal with him, same as you're doing one with me. You're fighting for your life, Mr. Koehler, I can see that."

"I'm fighting for my daughter."

"Same thing," Ma Price replied, wincing.

"Does Rossett know about Sterling?"

"What I've heard about Mr. Rossett, it won't take him long to find out if he doesn't."

Koehler nodded, glancing over his shoulder at the two others on the curb, and then leaning back in to Price.

"If I manage to get Hartz, if I manage to clear this up, the slate is clean between us. If I don't, if I'm questioned . . . I don't know what will happen. I gave you my word, but—"

"I'm a big girl, Mr. Koehler. When you see your daughter you hold her tight. Mark my words, you don't ever want to let go again."

Koehler nodded, then stepped back from the taxi and turned to the driver. "Go."

"Where's she going?"

"Out of this shithole."

CHAPTER 48

BILL FRASER HAD his shoulder and his foot to his front door, but still it moved toward him.

"You can't just push your way in here, this is my home."

Rossett shoved again. This time Fraser rocked back a step under the pressure.

The door was now open wide enough for Rossett to walk through, but he didn't.

He stared at Fraser from the front step.

"I've known you for ten years, Bill. Ten years, and you try to slam a door in my face?"

Fraser looked at Ruth, who was standing behind Rossett.

"I don't need this."

"You slam the door on me?"

Fraser scratched the back of his neck.

"I've had a hell of a morning, John."

Rossett and Ruth both raised their eyebrows.

Fraser sighed and shrugged, then took a step back and lowered his head.

They stepped into the hallway. Rossett ignored Fraser and walked past him toward the door at the end. Ruth watched Rossett look into the kitchen, then open the door to the back room of the house.

Ruth could hear a voice on a radio somewhere; it sounded like one of the political discussion programs that featured a lot on the BBC nowadays. She remembered how they had been piped into the labs at Cambridge when she first had first arrived. That lasted a few months, until various members of staff complained they were unable to think with the constant twittering of "Nazi intellectuals."

The radio had been switched off at Cambridge, and some of those staff had moved on a short time later, never to be seen again.

She looked at Rossett, standing at the far end of the hall, hands in his coat pockets, staring at Fraser. Fraser was still stationed next to the front door, nervously toying with a button on his cardigan.

Ruth broke the silence.

"Could I use your bathroom?"

Fraser nodded, pointing up the stairs.

"First door on the left."

"Thank you." She started up the stairs, then leaned over the banister.

"John?"

Rossett looked back at her.

"We're guests."

Rossett nodded. "Put the kettle on, Bill."

THE RADIO WAS still mumbling to itself in the corner of the front room when Ruth came back downstairs. She had washed her face and run wet fingers through her hair in an effort to encourage it into behaving.

Rossett and Fraser were sitting silently together in the front room. The door was open and Ruth stood framed in it. Rossett smiled.

"You look better."

She looked beautiful.

"You look awful," Ruth said. "You should take off your coat, make the most of the fire."

Rossett looked at the fire, then at Fraser, who was sitting on the other side of it.

"Give me your coat, John. You can relax now," Fraser said gently.

Rossett's eyes lowered to the rug. His broad hands lay wearily on the arms of the armchair, white, like marble, lined with blue veins.

The kettle started to whistle in the kitchen, and Fraser rose out of his chair.

"Ruth will make it," said Rossett quietly before turning his head toward her. "Please?"

Ruth nodded and left the room. Fraser remained standing. Rossett stared without emotion back at him.

The voices on the radio were talking about the danger of communism and the Jews; someone called William Joyce was declaring that Hitler was the savior of the human race, a man who would be remembered by future generations as a great British hero.

Fraser switched the radio off and took up position by the window, staring through the net curtains at the empty street outside. Eventually he turned and looked at Rossett.

"Do you want a drink?"

Rossett nodded.

Fraser crossed to a silver tray on a small table in the corner of the room, where three bottles sat. The bottles chinked and rattled as he took one from the back, then held it up for Rossett to see.

"Scotch?"

Rossett just stared at the bottle until Fraser shrugged.

He poured half an inch into two tumblers and handed one to Rossett.

Rossett looked at the Scotch.

"I had to water it down, to make it last," Fraser said, reading Rossett's eyes.

Rossett took a sip, frowned, and placed the glass on the arm of the chair.

He breathed out through his nose, feeling the whiskey warm his throat and his sinuses; he blinked and licked his lips.

"When is your wife home?"

Fraser looked at the clock on the mantelpiece.

"Four hours. She finishes at five, and then it takes half an hour to get home."

"When do you need to be at work?"

"I don't, it's my day off."

Rossett nodded, took a breath, and looked at the fire.

"I'm bleeding."

"What?"

"I've been stabbed. I'm bleeding." Fraser took a step forward, but Rossett held up a hand to stop him. "I need your help, Bill. I'm tired, I'm struggling, I need your help."

Fraser looked at his own whiskey, then sat down.

"John, I—"

"I can't look after her for much longer. Koehler needs her; I think he's going to kill her. I'm not sure I can hold him off."

"I thought he was your friend."

"So did I."

Ruth entered the room carrying a tray with a teapot and cups on it. She noticed the whiskey, and frowned as she put the tea down on the small table next to the radio.

"It's a little early, isn't it?"

"It's more water than whiskey." Fraser sounded like a schoolboy caught smoking.

Ruth took the whiskey out of Rossett's hand. She sipped, savored, then smiled at him and handed it back.

"It's good," she said.

"It is," replied Rossett as he watched Ruth start to pour the tea.

The low winter sun was shining through the window, silhouetting her, highlighting every feature in a perfect contrast of light and dark.

Rossett could see a wisp of hair that had dropped forward.

She turned and looked at him.

She tilted her head, the sun so bright he couldn't see her face.

"Are you okay?"

"I'm tired."

"Not long now, we can sleep soon."

"Yeah."

Rossett couldn't see her smile, but—whether it was the fire, the whiskey, or the sun coming through the window shining on him—he felt warmer.

RUTH STOOD BEHIND Fraser in the hallway while he made the call.

"I need to speak to Sir James." Fraser turned and nodded to Ruth. "It's very important . . . Trust me, he'll want to be interrupted . . . It's Bill Fraser, tell him I'm calling about John Rossett . . . Thank you."

Fraser put his hand over the mouthpiece.

"He's gone to get him. I was starting to panic. I was running out of telephone numbers to try."

Ruth realized she was clenching her fists, so she opened her hands, trying to stretch the tension out of them.

"Hello?" She heard the tiny voice on the end of the line and held out a hand for the receiver.

Fraser passed it over and took a step back.

"Sir James?" Ruth said quietly.

"Who is this?"

"Ruth Hartz."

A smile entered Sterling's voice.

"Is it, by God?"

"We had trouble finding you, Sir James. I was starting to worry."

"I've been rather busy, getting ready to go on a little trip."

"Is there space for me to tag along?"

"Of course, my dear, you are more than welcome."

"Shall I come to you?"

"I'd imagine it would be best if I came to you. We'll not be long. Are you with Fraser?"

"Yes."

"Good, stay there."

"Sir James?"

"Yes?"

"There will be two of us traveling."

There was a pause on the line before Sterling spoke again.

"Are we talking about our friend the detective inspector?"

"We are."

"That might be difficult."

"It'll be more difficult if he doesn't."

"The inspector and I have a history."

"I like to think the inspector and I may have a future."

"Can you ensure his cooperation, Miss Hartz? He has a reputation for belligerence."

"It is Dr. Hartz, and he'll cooperate. I'll see to that."

ROSSETT HAD DOZED off. His head was resting against the back of the chair, and his mouth had fallen open. The fire had died down to embers, but the room had managed to retain the heat of the afternoon sun, which had long since sloped off to disappear behind the houses opposite.

Ruth stood by the window, lost in thought as she looked through the net curtains. Fraser sat half listening to the regular beat of martial music on the wireless.

Ruth watched the taxi slowly cruise past the low hedgerow that bordered the front garden.

She knew it was them.

Their faces were white at the windows, watching Fraser's house and then spinning and checking for signs of ambush from the empty front gardens, or passersby on their way home from work.

The taxi passed twice more before she finally spoke.

"They are here."

Rossett started in the chair and then grimaced, opening his eyes and blinking.

"Who?" His voice was husky and heavy with sleep.

"It looks like Sterling and a few of his men."

Rossett shifted in his seat, trying to push himself up with his elbows but unable to do so due to his wound.

Ruth crossed the room, knelt in front of him, then unbuttoned his coat.

Rossett's white shirtfront under his jacket was soaked dark red with dried blood.

He managed to almost smile.

"I cut myself shaving."

"Why didn't you tell me?"

"What's the point?"

"I could have cleaned you up."

"It's stopped bleeding, I'm okay."

Ruth lifted the jacket, gently touched the wound, and looked at him.

"I'll be okay," he said again.

There was a knock at the front door. Ruth paused, looking at Rossett, her hand still on his chest.

She smiled.

"We're nearly there."

"We?"

"You're coming with me."

Rossett smiled back.

"We'd better get going."

FRASER AND RUTH helped him out of the chair. Rossett stood still for a moment, collecting his remaining strength, and crossed to the window. He pulled back the net curtain and saw a tall man, dressed in a suit, standing by the front door.

The man jerked a thumb toward the taxi; Rossett nodded and let the curtain fall back.

He turned to Bill Fraser and held out his hand.

"Bill."

"John."

They shook.

"Thank you for being a friend," said Rossett, still holding Fraser's hand.

"I'm sorry I wasn't a better one."

Fraser turned to Ruth, holding out his hand.

"Look after him."

"I will."

They walked to the hallway, where they could see the outline of the man through the glass.

Rossett took out his Webley; he checked the load before nodding to Fraser to open the door.

The man outside smiled at Fraser, then saw the Webley and frowned.

"You'll not need that, guv'nor."

"Let's hope not," replied Rossett as he slipped the pistol into his pocket.

It was cold; the early evening was still, the wind having tired itself out. A few slow flakes of snow drifted down from the heavens, passing the dim streetlamp that had just flickered and buzzed into life. The taxi engine was clattering away and there was another man standing on the curb, holding the door open, while checking the street for potential threats.

Rossett paused in the driveway.

"Where's Sterling?"

The taxi driver turned toward him.

"I'm here, you idiot. Get in."

Rossett smiled again and wondered if it was becoming a habit.

He looked at Ruth over his shoulder and nodded.

She walked past him toward the taxi, touching his arm as she went; Rossett paused and looked at Bill Fraser for the last time.

"Cheerio, Bill."

"Cheerio, John."

CHAPTER 49

STERLING WAS A terrible driver.

In the rear the four passengers sat in silence, Sterling's two men facing forward, Rossett and Ruth facing back. The windows in the back of the taxi had misted to such an extent that the outside world was a mystery to them, as they edged across London heading for Paddington Station and freedom.

"We have tickets and false papers that will get us as far as the Welsh coast," said Sterling. "Once we are there it has been arranged for us to be picked up by a small boat, and then we'll travel onward to Ireland and beyond."

"You make it sound so easy." Rossett was almost shouting over the sound of the engine, which was being held in too low a gear by Sterling.

"We do this sort of thing more often than you'd think," one of Sterling's men spoke up for his boss, who was too busy concentrating on the road to reply.

"Let me see the papers." Rossett held out his hand.

The man slid a small leather holdall across the floor of the taxi toward Rossett.

Rossett looked at Ruth, who realized he was in too much pain to lean down to the bag. She lifted it onto her lap and undid the snap fasteners.

The papers were lying on the top of various clothes. There was also a wallet and a leather purse. Ruth opened the ID cards and held one out to Rossett. He held the card up to the window, inspecting it in the misted light of passing streetlamps.

"John Roberts," he read out loud, before turning toward Sterling up front. "How did you get my picture?" he shouted.

"I have many friends, John; it shouldn't surprise you to know some of them are at Scotland Yard."

Rossett looked at Ruth, who held up an ID card with her photo on it.

"I'm impressed," she said.

"You should be," said Sterling. "This has all been arranged at extremely short notice."

"Shouldn't we have waited until things have died down?" Rossett was putting the ID in his coat pocket.

"We don't have the luxury of time, Inspector. Koehler's daughter knows my name; also, I would imagine the Americans will be looking for us. I think it best that we exit London as soon as possible, I'm afraid."

The taxi slid to a halt at a traffic light. Sterling turned in his seat so he could look through the partition that separated the driver from his passengers.

"Our friends on the train will hold it for half a minute at the platform, after all the other passengers have boarded and just before it is due to leave. The guards in the car at the rear will be expecting us, and they will ensure we maintain a low profile during the journey."

"What if there is an inspection by the Germans? We'll be stopping at plenty of stations before we hit Wales, won't we?"

"We use these trains on a frequent basis; it is a long-standing arrangement. You can rest assured there will be somewhere on board where we can hide until we arrive at our destination."

Rossett nodded, happy to let it lie.

Sterling glanced at the traffic light, then looked back at him and continued.

"We'll go through the goods entrance at the side of the station; it is almost adjacent to our platform. We will need to move quickly once we arrive. Are you able to do that?"

Rossett nodded, then realized that everyone in the cab was staring at him. He looked down at his shirt and for the first time it struck him how bad he looked, and how bad he actually was.

"I'll be okay."

"You're sure?"

"I'll be okay."

The lights changed. Sterling nodded and swiveled in his seat, and they started moving again.

"My men will escort us to the train and then leave us. At our destination we have others who will help us onward."

"You might want to change that shirt," said the man next to Rossett.

Rossett looked down again and then nodded. He passed his Webley across to Ruth, who took the gun confidently, smiling at the two men opposite.

"He might need a hand," she said. "He cut himself shaving."

Sterling's men were surprisingly gentle with Rossett as they helped him change. His shirt was clotted to the bloody wound in his shoulder, which started to bleed again once the cloth was pulled away. One of the men produced a white handkerchief, then ripped a sleeve off the old bloodstained shirt. He gently eased Rossett forward and tied the shirt and handkerchief over his shoulder, bandaging the wound.

"Good field dressing," Rossett said through gritted teeth.

"I've had lots of practice," the man replied as he eased the fresh shirt across Rossett's shoulders. "You need to keep that arm as still as you can; if it starts bleeding heavily, you'll have some explaining to do if we are stopped before we make it to the train."

"I'll be okay."

One of the men brushed Rossett's suit jacket with his hand and then shook his head.

"You can't wear this. Take mine." He passed Rossett's jacket to Ruth. "Take his things out of the pockets, we'll swap."

The man started to empty his own pockets, as Ruth did the same to Rossett's jacket.

"Nearly there," called Sterling from the front.

Rossett watched Ruth as she took out his warrant card and his wallet.

She smiled at him.

He smiled back.

Then their world turned upside down.

THEY FELT THE impact before they heard the sound of a car hammering into the taxi. Everyone in the back pitched out of their seat, then spun in midair as the taxi seemed to rotate around them. Gravity took hold, suddenly slamming them into each other, like buttons in a tin box. They seemed to be turning and pitching forever. Dizzying flashes of streetlamps and headlamps came and went. The light strobed through the windows as the taxi pirouetted like a skater on ice before finally, catching on a curb, it flipped onto the pavement and landed on its side.

There was silence.

In the back of the cab Rossett was at the bottom of the pile, his back against the side window, his legs twisted and above him somewhere on the backseat. He'd hit his head against the glass and the pillar of the window, and sharp white pain was drilling into his senses and crazing them.

The taxi seemed to be rocking.

Rossett thought he could hear the sound of someone climbing out.

His ears were ringing. He blinked, slowly, and when he opened his eyes he wasn't sure how much time had passed. A slow realization of pain started to ring in his shoulder as he tried to inflate his winded lungs. It was dark; he blinked again and tried to move one of his pinned arms to wipe his face.

He forced another deep breath and lifted his head, realizing they were lying in shadow, up close to the station wall.

He tried to speak.

"Ruth . . ." His jaw ached. He swallowed, then felt someone on top of him moving and pushing down. "Ruth?"

Rossett felt her hair touching his face as she turned her head and lifted herself off him.

"What happened?" he heard himself say. His voice sounded far away.

One of Sterling's men started to twist and turn, trying to push himself off Rossett toward the window above. The pain in Rossett's shoulder caused him to cry out, and he felt Ruth's hand on his face.

Comforting him in the darkness, as something warm and wet ran into his left eye.

Suddenly there was no weight on him. His legs dropped, and for a moment he had his back to Ruth in a fetal position, gravity pinning him, his strength exhausted.

Ruth pulled at his legs, trying to twist him so that she could help him up.

He realized they were alone in the cab.

He heard shots.

Gunfire, the regular rhythm of his life.

When would it ever end?

"John, we need to get out!"

Rossett blinked again. Ruth was shouting at him as she pulled his legs, twisting him into an upright position.

Rossett wondered was he dreaming.

He wondered if he was still asleep in Fraser's armchair, music on the radio, fire in the hearth, warm whiskey in his throat.

He thought he could hear the radio.

Was he dreaming?

"John, we need to get out!" Ruth shook him. He was on all fours in the back of the taxi, but he couldn't remember getting into that position. He could see a white wall of snow pressed against the side window of the taxi. He stared at it, unable to understand why it was there.

"John!"

Ruth was shaking his shoulders. He realized he was wearing a shirt but had no coat on. He looked at his hands, then smoothed the front of his shirt, which was blood soaked again.

"A car crash," he said to himself. "I'm concussed," he said drunkenly to Ruth.

The back window of the taxi exploded to his right, and Rossett turned to look through it dumbly.

One of Sterling's men was knocking out the sharp edges of the broken glass with the butt of a Thompson submachine gun. Rossett tilted his head. The world was on its side. He could see a building lying down through the back window of the taxi.

"Where are we?" he said out loud.

Sterling's man reached through the back window.

"Come on, miss, we need to get you going."

"I'm a man," Rossett replied, as the leather bag went past him and out of the window.

He felt Ruth pushing him.

Ruth?

Clarity drifted back to him like a wave on the shore.

Ruth pushed against him.

He turned and looked at her.

Ruth, of course, Ruth, he needed Ruth.

No.

He looked at Sterling's man, then back at Ruth as she shoved him again.

"I need to save Ruth," Rossett said to her, patting his shirtfront looking for his pistol. "I need my gun."

Rossett looked down at his empty hand as if expecting the gun to be there. He remembered his shoulder was hurting, except . . . it was his head.

Reality drifted away again.

"Ruth?"

There were more shots; old instincts caused Rossett to look up at Sterling's man.

"Someone is firing a gun," Rossett said solemnly.

The man frowned, then reached through the window and grabbed Rossett's arm, dragging him unceremoniously through the gap.

"That hurt," said Rossett, once he was lying in the snow, flat on his back, looking up at the sky and the snow falling out of it.

The world suddenly seemed to have turned over again. He felt dizzy and closed his eyes.

He felt cold, very cold, or was it hot?

He opened his eyes and lifted his head.

Cold, it was cold, he felt cold.

It was the snow. He was lying in snow.

He was cold.

He lifted his head and then felt a little sick. He closed his eyes and waited for the nausea to pass. He grimaced, screwing his eyes tight, feeling his senses coming back again.

He opened his eyes.

He saw the taxi lying on its side and one of Sterling's men crouching next to it, a Thompson at his shoulder, aiming across the road at something out of Rossett's sight.

Rossett rolled onto his side and saw the others, a few feet away, crouching next to the taxi, alongside a tall red-brick wall.

His mind was clearing. He noticed something in the snow. It was blood, his blood, dripping from a head wound.

He looked at Ruth and saw she was holding his pistol.

She needed him.

Rossett got off the ground onto his haunches, breathing deep, one hand in the snow.

Ruth needed him.

He stood up.

Uncertainly at first, he touched his temple, felt a flap of skin and then a sharp sting.

"We need to move," he said quietly.

"We're pinned down. It's Koehler." Ruth sounded calm, in control.

The man at the corner of the taxi turned his head, glanced at Rossett, then turned back toward the street.

"He's over the road. They shunted us, made us crash," the man said.

Somebody fired at them and Rossett saw a puff of red dust come off the wall above the taxi.

Everyone flinched.

Everyone except Rossett.

"How far to the station?"

"We're almost at the goods entrance," Sterling shouted. "The train will be leaving!"

"Give me the Thompson." Rossett gestured to the other one of Sterling's men, who had taken up position next to his boss to protect him.

The man looked at Sterling.

"Give him it."

"No," said Ruth.

Rossett clicked his fingers impatiently for the gun. "Go get the train; I'll see you on it."

"You have to come."

"I can barely stand, let alone run, and you need to move fast."

"But . . ."

"Go get the train."

Ruth tried to go to Rossett, but Sterling caught hold of the back of her coat, dragging her down into cover. She struggled, showing Rossett she had his Webley.

"I can help."

"You're too important." Rossett tapped a bloody finger to the side of his head. "The war machine, remember?"

She started to speak, but no words came.

She looked so terribly, beautifully sad.

Rossett smiled.

Somewhere in the station a whistle sounded.

"Go save the world," he said as he worked the bolt on the Thompson.

Ruth nodded.

Rossett leaned down, almost overbalanced, and picked up a handful of snow. He wiped it across his face, took a deep breath, and then crouched next to the man at the corner of the taxi.

"Where is the entrance?"

"Twenty yards on this side of the road," the man glanced at him.

"When they start moving, we both open up with the Thompsons. We pin whoever is out there down so low, they'll need a ladder to get up again."

Rossett checked over his shoulder at the second of Sterling's men.

"Move fast with them, save your pistol ammo. If you're still out in the open when we stop firing it's your turn. Just make sure she is well clear of you if it comes to that, understood?"

He nodded.

"Get them into the station and on that train."

"I will."

"Go," replied Rossett as he pushed himself up and stepped out into the road on rubber legs.

KOEHLER HAD GUESSED that Rossett would head to Fraser's house.

A guess.

All he had left, one desperate guess, a last throw of the dice to save his life, to stay alive for Anja.

He knew that Rossett would somehow have to reach out to Sterling. He knew that Sterling had gone to ground, and he also knew that Fraser was the only link between Rossett and Sterling.

So it had been an educated guess, but a guess nonetheless.

It had taken almost an hour to get Neumann to go along with it. The policeman had cold feet, and not just because of the snow.

After witnessing the carnage at Finsbury Circus, March being shot, and the release of Ma Price, Neumann had wanted to call a halt to the whole affair and inform their superiors.

"You're out of control!"

"I'm maintaining control; by doing this I'm containing this situation. We sort the scientist, we pin this on Sterling, and you'll be a hero, in the clear and back to Germany as the man who saved the Reich."

"We need more men. Please let me call in a team to assist us?"

"What happens if that team gets to Hartz or Sterling before us? What happens if the truth gets out before we can contain it? If it were just you and me in this, Neumann, I'd say yes, I'd say we call in every man in London to help us get back the scientist . . . but it isn't just you and me. There is no other way: we keep this small, between us, me and you; that way we maintain control. That way we look good."

"I can't go on. At least let me walk away? I'll not say anything to anyone, there is nothing to tie me into this except a forged travel warrant I can talk myself out of."

"I need you. I can't do it alone. Please, for Anja, just one more step."

"My family, I—"

"If you walk away, all this was for nothing. Please . . . if you walk away, I lose her."

They'd gone to Scotland Yard, and there they'd established Fraser's address and booked out a car. They'd stayed away from the detectives' floor and control rooms, being careful to avoid the Finsbury Circus fallout. Throughout their time there Koehler hadn't left Neumann's shoulder as they had walked through the corridors, each step leading Neumann further into the abyss.

IT HAD BEEN the snow that had given Rossett and Ruth away.

Two sets of footprints, a man and a woman's, had led Koehler to the door on his first pass. He'd thought about Lotte, about the stories she had told him, about her father and how they had hunted together in the forests around their farm.

He had almost heard her voice, talking about reading signs in the snow, as he had turned his head and saw the fresh prints leading up the path to Fraser's front door.

Koehler was the hunter now.

Lotte was with him, helping him save Anja's future. He liked that thought, and he held on to it as he and Neumann sat quietly in the unmarked police car watching the house.

Waiting for the right moment.

Koehler was desperate, but he wasn't crazy. He knew that assaulting a house with Rossett inside would be madness. Koehler was good, but he was smart enough to know he wasn't *that* good.

Rossett and Ruth would eventually come out, and that would be the time.

In the open, fast, hard, then finish the job.

Koehler hadn't doubted himself until he saw the men in the taxi. Hard men, alert men, trained men. Not the usual stumbling scruffy resistance types tied up with string. These men were good; Koehler could see it as soon as they pulled up.

He and Neumann had been crouching low, watching as one of the men went up the path and the other stationed himself by the taxi door. Hands in pockets; smartly dressed, clean-cut killers.

There was too much risk, too many chances to get pinned down, caught up in a drawn-out gunfight that would give time for others to respond.

More police, more soldiers, clogging up his plan, risking it all, coming between him and what he wanted.

Anja and him, all that mattered.

KOEHLER AND NEUMANN had driven across London, following the taxi, keeping close, waiting for the right moment to strike. Then Koehler had seen the road sign for the station and realized they had nearly run out of time.

"We can stop the train," Neumann had tried to reason. "Down the line, we can tell them Sterling and Rossett are dangerous and should be shot on sight."

"I can't risk them being captured. It's now or never."

The side street that led to the goods entrance was quiet due to the bad weather, and it was sealed by a boxed dead end. On one side the high walls of the station, and on the other a solid office building. Halfway down on the right, the wide-open goods entrance to the station sat like a missing tooth, empty and black, waiting.

The snow, slushing and slippy from all the days' trucks, had created the perfect conditions for the final throw of the dice.

Koehler had accelerated, closing on the cab and sensing Neumann grabbing the doorframe to brace himself. He'd swung the wheel, catching the taxi on its rear quarter and slamming it into a lazy, lurching waltz across the road.

Koehler hadn't expected the cab to flip onto its side.

But he'd been glad it had.

His own car had slid to a halt almost sixty feet beyond the crash, across from the goods entrance of the station. Between them they had two Mauser pistols and one MP40.

Not much to stop a man like Rossett.

Koehler had climbed out of their car and looked into the goods entrance. One railway employee was standing with a trolley, openmouthed, watching the wrecked taxi up the road, one wheel still spinning.

Koehler had waved him away.

"SS! Get inside!"

The man had dropped the handles of his trolley and done as he was told.

One of the taxi's headlamps was out and the other hung from wires rocking back and forth, its beam like a lighthouse, occasionally shining into Koehler's eyes as he crossed the road toward it slowly.

Someone fired from the front of the taxi.

It was close, a good shot that caused Koehler to flinch and take a step backward.

There was another shot, which kicked snow next to Koehler's right foot. He turned and ran back to the other side of the bonnet of the police car.

"Shit," he exclaimed.

He looked for Neumann; he couldn't see him and wondered if the policeman was hit or, even worse, had run away.

Koehler aimed at the taxi and let off a couple of rounds, aware he only had one magazine for the MP40.

The taxi lamp stayed lit, blinding him, then lighting the snow as it swung back and forth.

Koehler saw someone climbing out the window that was on the top of the cab.

He let off a few more rounds.

They went high.

He cursed again.

"Come on," he said out loud to himself.

He heard Neumann nearby firing a few shots. He ducked as fire was returned from the cab.

Koehler glanced toward the goods entrance: it was empty. Maybe he could block their exit, show them there was no way out, and get them to surrender?

If they dropped their weapons he could finish them off with no problem.

He looked back at the taxi, took a breath, and started to run for the goods entrance.

The snow exploded around him.

Machine gun fire, heavier than his MP40, tracking him as he moved, drawing a bead, getting closer. He stopped, dropped, and scrambled his way back to the police car.

"Fuck!" he shouted, panicked breath catching in his throat. "Neumann?"

"What?"

"We need to advance on them, work as a team."

"Are you mad? There is sixty feet of open ground between us; they'll cut us to ribbons. We need to wait for reinforcements!"

Another round hit the police car.

"We aren't waiting for fucking reinforcements!"

Koehler rested his forehead against the cold metal, blew out his cheeks, and looked back toward the swinging lamp.

This couldn't go wrong, not now, not when he was so close. There had to be a way.

He could see shadows moving on the far side of the taxi. He lifted the MP40 and rested it on the front wing. He squinted past the lamp, fired two rounds, then cursed, certain they had gone high as the machine gun lifted in his hand and then settled back on the wing, chipping the paint.

He let go of the magazine and smoothed his hair, then looked toward the goods entrance and whistled.

"I'm going to them. I'm going to end this. Cover me."

Koehler rose, bringing the MP40 up. As if in slow motion, he presented himself to the bright light from the lamp as it danced shadows in the snow.

He fired a round, took a step, fired a round, and took another step.

And then saw Rossett coming toward him, out of the light, lit from behind, a long shadow, Thompson at his shoulder.

Silhouetted death coming to take his due.

CHAPTER 50

ROSSETT WASN'T CRAZY, he wasn't reckless, and he wasn't a fool.

He also wasn't afraid of dying.

Rossett had a role. He knew his place.

He was a protector, a policeman, a doer of what was right.

If he died, he would die well.

Rossett knew he wouldn't stop fighting till Ruth was on that train, or until those trying to stop her were dead, or until he was dead.

He would do whatever it took.

Rossett heard the train whistle.

He saw Koehler.

His friend, walking toward him. Not scared, just determined, desperate, and definitely coming toward him.

Rossett fired and tried to move to the left.

He'd figured that with both Thompsons firing at the same time, he'd have a chance to outflank whoever was attacking them and get to a position that would enable him to shoot around the car.

And then he'd seen Koehler.

Rossett would have run if he could, but his head was still groggy and his balance doubtful.

So he walked.

As Koehler ran.

Back to the cover of the car.

Rossett adjusted his aim, turning a fraction at the waist, three rounds, three steps, slow, plodding, struggling to keep his balance as the concussion of the crash kicked the inside of his skull, and the blood loss from his wound slowed him further. He could hear the other Thompson firing at Koehler and Neumann, rhythmic shots, not too fast, just enough to keep their heads down, same as his own.

Rossett kept moving, then saw Neumann, edging out of cover, aiming at him.

Neumann fired once and then ducked, turning his back to Rossett and the car, and sinking down until he was sitting on the wet slush and cobbles.

A rattle from Koehler's MP40 fired widely in the general direction of the goods entrance. Rossett turned and looked through the falling snow for Ruth.

Neumann reached around the corner of the car and fired again.

Rossett felt the burn, sudden and sharp, right through his forearm. Like a shaken rag doll he took a step to the right, then another. Out of the corner of his eye he caught movement by the goods entrance. He looked and saw Ruth with the others passing through, into the darkness of the station.

Ruth gave one last look back, dragged by Sterling, shouting, reaching out toward him.

Rossett tried to steady himself, but it was like he was wading through mud. His limbs felt heavy, his feet were like lead, each blink seemed to take seconds as he stumbled, fighting to get his balance.

He realized the other Thompson had stopped firing but didn't look to see if Sterling's man was all right. Rossett breathed deep, feeling the concussion sap his strength. He dropped to one knee, his head hanging heavily, sleepy.

Rossett paused, gathered his strength, sucked in more air, and turned back to the car.

The Thompson seemed to weigh a ton, but he lifted it again, one more time. Time to end all this.

He fired.

He saw a flash of Koehler's blond hair dip below the wing.

Rossett's Thompson clicked.

Empty.

He heard the train whistle, calling through the night.

Saying good-bye.

He let go of the barrel and tried to work the bolt but found he didn't have the strength. The muzzle of the gun dropped into the snow next to his knee, and Rossett sank back onto his heels, his hand falling to his side, blood in his eyes.

His head dropped forward, and he saw more blood in the snow.

He heard the whistle once more, but this time he didn't look.

Someone fired a gun somewhere, and Rossett noticed his shirt was soaked in blood from the stab wound as his chin rested on his chest. He heard the shunting and the power of a steam engine, and another whistle wailed.

A train was leaving the station on the other side of the wall.

He dropped into the snow and rolled slowly onto his back.

He lifted his head and saw Koehler, halfway across the road, running toward the goods entrance, slowing, then stopping.

Rossett knew he had done enough.

She was gone.

KOEHLER DROPPED THE empty MP40 and drew his Mauser.

He'd only made it halfway to the station entrance, and he knew he'd failed.

He stopped, lifted his hands, and dropped them to his sides as he heard the train powering out of the station. He stared at the goods entrance, and then slowly turned to Rossett.

His friend.

Neumann was emerging from behind the car. The policeman looked like he was in shock, half crouching, pistol pointed at Rossett.

"Leave him," called Koehler, his own pistol at his side as he walked across the road.

When he got to Rossett he found that he was staring up at the sky with glassy eyes.

Koehler dropped to his knees. Rossett was in a bad way. His shirt was soaked with blood, and there was another leaking wound on his forearm, staining the white wet snow. More blood was seeping from Rossett's scalp, and Koehler gently touched the flap of skin and tried to close the wound with a fingertip.

"I'm sorry it has come to this, John," Koehler whispered, even though he knew Rossett probably couldn't hear him.

"How is he?" Neumann came up behind him.

"I think he's passed out."

"Is he dying?"

"He's lost a lot of blood."

Koehler wrapped his hand around Rossett's arm to try and stop the bleeding.

"We need to get out of here," Neumann said quietly.

"I can't leave him like this. You go."

"If they find you here . . ."

"Go."

Koehler looked up and saw Neumann staring at the police car parked behind them, riddled with bullet holes.

"I signed for the car; there isn't much point in my running."

"I'm sorry for this, what I got you into. I'm sorry."

NEUMANN PASSED KOEHLER his handkerchief.

"Can you trust him not to say anything? He's just been trying to kill you."

"If he'd wanted to kill me, he would have done. He was just giving her the chance to get away."

Some station staff appeared at the goods entrance, watching Neumann, Rossett, and Koehler.

"They'll have called the police." Neumann nodded his head in the direction of the staff as Koehler wrapped the handkerchief around the wound on Rossett's arm.

"Yes."

"What do we do?" Neumann looked at Koehler. "Me and you, where does this leave us?"

"I got you into this, Neumann. You say what you need to say to stay alive and get back to your family. I'll agree to it, I owe you that."

Neumann looked at the pistol in his hand, then slipped it into his coat pocket. He stared at the upturned taxicab and the resistance man lying in the snow next to it.

Neumann walked across to the taxi as the first of the responding police cars slid into the top of the road, stopping well short of the scene of the shooting, holding back in case more rounds were about to be fired.

Neumann dropped next to the dead resistance man on the ground. Two feet away lay Rossett's warrant card, open in the snow. Neumann picked it up, shielding it from the view of the policemen cautiously making their way up the road behind him, and slipped it into the jacket pocket of the dead man. Then he climbed to his feet, arms rising above his head, just as the bobby behind him knocked him back to the ground.

CHAPTER 51

SCHMITT, THE GESTAPO man, pulled back the curtain and entered the cubicle. His leather coat creaked when he leaned over and looked into Neumann's eyes.

"You're awake?"

"Yes."

Schmitt peered at him.

"You're uninjured?"

"I'm in shock, and have a concussion," Neumann lied. "They say it was from the crash, but I think it was that copper and his truncheon."

Schmitt nodded, still unnaturally close, still peering.

"I'm Schmitt, do you know what I am?"

"Gestapo."

"Correct."

Neumann blinked and swallowed. The smell of the leather was making him feel nauseous.

Schmitt noisily dragged a chair to the side of the bed and sat down.

"You had quite an adventure this evening." Schmitt's coat creaked as he spoke.

"We were following up a lead into the death of Koehler's wife."

"What lead?"

"We had information the resistance were involved."

"What information?"

"That the men who killed her were trying to flee the capital by train."

Who gave you that information?"

"It was an anonymous tip."

"Anonymous?"

"Yes."

"Convenient."

"It's often the way, Herr Schmitt. I'm sure you understand."

"Do you know where Rossett has been these last few days?" Schmitt tried another tack.

"He's been with us."

"Us?"

"Me and Koehler."

"Doing what?"

"Being a policeman. It's his job."

"He hasn't left your side?"

"No."

"He's stayed in London?"

"Yes."

"And Koehler?"

"What about him?"

"He's also stayed in London?" Schmitt's eyebrow edged up a fraction.

"He's been helping us with the inquiries into his wife's death."

"He was a suspect?"

"Initially."

"But not now?"

"No."

"Why?"

"The evidence points to resistance involvement."

"Evidence?"

"The scene, the circumstances, his alibi, yes."

"And his daughter?"

"We think she was kidnapped, then released by the resistance."

"At Finsbury Circus?"

Neumann paused before answering, collecting his thoughts.

"We had a tip-off that Koehler's daughter was being taken to the circus.

The informant told us that she was being passed by one faction of the resistance to another, so we intercepted that handover."

"I take it this informant was also anonymous?"

"He was."

"Hmm."

"I can only tell you the facts, Herr Schmitt."

"I wish you would."

"I'm sorry?"

Schmitt adjusted position in the chair again, his coat creaking even louder.

"There was an American at Finsbury Circus."

"Was there?" Neumann tried to sound surprised. "Have you spoken to him?"

"He's dead."

"Oh, dear."

"Indeed." Schmitt sat back in the chair. "The American's involvement and subsequent death has caused us . . . problems."

"Problems?" Neumann detected a shift in Schmitt's voice that caused him to turn his head and look at him, for the first time since he had sat down. "What kind of problems?"

"Embarrassing problems."

"The worst kind."

"Indeed."

"Can I help you with these . . . problems?"

Schmitt scratched his nose before continuing.

"It would be . . . useful, if you could confirm something for me."

"If I can, I will." Neumann adjusted his shoulders, raising himself slightly higher on his pillow.

"If it turned out this dead American was working against the Reich, it could be highly embarrassing for both governments."

"Of course."

"Ambassador Kennedy has assured Prime Minister Mosley and General Hahn that the dead American was working with us, trying to rescue Koehler's daughter from the resistance. Is that true?"

"It is." Neumann nodded to back up his words.

"If it was confirmed that this American was also the source of your information, that would also be of assistance."

"He was."

"So you're saying the dead American was doing his best to help German-American relations."

"He was."

"And that he died heroically."

"He did."

"Even though a moment ago you didn't know he was there?"

"I'd say and do anything for the good of the Reich, Herr Schmitt."

"Hmm." Schmitt sat silently a moment, both hands on his knees, until he rose suddenly and crossed to the curtain. He pulled it open and looked back at Neumann.

"I'll have a full report written that you can sign to this effect."

"Of course."

Schmitt stared at him, then looked at the floor, then looked back at Neumann.

"Neumann . . . I know all this is bullshit. Just because I am standing here, saying it, doesn't mean I don't know."

Neumann swallowed but didn't reply.

Schmitt sighed and then spoke again.

"Koehler is toxic. He infects those around him like rabies and makes them do crazy things. You'd do well to remember that. Just sign this paperwork, stick to this story, and then, for your own good, put as much distance between yourself and Koehler as you possibly can."

"I'll do what is best."

"Koehler is walking a tightrope, and the wind is picking up. He'll not manage to stay on his feet much longer."

Neumann nodded and Schmitt turned to go.

"Herr Schmitt?"

Schmitt stopped and looked back in.

"Rossett?" Neumann tilted his head.

"What about him?"

"Is he dead?"

"Rossett?" Schmitt shook his head. "He's alive. Concussed, busted up, but he'll live."

"I thought he was a goner."

"Rossett?" Schmitt shook his head again and almost smiled. "It would take an army to kill that bastard."

ACKNOWLEDGMENTS

THE **B**RITISH **GOVERNMENT'S** MAUD Committee, and the later Tube Alloys project, were the stepping stones to the destructive outcome of the U.S. Manhattan Project. I'm afraid I don't have the space (or for that matter the intelligence) to fully detail their work, but what I can say is that their theorizing and calculations were instrumental in changing the British, and later the American, government's mind regarding the feasibility of an atomic bomb.

There has been conjecture for years as to whether Great Britain, on her own, could have manufactured an atomic bomb during the early years of the war. Without doubt there was no shortage of brainpower and ingenuity, but I think it is fair to say that the country was stretched a little too much to dedicate the manufacturing capacity required to put the plans into action.

Another question is whether a bomb would have stopped Hitler. The answer has to be that unless it killed him, probably not. We saw the depths he was prepared to go to in trying to win, even when the rest of the world knew it was lost. A nuclear explosion over Germany may have shortened the war by damaging infrastructure and causing untold deaths, but I doubt that it would have ended it as dramatically as the terrible events at Hiroshima and Nagasaki did with the war in the east.

The solace we can take is that the great minds behind the MAUD Committee, the men who had the intelligence to look over the horizon and see what other scientists couldn't, were on the side of good, and not evil.

I'll ask you to remember that this book was a work of fiction, and I hope you have forgiven me any flights of fancy upon which I've been carried in bringing you this story.

ACKNOWLEDGMENTS

SO MANY AMAZING people put this book in front of you; honestly I'd be here all day if I thanked them all, so I'll try and keep it as short as I can.

In the U.S. there is the amazing team at Sobel Weber, and specifically my agent Nat Sobel, whose wisdom and experience has been invaluable.

The team at HarperCollins U.S.: David Highfill, my editor, who has to slog through my poor grammar and lazy attempts at spelling. Lauren Jackson, who deals with my whining emails, poor taste in music, and empty boasting about my pool-playing skills. I can't forget the wonderful Chloe Moffett and Ashley Marudas, whose patience in dealing with a generally confused English idiot without visiting the crying room too often is also invaluable.

In the UK the wonderful team at Harper 360: Karen Davies, Helena Towers, and Alice and Ellie, who have to put up with me visiting occasionally and leaving sticky finger marks on their office windows.

Outside of publishing are my friends Tracey Edges, Jane Buchanan, Ruaridh Nicoll, Jo Hughes, and Ian Collins. All of them are supportive with a word of advice or encouragement in the small hours, when my head is hurting after hitting it too hard and too often on my desk.

I could never forget my dear friends and family in Liverpool: Sweeney, Terry, Tony, Denise, Jim, Philip, John, Wendy, Cliff, Dave, Glenda, Sarah, Angie, Trace, Ian G., Ian M., Rob, Graham, Barry, and the boys at the tip.

I love you all (except Sweeney) and I'm sorry I don't say it more often.

Last but in no way least, thank you, the person reading this. You've helped make my dream come true, give yourself a pat on the back.

ABOUT THE AUTHOR

Tony Schumacher is a native of Liverpool, England. He has written for the *Guardian* and the Huffington Post, and he is a regular contributor to BBC Radio and London's LBC Radio. He has been a policeman, stand-up comedian, bouncer, jeweler, taxi driver, perfume salesman, actor, and garbage collector, among other occupations. He currently lives outside Liverpool.